Coldharbour Gentlemen

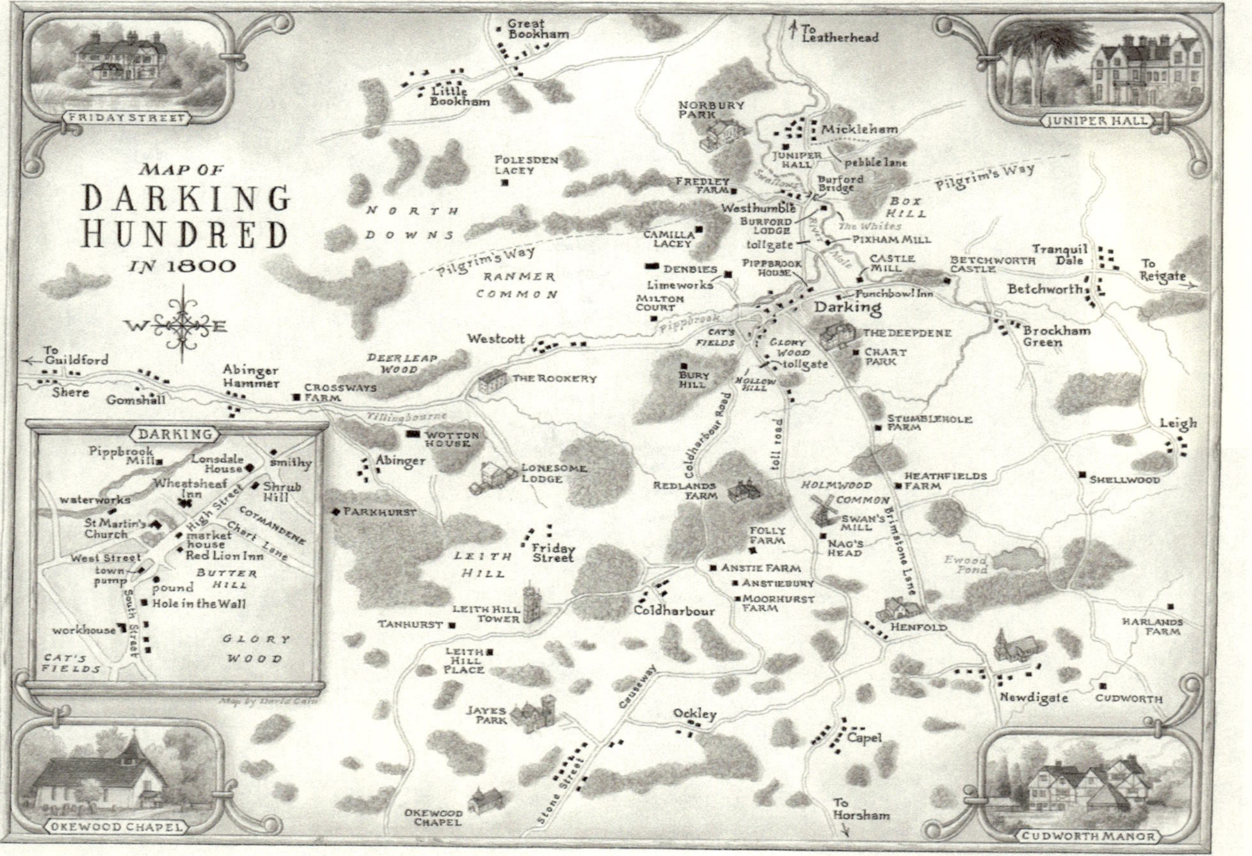
FRIDAY STREET
JUNIPER HALL
MAP OF
DARKING HUNDRED
IN 1800
W N E S
Great Bookham
To Leatherhead
Little Bookham
NORBURY PARK
Mickleham
JUNIPER HALL
pebble lane
Pilgrim's Way
POLESDEN LACEY
FREDLEY FARM
Burford Bridge
BOX HILL
NORTH DOWNS
Westhumble
Swallow
The Whites
River Mole
Pilgrim's Way
CAMILLA LACEY
BURFORD LODGE
tollgate
PIXHAM MILL
CASTLE MILL
BETCHWORTH CASTLE
Tranquil Dale
To Reigate
RANMER COMMON
DENBIES
Limeworks
MILTON COURT
PIPPBROOK HOUSE
Punchbowl Inn
Darking
Betchworth
Pippbrook
CAT'S FIELDS
GLORY WOOD
tollgate
THE DEEPDENE
CHART PARK
Brockham Green
To Guildford
Shere
Gomshall
Abinger Hammer
Westcott
DEER LEAP WOOD
THE ROOKERY
CROSSWAYS FARM
Tillingbourne
BURY HILL
HOLLOW HILL
Coldharbour road
toll road
STUMBLEHOLE FARM
Leigh
DARKING
Pippbrook Mill
Lonsdale House
smithy
Wheatsheaf Inn
Shrub Hill
waterworks
High Street
Cotmandene
Chart Lane
St Martin's Church
market house
Red Lion Inn
West Street
town pump
BUTTER HILL
pound
Hole in the Wall
workhouse
South Street
CAT'S FIELDS
GLORY WOOD
Map by David Cain
WOTTON HOUSE
Abinger
PARKHURST
LONESOME LODGE
REDLANDS FARM
HOLMWOOD COMMON
SWAN'S MILL
HEATHFIELDS FARM
SHELLWOOD
LEITH HILL
Friday Street
FOLLY FARM
NAG'S HEAD
Brimstone Lane
Ewood Pond
ANSTIE FARM
ANSTIEBURY
MOORHURST FARM
LEITH HILL TOWER
TANHURST
Coldharbour
HENFOLD
HARLANDS FARM
LEITH HILL PLACE
Causeway
Newdigate
CUDWORTH
JAYES PARK
Ockley
Stone Street
Capel
OKEWOOD CHAPEL
To Horsham
OKEWOOD CHAPEL
CUDWORTH MANOR
Map © 2017 by David Cain

DARKING HUNDRED BOOK ONE

Coldharbour Gentlemen

A NOVEL OF GEORGIAN ENGLAND

ANN LEE

Interior design by Damonza
Cover design by Damonza
Cover illustration: John Hassell, Newdigate Church (1823), watercolour. Surrey History Centre 4348/2/60/3, reproduced by permission of Surrey History Centre.

First Edition: December 2021
Library of Congress Control Number 2021920244
Library of Congress Cataloging-in-Publication Data
ISBN: 978-0-96406-5
ISBN (ebook): 978-0-578-96405-8

*The Darking Hundred series is dedicated
to all the historians of the Dorking Local
History Group, whose many studies of the
towns and villages of Wotton Hundred have
inspired my characters and their stories.*

Chapter the First

Wednesday, June **11, 1800**

The Walking Dunghill was dead.

Three days previously, while out on his customary walk through the town, the Dunghill—more conventionally known as Major Peter Labilliere—had abruptly stopped in the middle of the street, spread his arms wide to embrace the sky, and fallen where he stood.

As Harry Steer rode in to Darking that morning, the news was all around him. For a twelve-year-old boy who rarely left his father's farm, even the death of an eccentric old man was a notable event; and this one came laced with intriguing circumstances.

The first he heard of the matter was when he was halted in his progress by two fat gentlemen whose open carriages were blocking all traffic in South Street as they conversed at leisure, lolling indolently upon their cushions. "I understand old Major Labilliere will be laid to rest this day, Sir Nugent," said the first.

"And not a moment too soon!" cried Sir Nugent, his indignation setting the watch chain spread across his enormous waistcoat to quivering. "That creature was a blight on the streets of Darking, a filthy beggar. Ranting and

1

carrying on with his Jacobinical sedition, filling people's heads with notions of revolution. He belonged in Bedlam, if not worse."

The other gentleman was inclined to be more indulgent. "I never saw him beg; he had his own pittance to live on. A military pension! That is surely respectable. And you cannot say he intended any real mischief. His ideas were more of a spiritual nature, would not you agree? I always took him to be speaking of a revolution of the spirit, not of torches in the streets."

"That's where you're mistaken, Mr. Perrin," said Sir Nugent. "If you passed more of your time in London, the name *Labilliere* would be familiar enough to you. He opposed the Crown during the rebellion of the American colonies and was a well-known crony of Wilkes and Sayre. They say he was even a fellow conspirator in Sayre's attempt against the King, and it's a wonder he escaped punishment. I shouldn't be surprised if all his quotings from the Bible were simply intended as a concealment for seditious activity. I thank Providence he has removed himself from the neighborhood."

"God rest his soul," said Mr. Perrin drily.

Harry at last squeezed his horse past the carriages and proceeded on his way, reflecting on the deceased. He supposed that—to show proper respect—he ought to refer to him as Major Labilliere, but once a man has come to be known as the Walking Dunghill, it is altogether too much to expect such a young person as Harry to remember him by any other name.

The Walking Dunghill had been one of the principal personages of Darking town, as notable after his own fashion as the giant stuffed hog in the Wheatsheaf Inn or the lord of the manor, the Duke of Norfolk. The major indeed shared with both of them certain personal proclivities: he disdained cleanliness as wholeheartedly as did the duke (and no doubt the hog, though possibly for different reasons). But a lively twelve-year-old like Harry could scarcely condemn him for being unconcerned with washing.

At one time perhaps the Dunghill had been a man like other men—not within the span of Harry's memory, of course, but maybe long before. He had died at a ripe age and must have been less peculiar in his earlier days—for how else could he have achieved the rank of major in the army? Harry tried to conjure an image of this younger Major Labilliere, a dashing man of promise in a fine uniform, a man into whose care a company of soldiers could be entrusted. But Harry found it impossible to connect such a figure with the filthy creature who had sounded in the streets of Darking his perpetual yawp of sin and redemption, tyranny and liberty, calling on Jesus as the Prince of Peace and of Patriots—a baffling amalgam of political and spiritual radicalism cogent only to himself. And his smell—it was an unkindness to dunghills to liken them to the unholy brew of grime, bodily effluence, and decay that drove many townspeople from his presence. Time, or events; decay of mental faculties, or excessive devotion to a single idea—*something* had transformed the major into the Walking Dunghill, a creature part comical, part terrifying, part heroic in a way that seemed dreadful or sad.

And now the major was dead, and the sad aspects of him seemed to grow all at once into something solemn and noble. The words of admonition he had distributed so liberally among the youth of Darking appeared to carry a greater weight.

It soon became apparent to Harry that the lesser inhabitants of the town were no less obsessed with the event—though Sir Nugent might have been relieved to learn that the major's politics formed no part of their debates. What interested the common man was the mystery surrounding his end, particularly his landlady's allegation that he had foretold it. As Harry stabled his horse, he heard a stableboy say to the ostler, "I heard it from young Jacob Watford hisself. Two days after Twelfth Night, the major says to Mrs. Watford, 'Mrs. Watford,' he says, 'in six months I shall be dead.' And dead he was, six months to the day after. So you see, he must've been a saint, for how many on us do be able to know the time of our own death? Sure as sure, he were touched by the Spirit."

The ostler grunted his disdain. "More like he were punished for the sin of pride, for thinking he could look so high as to decide when he would be taken."

"But he seen it in one of his visions!" protested the stableboy.

"It's not God alone as sends a man visions," said the ostler darkly. "They comes from the Other Place as well. It's said we're not to know the measure of our days, and that pride goeth before a fall. For all his penances, the Walking Dunghill had his pride, with his brass buttons and his visits to a ducal estate. And now he has fallen—and they say he won't even be buried in consecrated ground."

Walking from the stableyard toward the High Street, Harry was faced with a quandary. The mystery of the Walking Dunghill's death and the question of his burial had taken strong possession of his imagination—did he really fortell it? And why could he not be buried in the churchyard? His speculations were doing battle with what he knew to be his duty, which was to take himself homeward as soon as his errand was complete. His father, who enjoyed the ritual of smoking a cheroot every evening, had that day made the unhappy discovery that his supply of cigars had run out. So he had granted Harry leave to escape his tutor for the length of the morning and ride in to Darking to replenish his stock. Considering the importance his father attached to Harry's academic preparations—he was to be sent away to school in only a few months' time—Harry knew that only dire necessity could have justified suspending his studies for even a few hours. The fact that market day was tomorrow, so that with only a day's delay his mother could have made the purchase in the course of her regular shopping, made it clear to Harry that in his father's mind the errand of the cheroots was a matter of great urgency. At home his father's word was law, and enforced by draconian measures; clearly it behooved Harry to hasten his steps to the tobacconist's and ride home as fast as his horse could carry him.

This Harry did not do. True, he did buy the cigars and stow them safely in his satchel, but afterward he could not resist loitering about the High Street listening to the talk of the Walking Dunghill's impending funeral. A crowd was gathered in front of the Three Tuns, some taking their ease on the settle and others lingering, like Harry, to relish a momentary interruption in the pursuit of their daily labors. The broomdasher had pulled up his cart, and his donkey stood with head lowered and one hind leg cocked, enduring. Mollie Fish was there, sporting her treasured sky-blue apron, the wide basket of her wares resting on one hip. Mr. Rudge, who owned the malthouse, had brought out a stool and settled onto it, his ample belly dangling down between his knees. Old Woodger had got a place on the settle and set down his tray of muffins and crumpets beside him, though many a housewife of the town was left standing. Several Puttocks were clustered in a clump as always, avidly drinking in the conversation.

There were sheep to be sheared and horses to be shod and ribbons to be sold to schoolgirls, but all work was suspended. Major Labilliere had been a notable presence, a constant source of pride and derision and compassion, a treasure and a blight, and his death must receive its due consideration.

"His passing leaves a gap. There's no gainsaying it, we feel a gap," said Mr. Rudge.

"He made me think Christian thoughts," said Mollie Fish, implausibly. (Mollie was no better than she should be, and her family, being respectable folk, had cast her off after her third fatherless child was born before she had achieved the age of twenty.) "Not acos of his words," she continued, "but acos of his kind ways toward folk. He made me think on Love Thy Neighbor and the Golden Rule. I compassionated the poor soul, I won't deny."

Harry could hear the Puttocks muttering among themselves something about the form Mollie Fish's compassion too often took and the possible resemblance of her second child to the major, but John-Paul Cleere, the clerk at Saint Martin's, was not about to allow the occasion to degenerate into the basest form of gossip. "He was indeed a tragic figure," said he; "with all his accomplishments, and his friends in high places, to be reduced at the end of his life to a filthy simpleton, spouting nonsense half the time—it makes one humble."

An ancient dame unknown to Harry removed the pipe from her sucking lips. "I wouldn't say 'twere nonsense," she retorted, still articulate despite the nearly toothless state of her gums. "His words were deep—too deep for most our minds to fathom. When he spoke on the Holy Spirit, you could see in his eye he spoke true."

"Which eye would that be?" jeered old Woodger. "The

one as got poked out by a stick when he fell down in a fit on Box Hill?" This sally drew guilty laughter from many present, including Harry. Pleased to have captured everyone's attention, Woodger added, "He were an owd fool. And if so be as we all live to be that owd, most on us'll see our own brains as gollymoggled as his was."

They all observed silence for a moment, pondering the absurdity of life and the inevitability of the tomb. But in an instant the mood was transformed, for Mrs. Watford, the Dunghill's landlady at the Hole in the Wall cottage, was seen to be approaching. She was not, as might be expected, attired in her blacks, but wore with an air of defiance her most festive garb—a long-sleeved gown in a striking hue of green, which had clearly been handed down to her by a charitable maiden of less ample proportions. This unusual garment sported panels of fabric in different colors that had been added under the arms to let out the bodice; a deep ruffle, to increase its length; and all the ornaments of lace her means permitted. Harry eased his way closer as several of the assembled drew breath at once to demand information. As the ranking expert on the deceased she should naturally be able to satisfy their curiosity. But she was on the instant accosted by the young vicar, eager to learn the truth of the rumors that were flying about the town.

"Mrs. Watford," said he, "I have heard that Major Labilliere is to be buried today without the proper rites. What can you possibly be thinking of?"

"We are following his own expressed wishes to the letter," she retorted stoutly.

"My dear lady, even had the major stated such wishes— which I find hard to credit, for he was a man of education and no small degree of piety—we cannot be expected to follow them to the letter. Allowances must be made for the poor gentleman's infirmities, for the weakening of intellect that is so often the regrettable concomitant of old age—"

"He'd no need to be pothery to want none of your sermons," retorted Mrs. Watford, to Harry's scandalized delight. "You knows as well as me the major ne'er darkened the doorstep at Saint Martin's, and him as inclinable to saintliness as any man you'll meet—more than many I know, surely. And if he said he didn't hold with no parson jawing over him, then I reckon no parson shall he have, for all you say!"

"But I cannot stand by and see one of my flock interred without benefit of the funeral service," protested the young reverend. "I could not vouch for the safe passage of his soul—will the doors of heaven even open for him without the proper rites being observed? We humble mortals cannot judge such matters for ourselves. I'm sure you believe you are doing right, good lady, in following the wishes he expressed, but can we truly believe he knew what was best for himself? No doubt your impulse toward your former tenant is kindly meant, but—"

"Don't you worrit yerself about *my* impulses, sirrah!" cried Mrs. Watford, bridling. "I may be no more than a seamstress, but I attend Chapel regular every Sunday, and if the pastor in charge has no fault to find, it ain't for you to do so neither. I reckon what frets you is not getting your burial fee!" The vicar gasped but she plowed on. "And as for the major's wishes, you don't has to listen to the likes of me. The major done settled every detail of his earthing aforehand with his friend Mr. Peters, and got his say-so to be buried up there on Box Hill. You can just ask *him*, if you like. It'd do me a sight of good to watch you at it, it would so. You could talk his dog's hind leg off, and it wouldn't do you no manner of good."

At the mention of Mr. Peters, many of the audience who had inclined toward supporting Reverend Feachem's view of the matter were visibly shaken. Next only to the Duke of Norfolk or Sir Frederick Evelyn, there was no personage in all of Darking Hundred more deserving of respect and deference than Mr. Peters, who had inspired universal awe two years previously by laying down the cash to purchase Betchworth Castle and an estate measuring upwards of a thousand acres.

But her words had a very different effect on the vicar, whose youth perhaps deprived him of a due appreciation for the rival claims of ecclesiastical and secular influence. Indeed, his own precarious position of authority demanded a more emphatic assertion of it.

In any case, he was not to be diverted from the fresh outrage falling upon his ears. "*He is to be buried on Box Hill?* Do you mean to say that you, or whoever may be making these decisions, intend to deny him burial in consecrated ground, as if he were a common felon? It is not to be tolerated that even the meanest of us be consigned to the soil in a place where parties of pleasure-seekers take their picnics—a place to which every jumped-up squire and clerk resorts when he wishes to dally with some common wench!"

The notion was shocking to Harry, but Mrs. Watford remained unimpressed with the scenes of dissipation and vice conjured by the vicar. "The major cared naught for none o' that. Box Hill were his church. That were the place where he had his visions. Time and again he says to me, after the time he fell down there and a-poked out of his eye, that it were a holy place, on account o' what it says in the Gospel: 'And if thy right eye offend thee, pluck it out, and cast it from thee; for it is profitable that one of thy members should perish, and not that thy whole body should be cast into hell.'"

The vicar was momentarily struck dumb by this personalized reading of Scripture, and Mrs. Watford took advantage of his silence to produce her final revelations. "He wished for everyone pleased to attend, man, woman, and child, to join him on his final journey. *And* he asked to be buried arse-uppards, with his head below and his feet skyward, like Saint Peter, along of how he was too humble to be buried as his Lord were; and besides, he said, the whole world is topsy-turvy, and when the end times come he'll be the only one standing upright! And that there is what shall be done." Mrs. Watford folded her arms and stood back to enjoy her dual triumph, having simultaneously vanquished the forces of conformity and provided her audience with pleasures to be savored for many days to come.

There was more than sufficient in her description of the event's wonders to complete Harry Steer's beguilement. He could no more have ridden tamely home to his tutor at this juncture than he could have taken a seat in the House of Lords; he must and *would* attend the funeral of the Walking Dunghill, two miles away on the top of Box Hill, though it meant he could scarcely reach home before nightfall and would without question get his coat dusted for him by his papa.

It appeared that most of Darking and the surrounding countryside felt the same; it was as if a holiday had been declared. One shop after another closed its doors, the calls of vendors crying their wares were silenced, and laborers shed their workday smocks for Sunday finery and poured into the town. Soon two carts began to rumble over the paving-stones bearing sprigs of box and yew, from which people were invited to select a branch to carry in the funeral cortège.

The air of furtive jollification in the crowd was imperfectly suppressed by a guilty awareness of the occasion's solemnity. But from this discomfort also Mrs. Watford was eager to relieve them: for she explained to all who might listen that Major Labilliere had insisted his funeral should be treated as a celebration, marked by the observers with singing and dancing. "He allus said as how his leaving this world ought to be a cause of rejoicing, not of sadness," she confided.

Harry, who yearned after food like a miser after gold, fortified himself against whatever the afternoon might bring by purchasing a hot meat pasty out of the funds remaining from the acquisition of his father's cheroots. Then he fell in with the townspeople, now coalescing into a procession behind a dray that had emerged onto the streets bearing a plain wooden casket. This repository struck Harry as curiously inadequate to serve as the final home for a larger-than-life figure such as the major. He could only guess that this plain box had been another of the Dunghill's eccentric directions regarding his interment.

As the procession wound its way out of the town, past the millpond, the nursery, and the ripening fields of corn, Harry attempted to rise to the demands of the occasion by waving his yew branch about over his head. He eyed his companions sidelong and observed a number of them doing likewise— both waving the greenery and observing one another doing so. Harry could not but feel that the young vicar, Mr. Feachem, for all the priggishness of his objections to the irregularity of today's proceedings, might have had a point: that the absence of established words and rituals left people at something of a loss to determine what conduct was expected of them. The end was that everyone appeared to be thinking more about themselves than about the Departed.

The procession was approaching the River Mole, at the foot of Box Hill. The waterway was narrow at this point and spanned by a simple footbridge consisting of no more than a few planks and a handrail. The dray in consequence could travel no farther. The crowd milled about, debating this problem. It would take all the rest of the day for the coffin to be hauled around by the carriage road on the far side of the hill. There was confusion for a time until half a dozen stalwarts from among those assembled stepped forward to serve as pallbearers for the ascent. This obstacle having been surmounted, the cortège continued on its way.

It was a warm afternoon, and the volunteers soon regretted their offer to convey the Walking Dunghill to his chosen resting place, which was high up near the crest of Box Hill. The path was steep and the flies were bothersome; the roots of ancient yews snaked out underfoot to trip them up. But they kept to their duty with dogged, if sweaty, persistence until the summit was achieved.

Here it could be seen that, contrary to previous appearances, a measure of forethought had been applied to the planning of the solemnities: for there was already a hole dug, ready to receive the remains of the major. This hole, in deference to the deceased's wish to be buried headfirst, resembled more a well than a grave, being circular, quite narrow, and fully ten feet in depth.

The landowner, Mr. Peters, was already present, chatting affably with the muscular lads responsible for the digging. As the crowd gathered around the hole, enjoying the relief of a gentle breeze rising up from the southwest, Harry—a countryman at heart—could readily understand how this spot might have been for the major a place of divine visitation. Below the brow of the hill, all Darking town was laid out before him, its buildings and its commerce alike reduced to miniature by distance and height, while the dark mass of Leith Hill rose opposite and the sky spread infinite overhead. A windhover rode the upwelling currents of air directly over the hilltop, and even a less God-fearing person than Harry might have seen in its presence a sign of sanction from on high for the irregular memorial. The sole desecration of the grave site was found in the presence of the crowd, trampling the betony underfoot and waiting with avid gaze to be entertained.

Mr. Peters appeared gratified by the arrival of so numerous a contingent of mourners—or, as Mrs. Watford would remind him, merrymakers—and proceeded to explain the next event planned for their amusement. Mr. Peters particularly welcomed the landlady, Mrs. Watford, and her progeny, declaring it to have been Major Labilliere's wish that her two youngest children, a boy about Harry's age and a younger girl, should dance atop the coffin before it was lowered into the earth. This was a development too pagan for the sensibilities of a few dames, who gasped and turned away. But the Watford boy seemed willing enough to oblige: he promptly scrambled atop the wooden box and commenced dancing a little jig with a liveliness that considerably exceeded his grace. His enthusiasm was only encouraged by the hurrahs and aping dance steps performed by some members of the assembly and he evidently enjoyed being the center of attention, even in such a macabre cause. His sister, however, being of a more discreet or possibly superstitious nature, could not be inveigled onto the top of the coffin. Instead she sat gingerly on its edge, dangling her feet and looking apprehensive.

At length it seemed her mother came to share the little girl's view of the enterprise, for Mrs. Watford finally stepped forward, adjuring her son to stop and dismount. And now it appeared that the major's creative ideas about his send-off had run their course, and nothing remained of the ceremonies but to deposit him in the earth.

The pallbearers lifted the casket one last time and tilted it toe-end up in preparation for lowering it into the hole. Harry, who had squirmed his way into a position near the fore, could distinctly hear a rather sickening sequence of thuds and slithering noises as the corpse of the major shifted its position within the box, apparently collapsing in a heap at the head end. It seemed the Walking Dunghill was going to greet his maker when the Last Trumps sounded in an even more undignified posture than he had envisioned. But the adults surrounding Harry all pretended to hear nothing of these noises, so he tried to stop alike his ears and his speculations regarding developments inside the coffin.

The casket was lowered, with much grunting and a final thump, into place, and the onlookers were told to cast their fronds of box and yew into the opening after it. Harry was one of the first to do so and he speedily backed away to the periphery of the crowd, only to come face to face with one of his cousins.

Dick Steer, a cheerful, well-grown lad of sixteen, was from a branch of the family generally slighted by Harry's father. Steers were numerous in Darking Hundred, the family being one of great antiquity if, for the most part, little distinction. Their place in society ranged from the Lee Steeres of Jayes Park—who had kept their name unspoiled by a titular prefix but were nonetheless qualified to rub shoulders with any peer of the realm—to a lowly George Steer, currently resident in the Darking workhouse. Harry's father aspired to belong to the Lee Steere end of this spectrum—indeed, the question of whether to append the all-important *e* to their name was a frequent topic of dinner-table argument—while Dick, the eldest son of a tenant farmer with a tidy copyhold on the eastern side of Holmwood Common, stood only a few bad harvests away from the luckless George's state. Harry was being taught Latin and the elements of Greek before being sent to Winchester College for his education; Dick had learned his letters in the parish vestry and now helped his father on the farm.

Harry looked up to Dick and wished his own parents allowed him greater intercourse with Dick's branch of the family, for they seemed to be a jolly, contented lot who kept their farm in good order and led an easygoing existence untroubled by concern for the proprieties—much less the classics. Dick in particular was an enterprising fellow, always ready to kick up a lark with his cronies. If it came to any form of sport, from orchestrating a backwards race on mules to pretending to be a press-gang and seizing unwary boys of less adventurous proclivities, Dick and his friends were game. Harry could see at a glance that Dick was up to something now, despite the presence on the scene of his father's landlord, Mr. Peters. So Harry's interest in the obsequies, already flagging as the earth was shoveled over the Walking Dunghill, was easily won away.

"Hoy, Harry," said Dick, employing in deference to the occasion a slightly less stentorian tone than was his habit, "what'd you think?"

"Better than an ordinary funeral," replied Harry judiciously, though he had never in his life attended one, "but—but—" He felt unable to articulate exactly how the funeral of Major Peter Labilliere had fallen shy of his expectations; he only knew that it had.

It was enough, however, to earn at least Dick's temporary esteem, for he said, "I know. Curst flat. But some folk and I have an idea that ought to make things more interesting. You in?"

Harry hesitated. The afternoon was already lengthening, and he was not certain he wished to get caught up in any of Dick's sort of knavery, which could only earn him even more severe punishment than was already destined to be his lot.

That brief hesitation was instantly perceived by his cousin, and the moment was lost. "Oh, well, reckon you're too little to be of any use with what's afoot, anyway. Mind you don't get yourself a dunking, that's all." And on this cryptic note Dick was off, joining a small cluster of his intimates as they loped down the path toward Darking.

Harry glanced back at the funeral party. The hole had been filled in and a portion of those gathered, reluctant to end their afternoon's release from daily toil, were dancing to a rough music being hummed and stamped out by several of their number; but most of the townspeople were simply milling about, discussing the events of the day in lowered tones and wondering what to do next. Harry saw little point in remaining on Box Hill any longer; he took to his heels in pursuit of Cousin Dick.

He caught up to the older boys at the bottom of the hill, on the banks of the Mole, and the meaning of Dick's parting shot was immediately apparent. The young men were in the act of removing the last of the planks from the footbridge across the river. A moment later and the entire funeral party would be stranded without a crossing.

Harry gave a shout of delight and raced for the final plank. He had excellent balance and was halfway across, even without the handrail (which had already disappeared), before the lads on the other side were able to seize their end of the plank and begin to heave it from side to side, loosening it within its resting place. Harry dropped to all fours and clung to the wood, only to discover the flaw in this stratagem as the boys raised their end and flipped the whole plank over, Harry and all. Harry's hands slipped and he dropped into the water.

He resurfaced in the stream, laughing, and struck out for the Darking shore, hurling cheerful threats of retribution as he came. The older boys responded in kind as they hauled in the plank and laid it down with the rest upon the bank. Harry's good-nature about his mishap earned him a quick smile from Dick and an offer to hide with them in the undergrowth while they waited to observe what befell the members of the funeral party once they returned to discover the missing bridge. Harry was about to fall in with this plan when he realized that along with himself and his garments, the satchel holding his father's cheroots had gone under the waves and was soaked.

"Oh, I'm going to catch it now!" he cried, frantically pulling at the strap of the bag to inspect its contents.

The boys all gathered around to consider the box and hear the tale of Harry's errand and its unfortunate denouement. It was decided that the cigars were not so very wet after all, and the best thing Harry could do was to spread them out to dry for a while in the sun before attempting to take them home, since he had insufficient funds remaining to buy more. The sun was still hot and the tobacco might very well be as good as new after an hour or so; and if not, Harry could always blame the condition of the cigars on a careless shopkeeper, so long as his clothes dried completely in the interim.

This seemed like excellent commonsense to Harry, so one of the boys obligingly spread out his coat on the grass, a little distance away from the path, and all the cheroots were arranged atop it. Then the group retired to a thicket beside the riverbank and settled down to wait.

It was not long before the first members of the mourning party appeared on the scene. These early comers seemed to feel that perhaps they had mistaken the way and thus reached the Mole at a spot some small distance from the location of the bridge; they spent a few minutes clambering through the riverside tangle on a hunt for the crossing, to the suppressed hilarity of the watchers on the other side.

"You'd think they were birds whose nest had been moved to another branch!" whispered one young blade. The wood-pigeon overhead hooted its sympathy, and a yaffle farther away uttered a heartless laugh.

"Where can it be?" hissed another, aping the distress on the face of a matron on the other shore. "It must be here somewhere!"

"Shh!" The boys continued their watch.

Soon greater numbers had joined the first victims, however, all having taken the same path, and it rapidly became plain to everyone that the bridge was indeed gone. Much agitated colloquy ensued on the Box Hill side of the stream, and the responses to this unexpected setback were as varied as the people experiencing it. There were the outraged, who huffed and puffed before they could submit to the indignity of wading fully clothed into the water; and the good-humored, who were prepared to laugh their way through the stream before continuing on to Darking. Some young and playful members of the party found amid the inconvenience an opportunity to cast aside restraint and enjoy forbidden intimacy—young men offering to carry a fair lass from one bank to the other, young women agreeing with blushes and laughter to being carried. And there were still others whose notion of decorum or self-worth forbade them to submit to crossing in any such manner; they set off with stiff backs to walk three miles around by way of the Burford Bridge crossing.

The hidden authors of the scene observed these debates with glee. But soon controversy arose among them as well: Should they declare the joke complete and replace the bridge? Should they remain where they were and wait to see what all their victims decided to do? What if some of the mourners achieved the crossing and discovered them in their hiding place? Perhaps they ought to emerge, one or two at a time, as if they had simply happened upon the spot, and offer assistance? What if they were not believed? The whispers flew back and forth in the thicket where they were concealed.

Harry held his peace throughout this controversy. He felt it was for his elders to decide—having created the dilemma, they bore the burden of its resolution—but also, he could not readily see how he was to retrieve his cheroots without being spotted by those on the other side of the river, and then he might be blamed for the whole. So he remained where he was and, unable to reach consensus on a course of action, the other boys did the same.

The leisure of inaction was not possible for the unfortunate mourners gathered on the opposite bank, however, and the crossings had begun. Though shallow at this point the water was fairly swift, and a few suffered ignominious dunkings and struggles before reaching safety. One or two of the boldest youths may have intentionally lost their balance midstream and dropped their fair passengers into the water, for the honor of rescuing them and perhaps for a glimpse of their figures under sodden, clinging garments. The sight of the good townspeople of Darking thus submitting to the ruination of their best festival-day clothes was irresistibly amusing to Dick Steer and his cohort, and the prank was held to be a great success.

At last Harry judged the scene of commotion to be sufficiently chaotic that he might be able to slip out of his place of concealment without drawing unwelcome attention. He did so and, being already soaked to the skin, was able to give the impression of having just emerged from the waters himself. He approached the edge, assisted one shopkeeper's wife of imposing girth to clamber up onto the bank, and then made off for the field to inspect his cheroots. These were still unfortunately a trifle damp, but he judged the perils of waiting any longer to exceed those of presenting them to his father without further loss of time, so he repacked them in their box and hurried off with the other bedraggled mourners toward the town. There he collected his horse and rode to the southward for home.

The Steer family's house, Henfold, was a rambling structure, the greater part of which dated to the reign of the Virgin Queen. It had started life as the home of a man of property, declining over time to become a farmhouse and then growing again over the centuries to an abode of somewhat greater stature, though it retained a curtilage designed more for function than for beauty, with barn, storehouses, and dairy all close to the house. It might by the liberally inclined be described as a manor, though without any historical justification for the title. Henfold was located nearly five miles from Darking, on the other side of Holmwood Common. Between the two lay great stretches of rutted, ill-maintained roads as well as woodlands and waste lands filled with hazards that ranged from bogs to banditti. It was imperative that he reach the safe harbor of his home before full dark or anything might befall him.

The idea of such perils made the journey more thrilling than daunting for Harry, who had always considered his life to be burdened by excessive monotony; and a ride across the Holmwood, with its reputation as a haunt of desperadoes and highwaymen, offered promise of adventures of the most nerve-tingling variety. Not for nothing had he dubbed his horse—in reality a strengthy beast retired from farm work—Parsifal, in honor of the quests and adventures he often undertook in his imagination.

The more direct road, passing along the eastern side of Holmwood Common, must be avoided on account of being deeply mired at most seasons of the year, and thus too hazardous in failing light for Parsifal. After considering what coins remained in his purse, Harry opted instead for the turnpike road toward Capel, which drove straight along the common on the western side—still muddy in spots, but navigable at least on horseback.

He passed by Cat's Fields and the workhouse without incident. The sun had fallen below the horizon and the long twilight was begun by the time he had paid his tuppence at the first tollgate and was riding across the flank of the Hollow Hill, with its dark tangle of elms, hollies, and firs looming above the road. Wednesday not being market day, the way was deserted and he rode at his ease, taking care only to direct Parsifal's steps into the portions of the road that suffered least from ruts and puddles.

Before long, however, both Harry and Parsifal became aware of some unusual movement in the undergrowth, the old horse's ears pricking forward in inquiry and Harry sitting up a bit straighter. No sooner had he dismissed the movement as the stirrings of a fox or a pig than a rider emerged from the trees a little way ahead of him. This person spurred his horse into a gallop, riding straight toward Harry at breakneck speed. As horse and rider bore down upon him, Harry could see first the man's worn clothing, then the cloth drawn up to cover his face to the eyes, and lastly the cold nose of a pistol aimed at Harry's own head.

Chapter the Second

For a brief moment Harry wished he were not such a grown-up boy as to be sent alone into town to buy cheroots. But however disagreeable, his predicament, and the weapon pointing at him, were real enough and must be faced. At the very least he was about to be robbed. Seeing no immediate avenue of escape, he reined in Parsifal, feigning a calm he did not feel.

"Raise your hands in the air!" commanded the highwayman, dragging hard on the reins to bring his horse to a halt just inches from Parsifal's nose. Parsifal fretted at being so accosted, but Harry held him well in hand. At this close proximity, Harry was able to see plainly the man's reaction when he saw he had waylaid, not some prosperous merchant carrying home the day's purse, but a mere boy. The ruffian's eyes widened momentarily, then became guarded. The direction of his thoughts was easy to read: he first considered simply turning and riding back into the trees, and next realized that if Harry were allowed to depart, he could well lay information with the nearest magistrate. Harry quaked inwardly as these ideas flitted across the highwayman's face, and he obediently raised his hands and laced his fingers behind his head, hoping that the trembling in his limbs was undetectable.

"I have nothing that could be of use to you," said he in the calmest voice he could muster. "I have only thruppence and some damp cheroots."

Whatever the highwayman had expected, it was hardly this. Victims were expected to beg or cajole. He could not resist making the inquiry: "Why are they damp?"

"My cousin gave me a dunking in the River Mole," said Harry, and he waited patiently for the highwayman to decide what to do.

"Only thruppence, you say?" The man was evidently stalling for time.

"Only thruppence," confirmed Harry, "because I bought a meat pasty."

"Have you still got the pasty?" the highwayman asked, confirming Harry's dawning suspicion that he had been waylaid either by an amateur at the robbery game or by the stupidest highwayman ever to walk the earth. The man was not even physically imposing: he was slight almost to emaciation and not much taller than Harry. As his fear abated, Harry composed his features into neutrality and slowly lowered his hands to rest again on the reins, a dis- obedience that went unremarked by his captor.

"I do have the pasty," answered Harry, "in my belly." The highwayman appeared so crestfallen that Harry was moved to add sympathetically, "You haven't always been a highway- man, have you? What led you to take to the King's Road?"

"No more nor a year agone I had a tidy farm over Hampshire way, but the black harvest done me in, and the lord took it away from me. There's been precious little in *my* belly since then, but for the nettles and dock I can pick by the wayside."

"I'm sorry I can't help you," said Harry; "work is scarce enough hereabouts. And in the future if you wish to hold up well-breeched victims, I suggest you watch the Wotton road to the west of town. Coast Hill is reckoned very fruitful by the local highwaymen, or so I hear—though others may contest your right to ply your trade there. This turnpike is very little traveled in the evening hours. Or you might visit the Nag's Head, down the way a few miles; I'm told it is a haunt of criminals, and those who pass the time there might be able to put you in the way of employment."

Without further ado, he prepared to urge his horse forward. The highwayman started out of his own thoughts and seized Parsifal's rein near the bit, his horse jibbing at the sudden assault.

"Not so fast, little nipper! Did I give you leave to go?"

"No," said Harry, "but as I am already extremely late getting home and my father knows the route I took, it seems likely that he will have sent out a servant to look for me. I imagine you shouldn't wish to be seen with that pistol, and a kerchief pulled up over your face."

The highwayman was much struck by Harry's sensitivity to the delicate nature of his situation. He released the reins. "That I would not," he acknowledged. "You're a canny one for your age. I'd best make off now—but mind you don't go telling no tales about me to your dad."

Harry assured him truthfully that nothing could be further from his intentions—telling his father about being held up on the road would only serve to focus his father's attention on the lateness of the hour, which would do nothing but increase his sire's wrath. Accepting Harry's sincerity, the highwayman wasted no time withdrawing again into the cover of the trees.

Harry, proceeding on his way, was left prey to conflicting emotions. On the one hand, he felt he had conducted himself well in a crisis; he had not shown fear, and had quitted the field of conflict still in possession of thruppence and the cheroots. On the other, his first meeting with a highwayman had proved to be a signal disappointment, the ruffian having been both undersize and not very threatening. As an adventure, the encounter had left a great deal to be desired.

Riding on through the crowding darkness of the warm June evening, Harry beguiled the time by imagining instead how the highwayman of his fancy should have behaved, weaving lurid scenes of drama and gore. Before he had traveled half a mile, the reality of the encounter had been supplanted by a thrilling narrative of bags of gold kept safe by means of his valiance and wicked swordplay. Soon he was overcoming life-threatening wounds to knock the pistol out of the highwayman's hand with his saber and then graciously sparing the man's life after commandeering his steed.

As the moon would not rise for some time to come, it was perhaps fortunate, considering Harry's state of distraction, that Parsifal knew the way to his stable very well indeed. The Nag's Head tavern and Swan's lonely windmill passed over Harry's vision unremarked, and luckily no more fearsome desperadoes lurked in the wastelands of the common that evening, or he would have been in real peril.

At the Holmwood tollgate, Harry scarcely heard the gatekeeper's remark of "You're abroad full late, Master Harry," as he surrendered two of his remaining pennies and rode on. Just past the second crossing of the Ashbrook, Parsifal turned in at the path that passed between the lower fields of Henfold's farm, his weary pace quickening as he climbed the last hill to the house. Here, however,

Harry was rudely awakened from his reverie; before he could reach the shelter of the stable, the side door of the house was thrown open with a bang and his father appeared, holding aloft a lantern.

No sooner had Harry tumbled off Parsifal than he found himself the recipient of a series of mighty whacks about the back and legs, delivered by means of the shaft of a rake that had been leaning most inconveniently against the stable wall.

"Where do you think you have been?" Mr. Steer shouted. "You should've been home a good seven hours ago! Your mother has been picturing you dead since nightfall! What have you to say for yourself?"

John Steer was a slim man, but wiry and powerful from years of toiling alongside his hirelings on the farm, and Harry's eyes stung from the force of the blows. He huddled close to Parsifal and took a few deep breaths while considering his best reply.

"It was a funeral, Dad—"

The unfortunate use of the word *Dad* only increased his father's fury. "Address me as sir, young good-for-nothing! Are we rustics?" But then, as Harry's meaning penetrated his wrath, he added, "Whose funeral? You were sent for my tobacco—what has a funeral to say about the matter?"

"I'd bought your cheroots, sir, when I learned that the major—Major Labilliere—had died, and the whole town almost was turning out to attend his funeral. I felt I should pay my respects."

"Major Labilliere, eh? Well, that could account for no more than an hour or two of delay. What did you do after?"

"It was much longer than that, sir. The burial was all the way up on the top of Box Hill—"

"Nonsense! There's no churchyard on Box Hill."

"No, sir, but that's where the major asked to be buried, and Mr. Peters gave his permission." If even this detail were to be considered incredible in his father's eyes, then Harry saw no benefit from relating any of the more extraordinary aspects of the event. "Everyone was going, so I thought I should go as well. And then on the way back—" Harry eyed the rake shaft with misgiving—"the bridge across the Mole had been removed, so we all got wet returning to town. The cheroots were in my satchel and were a little damp, so I spread them out in the sun to dry for a while, but it was getting late and so I put them back in the box and came away."

His father's attention was immediately diverted. "Show them to me!"

Harry produced the box.

Mr. Steer examined the cigars and appeared to a small degree mollified. "They are not completely ruined. It was a good notion to dry them out immediately; I will set them on the kitchen hearth overnight. But explain to me again about the wetting—the bridge was present when you crossed it on the way to Box Hill, and absent when you returned?"

Here was yet another hazard for Harry to navigate. Any mention of Cousin Dick would certainly arouse further ire, as well as calling into question the veracity of the whole. "Some older boys were playing a prank. They left the funeral early, went on down the hill, and took up the planks of the bridge. I arrived just as they were finishing and tried to get across on the last plank, but they picked it up and shook me off. Everyone who came down later had to swim for it."

"And you expect me to believe this farradiddle?"

Fresh from his triumphant encounter with the highwayman, Harry decided to put a bold face on it. "I expect half the county will be talking of it by now, sir—and most likely in embroidered versions, not the round tale as I have given it to you. Mama will doubtless hear of it tomorrow at market."

"We'll see, we'll see." Mr. Steer's wrath was subsiding, but he was still unwilling to let his son off unpunished for the worry he and his wife had suffered. "I can't say you should not have stayed on for the major's funeral, but it would better have happened on another day, and us none the wiser. Get you off now and see to your horse. I won't rouse Nat to help you, nor will you find any supper waiting for you indoors. Go straight off to bed after Parsifal is settled."

Harry did as he was bid. He performed the requisite tasks with the greatest thoroughness, rubbing down Parsifal with a straw, pumping up a bucket of fresh water for him, and settling him in his stall with a forkful of hay. The familiar motions soothed horse and master alike and allowed Harry for a bit to postpone his return to the house. It was by no means certain that his father would not work himself back into a rage, and speculation over what he might do much occupied Harry's mind and tightened the muscles of his gut. Pride and dignity must be summoned and fortified before he could reenter the family circle with equanimity.

At last, however, everything that might be done in the stable was done, even the restoration of the rake to its proper corner. Harry directed his steps to the side door and entered.

The rooms on the ground floor were all dark and no candle had been left for him, so he felt his way to the stairs and climbed. He was tempted to plunder the pantry shelves but refrained for fear his raid would not go unremarked. The ancient oak of the staircase creaked underfoot, but no one came out to see who was abroad.

He gained the sanctuary of his own room, there to discover that someone had placed a single tallow light on a table—and recently, for it had not yet begun to gutter. Harry was not inclined to stay up any longer, however; he undressed in haste and climbed into bed, his body stiffening and beginning to ache from the combined effects of riding, climbing Box Hill, and blows from the rake. His hands and face could just as easily be washed in the morning.

He was lying in the dark, entertaining rather melancholy thoughts about the day and its conclusion, when his door suddenly opened and his mother entered in a rush, closing the door silently behind her. Jenny Steer was a little sparrow of a woman, all swift movements and impulse. She scurried now to his bedside, scarcely setting down her candle before enveloping Harry in a hug.

"Oh, sweet boy, sweet boy," she whispered into his chest, and perched on the edge of the bed. "I was so frightened that you had met with some misadventure! I cannot imagine what I should do if you came to harm."

This assault on Harry's sensibilities was a good deal more dangerous than his father's wrath, and it was a struggle to suppress the desire to cast his arms around her and sob. But Harry was twelve—too old for such little-boy weakness—so he sat primly upright and apologized to her for causing anxiety. "I discovered upon arriving in Darking that the Walking D—that Major Labilliere had died and his funeral was just then about to begin. It didn't seem fitting to come away without paying my respects."

"And very proper to do so, I'm sure," said Mrs. Steer. "We won't regard your father; he was only angry because he wanted to smoke after dinner. He is asleep now, so I tiptoed down to the kitchen. You must be famished after such a day." And from a pocket in her gown she produced large hunks of cheese and bread.

This fresh kindness was almost too much for Harry to bear, had his hunger not been too acute to permit the indulgence of emotion. He seized upon the food and began bolting it down without a word.

Mrs. Steer smiled upon her firstborn. "We can't have you wasting away to nothing when you have so much learning yet to accomplish before you go away to school. I expect your papa will be even more insistent now that you keep to your studies." Their eyes met and both gave a little sigh, Harry for the summer pleasures to be forgone and Mrs. Steer for the prospect of his departure. "In the meantime, should you like to have a story before bed?"

Harry nodded as he chewed.

"Very well. What shall it be? Donkeyskin, or Hop o' My Thumb?"

"Bevis of 'Hampton among the pirates," replied Harry thickly.

"Very well. Bevis was the son of Guy of Southampton, and he had a very wicked mother. She was originally from Scotland, and had had a suitor there before she married. This suitor came to Southampton and she plotted with him to kill her husband, Bevis's father, which he did. She wanted him to kill Bevis as well, but Bevis escaped from the castle in the dark of night and was taken up on a pirate ship and sailed far, far away, to lands that you and I will never see. . . ."

Harry was asleep before the story was well under way.

CHAPTER THE THIRD

The next morning, after a night in which the Walking Dunghill kept uncoiling awkwardly from his pit of a grave to pursue Harry, haranguing him in a most terrifying manner about love and liberty and hurling coins at his face, Harry was awakened by the sound of his mother clapping her hands in the kitchen garden to frighten off the magpies. In the past he would have leaped out of bed to join the sport, but today he was moving more slowly, stiff from the blows he had suffered. So he sat by the window and watched her with affection while she cast grain for her fowls; as the corn caught the earliest shafts of sunlight in flashes of gold she seemed to be dispelling the darkness of his thoughts, scattering glory from her fingertips.

By the time he had dressed, she was already gone for the day in the farm cart, bearing her eggs and a selection of her fine Darking hens to market. This left only Harry, his father, his tutor William Marshall, and his younger sister Isabella to gather around the breakfast table. It was immediately apparent that as his mother had predicted, his father was even more implacably committed than before to having the classics pounded into his head.

Mr. Steer's sensibilities were not of such an order as to perceive that any harm might arise within the family circle if he berated one child in the presence of another, or even in the presence of such persons as Janey the kitchenmaid or Mr. Marshall. Accordingly, once he had returned the cheroots to their box and set it in the cupboard beside the kitchen fireplace, he felt no compunction about picking up his harangue where he had left off the night before.

Harry was attempting to swallow as much breakfast as he could while remaining invisible, but there was no hiding. "So, young scapegrace, you think you can sleep under my roof and eat at my table, and yet suit your own pleasure, just as if you were your own master?" Mr. Steer demanded.

"No, sir," said Harry meekly.

"I should think not! While you are in my house, you'll dance to the tune of my piping. No more running off to Darking, or to Box Hill, or out into the woods, or anywhere else your fancy takes you, young man: you have forfeited the trust I placed in you."

Harry chafed inwardly at the injustice of this characterization of events—his father had, after all, *sent* him to Darking, and all the subsequent events had flowed from that errand. But he knew better than to interrupt.

"One would have thought you would be grateful for the opportunity you've been given: it's not every boy who is admitted to Winchester, or whose family can afford to send him there! Your duty to our kinsman, Mr. Steere—the obligation he has placed you under for using his influence to secure your admission—ought to be enough to make you take your studies seriously. But no! All you want is to seize your pleasures where you find them, like some young lord of the manor."

Isabella snickered, her eyes bright as she stored up

fodder for teasing and tormenting her brother when her next opportunity arose.

"From this day forward, I'll have no more of it," pursued Harry's father. "You will spend every day at your books until the start of term, and when you are at school you will conduct yourself with proper appreciation for the privilege that has been extended to you. Do you think it was easy for me to earn the money to send you there?"

"No, sir."

"It has been the labor of years to make this opportunity possible! Extending my property, increasing my stock, studying the best methods for extracting every penny of value from my land, scrimping and laying by so you will have a chance to improve the family's lot. But do you care? No! All you think of is your own amusement."

"Shame on you, Harry," said Isabella, forgetting herself.

Her father rounded on her. "Nobody gave you permission to speak!" She quailed and Mr. Steer, after staring her down for a few moments, reverted to his subject. "You have earned what is coming to you. Parsifal will no longer be at your disposal; I have told Nat to deny him to you. You shall not leave the yard without permission. You will not take part in the haying or the harvest, even if I have to hire more hands. And I repeat: you shall study every single day until you depart for school."

To Harry's tutor Mr. Marshall, a son of the curate at Horsham, no pronouncement could have afforded greater satisfaction. It was a continuing mystery to this young man—who had received from his father an education that ill-suited him to pursue any profession he could afford to enter—how Harry, privileged to receive induction into the mysteries of a classical education, could instead favor unearthing a badger, robbing a bird's nest, or even laboring in the fields over reading Homer or Horace. Mr. Marshall would have given anything to have been educated at Winchester College. Instead he faced a dreary future as a shop clerk or scribe to a country attorney, his fate only postponed by this temporary employment, at a paltry wage, as Harry's tutor. For even this small reprieve he was grateful, and he felt a hurt bafflement in the face of his pupil's recalcitrance. To inculcate in Harry the elements of Greek and Latin grammar and philosophy was alike his duty and his delight, but Harry was all too prone to falling into abstraction, staring out the window at the swallows diving around the eaves just when Mr. Marshall was revealing the precious keys to unlocking Cicero's arguments.

Harry had hoped that his father's determination would wane over time, but more than a week passed and still Mr. Steer remained adamant. Daily he interrogated Harry at the dinner table about what he had learned, though Harry suspected he understood little of the answers. Harry was careful to betray no sign of awareness that his father's education had been inferior. He was all too conscious of the fragility of his father's pride, of how deeply he resented his ambiguous position in the world—placed too low to be noticed by the gentry, yet far too high to receive their largesse. His retired style of living, his lack of intellectual attainments, and the duties of maintaining the farm prevented any escape from his situation, so all his views for the elevation of the family had come to rest on Harry's reluctant shoulders.

As the days succeeded one another, the heat pressing against Harry's window and the intoxicating scents of summer trickling around the casements, Harry grew more and more restless, certain that his life was ebbing away while grand adventures lurked in the nearest copse and the world grew stale for want of his youthful spirits. Even the bee bumbling along the windowsill was free to take wing and seek its nectar elsewhere, while Harry was imprisoned by declensions and the optative mood till not even his fancy could wander.

The first hint of reprieve was not a promising one. The mandate of daily study was not to be the end of Mr. Steer's dispositions for Harry's betterment: no sooner had the surplus wool been hauled to market, in the brief pause before haying was to begin, than Mr. Steer declared one of the horses at liberty to convey Harry and himself in the gig on a visit of ceremony to their kinsman at Jayes Park, the grandly and redundantly styled Mr. Lee Steere Steere— the distant cousin who had arranged for Harry to attend school. "We mustn't be backward in showing him proper attention," was his assertion.

Harry would rather not have had *anyone* to thank for this favor, of course, but he knew better than to dispute the point with his father. Neither would his mother set herself in opposition to her husband's further decree that a brace of her beloved guinea fowl must be sacrificed and presented as a votive offering to the god of Jayes. If visiting were to be done, both mother and son would have found it far jollier to pay a call on their lesser Steer relations, but since they were not consulted in the matter there was nothing to be gained by dwelling on their own preference.

Isabella, however, was loud in her protestations that she should be allowed to go to Jayes. Unlike Harry, she shared her father's aspirations to rise in the world; her ambition appeared to center on becoming as ornamental and useless as the heroine of a romance. She had a taste for finery and grand furnishings that could not be satisfied by rare glimpses at periodicals such as the *Ladies' Monthly Museum,* which might on occasion come into the possession of a friend or neighbor. Although Jayes was far from being the grandest house in the country, to Isabella it represented all the elegancies that lay out of her reach, and she was seized with envy of her brother's luck.

"Why should Harry go?" cried she; "I should enjoy the visit far more, and I'm sure I would be much more polite than Harry will be, for he has no manners at all!" Ignoring her mother's attempts to hush her, she followed her father down the hall, pouting in her most angelic manner. "Our cousin has already done Harry a favor and isn't likely to do him any more, but if he took a fancy to *me*, perhaps he could send me to a Bath seminary. Why should Harry receive a fine education while I am left behind?"

Her father was obdurate, though, and she had no recourse but to enjoy a hearty bout of tears as she was pulled away to her room by her mother. So Harry would have no escape from the visit. At least, he reflected, it meant a day away from the books, and as the gig was not often used, a ride in it might be construed as a treat. This conveyance—which had seen its better days in the household of a gentleman whose idleness had justified its expense until his vices had necessitated its sale—required considerable washing and polishing up by Nat before it could be deemed respectable enough to grace the precincts of Jayes Park. But it was ready at last.

They were dressed in their Sunday finery and on the point of mounting into the gig when an unexpected interruption occurred: a handsome curricle and pair drove up to the door, and a gentleman, a stranger to them all, climbed down from it. He was a tall man in the prime of his years, handsome but foreign in his appearance, with an olive complexion and dark eyes flashing under black brows. Upon descending from the curricle he carelessly demanded that Harry go to the horses' heads; Harry, unaccustomed to being treated like a groom on his own doorstep, was little inclined to comply, but at a nod from his father he obeyed.

Mr. Steer, impressed by the stranger's prosperous appearance, offered a bow and asked, "May I be of service?"

The dark man strode forward, his driving cape billowing behind him. "My name is Barclay. Is this your farm?" he asked abruptly.

Even Harry's father stiffened a little at this brusque approach. "And my name is Steer, sir. How do you do?" He put out his hand and, after hesitating a moment, the man took it. Only then did Mr. Steer continue: "I own this property and the farms associated with it."

"Freehold?" demanded Mr. Barclay.

"Yes, though I cannot see what business it is of yours."

"I'd like to purchase it."

Mr. Steer was all astonishment at this haphazard method of conducting business. "Purchase my property? Why, you don't even know its extent, or the condition of the house, or what the acres yield. How—"

"I've no doubt you will enlighten me on all those matters in due course," said Mr. Barclay indifferently.

Harry's father stiffened. "And I am certain I shall not. This property is not for sale." Harry discovered he had been holding his breath, and he let it out in a long sigh of relief.

Mr. Barclay, however, was unimpressed. "I want it, and I have no doubt I can name a price that will make it worth your while. I intend to have it."

Mr. Steer had had enough. "I shall be charitable and take you to be a madman who has eluded his keeper," said he. "Harry, it is time we departed. If you will pardon us, sir, we have an errand and you are blocking our drive."

Harry released the reins of Mr. Barclay's horses, so the man was compelled to leap into his carriage to control them. "I shall not be so easily dissuaded!" he cried. "You shall hear from me again." He jerked at the reins and his horses leaped into motion, almost colliding with the Steers' gig before he got them turned, and dashed away toward the lane.

On account of this peculiar incident the morning was considerably advanced before Harry and his father set off to visit their cousin. Harry was bursting with questions about what had happened, though a glance at his father's scowling face as they bowled along was enough to urge caution. But at last he could contain his curiosity no longer. "Had you heard of this Mr. Barclay before, sir?"

"Hah! I'd neither met him nor heard his name in all my life. He bore the appearance of one of those new-made men from London, come down to the country to set up as a weekend squire. Perhaps the customs pertaining to matters of business are different in town from what they are here, but with manners like his I can't imagine he'd have much success."

"Why would he not employ an agent to seek out available houses? It seems odd to ride slap up to us and order you to sell."

"*Odd* is an inadequate way to describe it. I have never heard of such a thing. If he hopes to achieve his ends, he would do well to adopt a more ingratiating approach."

Fear assailed Harry. "Would he have any hope of succeeding with you, sir?"

"Of course not! Why would I sell Henfold, after all the labor I have put into it? Where would we go?"

"I am very glad of it, sir," said Harry, feeling the ground beneath him become solid once again.

"But why should he wish to buy?" his father mused. "He had no interest in the land, or even the house. What was he after?"

Harry waited in silence for his father to say more, but after a long pause, he ventured to say, "I am very glad you sent him away with a flea in his ear, sir."

This, however, was too great a familiarity to please his father, who passed the remainder of their journey in lecturing Harry about his use of cant expressions. "I expect you to speak in proper English when you meet our cousin Steere," he concluded as they approached the gate of Jayes Park.

The cousin in question might have been startled to learn that he was a person deserving of such formality. Mr. Lee Steere Steere had succeeded to the dignities of his position at a very young age, some five years previous. Born Lee Steere Witts, the grandson of an earlier master of Jayes, he had not been raised with any certain prospect of inheritance, for his mother had been cast off by his grandfather after marrying a tradesman. But that grandfather having died without any other heirs, young Mr. Witts had been obliged to surrender his surname in exchange for the large, rambling house more than a century old, the several hundred acres of woodland, pasture, and farmland, the quaintly decorated barns and cottages, the advowson of Ockley parish, the raised pew in the church there, the rent rolls, and everything else that went with being a Lee Steere of Jayes. It was said that nobody but a Steere had ever owned the manor since the Conquest, and this was to hold true even if a change of surname were required to make it so.

Any awe he may have felt, however, at this elevation to the highest honors redounding to his house was rapidly subsumed into a conviction that he had found his rightful place in the world. So now, at the age of twenty-five, Mr. Lee Steere Steere had engaged himself to be married and settled into an existence bounded by his plans for the enclosure of his fields and the increase of his house, alike through renovation and reproduction.

That he was pleased with the turn in his fortunes could not be gainsaid, but as his sense of self-worth also mandated that he serve his lessers and dependents according to the principles of noblesse oblige, he had speedily earned the goodwill of his dependents. He was wise enough to understand that naked envy and resentment did not provide a sturdy basis for respect, so that whenever the occasion arose, he took care to extend any assistance or attentions to others that his prudence might allow. Among these was the service he had rendered Harry in representing to the master of Winchester College that admitting his young connection as a Commoner to receive a public school education would lay the basis for an agreeable future relationship between the Steere family and the school, which might bear fruit in who knew what sort of endowments and secondary benefits. The master, well aware of the situation of Jayes Park and the standing of its overlord, was only too happy to oblige.

It cannot be said that Harry shared in the general satisfaction: the prospect of attending Winchester hung over him like the sword of Damocles. Harry was happy in his home and in the rural pursuits that had heretofore occupied his days; he was content to be scrambling his own way into an understanding of the world. He lacked an ambitious nature and could see no allure in the professional avenues that would be opened to him through a classical education, or through rubbing shoulders with boys from higher-bred families. Had he been offered the promise of a commission in a cavalry regiment, that might have been something to look forward to! But absent such an opening onto a life of derring-do, Harry was perfectly content to envision an adulthood conducted along the same lines as his father's—as a freehold farmer with a few laborers to work in his fields, pasturage for cattle and sheep, and peace to enjoy a smoke by the fireside of an evening while reading the newspaper.

His father, however, could not doubt that in sending Harry away to school he was offering him his best—nay, his only—chance at betterment. With that education he would be no longer a gentleman farmer, but a gentleman *tout court*.

And so the gentleman-farmer and the young gentle-man-in-the-making rattled their way up the well-tended drive of Jayes Park, Mr. Steer exhorting his son to make himself tidy. Harry was paying him little heed, however; he was entranced by the scene now unfolding before him. High on the ridge to northward, Leith Hill Tower loomed above the estate in all its mystery. Harry had heard of the place and had been regaled with tales of wicked goings-on there, but he had never seen it. *Might we not go there instead?* he wondered—but not aloud.

Knowing such wishes to be futile, he abandoned hope of escape and studied the house, a rambling jumble of loosely connected red brick wings marking the accretions of several centuries. It was for the most part a plainly built structure, no more than two stories in height and little ornamented—not nearly as grand as he had expected from the awe with which his father had spoken of it. But to his country-bred eye the barn and the farm buildings were of a superior character, some built solidly in stone and decorated with fancifully carved bargeboards, iron spikes ornamenting the peaks of the roofs, and pointed arches over the doors and windows. It would seem that at Jayes, the horses expected to live in a better style than the people. Even the granary was a grand affair of ornamented brick and diamond-paned mullions that Harry would not have scorned to call his home. To one side was an ancient-looking crenellated garden wall complete with arrow slits, as if the gardener expected to be called upon to defend his cabbages by force from an unruly mob. Harry was keen to leap out of the gig and explore the gardens, but his father had his sleeve in a tight grip and he was marched firmly up to the house, clutching the brace of guinea fowl by the legs.

Their host, Mr. Lee Steere Steere, greeted his humbler kinsman John Steer with the deference due to his superior age, and declared himself happy to improve his acquaintance with such a fine young man as Harry. He was a jovial young man, less grand than his imposingly dynastic name might suggest, and welcomed them into a sitting room that had been furnished by some earlier generation and never updated.

"You'll take a glass of wine, I trust?" he asked Harry's father, adding with a wink, "We'll liven it up with a tot of brandy, eh? I received a keg of some capital stuff only a day or two ago—left on the kitchen doorstep one morning, you know."

Mr. Steer, who was content with the ale that came from his own brewhouse, was startled. "You mean, left there by the *smugglers*?"

"Free-traders, we should say, to give them their proper respect," rejoined his cousin. "Of course! I wish to be on good terms with *all* my neighbors, and those enterprising gentlemen most of all. One must have something to drink, you know; and in these times, who can afford anything once duty has been paid on it? Keeping the traders content is a matter of prudence, wouldn't you agree? They are a rascally lot, after all—it doesn't do to be on their bad side. *I* don't want my horses stolen or my hay ricks set alight!"

Mr. Steer was unable to take such a cavalier view of the case. "They have never troubled me, and I have never chosen to have any dealings with them, cooperative or otherwise."

"How can you be certain you have not? When you select the lowest-priced tobacco at the tobacconist's or tea that has not been cut with blackberry leaves at the grocer's, or your wife purchases cambric for a gown, do you inquire into how the shopkeeper obtained his stores? Between the coast and the metropolis, I daresay, there's few enough bargains to be had that were not delivered to the back of the shop in the dead of night. And have you never found laborers scarce at harvest time?"

Mr. Steer allowed that he was finding it difficult to hire enough men willing to cut his hay the next week.

"And the wagoners none too eager to oblige you with portage either, I suspect. Do you not imagine that many believe they can earn better wages in the pack trains, running smuggled goods to London? I pay my laborers a higher wage than is customary, ay, and provide the best-kept cottages I can afford; but the temptation must be very great for the young men of that class to throw in their lot with the free-traders. It is not to be wondered at if no one feels the slightest shame at violating laws which everyone believes to be absurd and unjust."

"Do you not fear the contagion of such ideas? If a man thinks nothing of violating a law that makes no sense to him, will he not proceed from one seemingly minor infraction to others more serious?"

Harry listened to this exchange with round eyes; he had little expected so much interest to arise from the visit. Tales of smugglers were always thrilling but had seemed far away in space and time, centering as they did on the seacoast and the notorious Sussex gangs of fifty years earlier. It had never occurred to him that there might be smuggling in Surrey! But when he thought about it, it made sense—for the smugglers could hardly dispose of all their goods in the seaside towns. It stood to reason that much of the tea and tobacco, spirits and silks they brought in should have to reach the markets of London and beyond.

Unfortunately, his father was bent on turning the conversation. "We must not waste this fine wine on questions of politics, but instead lift our glasses in honor of your bride-to-be," he said. "We heard of your good fortune even in our remote corner of the world. Indeed, sir, my wife joins me in offering you our congratulations! Shall you be married soon?"

"Not so very soon; we look to be wed at Christmas. Miss Sarah is eager to make a start on her life as mistress of Jayes, so I must rejoice in my bachelor state while yet I may. She is full of plans for improving the house—and no doubt myself as well. If she is to be believed, Jayes will soon present an entirely new aspect to passersby, with a limestone front, bays of enormous windows, and an imposing Grecian pediment. We shall see! It is difficult to imagine that such appurtenances of grandeur would look well plastered to the front of this old brick pile. The Steeres are not accustomed to cutting such a dash in the neighborhood."

"No, indeed. Leave that sort of display to the rich tradesmen who come here bent on setting themselves up as squires," said Mr. Steer, thinking of their unwanted visitor of the morning. "The name of Steere is too ancient, too well respected for such ostentation to be necessary."

"I cannot say as to that," replied the younger man with some discomfort. "My grandfather would have agreed with you, but I was happy enough growing up under the name of Witts till events decreed otherwise. We are, after all, embarking on a new century, where doubtless new manners will prevail. If the new men behave gentlemanly, I shall treat them as gentlemen and not hold myself aloof. And as for my bride, we must keep the ladies happy, after all—and finery and fine houses appear to be all they can think of. If she is determined to turn Jayes into a grand modern house, I fear I must indulge her."

"How could it not be enough for any lady to be Mrs. Lee Steere Steere of Jayes? You honor her with your favor—as you have honored us as well, which we do not forget. Harry, step forward and express your obligation to your kinsman."

Thus urged, Harry did his best to articulate his appreciation for the opportunity being afforded him; but as he could find little to rejoice over on the occasion, it was fortunate that Mr. Steere was not much inclined to enjoy toad-eating. "None of that, none of that!" he cried. "We must all receive an education—though some of us might prefer *not* to spend our days sitting at our books—at least not until we are too old for other amusements, eh, Harry?"

"Yes, sir," agreed Harry warmly, but then added "No, sir," after catching a glimpse of his father's darkening countenance. His kinsman smiled in sympathy with Harry's dilemma. "I believe you will find your schooling to be more diverting than your preparatory studies—especially at Winchester. The headmaster there, Dr. Goddard, impressed me most favorably when we met with his commonsense notions about the education of young boys. He was remarkably eloquent about the necessity of balancing intellectual improvement with physical activity. He outlined his ideas with a degree of trepidation that led me to surmise some parents were unpersuaded of the benefits of his approach; but were I about to enter Winchester, his educational philosophies would considerably relieve my mind!" And then he good-naturedly rescued Harry from further confusion by turning his attention back to Mr. Steer. "Do you believe the weather will continue to smile on us throughout the haying?"

Harry's father considered the question. "At present it appears settled, but having no rain at all for an entire week seems too much to hope for. At least this year promises to be an improvement over the last. Unless the weather turns tomorrow and we see unusual downpours, I am optimistic—not only about the hay, but about the crops. If we can maintain a regular summer climate, the harvest seems very promising indeed."

"I am glad of it, for the sake of the people. They have had far too much suffering in the past two years; any more setbacks and I don't know what will happen."

"Do you fear uprisings, like those on the Continent?"

"I know many men of property go in dread that their tenants and laborers will borrow ideas of revolution from the French or the Irish, but I am more sanguine. We Englishmen have always had a closer relationship with our people. Give them cause to love us and they will remain our friends. I am more worried about their chances of starving. It's my view that a flitch of bacon on the rack does more to keep a man content with his lot than whole volumes of penal statutes." He smiled. "Perhaps the nation has more to fear from our gentry, when faced with all the new taxes—not simply on our land, our servants, our dogs, and our glass, but now on our income! Why should *we* not rise up to defy our oppressors? And the ministers have proposed yet another window tax. Where will it end?"

Harry's father had little to say on this subject, as he lacked sufficient property for such taxes to be a heavy burden. But he agreed that taxes were in general excessive, and galling when imposed to support a war that seemed far away from home and from local concerns. Mr. Steere took the hint and redirected the conversation toward the prices they could hope to get for their corn; the merits and demerits of Robert Bakewell's new Longhorn cattle and John Ellman's Southdown sheep; and other matters of import to country gentlemen. Though not raised to the management of an estate, he was eager to learn, and turned the tables of flattery on his kinsman by soliciting the wisdom of the more experienced countryman.

Harry was happy to be ignored, though his host was considerate enough at the end of the visit to conduct him upstairs to view a monstrous stuffed badger on the landing ("Perhaps I shall make you a gift of it on my wedding day," said Mr. Steere; "I don't imagine my wife will allow me to keep it"). Although Harry was obliged to come away without exploring the crenellated garden wall or the magnificent stables, he departed feeling that, all things considered, his cousin was not so very bad, despite having been so cruel as to arrange for his education.

Chapter the Fourth

After his visit to Jayes Harry's life of drudgery resumed, with Sunday's journey to church in the village of Capel the only variation in his days. His father became preoccupied with the haying, and Harry chafed at the cruelty of being kept away from the fields. The toil of the haying season had faded into dim memory, but he could vividly recall his pleasure in playing among the stooks with the laborers' children and riding home on the jingling hay wains at the end of a long day, as he had always done before. After days of watching his father set off for the fields at first light and return to his rest at nightfall, Harry could dwell in frustration no longer. Without being fully aware of the change, he began to move from resignation to resentment to dreams of escape. He was not always watched by his jailers: Mr. Marshall could not be teaching every hour of the day, and at night his parents, believing him to be asleep, slumbered themselves. Surely on some of these occasions he might be elsewhere, and they none the wiser! A little imagination, and he might discover the means and opportunity to slip his leash.

And yet when the opportunity finally arose, there was little enough foresight or strategy involved. Harry awoke one night from a shallow doze to hear an untoward sound outside, somewhere in the dark. The crescent moon had long since set and his window was open to the warmth of the evening; some slight shift in wind direction carried the sound to his ear and brought him fully awake.

Harry tiptoed to the window. He sat there for a few moments wondering if he had dreamed of hearing something, but then in a fresh stir of breeze the sound came again. He peered out toward the woods to the west of the house and thought he caught a glimpse of something: a tiny flicker of light, then another about thirty feet behind the first. And between these pinpricks of illumination the darkness appeared to be convulsed with vague movements just beyond the power of his mind to interpret.

He listened hard and finally heard it again. The sound was not in itself unusual; he identified it swiftly as the soft clop of many horses' hooves, accompanied by the muffled chiming of their harness. But what made it strange was the hour—that and the location, because toward the west Henfold lay too far from any public road for such a thing to make sense. Who were the phantom travelers passing so close by his house in the middle of the night?

Harry's decision was made without thought. In a moment he had thrown on his breeches over his nightshirt and was carrying his shoes down the stairs, relying on bare feet to keep his descent quiet enough that not a whisper of his intention would be betrayed to the household. He gently unbolted a side door and was off.

Harry flitted across the stableyard and squeezed over the wall where it was shadowed by the eaves of the granary, eschewing the gate lest it squeak. In the lee of the wall he paused a moment. At ground level the lights of the travelers were no longer visible, and a variety of other sounds vied for his ear—a gentle waft of breeze sliding through the treetops, his father's horses restless in the barn as they sensed the presence of unknown animals nearby. He looked back toward the house to identify his window, and then projected outward into the gloom the direction from which the lights had come. Then he was off again, slipping through the puddles of deeper darkness in search of mystery.

As Harry well knew, there was an old way that lanced through the woods nearby, the relic of a cart track leading from the main Capel road to a long-abandoned copyhold. Cottagers sometimes herded their commonable pigs along that way, seeking the abundant pannage of the southern Holmwood. Harry assumed this to be the path taken by the nocturnal travelers, so thither he directed his furtive steps.

The underwood close to the house was easy going, for the servants regularly plucked it clean of twigs and small branches for the kitchen fire. The bracken swished against his legs, and he took care to move in fits and starts as a four-legged creature might. The slow pace of his progress, however, was frustrating: would the horses have moved out of reach before he came to the spot? He increased his speed, only to trip and lie panting in fright on the ground for some moments, awaiting discovery. But no hand seized him out of the night, so he finally picked himself up and moved on.

Throughout his passage toward the old track, no further glimpse of the lights had befriended him; nor could his ears, preoccupied as he was with concern over the small noises he was making, discern any repetition of the sounds that had drawn him from his bed. Eventually in his impatience he abandoned any attempt at caution and simply pushed his way down to the path, disregarding the snapping of twigs and the thump of his feet.

As he feared, there was no longer anything to be seen. But Harry's spirit had broken loose from its confinement and would not suffer him to return tamely to bed. The horses and their attendant lights had seemed to be moving northward along the old way; Harry set off at a trot in their wake.

Even in darkness the track was easily navigated, and he made rapid progress. It was not much more than ten minutes before he imagined he could see a flicker ahead. He slowed to a fast walk and listened again. A horse nickered a furlong up the path and was answered by another.

Their passage through the wood seemed not to have disturbed the night creatures, for an owl hooted just behind Harry. He barely had time to register some oddity in its call before there was a sudden rush of motion and an arm was thrust out of the dark to fetch him a clout on the side of his head. Harry went sprawling and found a knee pressed into his back.

"What do ye here?" demanded a voice in a guttural whisper.

"N-nothing," replied Harry, trying to catch his breath with his face pressed into the dirt.

His assailant set down next to Harry's face a curious device that looked rather like a watering pot. There was a faint scrape as the man turned a cap on the pot and a light shone down the spout, pointing ahead down the track. Several pairs of feet came running back toward them.

"Wotcha got there, Jack?" demanded one.

"Some lad. Seems to be alone," said the voice belonging to the knee.

"Well, get him on his feet," said another.

Harry was dragged up and set on his trembling legs. The watering-pot lantern was again deployed, this time to direct the narrow beam of light onto his face.

"It's nobbut a nipperkin!" cried one of the men surrounding him. "Is that your nightshirt, boy? Why ain't you in your bed?"

Harry recalled the success he had enjoyed from taking a high hand with the highwayman and decided to try the same tactic again. "Why aren't you in *your* bed?" he replied.

This earned him another clout that made him stagger, though this time the hands clutching his arms held him upright. Still he refused to show his fear, and despite a rising nausea, he met their eyes squarely without speaking. They were a grotesque-looking lot, their dirty farmers' smocks covered with dark coats despite the warmth of the night and their hats pulled low over faces smudged with soot. His captor, Jack, was particularly ill-favored, with teeth as crooked as ancient gravestones and a nose that listed several degrees to port.

Harry's silence drove them to speech. "Who told you to look for us?" demanded Jack.

"Nobody. I woke up and saw some lights bobbing in the woods and wondered what was afoot."

"'Tain't healthy to be curious about things you might see in the woods at night," said another man, a heavy-set fellow dangling a club in one hand. "Who kens you're here?"

Harry pondered the consequences of one answer or another, but ultimately decided veracity was best. He admitted that he had left the house without his parents' permission or knowledge. "My life is so very dull, you see," he added.

"You thinks to might find excitement out in the woods, eh?"

"Bound to," said Harry. "Nobody going about legitimate business would be on this track at this hour, after moonset."

"You're one to prate about 'legitimate business'! You ain't afeard that folks not on 'legitimate business' might take it in bad part if you spied on 'em?" asked a younger man. Harry started; the voice sounded familiar, but without a sight of the face, he couldn't place it.

Just then someone from up the track called out to them, "Is all well?"

Jack called back, "It's nobbut a boy out alone, Cap'n. You wishful we should kill him?"

There was a pause, dreadful for Harry in its suspense. "Fetch him here," said the distant voice.

"But he'll see the cargo!" objected the man with the club.

"We can always kill him later."

CHAPTER THE FIFTH

So Harry was dragged up the way to where the rest of the travelers were waiting. He saw more of the curious watering-pot lanterns as well as some dark lanterns, each with only a single panel ajar, set on pikes. By their fitful light he could just make out a large company of packhorses, perhaps as many as fifty, all laden with bundles and two large casks apiece. Men milled about the pack train, some also carrying burdens and others brandishing an assortment of simple weapons, ranging from knives and crooks to large clubs. Eyes gleamed at him out of soot-blackened visages in the lanterns' flicker; these men also wore dark coats and some had kerchiefs drawn up to hide half their faces.

He understood the situation immediately: these were the smugglers his cousin had told of! The idea brought panic, raised as he had been on tales of the ruthless gangs who tyrannized over the coasts through intimidation and murder. And the bobbing of the light lent the scene an infernal quality; he felt a moment's superstitious dread as if he had interrupted a gathering of demons. He sniffed the air to catch a whiff of sulfur about them, but all that came to his nose was the reek of old sweat and the byre.

The familiar odors calmed him. These were mere men, men of the sort he saw every day plodding to the fields, gnarled and leathered by their toil, and bound to labor under the direction of his father or some other landlord. Tonight, however, they were somehow transformed—not only by their disguises but by a certain loose vigor in their movements. Tonight, whatever their order, they were free men, raised by the night and the forest to equality with Harry, with Harry's father, with King George—anyone you choose. The exhilaration, the hazard they embodied was contagious; it ran through Harry in an invigorating current.

His observations were cut short as the men holding him cast him at the feet of a great, barrel-chested young man who seemed to loom so high above him that his head sat among the stars. And from out of the darkness came a sudden exclamation: "Harry! What's your business here?"

The voice was that of his cousin, Dick Steer.

Before he could reply, the tall man before him turned on Dick. "You know this boy?"

"He's my cousin, Cap'n," said Dick. Clearly feeling some further defense necessary, he added, "He's harmless. You can count on him not to rat."

Harry didn't much like being called harmless; but perhaps it was preferable to being killed by the ruffians who had seized him, so he reserved his objections for a more propitious moment—always supposing he should survive to see that moment.

The tall man peered down into Harry's face, his own obscured with soot like the others. "That so? Young 'uns crave having a tale to tell. Dead 'uns don't. I'd as lief he didn't get the chance."

Harry could see, from the way Dick remained still and all the others held their tongues, that his fate trembled on the knife's edge and this man held the power to decide it. With an effort, Harry drew his dignity about him before speaking. "If I told anyone," said he, trying to speak in a deep voice but succeeding only in sounding like a goose with a head cold, "I'd also have to tell that I left the house in the middle of the night and went running off into the woods. My dad would dust my jacket for that, no question. And besides, what could I tell? 'There were men and horses in the woods; I don't know where they are now.' *I* don't even know precisely where I am now, and I doubt you'll be here come sunrise."

The man called the captain eyed Harry with an air that reminded him alarmingly of a cat toying with a bird. "So you say we go our own roads and no harm done?"

"Yes, sir," said Harry, the jut of his chin belying the tremor in his voice, "—unless, perhaps, you could use another helper?"

A number of the men guffawed, and Harry relaxed a fraction.

"And what sort of help would you be of a mind to provide, lad?"

"I don't know. What do you need? I could be a lookout—I can certainly imitate an owl better than that Jack fellow there."

The men laughed again and dug Jack in the ribs. "There's for you, Cursemother Jack!" one cried, only to receive a playful knock in the teeth from the object of his mockery.

"Or I could lead the horses, or carry messages," added Harry.

The captain peered down at him, the soot on his face making his expression unreadable. "Why should you be wishful to do that?"

"Well, I'd be a smuggler," said Harry, stating the obvious.

"You think you'd like that?"

"Oh, yes!"

The tall man considered him. "You're just a bantling, but you're as bold as brass. I'll think on it," said he at last. "Where will you be if you're needed?"

"I live at Henfold," said Harry, but then wondered if he should have lied. Would these desperadoes burn down his house in the night?

"Well then, get yourself home now afore you're missed. And mind you say nary a word—or your cousin here will pay the price!"

Harry shot Dick a look he hoped was reassuring before sketching a little bow and setting off at a run, hurried on his way by a valedictory clout from the one called Cursemother Jack. He had no leisure to feel fatigue as he flew down the track, putting as much distance as he could between himself and the smugglers before they could change their minds and hunt him down.

At first all he could think about was getting away without falling flat on his face in the dark. But as he got closer to home, he felt he could slow down a little, his thoughts so crowding his mind he could scarcely place his feet. His cousin Dick Steer—in league with smugglers! Carrying their contraband through Henfold's own woods! And Dick had stood up for him, tried to protect him when his life was in danger. As for the voice he had recognized earlier, he was now certain it had belonged to one of Dick's friends who had removed the bridge over the Mole on the day of the Walking Dunghill's funeral. How many more of Dick's friends were involved? Or neighbors, men he had seen on the streets of the town? It was as if the ordinary world

Harry thought he knew was become a mere illusion, and this night had stripped away its disguise.

And what of the tall man who had decided Harry's fate, the captain—who might he be? Why had the man let him go? Would he truly allow Harry to become one of the band? It was all a puzzlement.

A sudden scream nearby in the underbrush brought him up short, his heart thudding—were they coming for him after all? But a moment's breathless listening told him it was no more than a vixen calling to her kits. Harry looked about and realized he had walked too far; Henfold lay behind him. He turned and retraced his steps to the spot where he had first set foot upon the track. Stepping carefully amid the roots and brake, he made his way back to the farmyard wall. He scaled it with practiced hands and slipped quietly across the yard to the kitchen door.

It was still unlocked, and he succeeded in returning to his bedchamber undetected. He laid his shoes carefully by a chair, then threw off his breeches and slipped back into bed in his dusty nightshirt, there to lie awake with all the same questions revolving around and around in his mind, too nervous and excited to fall asleep.

Harry was yet wakeful as the first lessening of night brought out the swallows to twitter and swoop about the eaves, and as they in turn awoke the sparrows to chatter in the latticed apple trees. He lay in bed, feeling the night's adventure as a dull ache in his limbs and listening to his father, out in the stableyard, calling to the laborers as they made their way to the fields for another day's work.

At length it was time for him to rise, and he stumbled downstairs heavy-eyed. His mother was instantly solicitous, pressing her hand against his forehead and asking if he felt any fever. He reassured her but remained so absent-minded during breakfast that her concerns were not entirely allayed until she saw how hearty was his appetite.

Afterward he dragged his way through his schoolwork, drawing a series of rebukes from Mr. Marshall for inattentiveness and stupidity. He wasn't sleepy, but bursts of memory kept sending hot flushes through his body, distracting him from his lessons. He longed for someone he could confide in but knew his encounter in the woods must forever remain a secret.

Fatigued despite himself by the end of the day, Harry retired early at his mother's insistence, sped along by Isabella's taunt that he was little more than a baby. He was so tired he lacked the will even to dispute the point. The long summer twilight was scarce begun as he undressed, and his father had yet to return from the fields. In his exhaustion the events of the night before began to assume an air of unreality, and he even allowed a tiny corner of his mind to be grateful for the return of normalcy.

No sooner was he under the sheet, though, than he was startled by a sound: an owl had hooted close by outside. And not just any owl, but the implausible-sounding owl of the smuggler known as Cursemother Jack.

Harry shot back out of bed and peered through the window. At first he could see nothing, but then a flicker of movement caught his eye. Just above the wall that surrounded the stableyard, a hand was waving.

Harry opened the casement and considered for a moment what his response should be. He rapidly concluded that the safest thing would be to hoot back. Excitement had so dried his throat that his first attempt came out as more of a croak; but he tried again and achieved what he considered a creditable effort.

Stillness reigned. He watched and listened eagerly but could detect nothing.

Just when he thought he had imagined it all, the hand appeared slowly above the top of the wall again. This time it was holding a scrap of paper. This was laid atop the wall, and a rock was placed atop it.

Harry waited for several minutes, breathing rapidly, but there were no further developments. Evidently, Jack's signaling was done. Harry stared at the rock. As he watched it, it seemed to grow larger and larger, more and more intrusive on the eye where it broke up the smooth line of the coping. Nobody, he was certain, could fail to notice it if they looked in that direction.

Just then his ears picked up the distant jingle of bells on harness. The first of the hay wains was returning from the fields! Harry ran for the door in his nightshirt. He pounded down the stairs, past the open door of the room in which his mother was sitting at her needlework ("Harry?" she called; "The necessary!" he gasped in reply), and wrenched open the side door. He flew across the stableyard, seized a bucket, upended it at the foot of the wall, and climbed up to reach for the rock and paper.

He was about to throw the stone away, but a moment's consideration made him put it back atop the wall. If any future messages were to be left in the same manner, the stone must become a common sight there, something so familiar it would draw no one's eye. Then he was off to the corner of the yard, banging the door of the privy as he hastened inside.

Peering at the scrap of paper in the noisome gloom, he could make out just four words, written in a childlike scrawl with a bit of charcoal: *Swans windmil. Eleven oclok.*

Harry studied this missive with a fast-beating heart.

The dirty scrap was a precious object, as treasured by him as a summons to the Court of King George might have been to his sister. He, Harry Steer, was being asked to join a band of smugglers! He could not imagine what value he might have in the captain's eyes, but whatever was expected of him he would strive with all his might to perform.

It was crucial to dispose of the message in case his father caught him in the yard or his mother intercepted him on the way back to his room. The easiest solution appeared to be the cesspit, so he dropped it through the opening.

The paper fluttered slowly down and came at length to rest on the bottom. He had thought it would sink in and disappear, but it remained on the surface, a bright white square on a dark background. It would certainly be seen by the next person to visit the privy. So Harry sneaked out into the yard, searching for some way to conceal it. He could hear the sounds of men and beasts in the stable as he cast about wildly for a solution. A small pile of last year's straw had been left untidily at the foot of the stable wall; in a moment he had dashed across to seize a handful and returned to the necessary. He fed it in through the hole bit by bit, and was pleased to see that the piece of paper could not be distinguished from the pale straw. By the time the cesspit was dug in a few months, he hoped, the message would have disintegrated. He returned to the house.

His father had entered the kitchen moments before and was putting off his hat and smock by the door. Harry muttered, "Good evening, sir," and passed on. His mother was still seated in the parlor at her needlework, but she was on the listen for her son and called out to him as soon as he entered, "Harry? Come, let me look at you."

He obediently approached her, and she examined his face closely. "You appear feverish—are you bilious?"

Harry blushed but declared himself well. Then it occurred to him that his mother's concern might be turned to good purpose. "I should feel more the thing if I could move my limbs more," he added. "After sitting at my studies all day I find it difficult to sleep at night, and then I am tired the next day."

Mrs. Steer eyed him with sympathy. "I know, it seems unnatural to keep a boy so tied to his books. But your father is very determined that you shall be well prepared for school." She gave him a quick smile. "I shall see what I can do."

Harry ducked down to give her a kiss. At that moment he heard his father's heavy footsteps approaching from behind, so he fled upstairs to his bedroom.

The hours crawled past as Harry waited for the house to quiet and darkness to close in. The household possessed no clock, and he could only guess at the appropriate time for his departure. Despite the excitement of anticipation, he had to fight the urge to nod off. But he succeeded, and at last judged it safe to embark upon his journey.

This time, instead of moving cross-country, he made his way boldly up Brimstone Lane under a setting quarter-moon to approach Holmwood Common from the southeast. He saw no need for concealment; it seemed unlikely that any of the laborers and farmers, all of them working so hard to get in the hay all around the neighborhood, would still be abroad at that hour, so anyone else on the road at night would no doubt be a fellow criminal. Harry was filled with a thrilling sense of camaraderie with all those invisible others stepping outside the bounds of decorum in the dark to pursue their common purpose.

As he walked, Harry wondered about the destination named in Jack's note. The former proprietor of the mill on Holmwood Common, Henry Swan, had always appeared to be a pillar of the community—a prosperous Quaker farmer and overseer of the poor. His son-in-law Mr. Bisshopp now managed the business. What could such an upright family have to do with the rough men he had met the night before?

Shortly after Harry passed Stockriden Farm and as he approached the green track that turned aside from the lane to cross the heath at the southern end of the common, his ears began to pick up sounds of activity. Horses were being led southward toward him down the lane; he could hear the soft clop of many hooves and the low hum of voices. At the turnoff he was met by the horses, as yet unburdened and being led by a group of men disguised as they had been last night. He turned without a word to cover the remaining distance in their company.

"You again!" hissed the man nearest him through a cloth drawn up to his eyes.

Harry recognized the voice this time. "You're Dick's friend Sam, aren't you?"

"Never mind who I am," replied Sam impatiently. "The less we know about one another, the better."

"We calls him Slug 'cos he allus finds us the slowest horses," volunteered the man behind them, a stumpy fellow with the beginnings of a hump in his back.

"You just try calling me that, Harry," growled Sam, "and see if I don't draw your cork for you."

"He's in the right of it," the stumpy man allowed. "You gots to earn the right to bandy names about—and you've earned naught, whelp."

In short order they were approaching the mill, a creaking bulk in the darkness. About a dozen men were already congregated there in low-voiced parley; Harry wondered how the miller and his family could possibly remain ignorant of what was going forward. But his question was shortly answered by the appearance of the miller himself, a stolid ox of a man bearing a close lantern. He walked slap up to the door of the roundhouse at the base of the mill and unlocked it. Harry wondered whether his master, Mr. Bisshopp, were aware that he was in league with the free-traders.

At that moment, the captain strode up to the door and gave a sharp whistle. Everyone gathered around and lent him an ear.

"Gentlemen, a fine evening to all. We have a good night's work ahead of us. This load's bound for Darking—rum all 'round at the end of the road!"

Cheers erupted among the men, quickly hushed by a hard stare from their leader. He resumed. "Last night we had to hang 'em high up at the top of the mill accos of an exciseman being spotted on the 'pike, riding all alongside of two of them militiamen."

"And broke my sack hoist chain in the doing of it," muttered the miller.

The captain ignored him. "It'll take a deal of doing to get the tubs down and loaded up. Then we'll follow the sunken way through the woods, not the high road. If that there cully be abroad again tonight, we might see some action."

One or two of the younger men gave a whoop at the prospect of breaking a head or two but were silenced again by the captain. "Them as wants to be paid reg'lar use their guile, not their pikes and pistols," said he. "We've done well so far thanks to outwitting and avoiding the Militia, not confronting 'em. We'll allus fight if they bothers us, but better if we're all safe in our beds by sunrise."

This speech was a source of some secret relief to Harry, and any doubts he had felt about the wisdom of the enterprise were fast receding. As if he had read Harry's mind, however, the captain slued about to survey the crowd and cried out, "Is the boy come?"

Hands of the men nearest him seized Harry's shoulders and thrust him forward.

"Our latest volunteer," said the captain, to the laughter of the crowd. He bent down and scraped up a handful of mud, which he smeared over Harry's face. "Gentlemen, I give you—Monkey."

Several men nearby clapped Harry on the back, none too gently. In answer to Harry's quizzical look, the captain explained. "I'm of a mind to need a monkey, Monkey. The last boy is recovering from his injuries." Harry wondered uneasily what injuries those might be and how they came to be inflicted, but the captain was pointing upward. "You see the shaft up there the sails are attached to?"

Harry looked up at the windmill's huge sails, stationary now and dark against the stars. Suddenly the mill seemed to be very, very tall. He nodded.

"You're to take this rope, climb up inside the mill, go out through the opening at the top, and out onto that shaft. Then knot the rope around the shaft—securely, mind! It must needs bear a deal of weight. We'll use it to let down the tubs."

"Accos of how you broke my sack hoist last night," repeated the miller, who was again ignored.

The coil of rope was large and extremely heavy as Harry hoisted it up to his shoulder, but he was not about to display hesitation or weakness. He simply staggered off under the rope's weight to the mill door.

There he was taken inside inside by the miller, who

lighted his way but made no offer of assistance. Together they trudged up the steps to the main floor with its large meal bin, the miller muttering about his sack hoist all the while, and then up the next flight, more ladder than stairway, to the second level where the millstones sat idle. Here the steps ended, and Harry peered inquiringly at the miller in the dim light, the stale grain dust tickling his nose. He could dimly see the grain hopper as a dark hulk to his left, and a faint light filtered in through the small opening for the shaft, well over his head, but he could perceive no way to get up there. On all sides, tubs and boxes were stacked in tidy piles three high—the smugglers' cargo.

"Here's your chance to climb, Monkey," the miller said, pointing up into the gloom. "Scramble up there and I'll toss you the rope." He opened a large barnlike window to admit a little more light. This, Harry surmised, was where the sacks of grain were let in for the grinding—when the sack hoist was operational.

Harry looked around quickly. The mill was of a simple post construction, the framing clad on the outside with weathered laths. There were chinks aplenty for enterprising fingers and toes, so he swarmed up the wall easily enough and threw a leg over the shaft. He pulled his torso over close to the opening, which was barely wide enough for him to squeeze through, and signaled his readiness to receive the rope.

The coil hit him with a force that nearly sent him tumbling, but he managed to seize an end and hang on while the miller laughed. "Lay yourself flat on the beam there, and put your head and shoulders out through the hole. You'll want to be tying the knot as far out from the wall as you can," he advised; "I don't want no tubs banging off the walls of my mill on the way down."

Harry did as he was told, trying hard not to look down as he poked his head through the hole. For a dizzy moment he felt hypnotically pulled toward the heath far below, as if impelled by an invisible force to leap out and fly—or, more likely, plummet to his death. Why on earth had he imagined working with smugglers would be a lark? But he could not remain frozen in place forever. Timidly he wriggled his upper body a little way outside along the shaft, keeping the remainder of his body secure on the comforting bulk of the beam.

"I see him!" came a cry from below. There was a quick flurry of activity on the ground, and suddenly Harry felt a horrible shudder and lurch: the men had put their shoulders to the tail pole and were turning the mill into the wind.

Harry could feel the shaft begin to rotate under him as the sails filled with air, and he heard the groan of the millstones starting to turn behind him. He scrambled hastily back to the beam before the shaft's rotation could send him slipping off to his death, trembling so violently he nearly dropped the rope.

Shouts of laughter rose from below, and cries of "How do you like your tree, Monkey?" But the miller was not amused, and he roared out through the window below Harry's perch, "I'll thank'ee not to make sport wi' my mill! Turn it back!"

After a moment's pause, the mill was rotated back into its original position, the framework creaking loudly, and the sails went slack. Harry stifled a desperate impulse to climb down and run home; with all the men watching, he had no choice but to proceed.

The worst part was having to throw the tail end of the rope under the shaft and catch it on the other side; Harry attempted several methods involving only one hand, but none was efficacious. It could only be accomplished with both hands free. So he hooked his feet securely around the frame of the aperture, played out the rope several arms' length, held it out as far as he could over the void, and then swung the end under the shaft. There was a dreadful moment when he began to overbalance, but then he caught the end and pulled himself back.

After that it was easy enough to tie the knot, and at last he was able to wriggle back to safety as he played out the untied end of the rope. The miller leaned out through the opening on his level, and Harry swung the rope back and forth till the miller could catch the end and pull it inside.

The miller set to work immediately lashing the first tub to it, ordering Harry to look sharp and send some men up to help him. Harry was delighted to scramble back down to the floor at last, and thence to solid ground.

There he was met by the captain, who clapped him on the back before moving off to direct the loading of the pack train. The tubs were let down swiftly two at a time, and other boxes and parcels produced from hidden corners of the mill. Of the greatest puzzlement to Harry were some odd brown ropes, which were borne, neatly coiled, to the laden horses and carefully arranged atop the casks and boxes already tied to their backs. Catching a glimpse of Dick at last, he ventured to ask why the smugglers were importing rope when it was so readily available for sale.

Dick laughed and ruffled his hair. "Bless me, Monkey, you *are* green! That there's tobacco, twisted to appear like rope to fool the Revenue men. Them as bring in the goods by sea, they coil it up on the deck under the real ropes, and if they're boarded, nobody the wiser!"

In short order the pack train was loaded and they were off, Harry greatly relieved when he was not asked to return to the shaft and untie the rope. Instead he was handed the rein of the first horse in a string of three and told to follow others who were already under way. He observed that the smaller men, and those who showed signs of infirmity, managed the horses while the larger and stouter members of the party, like Dick and his friend Slug, walked alongside as an armed escort.

Harry's successful exploit with the rope—and failure to succumb to his fear when the windmill was moved—appeared to have been sufficient for at least provisional acceptance into the band. The armed guard walking nearest him asked jovially, "So, nipperkin, is the free-trade to your liking?"

"Oh yes, sir!" cried Harry; but then, feeling such enthusiasm betrayed his naïveté, he added, "What else is one to do with one's evenings?"

The man laughed. "*Sir*, is it? The gents here knows me as Nasty Face; mind you inform them they haven't been according me my proper title."

"*Sir* Nasty Face it is, then," said Harry boldly. "But how can they know your face is nasty under all that soot?"

"A thinker we have here! How indeed? But I'll tell you true, Monkey: in going about our business, there be times when an ugly mug be useful. There's some meddlesome coves as pokes their noses in where they ain't wanted and needs to be frightened into minding their own business."

"I imagine those pistols you carry are as much to the purpose as your face."

"I'm of the cap'n's mind—the less call I have to use the barkers, the better it is for all. Why make a big noise when a hatchet-face with staring glims, popping up over a hedge at midnight, is enough to send most folks running for home? You think half the ghost stories you hears in these parts be true?"

Harry digested this, not sure whether to be glad or sorry to think that a spectral apparition might be no more than some ne'er-do-well bent on scaring people away from his criminal activities. And jumping up from behind a hedge was a child's ploy, not nearly so dramatic as firing off a pistol. "So have you never shot anyone?" he asked after a moment.

"And if I had, would I tell it, young Hemp?" said Nasty Face, and Harry was again aware of having violated an unspoken ruffians' rule. He apologized politely and thereafter held his peace.

There was certainly enough to listen to, though the men kept their voices low. He drank in avidly their tales of pitched battles with excisemen and dragoons; of hiding tubs of spirits in tombs and under false floors; of the ruses and disguises employed to conceal their activities. Here was a treasure better than any fairy-tale told him by his mother—for these stories were true, and he was entering this world of derring-do and living it!

The journey was for Harry an interlude of perfect happiness. The pack train wound its way to the north over greensward and sunken forest paths, lit by little but the stars and a few of the peculiar watering-pot lanterns. He listened hard to pick up the men's cant, learning that these odd devices were called spout lanterns and were excellent for signaling over long distances; that the tubs were ankers and the armed guards were known as batmen. Harry felt a deep satisfaction as they took their road along the wild ways of Holmwood Common. Beyond even the excitement of what adventures the night might bring, he felt all the honor of being, for the first time in his life, one of a band of men engaged on a common enterprise.

This blissful idyll was all too brief, however, for it was not above an hour before they were approaching the outskirts of Darking. Here there was a pause while scraps of cloth were wound around the metal parts of every horse's bridle and their hooves were similarly wrapped. Evidently, the entrance into the town would need to be made in the strictest silence. These preparations complete, the group moved on into South Street, halting at a gap between two dilapidated cottages that backed up against Butter Hill.

A quiet frenzy of activity began, as the men who had been escorting the pack train laid down their weapons by the wall of one of the dwellings and swiftly unloaded the horses one by one. The ankers, boxes, and ropes of tobacco were carried off into the darkness of the gap, to what destination Harry could not make out. As his own horses were unloaded he craned his neck to peer down that passageway but could perceive nothing at the end, and as soon as his horses were unburdened he was gestured to move on and turn them around. He tried to fix the appearance of the two cottages in his mind, hoping to return at a later date and explore the gap, but in the darkness he was unable to distinguish one building from another. In less time than he could have imagined possible the unloading was complete.

Now it seemed the party was to be divided, some remaining with the goods and others with the horses. The captain reappeared, and he moved among those members of the party who were with the pack train. Each one received a whispered word and a handshake; when it came Harry's turn, he heard "Well done, Monkey. Newdigate Church tomorrow night," and felt two shillings pressed into his palm. Never in his life had he been compensated for his labor like a man! If anything he felt the debt and obligation to be on the other side; but he pocketed the coins as if he had been expecting them.

He was sorely tempted to inquire about the fate that

lay in store for the run goods, but the captain moved swiftly along the line of horses, and once he had paid all the men they were in motion. They did not, as Harry had expected, return to the area of the windmill; instead they made their way eastward along back alleys to Chart Lane. There they stopped only for a moment to unwind the cloth from around the horses' hooves and tack before making their way boldly southward. The road was muddy as usual and great care was necessary to keep both men and animals on their feet, so progress was slow.

By this time the short summer night was nearly over, and Harry had begun to worry he had no hope of reaching home before dawn. What his parents might have to say, were he to be discovered creeping into the house by daylight, did not bear considering. Worse even than his father's inevitable wrath would be his mother's disappointment. And how could he ever explain the two shillings, should they be found? Still they plodded on, nearer to home yet not near enough.

Before long they had passed Chart Park and come abreast of Stumblehole, his uncle's farm. Harry saw Dick hand off his string of horses to another man and make for the gate. "Bide a moment, Dick!" he called out softly; Dick hesitated and then approached him. Harry explained his concern.

"Oh, for the Lord's sake, cub, one moment you're acting the man and the next you're a baby again! It has been a long night—do you truly need me to take you home?" But his good nature overcame his impatience, and he sang out to the man at the head of the pack train, "Hoy there, Joll! Monkey and I want to borrow a horse. One with a bit of pepper left in him, if you please."

There was some brief parley and then a young, healthy-looking beast was detached from the line and his empty packsaddle loaded atop another's. Dick mounted him bareback, then put down a hand to Harry, saying, "Up you get, now." Harry took a leap and scrambled his way up behind, wrapping his arms around Dick's waist. "I'll return the horse to Heathfields in my way home," Dick promised the man known as Joll, who merely nodded.

Dick was intimately familiar with this area of the Holmwood, so they set off at a confident trot and soon left the others behind.

"What is at Heathfields?" Harry asked.

"Stables," said Dick shortly. "It's a wonder the questions you carry about in that cockloft of yours."

"But there is so much I want to know, and if I don't ask, how am I to know it?" protested Harry. "Who is the tall man who gives the orders—the captain? What was in the boxes and tubs—the ankers? What will happen to the goods we delivered to Darking? Where did they come from?"

"The less you know, the less you can tell," said Dick. "If the cap'n wants you to know who he be, he'll tell you, won't he? Now, stubble it."

So Harry was obliged to weave his own answers to his questions. These became increasingly bizarre and tangled as exhaustion overtook him, so that he was more in the realm of dreams than in Surrey by the time Dick set him down a short distance from his home, with a promise to wait for him in the same spot the next night. Harry stumbled up the lane at the hour the badgers were making for their dens and let himself in again by the kitchen door, forgetting even to remove his shoes before climbing the stairs and tumbling into bed.

Chapter the Sixth

All too soon the day was upon him again and he had to drag his tired bones down to breakfast. Only the pangs of hunger, rendered severe by his exertions of the night before, could have induced him to rise. As he took his seat at the table, his mother took one look at him and exclaimed, "I declare I have no idea how it is that boys can make themselves so dirty all the time! Harry, you are a disgrace! Have you been wiping your face on the stableyard cobbles?"

Harry realized he had forgotten to wash off the mud that had been smeared on his face for a disguise last night! He muttered an apology and rushed outside to the pump, chased by Isabella's derision. When he returned his countenance was more presentable but fiery red, and he buried his face in his plate without a further word.

Midway through the morning he actually fell asleep in the middle of the fifth declension (*"Res, rei, rei, rem . . ."*) and had his shoulders whacked with a switch by the ordinarily peaceable Mr. Marshall. He was discovering that a life of crime was excessively fatiguing when conducted in secrecy, and wondered how he was ever to summon the strength to participate in the coming night's run. Fortunately for his plans, his mother was still on the alert for signs of ill health in him, and after eyeing him closely as he consumed his dinner, she ordered him to bed. Thus it was that Harry was feeling quite fresh when he awoke to the shouts of his father's men unloading hay in the stableyard at nightfall. He remained on the listen in his room for two hours more, however, till the house was quiet again before creeping down the stairs for his next night's work. Having missed his supper, he paid a visit to the pantry before departing to meet his cousin Dick over by Brimstone Lane, recruiting his powers with a cold pigeon pie and a hunk of cheese.

This time they rode south to the village of Newdigate. Harry knew it to be a sorry place, neglected by an absentee landlord and clergyman, with crumbling houses and poverty so widespread it was beyond the reach of the poor rates to care for all those in need. Small wonder, then, that the smugglers found it a congenial spot for the conduct of their enterprise—much of the populace must be grateful for any employment. Nonetheless he was taken aback, on their arrival, to see that unlike the night before on the common, nobody here was making the least effort to keep their activities quiet. Directly in front of the church men were shouting across to their compatriots at the Five Bells alehouse, openly organizing the horses and their cargoes.

"Are they not afraid of discovery?" he asked Dick.

"Lord no, not in Newdigate," Dick replied. "Milord might as well be the magistrate here. He's the publican's main supplier and even made a great loan to the churchwardens a few years back, so I hear tell. Half the town receives his wages, and the other half eats because of 'em."

"Who is Milord?"

"The cap'n's cap'n. Enough with questions!"

And indeed the captain, standing on the steps that led up to the church, had an air of confident mastery about him. Spotting Harry and Dick, he called out, "Monkey! Time for another rope scramble!"

So Harry was once again set to climbing, this time up inside the church tower among the bells, where he saw another collection of ankers stored. Having heard that a man could be permanently deafened by standing among church bells while they were pealing, he felt a moment's panic that the men might get up to more of their mischief, but evidently all were too much occupied this night to have time to spare for japery. His task was easier, as well, for he had merely to secure the rope around a beam of the ceiling; then Dick, who had gone up with him, removed a grating in the wall and men set about tying up the ankers and letting them down. The rope fitted perfectly into deep grooves worn into the sill of the opening, leading Harry to surmise that this hiding place must be used regularly for the storage of contraband.

Back at ground level, he found the captain in a cheerful mood. "Genuine Crowlink, this is," he remarked with satisfaction, patting one of the ankers as it went past. "We'll get a pretty price for this load."

"What is genuine Crowlink?" Harry could not resist asking.

"Lord, Monkey, you're as ignorant as a babe in arms! Crowlink be the best gin to be had anywhere. The Sussex boys brings it up to us, and we see it safe on its way to Lunnon. Or at least most of it—genuine Crowlink is well-liked hereabouts, and our local innkeepers do like to get their cut."

Observing the captain to be in an expansive humor, Harry pressed on. "Are you a real captain?"

"No more than calling you Monkey makes you an ape."

"What else do you transport?"

"Whate'er the Sussex boys choose to bring us: gin, brandy, hollands, arrack, tobacco, tea, silk, India muslin. Paper and soap, on occasion. Watches, salt, spices. What the Lunnon shops want, and don't want to pay duty on, we supply."

"So London is the final destination?"

"Mostly. The innkeepers and shopkeepers hereabouts do ask for goods, and we oblige 'em when we can. You've a deal of questions between those flapping ears, Monkey, and you're most owdacious bold in asking 'em."

Harry apologized, but the captain laughed and ruffled his hair. "You put me in mind of myself not so very long ago. We can use a sharp eye and a ready tongue like yours; most of these men are mutton-headed lackwits. Now, earn your keep, boy—help with the loading!"

Harry obediently set about rolling ankers from the base of the church tower over to the horses, lined up boldly in the street. The men were using torches and lanterns, and he could estimate the size of the pack train. There were close to fifty animals, and he wondered whose they were and how so many could be kept fed and maintained in secrecy.

Once they left the last houses of Newdigate behind, however, they moved more cautiously and kept quiet, the only sounds being the snort and stamp of the horses and the jingle of tack. The moon had not yet set, so all their lanterns were kept covered. Harry was near the head of the train, and from time to time he could see a man materialize out of the darkness, whisper a few words in the captain's ear, and melt away again.

Thus they passed by the lane leading to his own house, and the Peters farm, and at length approached that part of the common where woods gave way to heath. As they neared a side track, there came the sudden hoot of an owl, followed in short order by a man running along the track. Harry could just make out the words he gasped to the captain: "Cavalry by the mill!"

The captain whispered a few words to the lookout, who gave an unintelligible answer. Without further ado the captain swung his long legs over the back of the pack horse at the head of the line and kicked him into a canter, dragging the horses attached to his into following suit. One after another, men mounted and pursued him, the barrels on the horses' backs slapping and sloshing as they went, while the batmen turned to face the lane, weapons out. They waited till all the horses had passed and then followed the line at a run.

Harry, clinging to his horse's back and trying to hold the ankers off from crushing his legs, was impressed by the speed and silence of their flight. But if the militiamen were mounted and caught sight of the pack train, how could these laden beasts hope to outrun them? And where could they hide? Why had he never thought to bring a weapon in case of violence?

Before he had time to do more than wish he had left a note for his mother, however, the horses ahead of him swerved suddenly to the right and passed through a gate. They rode in at speed, the horses slipping under their loads, entering a large, muddy stableyard surrounded on three sides by farm buildings, visible only as patches of deeper darkness around them. Here the horses drew up, evidently assuming they had completed their work for the evening. From their demeanor Harry surmised that this must be the Heathfields Farm he had heard about the night before, and these stables their home. The men were dismounting and leading the beasts quickly around to a pasture at the back, where they were shut in.

Seeing everyone else creeping back to the corners of the stables to peer into the stableyard, Harry followed suit, his heart beating fast. He could dimly perceive the batmen arranged on both sides of the farmyard gate, weapons out, listening for their pursuers. So they remained for several agonizing minutes of suspense.

After what seemed an eternity, hoofbeats could be heard, and soon a small party of men rode by on the road at a trot, never thinking to pause at the farmyard gate. The man closest to Harry gave a low chuckle once they were past, muttering, "Gormless clods. They think to roll us up with nobbut eight men?"

Another growled back, "What I wants to know is, who put 'em on to the mill? Is that lout of a miller playing us false?"

A voice from somewhere behind Harry said, "What about that new boy—Monkey? He talks like carriage folk; what's he doing with the likes of us? Jest listen to 'im—who's to say those ain't a false pair o' jaws?"

Harry tried to flatten himself against the wall, praying for the rough shingle to swallow him up. He felt an impulse to run for it, but the batmen were still clustered near the gate and he had no idea what lay in any other direction.

But once again Dick was nearby and rose to his defense, saying calmly, "If he'd told anyone, he'd not be here with us tonight. I know enough of his father to be sure of that— he'd've got a bannicking and be locked in his room with a smarting backside."

The captain's voice was also heard, low but clear. "We don't even know for certain they was looking for us. Thirsty Chub, when he brought word of 'em, could see no sign of the exciseman among 'em. They might've been on the hunt for a highwayman or a thief. The mill's a natural place to look to as a hideout, or they might've been searching the Nag's Head. Anyroad, it makes little matter; we've more paths to take than they can patrol."

The batmen began to move back from the gate, their relaxed posture indicating that the militiamen were well gone. The captain gathered everyone around for their new orders. "'Tis a long night that lies before us," said he; "good thing we made an early start. We'll find our separate ways across the common and meet up with the Coldharbour road on the west side, then run straight in to Darking from there. We'll have these ankers safe-stowed in the caves while they're galloping about disturbing the toffs' rest at Chart Park and the Deepdene." There was grumbling amid the laughter; it was the long way 'round to Darking, and the Coldharbour road was narrow, rutted, and steep. But the horses were retrieved from behind the barns, grumbling a bit in their own fashion as they were led away from their stables again, and the pack train resumed its journey.

Harry was still feeling a good deal of alarm from this episode, and as the horses turned northward he had to master the impulse to take to his heels back the way they had come. His bed seemed very inviting at this moment. But he saw Dick was keeping close by him, and soon his curiosity overcame his fear. "Was that Heathfields where we hid?" he asked. "Does the farmer work in the free-trade, like the miller?"

"If ever there was a one for questions, it's you, Harry," said Dick impatiently. "No wonder some have suspicions about you."

"Yes, but what was that about *caves*?" Harry persisted.

"Shut your yap, Harry!"

Harry was obliged to swallow his curiosity, and soon enough he had other concerns to occupy his mind. As they cut across country, they encountered many of the boggy places for which Holmwood Common was infamous, the remnants of abandoned clay-diggings. He soon learned that every time the midges clustered around his face, it meant he was close to a low-lying wet spot and had to skirt along the sides of any rising slope he could find to locate solid footing for the horses under his care. The group became a little scattered as each sought his own way, though he could still hear sometimes the progress of others on either side of him. At last he found a woodland ride and decided to risk it for the sake of making progress. The ponies were happier, too, under this alteration in their circumstances, and followed his tug more willingly.

Before he had gone much farther, however, the ride emerged onto the open heath and petered out. By this time the moon had set, so his way became a hard slog through prickly furze, its seed pods startling him as they burst on the twig ends with a pop like miniature gunfire. He moved quietly around one or two inholdings and innumerable coppices underhung with holly, carefully guiding the horses across narrow streams. The night was filled with sounds, each causing him to start and peer nervously about him in the darkness: even the slither of an otter slipping underwater to avoid the unexpected nighttime visitors sent a shock of fear coursing through his veins. Harry was sweating though the night was cool, and it was with effort that he controlled the shaking of his hands.

When he came at length to the turnpike road, he paused for a few moments under the trees before braving the crossing, reflecting wryly that it was not far from this spot where the highwayman had lain in wait for him little more than a fortnight before. Now he was the one who had placed himself outside the law. On the other side of the road he located a well-tended track through the woods, where the going was easier for him and the horses in his care. By this route he at last descended into the low-lying farmland of the Bury Hill estate, through which the Coldharbour road made its way.

Others of his party had already achieved the road, and he joined them in silence as they resumed their northward journey. He drew no attention to himself, uncertain whether to be grateful for the presence of the batmen or afraid of them, should they decide again to blame him for the night's reverses.

Once they were near the outskirts of Darking, the band paused as they had the night before to wrap the hooves and tack of the animals. There was a little rise to the side of the road just at this spot, and although Harry could not see in the darkness he knew that above him loomed the town gallows. The smugglers seemed oblivious to this reminder of the consequences of discovery, but it gave Harry an uncomfortable feeling in the pit of his stomach. He was impatient for the remainder of the party to straggle into view, shifting from foot to foot as the captain quietly counted heads to make sure all were present before giving the signal to proceed.

As they drew up again in South Street, Harry could no longer contain his curiosity about the destination for the ankers. Quietly attaching his train of three horses to the one before him, he scurried to the head of the line on the side between the horses and the buildings, where the men could not see him, and slipped into the dark gap between the two cottages. He felt his way down the passageway until he came to a spot where his hand felt nothing as the space opened out into a courtyard. With halting steps he started to cross it—only to be seized from behind by a pair of strong arms.

He was thrown roughly up against the wall. There was a scrape of metal as the aperture of a lantern was pushed back and a beam of light momentarily blinded him.

"You've no call to be here!" growled a voice behind the light, and a fist fetched him a blow on the side of his head that crumpled him, head spinning.

"What is it?" He recognized the voice of the captain, low but sharp with tension.

"Some bantling," replied the man with the fist.

The light was trained down again on Harry. There was a moment's silence, and then the captain said, "Monkey, why ain't you with your horses?"

Trying to keep a whining tone out of his voice, Harry said, "You said the ankers would be safe-stowed in caves, sir. I wanted to see the caves."

The captain chuckled quietly. "That resty mind of yours'll get you killed, Monkey. How many times am I going to have to rescue you from the consequences of it? Up you get, then. I'll give you a glint and then off you go home." He reached down and pulled Harry to his feet.

Stumbling a bit, his senses still befuddled, Harry followed him across the dark courtyard to what appeared to be a large wooden cabinet. The captain and the Fist pushed it to one side, revealing a heavy-looking door. This was unlocked, letting out a sigh of cool, moist air like the final exhalation of a dying person; and the three of them stepped inside. With the door pulled nearly to behind them, the two men took the candle out of the lantern and began lighting tallow dips set up in a row on the floor, revealing a rough stairway carved into the sandstone that led down into the earth.

Harry gasped with delight, his spinning head forgotten. He followed them as they descended, lighting more dips as they went, till the way leveled off and they emerged into a large, well-lit chamber lined with empty shelves. Toward the back, young shopgirls from the town were working at tables, cutting up the ropes of tobacco that had been brought the night before. A large crate had been opened and bolts of fine cloth removed from it. Harry recognized Mollie Fish in her blue apron, and wondered for a mad moment if he had in actuality been engaged in nothing more thrilling than the transport of herring from the coast. But she was wearing a loose gown evidently intended for a woman of much greater girth; and under his horrified gaze she seized one of the bolts of cloth and pushed it up under her dress, poking and prodding it into a wad until she appeared to be heavy with child. Catching his eye, she gave him a saucy wink and moved toward the stairs, tweaking his nose as she passed. Nobody stopped her, so Harry could only conclude that this unorthodox means of transport was part of the plan of distribution.

"So they fetched the load all right?" inquired the captain of another who was rolling a lone cask toward them.

"Went smooth as you please," replied the man; "they were done and gone nigh on two hours past. This be the delivery for Mr. Cheesman."

"Very well then, let's unload. Monkey, you've had your look, now make yourself useful: go on back up and give the signal. Here's for you," the captain added, slipping two shillings into his hand; "now, you and your cousin get you gone home."

"Where do we meet tomorrow night?" asked Harry.

"We don't. Too much moon. We lie low for a fortnight or more. Cursemother Jack got you a message before, didn't he?"

"Yes, sir."

"He'll do so again. You're a good lad."

Harry sped up the stairs and out into the courtyard, his flagging energies momentarily refreshed by the captain's praise. He felt his way to the passage between the houses and back out to the street, where he found the pack train waiting where he had left it. "They're ready for you," he said in lordly tones to the man at the head of the line, and continued on to seek out his cousin. As soon as Dick had unloaded his goods and returned from the caves, jingling the coins in his pocket, they were off.

Boldly they washed the soot off their faces at the town pump and mounted up. Thanks to their newfound wealth they decided to ride home along the turnpike like honest men, leaving the rest of the pack train to make its way back to Heathfields by the more easterly route.

CHAPTER THE SEVENTH

A purgatorial period of uncertain length now stretched before Harry, whose recent exploits had ill suited him for submission to the tedium of his daily life. Twenty-four hours sufficed to restore his animal spirits, but no amount of time could reconcile him to the study of Latin and Greek. Harry's mind was fevered from the thrilling events he had experienced, and he craved a return to the exaltations of excitement and terror. His thoughts continually rebelled; there was no possibility of bringing them under regulation.

The satisfactions of family life were now as nothing to him; the free-traders were his all. Let lesser spirits be satisfied with plenty to eat and a comfortable bed: Harry's demanded a quest for derring-do alongside his corps of comrades. Even the kindnesses of his mother left his heart obdurate. He was a smuggler, not a child.

A few days brought diversion that in the past should have been the high point of his summer, as the haying was brought to a successful close. It was the custom of the household, after the conclusion of the laborers' work, to hold a regale for them in Henfold's large old-fashioned hall, little used for any other purpose throughout the year.

This chamber, the oldest part of the house, was adorned with two rows of trestle tables for the workers' accommodation and a vast hearth on which a fire was kindled not more than twice in a twelvemonth—certainly not for the haying supper, though Harry's mother lent a festive air to the occasion by placing a large urn of flowers from her own garden in place of the firewood. Three of the musicians from St. John the Baptist at Capel were hired in to play the fiddle and pipe, and a hearty dinner of roast beef, mutton, and suet pudding was laid on, Mrs. Steer and Isabella serving with their own hands and Harry passing the ale and the home-brewed beer. Here were gathered all the strong young men who had wielded the scythes, along with the women and children who did the raking and turning; and as always, old Thomas Weller of Capel was invited, though he was years past being able to work—for no one in the county spun a yarn the way Thomas did.

After the previous year's black harvest, when crops had rotted in the fields, Mr. Steer's spirits were high: not only the hayloft but also one of his storerooms was packed as full as it could hold, where only a week before the supply had been reduced almost to nothing. If the weather held through the harvest, there should be plenty for all to eat throughout the winter. The men too, sobered by a year of little work and even less meat, were grateful for their pay and for the generous repast. Even Harry, jaded as his palate was for the common amusements of the agricultural year, enjoyed the music and the dancing. And everyone was eager to hear what tale Thomas Weller had to tell.

The food was all eaten up and the last jig danced, and everyone gathered 'round to hear him. Thomas glared at the circle of expectant faces from under the thicket of his brows and waited till the room hushed. "There was an owd pirate named One-Eyed Joe," he began at last, to a rustle of anticipation—this was a new story—"tho' he did not begin life as a pirate, nor yet as a one-eyed man. Joe, he'd went to sea as a boy, and worked hard in his youth and was well liked among the captain and his mates. As a young man he were a great tall fellow, and strong withal, and when he was ashore the ladies lived for naught but to catch his eye—they did so."

"Did they catch his eye onct too many, Thomas?" cried a wag from the audience. "They catched it and wouldn't return it, and that's how he come to be one-eyed?"

Thomas frowned down this impertinence and drained his tankard before deigning to proceed with his tale. "All the ladies would throw themselves in Joe's path, but Joe had eyes for none but one, a fair young girl whose pa kept a tavern. Nan was her name.

"Now, Nan were comely, but she was one of them as has big ideas about their worth." Murmurings of disapproval sounded among the crowd. "Mayhap she set too much store by her looks, and so she were picksome and raised her eyes to look at a gentleman. Certain she was she could win herself a fine carriage and a big house to sleep in, one of these days. So she turns up her pretty nose at Joe the sailor, and she breaks his heart."

A few women spoke up here to call fie upon Nan's pride and aspirations, but Thomas enforced attention by proceeding. "Many was the wench who thought to relieve Joe of his sorrows, but he would look at none of them, and wouldna be consoled. He was sent back out to sea soon after, and fought under Howe on the Glorious First of June, and when he come back two year later, he had only the one eye. Not only that, but he was covered from head to waist in hideous scars, on account of being burned in the battle when the cannon he worked did explode." There were shudders of sympathy at this; several families in the neighborhood had sons who had gone into the navy and suffered a similar fate.

Warming to his grisly subject, Thomas added, in a guttural growl, "And he'd only one hand as well; for where t'other once was, there was nobbut an iron hook. But that weren't the worst of it, not by no means: for One-Eyed Joe had been scarred in his heart, and his spirit was burning like coals in the grate.

"Still he thought on his Nan, and he went to her father's tavern to look for her. All there shrank away from the sight of him, for none wished to look on a phiz or a soul so dark and ugly. But there he stood in the taproom, waving about the hook where his hand once was and roaring out, 'Where's my Nan? Where's my Nan?' till all who sees it was quaking in their boots.

"At last, for to make him go away, Nan's father told Joe the truth. Nan had found her gentleman, and he had enticed her with soft words and gifts, and she had gone with him for to be married and ride in a carriage and sleep in a fine house. But he was nobbut a foul seducer, and he ruined her and left her to starve. She bore him a child, she did, but the Almighty judged of her for her wickedness, and mother and infant alike died in childbed."

Here Thomas paused and demanded more refreshment, while his auditors clucked at the perfidy of their betters. Thomas fixed them with his eye and said sternly, "But this be'n't the tale of the tavern-keeper's daughter—this be the tale of One-Eyed Joe. Be Nan an innocent deceived or be she a sinner looking for her best chance, it makes no matter of mind. The point being, that once Joe did hear of her fate, his heart ceased to burn like coal and hardened to stone. He turned without a word and went out of that taproom, and he went straight down to the sea and got himself taken up with the crew of a pirate ship.

"He sailed with the pirates for three year, he did, and was no-tor-ee-us over all the oceans for his ruthless and cruel ways. There was nary an honest sailor anywhere did not fear One-Eyed Joe. He was the terror of the seas and of every island port, no matter it be in the West Indies or China or Egypt. The world over, One-Eyed Joe was know'd to be vexatious wicked and killsome.

"One day—none can say what day it was—One-Eyed Joe come back to England. He was such a black-hearted villain that even his pirate comrades was afeared of him— but they was loyal to the pirate code, and they would never give him up for his crimes, not even for murder. So he was suffered to come back to our shores, and to live among us.

"Now, at somewhen after this time, a tale come to be told along the Sussex coast. Whispers was heard that a gentleman, who'd taken his lady-love a-riding out in his carriage to a secret trysting spot, was found done to death, and alongside of him the lady—and not just kilt but torn to pieces, like it was done by a savage beast. They was left in the carriage awash in their own blood. And the coachman dead, too, toppled over right there on his perch."

Gasps went 'round Thomas's auditors at this; murders at sea were one thing, but such grisly violence committed in the next county was quite another. A glimmer of satisfaction showed in Thomas's eyes, and he was encouraged to elaborate. "Their faces was torn so bad their own families wouldn't of known them, and other parts I canna name ripped right off, and their insides turned out. The horses shut into the shafts, smelling all that blood, bolted and galloped all the way back to their stables, and that is how the bodies come to be found.

"But then it happened agin, and yet agin. Each time, a man and a woman and a coachman foully done to death, and nothing to say who—or what—might've done the deed.

"The pirates know'd, howsomever; they know'd it was One-Eyed Joe. But accos of pirates' honor, they couldn't tell a soul what they know'd. And so the murders happened agin and agin.

"After a time, there was nary a gentleman lover along the whole coast of Sussex who'd ask his love to ride with him to tryst in his carriage. So One-Eyed Joe, he couldn't find no one else to kill. But now the hunger for blood was strong in him and wouldna let him go. He only cared about murder, for that one day he might kill the wicked master who'd ruined his Nan. So he left behind the coast, and he began to move northward."

As he spoke, darkness was falling in the hall, but no one stirred to light the candles. They simply huddled closer as if it had suddenly turned cold; and the ones nearest the door glanced over their shoulders, just in case.

"On came One-Eyed Joe, going from town to town, watching for lovers in their carriages, so he could stalk 'em and leap upon 'em unawares, and tear 'em to pieces with that wicked hook what was where his hand had been. Why, jest last week there was a murder as near to us as Horsham—two lovers in a carriage in a pool of their own blood, and the coachman dead on his perch." Somewhere in the hushed crowd, a young woman began to cry.

"And all this time his pirate comrades held their peace. But the girl kilt near Horsham was kin to one of them pirates—a young man less black-hearted than the rest. And his conscience smote him that he could have saved her but did not. So he comes up from the coast to Horsham, though the other pirates was riled with him and said they'd revenge themselves on him for a-breaking of the pirate code. And for two days he went about from house to house, a-warning people about One-Eyed Joe.

"But what he found was, not all was wishful to believe him. He was, after all, the ne'er-do-well who'd gone off to sea for to become a pirate. So not all the lovers of Horsham was willing to give up their lovemaking, jest on his say-so.

"One such couple went off in the evening to a shaw some ways away from the town so they could do what lovers do when no one is by. They was paying no mind as the sun went down and their carriage was left standing in the dark. But then, all at once, it gave a little jerk, like as if the horses'd been startled. The man was for ignoring it, but the woman remembered the pirate's words, and she was all in a worrit. What if he had told them true, and was not playing some pirate trick on 'em?

"So she pushed her man away and would have none of him, and was wishful to return to the town. He begged her to give over, but she wouldna change her mind; so at last, to please her, he pounded on the roof of the carriage to tell the coachman to go.

"But the coachman didn't answer. The man pounded agin, and roared at him to whip up the horses and go back to Horsham. Agin there was no answer. But the hubbub he was making and the rocking of the carriage startled the horses, and off they went.

"When they was back in the town, the horses finally stopped. The gentleman waited for the coachman to come down from his perch and open the door for them, but he did not. At last the man, cursing at his servant, opened the door himself. He stepped into the road and looked up at the coachman's perch—only to see the man was fallen over on his side, stone dead. He went back to the door of the coach, and what he saw make him screech and screech! For what did he find, a-hanging from the door handle, but a big iron hook, with a few scraps of scarred flesh a-dangling from its base!"

Thomas peered from face to face in the gloom, making certain everyone grasped the import of this discovery. When he was satisfied by the looks of frozen horror on all sides, he added deliberately, "A'course, One-Eyed Joe may've lost his hook—but that's not to say he can't have another made for him." This observation elicited shrieks from several of the people present, and Thomas was finally satisfied.

After a respectful pause at the end of this recital, a babble of voices broke out as people debated with vigor the moral of the story. Mrs. Agate, who was of a religious turn, opined, "The true evil is the wicked sinfulness of the lovers. They're an affront to decent people! Did they but stay home conning their Bible and hold off their dalliance till they'd a marriage bed, they'd've been all right. It were a judgement on 'em!"

"Well, young folk has always been resty," said Jacob Holland in placatory tones, spreading his hands across his broad belly; "we can't allus be judging. But I've said before and I'll say now, no good never came of a girl's reaching above her station and trying to marry high."

Walter Rose, who aspired to philosophy, nodded at this and further deprecated the pirates' code of silence as detrimental to the greater good. "We must allus expose the sins of one person for to protect the commonweal," he declared.

"That's why you ain't liked, Walter!" retorted James

Underhill, who was large enough to get away with bluntness. "It's clear enough to see the point: 'tain't no use going for to work as a coachman, for who knows what the consequences might be!"

In the midst of this debate, Mrs. Steer suddenly realized that both Harry and Isabella had been present to hear this entire tale of horror, and she shooed them hastily off to bed. For once, Isabella was grateful for the presence of her brother, and she clung to his hand as they climbed the stair. Harry, for his part, was happy he did not have to walk home in the dark like the rest, and it was only with the greatest effort that he was able to hold his tallow candle steady. Isabella's was shaking so much he feared it might blow out.

He graciously saw her to the door of her chamber, saying with the most spurious kindness, "I wonder if One-Eyed Joe is as skilled at climbing walls as he must have been at climbing the rigging? You might wish to lock your casement tonight, Bella."

Isabella squeaked and rushed into her chamber; Harry could hear the window slam, and then a scraping sound as she tried to drag her wardrobe over in front of it. He laughed and retired to his room—though it must be said that he more than once peered out his window to look for a shadow slipping across the stableyard.

CHAPTER THE EIGHTH

It was but a day or two after the haying dinner and Mr. Steer was taking his ease for a stretch before the corn must be got in, doing little more than making repairs to his tools. The entire family, with Mr. Marshall, was assembled over their morning bread, bacon, and cheese when a knock was heard. Janey the kitchenmaid being sent to open it, the assembled company was surprised to see Cousin Dick Steer in the doorway, twisting his hat in his hands.

Mrs. Steer recovered first and rose to lay another place for him. "Why, Dick, aren't you a sight for sore eyes—so big as you've grown, you look more man than boy! How are your father and mother keeping? Come, sit with us."

Harry was staring at his cousin, horrified, over the rim of his tankard of small beer. What could this visit portend but discovery of his exploits with the free-traders? He turned red, then pale; but no one was looking his way to notice. Even Isabella's sharp gaze failed to penetrate his guilt.

"Thank you, Aunt," said Dick easily, taking his seat. "Uncle, how d'ye do? The family is all well, and my parents send their remembrances to you. I've already eaten, but I'm sure a little more can do me no harm." And he commenced with the greatest aplomb addressing his meal, ignoring the desperate appeal in Harry's eyes.

Mr. Steer waited for Dick to swallow a few bites—which he accomplished with nods of pleasure and a compliment to Mrs. Steer on the fineness of her bread—and then asked, "Well, my boy, what brings you all this way at such an hour of the morning?"

"Aside from my aunt's excellent cheese," said Dick, "my mother did ask whether you might spare Harry for a day. The cherries are that forward, and Dad and all the men still hard at it in the hayfields. As you know, we planted an orchard ten years back, and after last year's cold the trees do bear a treat. Harry and I could finish the task in a day—and a fine basket of the best fruit for your family into the bargain."

Mr. Steer was on the point of demurring in the name of Harry's education, but Mrs. Steer was too quick for him. Here was the chance she had been looking for, to give Harry a day out of doors to recover from his recent malaise. "We should be happy to send him; we don't see enough of all of you. And I've been wishing to present your mum with a cheese. Mr. Steer is dearly fond of your cherries, and it would be a kindness to receive some." Turning to her husband, she added, "Harry may ride Parsifal, mayn't he? The poor beast has been shut up in the barn through all the fine weather. It would do them both good, don't you agree?"

Outmaneuvered, Mr. Steer had no choice but to give in, at the hazard of slighting his own kin by remaining obdurate. Harry rushed to give his mother a kiss on the cheek and took to his heels before any objections could be made.

"Your mum's a good soul," said Dick as they saddled

up Parsifal, who was fairly dancing in his eagerness to be out of his stall. "D'ye think she believed me?"

Harry hushed him and whispered, "Are we not then going to pick cherries?"

Dick laughed. "And haven't I got a basketful, sent from my mum to yours, hidden under some bracken by that old cart track where you met up with the pack train a week gone? It's hard by a great branch fallen across the way. You can pick it up in your way home, and give it her with Mum's compliments."

"Then where are we going?"

"Sneck up for now; when we're well away, I'll tell you."

For the moment Harry was happy enough to ride alongside his cousin, swelling with pride at the unaccustomed sensation of having an older boy, so well versed in the ways of the world, look kindly on him and include him in his enterprises as if he were an equal.

The sky was threatening a break in the fine weather that had been so favorable to the haymaking, but the prospect of a soaking did not daunt Harry in the least. As they rode, Dick beguiled the time in laying out a plan he and his associates were forming. It seemed a large dray had been left outside the cattle pound in Darking; they proposed overnight to disassemble it, move the pieces into the pound, and reassemble it within, to the confounding of the driver when he returned for his vehicle in the morning. This idea made Harry laugh immoderately, but he was obliged to confess that he would not be able to contribute to the endeavor. With his father done with the haymaking, Harry risked discovery if he tried to escape the house at night just now. He had no wish to queer his chances of joining in when the smuggling runs began again a few weeks hence with the waning moon.

At last they had left Henfold far enough behind that Dick considered it safe to disclose their destination. Even though nobody was by, he drew close to Harry and spoke only in a whisper. "Milord is wishful to meet you. He has heard about you from Mr. James—"

"Who is Mr. James?"

"Have you learned naught?" Dick glanced around again. "Mr. James Tilt is the cap'n."

"Oh! And Milord is his commander."

"Yes. It's Mr. James's father who runs all the free-trading hereabouts. We call him Milord, but his name be John Tilt, of Redlands Farm. Now that you've heard it, forget it! Milord allows none to work for him without he meets them and takes their measure. Today's the day you're having your measure taken."

Harry could not help but be a trifle cowed by this prospect, and he humbly asked if there was anything he could do to convey a favorable impression.

On this point Dick had little to offer. "Cap'n appears to like you, so I expect you'll do well," was his only reply.

A gentle mizzle began as they proceeded in a north-westerly direction across the common. To Harry it seemed oddly tame to be taking this familiar way in daylight, chased by the calls of the pewit and the lark instead of the heave-jar and the owl. But warring with those feelings were the trepidation and excitement of meeting his secret employer, the mastermind of the organization in which he had played a minor part. Mr. Tilt must be no common man to have created such a massive yet covert enterprise, and Harry, forgetting he was the one to be examined, determined to ask as many questions as the duration of the interview allowed.

At length they quitted the common and proceeded

between tall hedges down a humble cart track, its muddy, rutted surface belying any notion that the owner of the property might be a successful man. The fields beyond the hedges lay mostly fallow and weedy, woods encroaching around the edges; the stiles and gates were in disrepair, and altogether Harry's farmer soul was disgusted by the neglect so obvious on all sides. When the farm buildings came into view, Harry saw that the principal structure was an ancient house of whitewashed brick, half-timbered, with slumping beams and a series of extensions sagging off the sides of the central block, as if the house had suffered an apoplexy. Its two stories were low-ceilinged and the windows were small. The building seemed an unworthy abode for a criminal mastermind.

As they dismounted, a young boy with a thumb in his mouth appeared briefly in an open doorway and then vanished back into the house. This led to the appearance of the captain, who strode out to greet them and show them where to stable the horses. Harry, who had never before seen him without a blackened face and a hat pulled low over his brow, now discovered him to be a well-formed and good-looking man of about thirty. The captain welcomed them with cordiality and conducted them into the house.

Harry's first impression was of bustling activity, as if he had strayed into a coaching inn by mistake. Women and children were everywhere, spinning about him in a dizzying variety of occupation. Two small boys dashed almost across his feet in pursuit of a kitten; a young woman who appeared to be at the point of her lying-in brushed past him with an armload of washing; another was descending a narrow staircase opposite the door with a baby nestled in one arm and a pile of shirts for mending in the other; two older boys stood in a corner of the main gathering-room, eagerly disputing politics, while a small girl pulled at her mama's skirts and complained of the toothache. The room was dominated by a large hearth, cold on this summer's day; and in the chairs set beside it, presiding over the melee with benignant calm, was an older couple. The lady was sitting perfectly still with hands folded in her lap and eyes downcast, her mouth sagging slightly to one side. Her husband, a man ample in both size and girth, rested a foot on the grate and gripped a large tankard of ale. He appeared as vital as his wife was lifeless, fit and strong for his years, which Harry guessed to number about sixty.

While Harry struggled to absorb this chaotic scene, the captain was leading the two boys forward to stand before the old man. "Dad, this here is Monkey, the young imp of Satan who's so determined to become a free-trader."

Harry made his bow to Mr. John Tilt. As he straightened, he found himself under the scrutiny of a pair of shrewd but friendly eyes. "Ann," called Mr. Tilt, "bring these boys a tankard to slake their thirst!" He added in an aside to Harry, "You wish for aught in this house, simply call for Ann. 'Most all the women in this house are called Ann! One of 'em will answer you." And then, to the political disputants in the corner: "Joseph, Will—seats for our guests."

Mr. Tilt clasped hands with Dick but it was the younger boy who held his attention. "So, Harry Steer, is it," said he. "You're living down close by Newdigate, at Henfold, eh?"

"Yes, Milord."

Mr. Tilt guffawed, setting the herbs that were drying in the chimney to swaying. "Listen to him, boys!" he cried to the room at large. "He gives me the title of a nobleman. You scapegraces could learn a thing or two about respect from this one."

No one paid him any heed. "That's all very well, young man," he continued in an easy tone, "and I know what I'm called, but I'm no gentleman, nor ever was, and no doubt my pa pulled his forelock to yours when they met in the street. When I begun, I hadn't so much as a pig in a sty. For all that, I'm now a warmer man than your pa, and a man of larger property to boot! I may not have my letters, but I've got my wits about me."

Harry liked him instantly and settled back to enjoy himself. Mr. Tilt, observing this, suddenly leaned forward and added, "Harry Steer of Henfold, I know where you live and who your family be. Betray me at your peril."

There was a silence; everyone in the room was paying attention. Harry's throat felt dry, but he managed to say at last, in something perilously like a squeak, "I would not, sir."

"Mind you don't, Harry. Now: why are you wishful to become a smuggler? Not to pad your family's income, I wager, like your cousin Dick here. Not to lighten the burdens carried by your sweet mother—her name is Jenny, I'm told? Charming woman, I make no doubt. You see, I know all about you. Speak up!"

For some reason the implicit threat against his family lost some of its terror through repetition, and Harry felt able to reply with tolerable composure. "For the adventure, Milord—sir. You see," he added mournfully, "my dad wants me to go away to school. He keeps me at the books all day with a tutor. It's more than a soul can bear!"

John Tilt gave a roar of laughter. "There's for you, Will!" he called to one of his sons, a boy about Dick's age, who hunched his shoulder resentfully. "Will's of a bookish turn," he explained; "dunno where he came by it. If I knew no better, I'd suspect my Ann played me false." He gently stroked the folded hands of the woman beside him, who remained unmoving. "My Ann's not been well these past months, but she knows when I'm just having my fun and don't take me serious. So you're out for adventure, is it? That's not enough of an answer, Harry Steer. And play no tricks on me, boy; I've too many sons to be gulled by a stripling."

Harry puzzled over this. "Would it be better if I came to the free-trade by necessity rather than by choice?"

"As your employer, it'd be better for *me*. I have a hold on them that puts food on their table thanks to what I pays 'em. You see, I speak straight to you, Harry, accos I likes you."

Harry declared himself honored.

"But if you're with us only for adventure and then find the work too hard, like a gentle-bred one like you might, what's to stop you thinking that giving us up to the Excise would be more exciting?"

"If a person serves you only because he must, what is to prevent his betraying you if that necessity is removed— if he receives an inheritance, for instance?" argued Harry. "My loyalty is voluntarily bestowed and based on gratitude. I cannot run away to sea and become a pirate because I live too far away from the coast. Knights no longer go off on quests, and I am not a knight in any case. How else am I to have my adventures and grow into a man without joining the smugglers? And the captain your son gave me that chance."

"Well spoken, imp," said James.

"Perhaps," said Mr. Tilt; "but you must understand what's at stake here, Harry Steer. Who d'you think are the great lords hereabouts?"

"Mr. Peters, the Duke of Norfolk, Baron Verulam."

"Aye, and others too; but not a one of 'em employs more men than I do in this neighborhood; not a one, I tell you. They collect their rents, be the harvest good or bad; if a tenant can't pay, they throw him out without the means to feed his children. They house their laborers in cottages so bad they're little better than no shelter at all, and pay 'em so meanly that most can't buy the coals to cook their dinner with. The Crown corners the market in grain to feed its soldiers, and a man can't buy his children a loaf of bread."

Harry sat still and silent.

"*I* pay in a night what a laboring man can earn in a week, toiling in the fields of those great lords. I pay every man the same, regardless of station. I own eight farms and use 'em to house those as serve me well, and build cottages for 'em too. Here in this room you see about me not just my own family but that of my wife's son Peter Peters and his friend Charles Cosens, who's served my business for years. We all see to each other. The so-called lords may may dress and speak as fine as they please, but a real lord is a lord on the strength of how he cares for them as lives under him. Make no mistake, Harry Steer: *I* am the lord of Darking parish, and the parishes roundabout to boot."

Mr. Tilt paused to drain his tankard, and then leaned in to stare at Harry. "The lords and the magistrates may say my trade is unlawful, and if they bubbled me I'd surely hang for my crimes, for I was a highwayman afore I was a free-trader. But if that came to pass, who would keep the people hereabouts in food and shelter? Them lords won't look about 'em and say, 'My people are starving, they must be fed,' or 'I won't foreclose because this man can't pay what he doesn't have.' They'll say, 'Where's the money to buy my next snuffbox?'

"I may have no book-learning, but I know what's what in this world. If so be as you ever betray me, Harry Steer, you betray half your neighbors. You betray your cousin Dick here, and his mother and father and brother and sisters. And for that I'd see that you pay with everything you hold dear."

Harry, his eyes shining with fervor, swore on his family that he would remain constant to the free-traders' cause; caught up in his enthusiasm, he ventured to amplify on Mr. Tilt's ideas. "You put me in mind, sir, of one of the Walking Dunghill's—Major Labilliere's—sayings: he would say that virtue is not rest, but action, and that a poor man should not be silent when oppressed with heavy burthens and taxes."

John Tilt leaned back in his chair and his fearsome aspect dropped away, replaced with his original attitude of benign calm. "A toast on that—and to the memory of Major Labilliere!" he cried, waving his tankard about to have it refilled. One of the Anns leaped to do his bidding, and Mr. Tilt, Harry, and Dick solemnly drank to the prosperity of all.

The rain had begun in good earnest some time since, so the Steer cousins were invited to stay on and take their mutton with the extended Tilt family. Accustomed as he was to the fearful quiet of his father's household, Harry was charmed by the noise and gaiety that prevailed in the low-ceilinged room. He was not above participating in a game of spillikins on the floor with the younger boys, while Dick, mindful of the dignity of his years, stood with Will and Joseph Tilt and listened with little comprehension while they debated the likelihood that the Acts of Union should receive their final approval and the dismaying news from the Austrian battlefields. A baby occasionally wailed and the women gossiped without restraint as they bustled to and fro from the kitchen, preparing the dinner. There was no table large enough to accommodate them all, so when the food appeared, plain but ample, each person took a plate and retired to the first chair he could find.

At last the storm relented and Dick told Harry in a whisper that it was high time they took their leave. The captain saw them out, whispering to Harry to "watch for a sign a fortnight hence," and they went their separate ways, with a reminder from Dick not to omit collecting the basket of cherries before returning to Henfold.

CHAPTER THE NINTH

Perhaps it was his pleasure in the cherries that induced Mr. Steer to relent in his severities toward his son, or perhaps it was simply that he needed help doing a job on the sly. The hares had been troubling him to such a degree this summer that even though his demesne was insufficient to qualify him for taking game, he could not stand idly by and watch his livelihood destroyed. In addition, the rabbits were got into Mrs. Steer's garden something fierce, and she was forever complaining of stepping in their crottle and finding her carrots dug up.

The situation posed a dilemma. Had it been September and the partridges, he might have asked his kinsman Lee Steere Steere to ride over and enjoy some sport, but for mere snaring such a request would have been an impertinence. Since the Duke of Norfolk was buying so much property in the neighborhood of Henfold, without ever spending a day on his lands, there were no qualified landowners nearby who could be relied on to kill Mr. Steer's hares for him; it must be done surreptitiously. If he engaged any of his laborers in the task, they might talk; and he could ill afford to pay the fines should his activities be discovered. Another year of losses might leave him at the mercy of the bankers. Mr. Steer needed help, and he needed it from Harry. Accordingly, for privacy the tutor Mr. Marshall was given leave to spend a few days in Horsham with his family. Harry saw him off with undisguised joy.

It was agreed the rabbits were the more pressing issue, and they had the advantage that they could legally be killed and sold, so long as they were not shot. Mrs. Steer's complaints were unceasing about the destruction in her kitchen garden, and out in the fields they were devastating the turnip tops. So Harry and his father set out a few hours before first light to watch, Mr. Steer among the turnips and Harry perched on the kitchen garden wall, remaining as still as he could bear despite a squally wind that brought in periodic showers. It was frustrating to do nothing while the rabbits made banquet, but as he well knew, catching rabbits is not done in a night.

At dawn the sated creatures made their way home to their forms and burrows, and Harry, sleepy but valiant, rushed about to mark all the spots where they had gone to earth. Soon his father was coming home from the fields, and they repaired to the kitchen for sustenance before the real work of the day began.

Back out of doors, they collected stones and con-structed bulwarks around all the marked burrows, covering them with grass from the fallow meadows. After dinner Mr. Steer pulled out his long nets; the entire family, even Isabella, worked to check and mend them.

Harry and his father seized a few hours of rest before Mrs. Steer came to awaken them after full dark. The moon was nearly full, so they were able to proceed without the encumbrance of a lantern. Taking up the first of the nets, they made for the kitchen garden, where the rabbits were again busy. At a signal from his father, Harry jumped up and down, shouting and clapping; the conies raced for cover, Mr. Steer in hot pursuit. Once they were below ground he cast the net over the bulwark they had constructed around the largest of the burrows, and Harry pinned down the corners of the net with stones.

At a call to Mrs. Steer, she emerged from the farmyard, her grimace visible even in the moonlight as she brought them a small basket with the rotten eggs she had been hoarding for the occasion. Harry had the doubtful honor of dropping one of the eggs into the burrow while trying not to breathe. They all stood back to wait.

As the reek of sulfur penetrated the passageways of their burrow, the rabbits bolted out one by one, only to find themselves entangled in the net. All three Steers moved in to snap their necks. When the burrow could yield no more, they disentangled the little bodies and stacked them alongside the stable wall.

Since the remaining rabbits in the kitchen garden would be skittish for some hours to come, the Steers then moved on to the turnip fields and attacked a burrow there in similar fashion; after that it was back to the kitchen garden, and once more out to the fields. Before moonset they had a stack of thirty rabbits and were free to retire for what remained of the night, Mr. Steer clapping his son on the shoulder with a "Well fought, Harry," that left him in a glow of satisfaction.

Here was entertainment enough to cast the long nights of plodding alongside the free-traders in the shade. The burning desire to impress the Tilts, father and son, sloughed off Harry like an old skin; he was in a glow of gratification for serving his own family well. Not that he was ashamed of his work with the smugglers: to the contrary, the sight of his father setting out so deliberately to contravene the game laws only reinforced the honor of their enterprise. The laws were, after all, written to benefit the wealthy at the expense of the poor—to defy such laws was a necessity when survival was at stake, and it was a matter of principle for a man to be a man for those he loved. It was a question of liberty and justice! But the thought of his father's pride in how he had done his work was what warmed his cheeks as he fell asleep.

The next morning was to produce an even greater satisfaction, for after Mrs. Steer set aside several of the rabbits for her pantry, Mr. Steer decreed that Harry was to accompany him on his errand to sell the remainder.

This was an undertaking of some delicacy. While he was permitted to sell the rabbits, his aim was to use them to pave the way for the illegal sale of any hares they might catch during the nights to come. Those who made a living out of poaching had standing arrangements with the coachmen on the turnpike, who would stop on their northbound journeys and purchase their catch so as to sell the game on to the London butchers and poulterers upon arrival in the metropolis. But not just anyone could wave down a mail coach and offer up illicit wares: these were relationships of trust, developed over years of transactions. The occasional offender like Mr. Steer required a middleman.

Fortunately, the entire neighborhood was familiar with that haunt of vice on Holmwood Common, the Nag's Head. If shady doings were to be done, this was the place to do them. Conveniently situated on the London turnpike, it was the ideal spot to sell anything that might be swallowed up by the insatiable demands of the city and none the wiser. The young widow Elizabeth Wood who was its proprietor had opened her establishment on the strength of the ill-gotten gains of her husband, who had ended his days on the gallows for taking to the High Toby. She was known to be tolerant of any sort of outlawry, and her public house thrived on the custom of ruffians and thieves.

Thither Harry and his father therefore directed their gig, the rabbits hidden under a stack of firewood at their feet. To Harry's private amusement his father, eager to avoid being noticed at the tollgate at the southern end of the common, retraced the route Harry had followed with the smugglers, up Brimstone Lane to the track leading toward the windmill, before joining the turnpike road just north of the Nag's Head and doubling back.

As they drew up, Mr. Steer admonished Harry to keep his mouth shut and his eyes open.

"Yes, sir." Harry needed no encouragement to look about him; he entertained the liveliest curiosity about this hitherto forbidden den of iniquity. His initial reaction was one of disappointment, for the taproom was no more shadowy, decrepit, or filthy than the average run of such places. Indeed, the east-facing windows let in enough light to illuminate the dust motes floating in the air and the ill-dressed men seated in the corners. The Steers were as much watched as watchful, and it was scarcely a moment after their entry before Harry locked eyes with one of them—none other than the impoverished highwayman who had accosted him on the evening of the Walking Dunghill's funeral!

Harry immediately withdrew his gaze and turned away, taking a seat on a bench next to his father. But it was too late; the man arose and approached them. Harry tried to send him a silent rebuff, but the man did not take his meaning and came to stand before them.

"It's that pleased I am to see you again, young nipper!"

he said, in what seemed an unnecessarily loud voice, waving his tankard about and dispersing some of its contents around his shoes. "You told me as how I might find gainful employment here, and how right you were! I was on the edge of selling my horse for food, and now I've a roof over my head and a change of clothing."

"I'm afraid I don't recall having the pleasure of making your acquaintance," said Harry coldly, frowning him down.

The man only roared with laughter, and more beer was scattered about in the rushes. "Listen to the lad with his breakteeth words! If you'd spoken to me so, that night on the road, I'd not have believed you when you said all you had was thruppence. I'd have had you off that horse and gone through your pockets, I would so; aye, and maybe slit your throat in the bargain."

"I don't know you!" cried Harry in desperation, feeling his father stiff with rage beside him.

"To be sure, we weren't formally introduced; it weren't that sort of occasion, were it?" replied the highwayman, imitating Harry's tone. "Allow me to rectify the omission. Will Tomkins, at your service." He bowed with a flourish, losing the remainder of his beer in the process.

"Get you gone, madman!" cried Mr. Steer with a fierce stare.

"Now then, there's no call for hard words," said Tomkins. "Your son—he is your son, I assume? He has a look of you—your son, I say, did me a kindness some weeks ago, and I'm one as is grateful where grateful is due."

Mr. Steer bent his stare on Harry, who hastened to explain. "Mr. Tomkins held me up on the turnpike, not far from here," he whispered. "The night I came home from Darking after the funeral for Major Labilliere. There was no harm done, I had nothing to give him; it didn't seem worth mentioning."

Tomkins added helpfully, "I didn't touch a hair on his head. He said he had nobbut thruppence, and I believed him. Despite how we met, he was good enough to suggest I come here. Put me in the way of work, he did."

Mr. Steer sought for words to express his distaste for this acquaintance of his son's, but could think of nothing to say and simply looked daggers at the man. Tomkins, observing his discomfiture, finally decided he had had his fun and took pity on Harry. "Well, well, I see you're occupied and will leave you be. But I was wishful to say I am in your debt and will repay you if the occasion arises." He bowed again and withdrew to his corner of the room.

"Well, *that's* cut it," said Mr. Steer in an angry whisper. "Now everyone in this den of cutpurses is staring at us. Did it occur to you that I wanted us to pass unnoticed? Didn't I say to keep your mouth shut?"

Stung by the unfairness of this reproach, Harry protested, "How was I to know he would be here?"

"Evidently you *sent* him here!"

"But that was weeks ago! And it's not as if I greeted him when I saw him. I tried to ignore him."

"See how well that worked!"

As this exchange threatened to devolve into a full-fledged quarrel, it was fortunate that Mrs. Wood chose this moment to approach them. "What d'ye want?" Her words may have been brusque but her attitude was welcoming enough, and Mr. Steer was persuaded to order small beer for Harry and a pint of ale for himself.

Under its influence he became a little calmer. The other patrons of the establishment seemed to have forgotten about them—in fact, all those who had recourse to the taproom at that hour appeared to prefer not to meet one another's eyes—so by the time Mr. Steer had drunk up he was prepared to conduct his business.

Calling Mrs. Wood to his side, he inquired in a low tone whether she had any use for some nice rabbits, freshly killed. He was about to embark on an explanation of how a large number of them chanced to die at once, and in the same location—a rigmarole, prepared in advance, about the sudden flooding of some burrows—when she interrupted him without ceremony.

"They bin mortal bad this summer, ain't they? Farmers coming in 'ere daily looking to sell for the Lunnon trade. So many it's forced the price down; not enough swells in town over the summer to eat 'em all. Three shillings the brace is all I kin do if ye shot 'em, four if not."

Blinking at the ease of this transaction, Mr. Steer allowed as how he had twelve brace of the finest, out in his gig, all with their necks broke.

"Then let's 'ave a look at 'em," said Mrs. Wood, and led them outside.

There they became aware of a cluster of young boys, about eight or ten years old, standing about the gig. As the party emerged from the Nag's Head one gave a shout and they all scattered, running as hard as they could with rabbits bouncing against their legs. Mr. Steer roared at them and ran for the gig, only to discover that this had not been their first visit and no more than six rabbits remained amid the scattered firewood. He cursed fluently while Mrs. Wood hooted with laughter and cried, "Bless me, you didna think to leave the boy outside to guard 'em?"

Mr. Steer was so enraged that he almost mounted the gig and rode off on the moment, but Mrs. Wood placated him, offering to pay for those he had left as well as any others that might happen to die on his land in the future; "for the coachmen stop 'ere regular, and I can allus cook up any I don't sell. An' if any 'ares should 'appen to die as well, I can give ye six shillings apiece for 'em, and not a word of where they came from."

So they shook hands on the deal and Harry and his father rode away, Harry doing his best to remain invisible. He knew well that any attempt at consolation would only exacerbate his father's wounded pride and earn him a clout or worse. He prayed his mother, upon their return, would not be so impolitic as to ask how they had fared.

Mr. Steer was enough of a horseman to understand that he could not give his anger full play while driving, but his sentiments on having this humiliating scene witnessed by his son could not be relieved without exacting some retribution. After a few minutes of silence, he seized Harry's ear and gave it a twist, reverting to the subject of Tomkins. "I don't like your secretive ways, boy! You're waylaid on the 'pike and don't even trouble yourself to inform me?"

Harry, conscious of even greater secrets he had to keep, hung his head and did not immediately reply.

"Speak up! How do you account for yourself?"

"Well, sir," said Harry, feeling his way carefully, "as the man said, there was no harm done. He took nothing from me, not even the cheroots. And I must say I did not find him to be a particularly frightening person. He's nothing but a farmer who lost his farm."

In spite of his desire to be angry, Mr. Steer had to acknowledge that he'd seen enough of such men in recent times. "Still, I had no wish to draw attention to us in there, as he did by accosting us in that public way."

"Perhaps in the end it was a good thing," observed Harry. "In such company, two law-abiding intruders might be viewed with suspicion. It may be that his welcome made us more acceptable to the other rogues."

Mr. Steer had to cede this point, but could not resist reverting to blame for the outcome. "If he hadn't drawn attention to us, we could have conducted our business sooner, before those damned thieving boys turned up."

"Next time," said Harry, "I'll stay with the gig while you go fetch Mrs. Wood."

"At least you had the common sense not to give that rogue your name."

Thinking guiltily about how many rogues in the neighborhood already knew his name, Harry remained silent.

Considering his father's ill-humor, it was perhaps an unfortunate circumstance that upon their return to Henfold, they should discover a fine curricle tied up outside—none other than Mr. Barclay's conveyance. Mr. Steer uttered an oath and leaped out of the gig, adjuring Harry as he strode indoors to unhitch the horse and pull the gig into the barn. But Harry was too curious to miss any of what was going forward, so he hastily sought out an idling Nat and turned the gig over to him before hastening in by the kitchen door.

There was a little alcove in the corridor where, Harry knew, he could eavesdrop on conversations in the parlor so long as the parlor door remained open. And to his delight, his father had been in too much of a hurry to close it. As it happened, though, Harry would have had no trouble hearing regardless of what corner of the house he stood in, for voices were already raised.

"A fine welcome you offer to guests," Mr. Barclay was saying, "threatening to kick me out without even so much as hearing what I have to say! Your manners, sir, are those of a rustic."

"It is no part of good manners to push in where

you're not wanted and introduce yourself to my wife in my absence!" roared Harry's father. "You'll be lucky if I don't draw your cork before I kick you out of doors."

Mrs. Steer could be heard to murmur a faint protest. "I asked him in, thinking you might conduct your business with Mr. Barclay upon your return."

"I have no business to conduct with Mr. Barclay, and well he knows it! Begone with you, sir, before my patience runs out."

"I mean to have my way," said Mr. Barclay. "It had been my intent to offer you a very attractive price, but with each incivility you utter the amount is reduced."

"You call me a rustic," said Mr. Steer with heat, "but I have a very good notion of what you are about. After your previous visit, I thought about your motives. Shall I tell you my conclusion? It's all about the Duke of Norfolk's plan to build a castle hard by at Ewood. You wish to buy up adjacent land for a pittance and then offer to sell the property to the duke for a fortune, do you not? You see, I am awake to your schemes!"

There was a brief silence and then the sound of a chair scraping on the floor. "I see you are not to be reasoned with," said Mr. Barclay in a sulky tone. "Another man will have to benefit from my generosity. You will live to regret your foolishness, I believe."

"Not so foolish as you thought, eh, Barclay?" Harry could hear that his rout of the persistent Mr. Barclay had restored his father's good humor. "You can make your own way out, cully."

Mr. Barclay came down the hall at a pace that prevented Harry's escape. Mr. Barclay caught sight of him, glared at him in impotent rage, and stormed out the door, chased by Mr. Steer's laughter.

Chapter the Tenth

Harry and his father returned to trapping rabbits that night and went back to the Nag's Head with a respectable number to sell. Harry took up his guard post while his father disappeared into the taproom. It was not long before Harry was approached by a group of four boys, who appeared to materialize from the hedges. He sat silently as they circled around the gig, rendering it impossible for him to keep them all under his eye at once. "Come down from there and we won't hurt you," said the largest of them, not much smaller than Harry.

"Ay," said Harry, "but what do you think my dad should do to me if I allowed you to rob us a second time?"

"What do I care, if at end of day I'm eating your fine fat conies?" said the boy insolently.

But Harry was prepared for opposition; he rose in the gig, took hold of the whip, and laid it neatly across the cheek of a boy approaching on the other side. The boy squealed and fell back, clutching his face. "None of this foolishness," said Harry sternly. He sat again, and continued in a softer tone, "I know you're hungry, and I'm sorry for it. If you come up to the gig one at a time, smallest first, you'll have a shilling each to buy yourself some food with." And he jingled the coins he'd earned with the smugglers in his pockets, as if he were a fine lord.

The boys showed some disposition to crowd up to him, but reaching for the whip again sufficed to discourage them and they lined up in the manner he had specified. He made sure each boy had time to make off with his shilling before giving the next, so the little ones could not be robbed by the bigger.

As he passed the coin to the largest boy, he said, "Scarper now—my dad will be out in a moment!" The boy touched his forehead, just as if Harry had been a gentleman, and obeyed.

Harry puffed up with a sense of his own self-consequence: he was a benefactor to the poor! The shillings he could but little regret, for he had nothing to spend them on and would soon be earning more. And they had both served to avert the violence he feared would be his lot as he defended the rabbits, and preserved his father from fresh humiliation. He felt considerable pride in his manner of dispensing both largesse and justice, as well as in the way he had maneuvered his would-be assailants. For the first time, he believed, he understood the power of money in the world.

At this moment Mr. Steer emerged from the Nag's Head in the company of Mrs. Wood and her kitchen boy, and the transaction was soon completed. Mr. Steer returned home this time in a more cheerful frame of mind than on the previous occasion, and as they drove he was full of strategies for mounting his campaign against the hares that night.

Upon their return to Henfold, Harry was set to searching out the hares' meuses through the hedgerows and blocking off the majority of them. Then they led Mrs. Steer's cows in off the stubble of the hay meadows, securing them in the barn so they would not be startled into losing their milk by the night's activities. As dusk fell, Mr. Steer draped his nets across the few remaining openings in the hedges and returned to the house. They reemerged several hours later under the full moon and made for the fields.

Both of them gathered up armfuls of stones as they drew near; the hares could easily be seen in the moonlight, feeding brazenly on the esh. Harry moved off to one side according to their prearranged plan, as his father moved off in the other direction. The task would have been easier with one or two more men and a terrier, but they had to make do.

After pausing for a few minutes to make sure the hares were not prematurely alarmed, Mr. Steer set forth marching across the field toward the hedgerow, waving his arms and shouting, with Harry following suit on the other side. The hares all froze in place until the humans were too close to be any longer avoided; at last one after the other burst forth in panicked flight. If a hare broke to one side, Harry or his father would pitch a stone out in that direction; the hare would veer back to run ahead of them. A few escaped, but a good number were driven forward to the hedge at the back of the field. They ran back and forth seeking their usual openings and finally dashed through the few left open, entangling themselves in the nets on the other side.

Harry and his father let some of the smaller leverets go, but the adults all met the same fate as the rabbits had. Harry thought it famous sport, and even Mr. Steer seemed exhilarated by their exploit, cheering and laughing as they struggled with the hares. *Why could they not always work together in this harmonious way?* Harry wondered, and he wished they had an endless supply of pests to capture.

The killing of the hares being the illegal portion of the undertaking, Mr. Steer would not allow Harry to go with him when he presented them for sale at the Nag's Head. Their take proved lucrative enough, on being presented to Mrs. Wood the next day, that even though Mr. Marshall returned in the afternoon, Harry's father ruled the hunt should continue for a few more nights. Of course, Mr. Marshall must be told nothing about it; Mr. Steer drew Harry out to the stableyard and decreed, "You will have to keep to your studies by day so he has no suspicion of our night's activities."

"But sir! When am I to sleep? And I had far rather help you about the farm than con my books."

"So say you now, but when you are old and every bone in your body aches, you would curse me for indulging you. You may not understand the value of an education at present, but you will when you are grown, I promise you. As for today—you are young, and will come to no harm over a few sleepless nights."

So for two more nights they continued to arise after the household was all abed for the prosecution of their slaughter. Evidently the deliveries to the Nag's Head were successful, as the cash box hidden in a high corner of the chimney was augmented each day upon Mr. Steer's return.

The day after their cull ended was a Sunday, and Mrs. Steer and her children were crowded into the gig for the journey to attend church at Capel, her husband riding behind on Parsifal and Mr. Marshall left to make his way on foot with Nat and Janey. Ordinarily the entire family walked, but Mr. Steer was feeling flush with his gains and desirous of enacting the role of gentleman before his neighbors. Unlike his wife he was not a man of religious feeling, and for him the requirement of Sunday attendance was more a matter of display than of spiritual improvement.

In his aim of striking the neighborhood with awe and envy he was, however, frustrated by how well he was known in the country. Although Mr. Broadwood, who had brought his family over for the service from Lyne House, might bow in an affable way and inquire how he did, Mr. Steer could scarcely rejoice in notice from such a quarter: Mr. Broadwood, for all his brass, was no more than a tradesman, whatever the quality of his pianofortés. And those whose acquaintance he might value, such as Mr. Gill of Temple Elfande and his kinsmen the Franklands, looked neither to left nor right as they made their way to the seclusion of their pews in the front of the church.

To make matters worse, those who had always considered themselves the Steers' equals did not fail to observe his attempt to rise above his station. A clutch of Agates, Ribbinses, and Longhursts gathered under the ancient yew in the churchyard after the service, their tongues clacking like the wind-tossed branches above them. As Mr. Steer passed them by in all his state, trailed by his family, Harry could distinctly hear remarks being passed: "He looks a regular mog"; "No call to get niffy—if he's wishful to hold himself so high, we want none of him!" For Harry, whose ambitions centered on following the plough as his neighbors did, it was an agony to be thus set apart, but his father's gaze was bent on the future and did not falter. Mrs. Steer moved as if to approach the group, but her husband took her arm and firmly led her away; she was able to do naught but look her apologies over her shoulder.

Their genteel solitude at home was relieved for a time in the afternoon, however, as their relation from Jayes, Lee Steere Steere, condescended to return their call, having ridden over their way to survey his properties in Newdigate parish. He sat with them for half an hour, and his attentions went far toward soothing Mr. Steer's sensibilities, lacerated by the snubs he had received at church. He had come, it seemed, with no object but to be pleasing to all—not least to Harry, who observed with delight that Mr. Steere had not forgotten his promise of the stuffed badger, which he carried in under his arm.

"Oh, thank you, sir, I will take the best care of it, I assure you!" he cried before Mr. Steere was even seated.

"Mind you do, Harry; a little spermaceti oil, rubbed into the fur from time to time, will keep the hide supple."

Harry could not bring himself to admit that spermaceti oil was beyond the means of the household, and merely clutched the badger with shining eyes. He now regretted his largesse with the young thieves at the Nag's Head and vowed that future earnings should be saved for the chandler's.

Meanwhile their kinsman was complimenting Mrs. Steer on her black-currant wine, just as if it were the finest product of France or Portugal, and exclaiming over Isabella: "Good gracious, I had no idea that your household was graced by two such lovely ladies! Miss Isabella, you begin to rival your mother for beauty, and will be breaking hearts in a trice. Mind you always wear ribbons in just that shade of blue; it is an exact match for your eyes."

Mrs. Steer, flushed with pleasure, inquired after his intended.

"Oh! Lud, Miss Sarah is well enough. I haven't the patience required to hear all about the bride clothes and such. I'll enjoy having a lady about the house once we're married, though; all those big rooms are too quiet for a single man."

"Do none of your friends come to stay with you?"

"In the winter they might, though for the most part they aren't men of property—so they can't refrain from being overawed by their surroundings, not being born into that way of life any more than I was. Their constant oohings and aahings wear on me, I confess. Growing up, of course, I had little notion of inheriting Jayes, and my companions were the sons of the other shopkeepers 'round about. It's hard to be jolly when one's friends are fawning on one."

Mr. Steer marveled silently at his kinsman's lack of shame about acknowledging his origins, but Mr. Steere proceeded, unconcerned. "I've been wishing to consult you, sir, about the rotations of my fields. Not being raised on the land, I've a lot yet to learn. The one thing I understand is that if I appear ignorant before my steward, I'll never take the reins! If you can point me in the right way, I'd be forever grateful to you. I had always heard of a three-way rotation of the crops, but lately I've been reading about Coke's innovations, and wonder if it should be four."

Harry's father was happy to oblige. "Four is certainly preferable to three—we follow a succession of turnips, wheat, clover, oats—but with the arable acreage you possess, you might wish to consider a bolder experiment. On the drier clay of the Weald, I've been told, there's talk of a six-year rotation: leave a field fallow the first year, treating it with lime and dung; plant it to wheat the next year, then clover, then oats (and mind you plough the stubble twice!), then vetches, and then wheat again, before lying fallow in the seventh year. I have not sufficient land of that character to attempt it, and it is far from proven that the scheme will serve, but the theory appears sound. You may turn your sheep out onto the field to feed when the vetches are grown and plow once afterward, leaving the roots to rot in."

Mr. Steere declared himself delighted. "That rogue of a steward cannot think me ignorant if I propose such a scheme! Do you speak of winter or spring vetches?"

"It makes little matter; you can choose depending on the weather."

Harry might suspect that this was not the first time his kinsman had heard of the six-year rotation, but his father was too pleased by the turn of the conversation to observe it, and he continued to expatiate on the scheme's advantages in a dry clay soil and on the superiority of white Dantzic wheat. He was attended to with every appearance of interest by the younger man, who finally brought the conversation to a close with a last profession of gratitude, adding, "The Winchester race meeting is next week; would you consider consenting to Harry's attendance under my escort? It would afford him the opportunity of becoming acquainted with the city where he is to live for the next several years."

"I am sensible of the honor you do him," said Harry's father, "but I fear his studies must be given priority. Mr. Marshall tells me he is by no means as forward in his Greek as I should wish him to be. I cannot wish him to have his head turned by the sorts of enticement a race meeting would provide."

Harry had appeared so delighted by this proposal, and now appeared so crushed by its denial, that Mr. Steere could not forbear making one further offer. "This Thursday the Gentlemen's Darking Club, whose ranks I have recently been invited to join, is holding one of its dinners. Perhaps you might grant the indulgence of allowing me to bring Harry along? It is only one afternoon, and he could pursue his Greek in the morning. At times I find the seriousness of the club's gatherings a bit of a trial, and as I am a relative stranger there, it would do me good to have a friendly face by me."

Mrs. Steer ventured timidly to worry about this proposal. "He seems full young to be admitted to such company. Will not the other members be offended?"

"Others are sometimes attended by their sons, and I thought it would do Harry no harm to make the acquaintance of some of the men of consideration in the country. Your situation is very retired here at Henfold," Mr. Steere suggested tactfully, "and perhaps you do not have many opportunities to exchange visits with more distant neighbors."

Harry's father confessed to being unfamiliar with the club. "Is it the men of affairs of the town who attend—the brewers and innkeepers and bankers?"

"Oh! No, only the landowners and other gentry. Lord Verulam we can scarcely expect, as he so rarely visits Bury Hill; but Mr. Peters, Sir Lucas Pepys, Mr. Lock, Sir Frederick Evelyn, and Mr. Denison attend most of the time; and it is said that His Grace the Duke of Norfolk may be in the neighborhood—"

"A duke!" exclaimed Isabella.

Her father frowned her down, but Mr. Steere was inclined to be indulgent. "He is indeed a duke, and a very grand duke to boot—but not perhaps the best of company for a young lady, I'm sorry to say."

"Why not?" demanded Isabella. "Is he not looking for a wife?"

Mr. Steere preserved his countenance. "I am sorry to say this one is not, Miss Isabella. His is a tragic story: his wife is mad, and confined for life in one of his houses.

And even were he on the Marriage Mart, I have to tell you he is notorious for being very smelly, so perhaps young ladies would not be so eager to be his wife, for all his grand estates."

Thus met with unexpected encouragement from an elder, Isabella ventured to seek the answer to yet a further question. "Why should he be smelly?"

"I believe he does not care to bathe." Mr. Steere refrained from mentioning what everyone in the room except Isabella was fully aware of, that the Duke of Norfolk was widely known for being washed only when he had drunk himself into a stupor and was unable to forestall the attentions of his servants.

"Is he not a gamester?" asked Harry's father with suspicion.

"He has that reputation—and indeed he could scarcely avoid it, being a great crony of the Prince of Wales. But I assure you, gaming is not a part of the festivities at the Gentlemen's Darking Club. Politics and public affairs are the order of the day, over a dish of the Red Lion's famous water souchy."

Mrs. Steer decided it was time to take a hand. "Harry should not depart the neighborhood without having had the chance to sample the Red Lion's water souchy," said she with a smile, but a hint of firmness behind it as she met her husband's eye. "You are very kind to invite him, sir, and he would be honored to accompany you."

Politics and grand gentlemen were not really Harry's métier, but he had by this time conceived such a slavish admiration for his kindly kinsman that he would have gone with him to a meeting of the Society of Antiquaries. He knew not why a fish stew should have been decisive in the matter but was relieved to have it settled.

Mrs. Steer then invited their cousin to stay dinner; this offer was politely declined, on the grounds of his having yet some miles to cover, and they parted, Harry waving the stuffed badger in farewell.

CHAPTER THE ELEVENTH

It had been settled that Harry would walk to the turn-pike on Thursday to meet Mr. Steere's carriage, and so he set forth dressed in his finest suit of clothing but barefoot, carrying a new pair of shoes to don after he had left behind the mud of the lanes. Mrs. Steer had traveled to Darking the day before and purchased these for the occasion, using some of the money from the hares, and Harry was just as happy not to wear them any longer than he had to, for they were stiff and a little too large.

Lingering along the side of the road under a lowering sky, Harry passed the time by watching the road traffic. He exchanged pleasantries with a drover bringing his cattle to London, gawped at a fine chaise with a crest on the panel, and fended off the derision of the son of one of his father's laborers, who was inclined to mockery of Harry's fine appearance.

Harry discouraged this youth from hurling clods of mud at him by the simple of expedient of throwing rocks back, but no sooner had the boy taken to his heels than Harry heard a "Psst!" from the roadside thicket behind his back. He turned and caught sight of Tomkins the highwayman, peering out at him through the leaves. At least Harry knew the individual in question to be Tomkins, but as he was clad in the garments of a female, Harry was uncertain what to make of him. Despite the skirts and petticoats of his disguise, Tomkins had not shaved off his whiskers and had merely attempted to conceal his face by donning a large bonnet, so altogether the effect was most disconcerting.

"Come here, boy!"

Harry drew a little closer and looked a wary enquiry.

"Is anyone coming?"

"Not just at this present; but the road has been quite busy."

Tomkins shrank back a little farther under the cover of the wood. "Where are you off to, looking so fine?" he asked.

"I am waiting for my cousin to take me to Darking."

"Darking, is it?" said Tomkins with interest. "Now, I would be going that way myself—on a matter of business with my employer. Would your cousin be of a mind to take me up with him?"

"I think not," said Harry firmly. Not daring to ask the question that was really on his mind, he inquired, "Where is your horse?"

"Thrown a shoe. I shall have to walk if you won't help me—and I'm not much inclinable to being seen on the 'pike."

Under the circumstances, Harry could easily credit this reluctance; but he said merely, "I am sorry for your trouble but cannot help you."

Just then Mr. Steere's coach, an elderly vehicle inherited from his grandfather, came into view and drew to a halt. Mr. Steere put his head out the window. "Hallo, Harry! I should have brought my curricle, but that it seems to be coming on to rain. Climb in and we'll be off!"

Harry glanced over his shoulder, but Tomkins had vanished. As he entered the coach, however, it gave a sharp lurch; Mr. Steere exclaimed, "You're a heavier boy than I should have thought, Harry! Mind my springs!"

Harry knew he had not caused the lurch and glanced at the small window in the back wall of the coach, just behind his cousin's head; there he saw, to his horror, the grinning face of Tomkins, who had seized the opportunity to scramble up onto the mudguard. Harry hastily averted his eyes and said nothing as he took his place beside his kinsman.

"Well well, Harry, it's a pleasure to have you join me for this dinner."

"I was honored you would invite me, sir," said Harry, adding wistfully, "though the race meeting would have been beyond anything great."

Mr. Steere laughed. "For me as well! But we must respect your father's wishes. His concern for your education is commendable. Today's entertainment is a poor second for you, no doubt. Yet I feel I should let you know a bit of what you may expect from the Gentlemen's Darking Club."

"Indeed, sir, I had never heard of it."

"Perhaps the best thing you can do is to remain silent and observe until someone condescends to notice you. It can do you no harm to make the acquaintance of the first men of the neighborhood; be civil and mind your manners, and you will make as favorable an impression on them as you have on me."

Though his mind, if not his eyes, kept straying to Mr. Tomkins clinging to the back of the coach, Harry felt obliged by civility to ask, "Who are the members of the club?"

"I cannot say precisely who will be in attendance this

evening. But we will, I imagine, see a variety of gentlemen. Some will be the squires from the parishes 'round about. In the past, such men would have predominated in the club, and local matters would have been the subject of the day. But the world is changing, and the polite society of Darking has not escaped the times. Nowadays, many of the men who own property hereabouts and ape the manners of the squires have risen through the professions and achieved a degree of respect through the influence of their wealth."

"Like Mr. Broadwood?" asked Harry, recalling the previous Sunday's ill-fated visit to church.

"Yes, perhaps like Mr. Broadwood, but he was a tradesman. A very fine one, but I was thinking of a different sort, those with more education. Several of the new men in the neighborhood are bankers in London. Their influence derives from their financial dealings in the City and on the Exchange. They are received in the first circles because of the ways they can benefit men of fortune and even the government."

"The government!"

"It is a truth rarely acknowledged that the government—in large measure because of the years of war—is perpetually starved for funds. And these are the men who can meet the need—if they choose to do so."

The carriage slowed its pace as the coachman blew the yard of tin to alert the keeper of the Holmwood toll gate to their approach. Harry fought panic, for surely the gatekeeper would notice Mr. Tomkins on the back of the coach and raise the alarm. But what could Harry do to prevent it? He turned his thoughts resolutely away from the crisis and cast about for an intelligent question. "But do the bankers have a choice in the matter? If the government commands, surely they must comply."

He heard the coachman exchange words with the gatekeeper and the carriage lurched into motion again. Miraculously, there came no shout of warning, and they proceeded on their way.

Mr. Steere, still oblivious, was saying, "Indeed they do have a choice; and if they should withhold their cooperation, the government could fall again, as it did in the eighties. Such is the power the bankers wield. King and parliament may declare war against France, but the bankers may prevent our waging it."

"I have heard there is talk of peace. Do you think we will be stopped from fighting France?"

Mr. Steere sighed. "I fear we shall not—and not only on account of the bankers, for they have discovered ways to make the conflict profitable for themselves. War is an engine of commerce. At times it appears to me that the aims of our government are held in thrall to the interests of the East India Company and the manufacturers of Leeds and Manchester. They see profit in war, so war we must have."

As he spoke, Mr. Steere turned his head slightly and Harry saw Mr. Tomkins's head duck out of sight in the window. Harry suppressed the impulse to giggle, leaned forward to alter the direction of his cousin's gaze, and schooled his face to solemnity as he remarked, "Profit seems an inadequate justification for loss of life."

"It certainly does," said Mr. Steere. "Mind you," he added after a short pause, "I do not disapprove of the new men per se. Too many noblemen are devoted to nothing but the dissipations of so-called polite society. Even so, I am an old-fashioned soul at heart, and I look rather to the land as the source of prosperity for England's people. Trade can supply the elegancies of life to those with the means to purchase; but it will not feed the cottager."

Harry thought of Milord and the captain, and wondered if their trade were not doing more to feed the cottager than all his kinsman's fields and flocks. But he was too civil to say as much to his host—whose mind in any case had taken a new direction.

"The other group of men who will doubtless be represented at our dinner are members of the political opposition. Did you know, Harry, that Darking is a hotbed of anti-government sentiment?"

"No, sir."

"Indeed it is," said Mr. Steere, smiling, "and these subversives are led by none other than the lord of the manor of Darking himself, the Duke of Norfolk. He is a steadfast opponent of our king's present ministry. He controls many seats in parliament and sees to it they are filled by men who share his views. These include several of our neighbors. You may hear some very sharp comments directed against the Crown and Mr. Pitt!"

"Is that not sedition under the new laws?" asked Harry, his interest more fully caught at last, even as Mr. Tomkins's face, his beard blowing in the wind and his bonnet askew, reappeared in the window. He tightened his jaw and fixed his eyes resolutely on his cousin.

"It may be, and if someone were to call it so, it would not be the first time His Grace has stood accused of it. He is much addicted to Jacobinical ideas."

"Do we not have a duty to report seditious acts, if we are witness to them?"

Mr. Steere laughed. "I cannot doubt that every one of the magistrates you might report it to will be already in the room and able to credit the evidence of his own ears! Some of them may not share the duke's views and will be offended enough—but would they have the backbone to press a public accusation against the first peer in the land? I see little likelihood of their making the attempt. No, my young friend, I am afraid that whatever we may hear, we must smile and regard it as no more than dinner-table conversation—not as a material threat to king or country."

These were yet more ideas that had never before come in Harry's way, his father not being a man much inclined to political discourse. It had reached his ears that plots had from time to time been laid against the King—in fact, a madman had fired upon his Majesty at the Royal Theatre, no more than a few months previously. And hadn't he heard that the Walking Dunghill had been involved in another plot to murder the King, years before? But Harry had never imagined that peers of the realm might be involved in treasonous activities. "Surely a man like the Duke of Norfolk has too much to lose if he were caught in a design to harm the King," he said.

"A shrewd observation, Harry. I believe he does, and therefore the King need not really fear him. For all his democratic sympathies, the duke would find scant comfort in a regime such as the French have endured in recent years. Despite his radical pronouncements, I think we may rely on his grace to stop short of advocating a true government of the people. The fact that he has renounced his Catholic faith in order to wield power and hold high office in the public sphere tells us that he is a man of calculation."

"Then why would he make such statements?"

"I can only suppose that the key to the duke's philosophy lies in his alliance with the Prince of Wales. The prince hates his father and all he represents, and so the duke as his follower is constrained to oppose the King in every instance." The carriage slowed for the toll gate that marked the southern border of the town; Harry prayed that Mr. Tomkins would have the good sense to jump off at this point, for surely he would attract attention on the busy streets! A page might ride the back of a carriage without being noticed, but a bearded fellow in female garments would be sure to draw people's notice. He wished he could risk a glance at the back window but felt certain doing so would lead his cousin to do the same.

Mr. Steere was still rambling on about the duke and his political affiliations. "Perhaps a decade ago, when it appeared the King would be permanently deprived of his reason, adherence to the prince's cause seemed a canny stratagem. But when fear for the King's mental state was removed, the prince's men were left with little ground to stand upon. And so they while away their lives with gaming, and horses, and wine while they wait for their monarch's health to fail. As little as I fear them do I envy their lot."

By this time the wheels of the carriage were rattling over the streets of Darking, and Harry's interval in Purgatory was nearly over. No outcry followed the coach, so he could only guess that Mr. Tomkins was gone. But another sharp lurch as he was climbing out alerted him. He jumped down nimbly and looked behind the carriage, just in time to glimpse the female that was Tomkins making off for an alleyway while several people pointed and laughed. Observing himself observed, Tomkins bobbed Harry a saucy curtsey and slipped away.

Harry turned to his cousin a bland face and followed him toward the entrance to the Red Lion Inn, wondering what business might have induced the highwayman to risk being seen in the town, and in so preposterous a guise; but he had no time for speculation, as his kinsman was climbing the steps to the door.

CHAPTER THE TWELFTH

Upon their entry into the vestibule, Harry discovered Mr. Peters already arrived, and in easy converse with two older gentlemen Harry did not recognize. Mr. Peters appeared even younger and more vital than usual beside them—for one was as round as the moon and the other held himself precariously upright on a pair of legs as thin as sticks, and both were powdered and bewigged in the old-fashioned style. Mr. Peters caught sight of Mr. Steere and hailed him: "One of our newest recruits! Mr. Steere, a pleasure to see you again. May I solicit your arm to escort Mr. Lock into the dining chamber?"

Harry's cousin stepped forward with alacrity to offer his arm to the thin-legged gentleman, nodding and smiling at the other elderly man as he did so. As they moved slowly along the corridor, Mr. Lock smiled graciously and inquired if he might make the acquaintance of the young gentleman.

"You're very kind, sir. May I present my cousin, Harry Steer, of Henfold? He is soon to depart the country and take up residence at Winchester College, and I thought he might profit from meeting some more of his neighbors before he goes. I wrote to our president, Sir Frederick, on the subject and he gave his leave."

"Winchester College, is it? Are you to be a Scholar or a Chorister, Master Steer?"

"Neither, sir," said Harry; "I am to be a Commoner."

Mr. Lock chuckled as if Harry's reply had been intended as a witticism. He replied, "If you intend neither to sing nor to study, you are doubtless wise not to set your ambitions too high. But perhaps once there you may surprise yourself."

The slow pace of their progress down the passage impeded other arrivals, and soon several more gentlemen were pressed up behind them. Mr. Peters and the fat man were there; Harry's notice was drawn to the latter by a creaking noise that appeared to emanate from his waistcoat, which he tweaked repeatedly as if it caused him discomfort. Observing the direction of Harry's gaze, his cousin bent down and whispered, "I believe Mr. Perrin's stays are troubling him."

Harry stared at the man until called to order by Mr. Steere; he had never heard of a man wearing stays, and wondered what might have induced two different men encountered in a single day to adopt female attire. Perhaps the constriction of the stays accounted for the sickly hue of Mr. Perrin's countenance.

From behind Mr. Perrin's bulk a voice cried out, "You are chased! Are we to dine in the corridor this evening? What is the delay?"

"You must hold me to blame for it," replied Mr. Lock equably. "My progress is deucedly slow. Have no fear, Mr. Denison, you will get to your dinner in the end. And I believe we have a dish of Captain Morris's own punch to anticipate as well."

Mortified apologies issued forth from the unseen Mr. Denison behind, but soon enough they had reached the dining parlor, a commodious room but austere in style, dominated by a long table plainly set. Mr. Steere escorted Mr. Lock to a comfortable chair close to the hearth, then moved with Harry to a corner hard by the door so that he could point out the new arrivals.

Captain Morris, standing at a small table near the fire where he was engaged with an enormous bowl, greeted them with good cheer. "Ah, gentlemen! Mr. Lock, your servant! Mr. Peters, Mr. Perrin, Mr. Denison, Mr. Steere, I shall be at your service in a moment, once the punch is ready. We are at a delicate stage in the preparation, or you should have my undivided attention. His Grace sent me on ahead to earn my supper. A moment only!"

"So the rumor is true: the duke is to be present tonight," said Mr. Steere *sotto voce*. "He is not often in the neighborhood, as he no longer has a home here—though I have heard he intends to construct one not far from Henfold." Harry nodded. "Captain Morris is a great crony of his, and holds the office of Punch Maker and Bard to the Beefsteak Society, which the duke and the Prince of Wales both honor with their patronage. You must be abstemious, Harry, in sampling it, or I shall have to carry you home on a trestle. Captain Morris's punch is notorious for its potency! And if we are fortunate, the captain may also favor us with one of his songs."

Indicating the other gentlemen who had entered behind them, he added, "You recognized Mr. Peters, I believe?"

Harry nodded. "He was the one who gave the Walking Dunghill—I beg your pardon, Major Labilliere—leave to be buried on Box Hill. I saw him at the funeral."

Mr. Steere laughed immoderately. "*Walking Dunghill* will do for me—with all due respect to the dead, of course. Well, the man whose stays appeared to absorb your attention is Mr. Perrin—of Parkhurst, so he is a neighbor of mine. He also owns Tanhurst and Leith Hill Place, as well as the tower which you may have observed, atop Leith Hill."

"Oh! Yes, I have always wished to visit the tower. I have heard it is used by—" Harry broke off, afraid to utter the word *smugglers* lest his percipient cousin divine his secret.

"By smugglers, yes, so I have heard," replied his cousin, untroubled by the association. "But sadly, they were driven out of the tower a few years past—and by the same Mr. Perrin who stands before you. He filled up the lower part of the tower with rubble and sealed the entrance, so that no further mischief could be enacted there. No longer can you see, on some moonless night, the flash of a lantern from its heights, or hear the muffled hoofbeats of the pack trains crossing the summit of Leith Hill." He heaved a mock sigh.

Concealing his real disappointment, Harry asked, "Do you know how Mr. Perrin comes to be so very . . . yellow?"

"I understand his fortune derives from estates in the West Indies—a most unhealthy climate from all I'm told. Perhaps he contracted one of the fevers so common there."

"The West Indies! I wonder if he was ever captured by pirates."

"If he notices you, you shall ask him. And now, behind him, you see the younger Mr. Denison; his father is master of Denbies. Like Mr. Peters he is a member of parliament, and very popular among the common people. The poor can always depend on the Denisons for relief."

Bustling in behind Mr. Denison, his movements suffused with a restless energy, was Mr. Barclay. He made as if to approach Mr. Steere with a greeting, but then perceived Harry and abruptly altered course to greet Mr. Denison.

Harry's kinsman grimaced. "You can see why I wished for a friend to accompany me," he said. "I am of little account in these circles, and there are those who won't hesitate to cut me."

He ceased abruptly to speak upon discovering himself overheard by another elderly arrival, slight and frail and bewigged like the other ancients in the room. Mr. Steere bowed and said, "Mr. Bouverie! What a pleasure to see you able to attend. How do you do, sir?"

"Well enough," said Mr. Bouverie, adding drily, "and better pleased to find you among the company than some others may appear to be"—with a knowing glance toward Mr. Barclay. "You must forgive Barclay's manners; his civilities are all too often reserved for those who can be of use to him."

"I am not well acquainted with him," said Mr. Steere. "We were inducted together into the club only recently."

"And you would account for his manner in cutting you by the slight nature of your acquaintance? You are gracious, Mr. Steere. Perhaps my greater knowledge of the—gentleman—detracts from my candor: Mr. Barclay and I have crossed swords in the House on more than one occasion. And I am an old man and find myself less in patience with City manners than I ought to be. But enough of him: surely this is not your son you have brought with you—a younger brother, perhaps?"

"My cousin, Harry Steer of Henfold."

"A pleasure to meet you, Master Steer of Henfold." And Mr. Bouverie passed on with a smile to pay his respects to Mr. Lock.

"Mr. Bouverie is a gentleman in the old style," murmured Mr. Steere after he had gone, "but don't be deceived by that. You could never guess it by his courtly demeanor, but he is one of the greatest radicals in the House of Commons. This past winter, he was once again entering motions to sue for peace with France, and he even holds that the royal family should not be exempt from taxation. Let us hope he does not begin upon the abolition of the slave trade, or half the company will walk out in a miff! Still, you cannot find a better model for the manners of a gentleman."

"He did not seem to approve of Mr. Barclay," said Harry. "But I fear it is not you who should hold yourself responsible for his behavior today. My father has had some encounters with him, and he is displeased with my family."

"You are not alone! I own to being astonished that this club extended an invitation to him. From what I hear, he is a very great rogue; they say his father was a Portugal merchant, for all he claims to be descended from the Collairnie Barclays, which not a one of them will confirm. But he has got himself a position as director of the Royal Exchange Assurance Corporation, which guarantees naval ships against loss—and in wartime, that makes him a valuable man to the government. You may be sure that few men here will risk offending him, or will resent his offensive manners. Most of the City men know enough to conduct themselves better."

With so many to absorb, names and faces began to be entangled in Harry's mind, but still gentlemen continued to arrive: next were Messrs. Stilwell and Fuller, so engrossed in their discussion of the paper currency that they nearly tripped over his toes on their way into the room. Then came a gentleman so resplendently dressed that at first Harry took him to be the Duke of Norfolk, until Mr. Steere informed him that the duke was by far less grand. No, this was the occupant of Pippbrook House—a dwelling on the eastern fringe of Darking town that had recently been expanded sufficiently to enjoy the dignity of a name—a baronet styled Sir Nugent Lumley-Dacre-Prudhoe.

Upon his appearance, an audible sigh of dismay went 'round the room, and gentlemen moved by common instinct into impenetrable clusters to preclude converse with him. Harry and his kinsman, being still close to the door and set apart from the rest, therefore came under Sir Nugent's eye. But as soon as he caught a glimpse of Harry, he muttered, "What? What? Is the Gentlemen's Darking Club become a nursery?" and stalked off.

Sir Nugent next closed in on the hapless Captain Morris, still imprisoned by the punch bowl. Mr. Steere whispered, "You see what a knacky idea it was to ask you to bear me company? You have spared me the greatest bore in Surrey!"

Eyeing Sir Nugent's tight pantaloons and silken redingote, Harry said, "But he is very grand, is he not? Is that how men dress for dinner in London?"

"None who believe, with Mr. Brummell, that taste is best expressed through modesty. Any man whose family tacks on an extra surname every time one of them marries is bound to rank very high in his own estimation—and for Sir Nugent, that means dressing the part. He is a country gentleman with no land to leave his children; a close ally of Pitt's whom the prime minister cannot abide; a wealthy man thanks only to his wife; a rider to hounds whose own horse loathed him so profoundly that it bit all the fingers off his right hand."

"*Truly?*" Harry could not forbear bending his gaze toward this extremity, and he craned his neck so blatantly to catch a glimpse of it that Mr. Steere was obliged to chide him.

"It seems unlikely to happen, but if he should deign to notice you, you must offer him your left hand, not your right, and do so with an air of unconsciousness. He is the chairman of the Darking bench of magistrates and has considerable political interest in Winchester to boot, so mind you don't offend him. I will say he has some effrontery to attend this meeting when the duke is expected!"

"Why, are they enemies?"

"If they were not before, they are now. Not a week ago a motion, brought in by Sir Nugent, was passed in the House of Commons, calling for émigré Catholic clerics to be investigated so as to ensure they are not recruiting British citizens into popery."

"But I thought the duke had renounced his Catholic faith! Why should that matter to him?"

"It is believed that he did so in name only, and still observes it in private. In fact, I'm told his confessor imposed on him a penance for his apostasy, that in public he must always wear the same old coat, in a most unfashionable shade of purplish blue. You may see if he is wearing it when he arrives! He is also known to be a source of support for Catholic families all across the country. The polite world feigns ignorance because he is so closely allied with the prince."

He broke off these indiscreet confidences as yet another arrival appeared, leaning on a cane. "Mr. Smith-Budgen, how do you do? You do us honor by coming all the way from Leigh."

"Ah! Mr. Steere," said Mr. Smith-Budgen, in a thin, cracked voice. "You have traveled no small distance yourself. Dare I hope we have more stimulating company than the usual fox-hunters and Cits?"

"Well," said Mr. Steere dubiously, "Mr. Lock is present, as well as Captain Morris."

Mr. Smith-Budgen gave him a severe look. "We cannot describe that inebriated versifier as an ornament to civilized society. I shall seek out Mr. Lock, however, I thank you very much." He suddenly caught sight of Harry and with obvious effort leaned over, his cane shaking precariously under his weight. Bending a fixed gaze on Harry he demanded, "Young man! What do you know about shells?"

"Nothing at all, sir," replied Harry, startled into bald honesty. "I have never been closer to the sea than Horsham."

"Ah," sighed Mr. Smith-Budgen, and tottered off in search of more congenial companionship.

Harry was beginning to wonder if he had strayed into Bedlam. He looked an enquiry at his cousin. "Mr. Smith-Budgen is a very brilliant man," explained Mr. Steere. "He attained his degree at Oxford when only four years your senior, and is renowned across Europe for his knowledge of marine life. I'm afraid he finds little to interest him outside the animal kingdom. I should not have expected him to take the trouble to attend this gathering."

The punch being now at last mixed to Captain Morris's liking, the company was called on to sample it. Mr. Steere set Harry to carrying the filled cups to all the oldest men in the room, that they should not be required to rise. This task he performed with goodwill, though his tolerance was strained in the end by the tendency of one or two of them to pat him on the head as he offered them their refreshment. For his own part, he was willing enough to do no more than sip at the concoction when his turn finally came for it made him cough, though he rather liked the fragrance of lemons and cinnamon that invaded his nose.

But what he wanted more than anything was his dinner. This meal, the ostensible purpose of the meeting, was nowhere in sight, though his accustomed hour of dining was by now long past. At last his belly could abide the suspense no longer, and after his kinsman had reached a pause in an exchange of civilities with Mr. Denison, he ventured to ask, "Is there to be no food, then?"

Captain Morris, overhearing this plea, said, "I am afraid our appetites are all at the mercy of our noble lord. His Grace shares with the Prince of Wales the conviction that a three o'clock dinner hour is vulgar. He believes one should never dine before six-thirty." At Harry's patent dismay he added, "I do not believe that, for all his indolence, he will keep us waiting half so long. He does make allowances for country ways. And we may rely on his host, Sir Frederick—no friend to town habits—to bring him up to the mark. The duke may complain and call it breakfast, but that won't keep him away from the table."

And indeed, so it proved. There was soon a bustle outside the room, and then a distinct odor penetrated to Harry's nostrils, followed by its source—a large, ungainly man of unkempt appearance, clad in the telltale coat which, despite its heavy wear and many stains, was discernibly purplish blue.

CHAPTER THE THIRTEENTH

The Duke of Norfolk entered the room with an air of nervous activity that sat oddly with his bulk, and had Harry not been prepared in advance to recognize him, he might have taken the duke for a blacksmith who had strayed in from the taproom. A bulbous nose sat foursquare above the purse of his mouth, and his unpowdered crop was plastered greasily to his head. As this noisome mountain shuddered to a halt beside Mr. Barclay, Harry could not help but wonder what made one unquestionably a gentleman and the other not—for the external distinctions were all on the side of the lesser man.

Nevertheless, the duke somehow cast everyone else in the room into insignificance. Conversations were cut short as all eyes turned his way. He appeared to take this attention as no more than his due and assumed the role of host despite the fact that the club's president, Sir Frederick Evelyn, was standing directly behind him. "Ho, gentlemen!" cried the duke. "You behold me fair dragged out of bed by my ruthless friend to partake of the water souchy. By Gad, there had better be a good beefsteak as well to make it worth my while! What a demmed thing, to be roused up at the crack of dawn to eat a fish." As everyone laughed politely, his porcine eyes took the measure of the room. "Denison, Barclay, Lock, Peters—your servant. Bouverie: still in favor of a peace, in the face of the news from Marengo? Sir Nugent—ah. And Captain Morris! What wicked brew have you concocted to put us all under the table? I'm counting on you to deliver me from reason." Evidently the remainder of the gentlemen in the room were not acquaintances, or were beneath his notice, for this speech appeared to mark the conclusion of his greetings, and he lumbered over to the fire to take a cup from the captain in a capacious paw. He downed it in a single gulp, and no sooner had its contents vanished than he reached for a second.

After a few moments more, when it became apparent that his attention was devoted only to the captain and Mr. Lock, interrupted conversations were slowly resumed—albeit in a more desultory fashion, for most of the ears in the room were on the stretch to capture whatever the duke might be saying.

Harry, shifting from one foot to the other in his stiff new shoes, could follow none of it. On one side, Messrs. Stilwell and Fuller continued unabated their exchange of ideas on the paper currency; Mr. Bouverie was kindly inquiring of Mr. Smith-Budgen whether he had acquired any new shells for his collection (but paying no heed to the convolutions of his reply); Mr. Peters and Sir Nugent appeared close to coming to blows over the question of establishing bounties for the benefit of merchants who imported wheat into the country; and the duke was apparently offending mild-mannered Mr. Lock by some coarse joke about the Irish populace's putative satisfaction with the Acts of Union. That the duke immediately guffawed, clapped this frail elder roughly on the back, and claimed he was only in jest appeared to mollify Mr. Lock not in the least.

Harry's cousin, who had been unashamedly eavesdropping on the latter conversation, appeared a little shocked by the duke's levity. He whispered to Harry, "The brother of Mr. Lock's daughter-in-law died in prison after leading the Irish rebellion of '98! It is badly done of the duke to remind him of family tragedy in such a fashion. And an odd choice as well, considering the duke's sympathy for the cause of Irish independence. Until the Irish Catholics attain the relief promised them under the terms of the Acts of Union, he seems little likely to be a friend to the measure."

Mr. Peters was taking up the duke on the subject of taxation. "The right of the King to raise revenue from duties on goods carried into this country can scarcely be in question, your Grace."

"So long as the duties are reasonable, perhaps he is justified. But the amounts demanded only increase with each year, regardless of the people's ability to pay for even the necessities of life! And the income tax is a very different matter, with no weight of precedent standing behind it. Is not excessive taxation in the name of a cause not supported by the people—for you cannot claim this war enjoys popular support—the very essence of tyranny? So you are saying that you would tolerate a tyrant so long as he is a benevolent one; but if you do so, how then do you set about to defy him when he ceases to be?"

Harry was starting to feel that the entire evening was fated to remain a bafflement to him, even despite Mr. Steere's efforts to decode the cryptic conversations taking place on all sides. The gentlemen might be speaking French or Hindoostanee, for all he could make them out.

But soon enough a language he *could* understand was spoken—for, at a signal from an attendant, Sir Frederick Evelyn took his place at the head of the table and called them to order. They all stood behind their seats while Sir Frederick—a man almost as corpulent as Mr. Perrin, with a moon face capped by eyebrows that gave him a perpetual look of surprise—conducted the formalities. He welcomed them all, even Mr. Steere's young guest, and entertained motions from the floor. Sir Nugent proposed that the new vicar, the Reverend Feachem, be invited to join the club now that he had been installed by the bishop, and this motion was carried unanimously. Sir Frederick offered a toast—"To Darking: prosperity and peace!" At last they were permitted to sit and the famous water souchy was produced.

This proved to be no more than a fish stew, bland and rather high in odor. Harry's family did not eat much fish, having no ponds or streams of any note on their lands, so the taste was alien to his palate. It was not improved, he had to admit, by the fact that the stench of the fish mingled so richly with the stench emanating from the duke, down at the end of the table. Nevertheless, Harry was so hungry by this time that he gave the dish his full attention. He was seated, to his dismay, between Mr. Peters and Mr. Barclay; he could not but imagine this arrangement would be an exceedingly uncomfortable one, but as it chanced neither of them paid him any mind for several minutes. With relief he settled down to pick at the potatoes in his stew, which appeared to be the safest portions to consume.

No sooner had the water souchy been banished from the table, however (the duke draining off two more glasses of punch, to take the taste out as he claimed, before turning to the claret), than Mr. Peters turned to Harry and good-naturedly enquired about his family.

Harry duly explained how he was connected to Mr. Steere and said he had a mother and father living as well as a younger sister.

"And you are an only son? Your parents no doubt rest all their hopes for the future in you."

Harry agreed dolefully that this was so. Mr. Peters hid a smile and offered as consolation that "perhaps your sister will make a brilliant match and relieve you of some portion of responsibility."

"That should please her inordinately," said Harry.

"And you as well."

"Yes, sir."

"Your tone implies doubt. Yet it is in the nature of all of us to wish for something other than our present lot, and 'other' generally means more—more prosperity, more fame, a higher position in society."

"But must it be so?" asked Harry, in all sincerity. "Forgive my saying it, but I look about this room and see little enough of happiness, for all the riches enjoyed by these gentlemen. His Grace the duke could not have more of material plenty without being a king, but I can perceive little contentment in his air."

"So, Master Steer—I perceive you to be a philosopher! I think you are correct, both for His Grace and for men in general, that discontent with one's lot is often not allayed by improving material circumstances. Our striving spirit follows us every step of our rise; few of us possess the gift of recognizing sufficiency when we have it, or valuing it as we ought. Here I am, recently possessed of a castle—a degree of grandeur my father could never have imagined—but do I rest at my ease there? No! I must set my entire family's life all about our ears by making improvements to it, altering and adding to what seemed to be perfection when I acquired it. I could profit from cultivating a greater want of ambition."

While Harry was seeking to parse the ambiguities of Mr. Peters's words, there was a stir at the door and yet another gentleman entered, pursued by the platters of the second remove. He was a stately man whose high forehead proclaimed his intellect, and apparently he enjoyed a rank sufficient to merit the duke's notice, for His Grace interrupted his conversation with Captain Morris to cry out, "Sir Lucas! Are you come from the bedside of your royal patient? No sign of the return of his former complaint, I devoutly trust?"

As the men at the table gasped, Sir Lucas Pepys took a seat beside Mr. Lock, a deep flush betraying his disapproval. "I understand His Highness to be enjoying his customary good health."

"Which means, no health at all," retorted the duke, unabashed.

Harry heard Mr. Peters exclaim "Impudent dog!" under his breath, followed by, "He hopes nothing of the sort."

Mr. Barclay, on Harry's other side, caught Mr. Peters's words and leaned across Harry (digging an elbow into his arm) to mutter, "He devoutly hopes the King's illness *may* return, he means to say. His Grace takes his allegiance to the prince too far, and he will come to grief for it one day."

"The duke is all effrontery today," agreed Mr. Peters. "Do you suppose any of us will be spared his offensive sallies before the evening is done?"

"Not if he maintains his present pace with the wine."

But Sir Lucas, at least, was refusing to rise to the duke's bait; instead he set himself to engaging Mr. Lock in a civil exchange about repairs to a road that ran through both their properties, and the table's several conversations resumed.

The duke, however, could never long bear to be merely one among many; and so, seizing upon a word overheard from Mr. Perrin, halfway down the table, he again raised his voice. "What's that you say, Perrin? If you are speaking of France, let us all have our share of the conversation. I imagine there is nary a man at this table who has not an opinion or an interest at stake."

Thus adjured, Mr. Perrin spoke into the sudden silence. "I was saying to Mr. Stilwell, Your Grace, that although war is ever a great evil, when we are faced with an aggressor such as France—particularly under the direction of a brutal zealot such as First Consul Bonaparte—it cannot be evaded. When our nation is fighting for its very preservation, we must all be resolute."

"Pho pho, Mr. Perrin, these are high words," cried Mr. Bouverie, leaning across Mr. Fuller to enter the lists, "but are we indeed fighting for our preservation? There is no credible sign of invasion. And when the expense of prosecuting the war prevents relief from reaching the countryside after the distresses resulting from a failed harvest, how are we to measure victory or defeat? If we win never so many battles, on the waves or on our shores, while our people are starving, who can truly say we are the victors? A Pyrrhic victory, surely."

Mr. Perrin puffed out his cheeks. "And if we lose the seas to the French, they will succeed in blockading our trading ships; how then will Britain prosper?"

"It cannot be questioned that the war draws resources away from our domestic commerce," said Mr. Barclay. "The bread and timber and copper and wool required to supply the army and navy may cause scarcities in certain counties at certain times. And it must be admitted that the demand puts upward pressure on the price of such goods. But what are we to do? If we lose the revenue from our colonies, and lose the foreign markets for what Britain produces, the poor will be no better off than they are today. We cannot all simply retire to the countryside and grow enough corn to meet our wants. The world has changed, and we must defend our preeminent place in the new order."

"Besides," said Mr. Stilwell, "there is profit to be made from war. Perhaps it would be more accurate to say that war occasions a reallocation of prosperity. The distortions of economic activity may cause a degree of hardship for one man while another reaps benefits in equal degree, and the nation as a whole is no worse for it."

"Spoken like a true navy agent," said Mr. Barclay in a haughty undertone.

"*You* should understand that sort of speculation better than the rest of us," retorted Mr. Peters.

The duke smiled on the debate he had initiated but did not dignify the conversation with remark. Mr. Lock, noting that the expression on his face clearly implied a superior knowledge of the subjects under discussion, leaned over and asked, "From your position on the coast at Arundel, Your Grace, do you see any signs of the French bringing their aggression to our shores?"

"Not in the least. The spies bring tales of transports being built at all the northern French ports, ay, and ships of the line as well, but are they destined for England? I cannot foresee them rowing an army across the Channel even on the calmest day; the sailors in the coastal villages laugh at the idea. Such slow-moving vessels would be sent to the bottom, one and all, by our cannon. Even the smugglers know they must cross under sail."

"I should trust our free-traders to understand the risk better than any French sailor," said Mr. Barclay.

The duke paused to look down his nose at this interruption but went on, with apparent courtesy, "And how do *your* friends in that confraternity rate the likelihood of invasion, sir?"

Mr. Barclay flushed and protested. "I have no dealings with such men, Your Grace! I merely intended that, skilled sailors as they are and being in constant communication with the French ports, they ought to be an ideal source of intelligence on the subject. I should imagine a Sussex man such as yourself more likely to be privy to their thinking."

The duke gave no sign of offence. "And I should imagine them to be an excellent source of intelligence in your line of business as well. The smugglers provide so many benefits to our society, do they not?"

Mr. Barclay appeared enraged by the innuendo in His Grace's words but ultimately bit back the retort on the tip of his tongue; the duke observed his struggle for a moment and said merely, "Wise," before turning back to Mr. Lock to resume their conversation. "I should not be surprised if the First Consul's eyes were turned toward Russia, and if the buildup of troops along the northern shores were no more than a diversion, intended to keep us fearful of deploying our forces overseas to strike at him elsewhere."

Harry, sitting beside the sullen Mr. Barclay, had been intrigued by the mention of smuggling yet could make no sense of it. What had the duke intended by his remark about the "many benefits" of smuggling? The entire passage of arms between the two men was confusing. He longed to ask for enlightenment but was in no doubt it would be ill-advised to do so. He was certain that if he addressed Mr. Barclay directly, he would at the very least be thrown from the room.

Mr. Bouverie, on the other side of the table, was still

making the case that the war drained from Britain the resources and money that should be devoted to relieving the sufferings of the poor. Sir Nugent protested: "Nothing can be so mischievous as these exaggerated representations of scarcity, which have no other tendency than to create unfounded irritations in the public mind. If we encourage the poor to bemoan their lot instead of laboring to improve it, we shall soon find ourselves doing the work of the French for them! What is to keep the pitchforks from our doors, or the guillotine from our public squares, if the poor are encouraged to fancy themselves ill-used?"

Mr. Denison intervened. "I would not presume that acknowledging the sufferings of the poor must lead to an increase in hostilities between the orders of society. You cannot deny that the last two harvests were uncommonly bad, and that the necessity of feeding the army and navy has magnified the deprivations suffered by the least among us—even, I might add, by those of the middle orders. Surely it is denial of the problem that should incite anger, not efforts to alleviate it. The poor among us have a claim upon our purses, both on account of the material benefits they afford us and from considerations of simple Christian charity. Thank God the present harvest is promising a return to plenty; but until it is in the barns, laborers must have something to eat if they are to continue to work."

"Jacobinical claptrap!" uttered Sir Nugent and turned away to inquire of Sir Frederick how his horses had fared in the meetings at Epsom. This led the rest of the table to introduce less controversial subjects, and as soon as the cloth was removed and the decanters had appeared on the table, the duke was calling on Captain Morris for a song.

"Spare my modesty, Your Grace!" cried the captain, even as he rose unsteadily to oblige.

"You're no blushing Miss in her first season, you've no modesty to be spared," retorted the duke. "Come come, we've had enough of weighty subjects! I came for festivity and mirth, not for dreary debate and farmers' prattle."

"Ah, Your Grace," said the captain, in a mockery of woe, "I am so far removed from my first Season that even so slight a task as enlivening the table to mirth may lie beyond my powers. In fact, that is the very theme of the little ditty I have prepared for this occasion. I call it 'The Veteran Bacchanal.'" He removed a paper from his waistcoat and began to sing, in a loud but cracking voice,

I am an old Bacchanal, quite worn out,
Once leader of many a jolly bout;
But the game's all up, and the show's gone by,
And now an old bore and a twaddle am I.

Sad proof my body and mind could bring
That it's time to cut, and move out o' the ring:
The proofs are too many, alas! by far;
But a few are sufficient,—and here they are.

When I try to sing I but hawk and hem,
Through a choking struggle of husky phlegm;
Half-strangled, I hack it out, bit by bit,
And my chorus is always a coughing fit.

I daub my clothes when I feed my chops,
From my trembling fork my meat still drops;
Aside ten times in an hour I creep,
And when I'm not pissing, I'm fast asleep.

A warning shadow on Mirth I lie,
And when I am off it's a cloud gone by;
To all live spirits, that charm the room,
I'm a death's-head lesson of what's to come.

So I'll bid farewell to the jovial scene,
Where a fading figure should ne'er be seen;
I'll take a hint from my warning cough,
Quit my jade of a Muse, and—Morris off!

Harry thought all this very clever, though hardly as entertaining as the stories told by old Tom Weller at his father's haying dinners. To many of the gentlemen, however, it appeared inordinately amusing, though perhaps the free-flowing wines had as much to do with their laughter as the captain's wit. Sir Frederick had waylaid one of the serving-maids and was paying her extravagant compliments, punctuated by her screams of scandalized delight; Mr. Denison, suiting action to the song, had retreated to a corner to relieve himself in a pot; Sir Nugent was arguing with Mr. Smith-Budgen on a subject neither could clearly identify; and Mr. Barclay had disappeared altogether.

Mr. Steere, observing where the evening was tending, leaned over Mr. Barclay's empty chair to ask that Harry seek out the ostler and require the horses to be poled up. Harry, sleepy from a surfeit of food and punch, was nothing loth to comply and slipped from the room.

He made his way down the shadowy passage and opened the door to the stableyard behind the inn. He was about to step onto the wet cobbles when a furtive movement in a near corner gave him pause. He withdrew slightly into the corridor again and pulled the door almost shut, but some impulse of curiosity made him leave it open a crack and peek through the gap. He saw a swirl of skirt and thought it might be simply a housemaid bent on trysting with a stableboy. But something in the awkwardness of the movement sparked his memory, and in an instant he knew: it was Tomkins in his disguise! And he was not alone, for just then another voice spoke—an educated man, to judge by the cadence of his speech.

"It is arranged. The shipment is to move next week, on Saint Swithin's night."

"Very good, sir, I'll be ready. Where's the exchange to be?"

"You will wait on the near side of the Mole, under the Whites. The password is 'The King's shilling.' Ten good horses should suffice and Tilt has pledged them, along with four of his best batmen. Be there no later than midnight and move as quick as you can to Tilt's farmhouse at Harlands in Newdigate. There's a panel at the side of the hearth; open it and place the shipment in the space behind. Once the bags are stowed, kindle a fire on the hearth and remain there till the next night, when the Sussex men will come to take them on."

"I'll follow your orders to the letter, sir, never you fear!" said Tomkins in a guttural whisper.

"Mind you do, or we'll all hang," said the other man, in a tone of voice that made Harry shiver from his hidden place behind the door. "Now, in case there are watchers—" and he swept Tomkins into an embrace, reaching around to squeeze his backside till Tomkins squeaked a protest. The seeming couple separated, Tomkins to settle his disarranged bonnet and the other man, chuckling, to move rapidly toward the door where Harry lurked.

Concealment was impossible; there was no time for Harry to flee back up the passageway. So he threw open the door boldly in the man's face and gave him a wink, as he if had observed only the last moment of the encounter.

This was a mistake; Harry's leer changed ludicrously to a gasp of horror as he recognized Mr. Barclay. "I—I beg your pardon, sir," he stammered, as Mr. Barclay glowered. "I thought you to have been one of the stableboys."

"*You!*" cried Mr. Barclay. "What do you here?"

"My kinsman, Mr. Steere, sent me to order the carriage."

"Well, show me any more cheek and I'll draw your cork for you," said Mr. Barclay, and he pushed past Harry to stride away down the passage. Harry ran across the yard, noting that Tomkins had vanished, and found the ostler to give him Mr. Steere's message.

Upon returning to the dining room, he saw that a number of the bottles on the table were already empty. Several of the older men were preparing to depart, leaving behind a corps of more serious imbibers, the duke showing them the way. Mr. Steere, catching sight of him, rose with alacrity to make his farewells. Both Harry and his kinsman were all too ready to quit the scene before any fresh hazards befell them.

Harry saw no sign of Tomkins as he mounted into the carriage, so it was evident the highwayman was finding his own way home. But his physical absence did not make him loom any the less large in Harry's mind. Harry was so taken up with what he had overheard in the stableyard that he could give only mechanical answers to his kinsman's inquiries about how he had profited from the evening. Fortunately, Mr. Steere put his abstraction down to fatigue and forbore to press him. That was lucky, since Harry could no more have put aside the questions weighing on his mind than he could buy an abbey.

Tomkins, engaged in an illicit trade of some kind with

Mr. Barclay, who appeared to be in league with Milord and the smugglers! What could it all mean? He knew many of the common laborers and farmers in the neighborhood were involved, but that one of the gentry should do more than look the other way when a cask appeared on his back doorstep, or a horse disappeared for a night, was scarcely to be credited. Yet his own ears had told him it was so.

The chief oddity to occur to Harry was that Mr. Barclay's goods, whatever they might be, were moving *southward* instead of north toward London. This defied all his understanding of the free-trade. What could possibly be of sufficient value to smuggle *out* of England? And in small quantity, for only ten packhorses were required. It must be something priceless for Milord and the captain to give up four of their batmen to the undertaking. He wished he could find Tomkins and interrogate him on the subject, but Tomkins seemed better able to find him than the reverse. Harry's father would never suffer him to go on his own to the Nag's Head in search of the highwayman. But perhaps he could discover something about the matter when the smuggling resumed—which must happen soon, for the moon was on the wane.

Their journey was undisturbed by any of the desperate men haunting the Holmwood, and soon they came to the parting of their ways. Harry, well schooled by his parents, was able to drag his mind back sufficiently from fruitless speculation to thank his cousin prettily for the outing. But the same questions revolved in his mind for hours.

<h2 style="text-align:center">CHAPTER THE FOURTEENTH</h2>

"How did you find the duke, really? Was he as fine as fivepence?" Over the breakfast table, Isabella opened her assault on her brother before he had been able to enjoy more than a bite of bread and butter. Evidently she had not entirely abandoned her matrimonial aspirations.

"He was not fine at all, Bella! He wore a dirty old coat and there was food on his neckcloth, and he smelled strongly enough to put you off your dinner."

"I don't believe you!" cried Isabella, and "For shame, Harry!" cried his mother, in unison.

"It's true, though. There were several men present much finer than he."

Isabella brightened. "Tell me about them!"

"Well, the one with the most impressive clothes was Sir Nugent—Dacre—Lumley—no, Lumley-Dacre-Prudhoe," said Harry, recovering the gentleman's multifarious patronymics after considerable effort of thought. "He was all in brightly colored silks and lace; you might have taken his clothes and made a ball gown from them. But don't imagine you have a hope of marrying him: my cousin says he has fourteen children."

"And his wife yet lives?" inquired Mrs. Steer, appalled.

"Mr. Perrin was grandly attired as well, but so fat he would crush you if he rolled over in bed." Mr. Steer said "Ha!" but then clouted Harry on the side of the head after encountering a glance from his wife.

Mrs. Steer thought it time to redirect the inquiries. "What was served at table?"

"We began with Captain Morris's punch; my cousin told me it was famous in London. I liked the taste of the spices, but it made me cough. Then there was the fish souchy, which was no more than a stew." Harry thought of referring to the unfortunate concatenation of odors produced by the fish souchy and the duke occupying the same space, but decided enough had been said on the subject already. "And then there was beefsteaks, and some dish with potatoes, and wine, and sweetmeats. The beefsteaks were very good."

Mr. Steer wanted to know who was in attendance. Harry did his best but bogged down somewhere around Messrs. Stilwell and Fuller. "Mr. Smith-Budgen was interested only in seashells, but Mr. Peters was very affable to me."

"And so he should be," retorted Mr. Steer. "Who is he to be looking down on the likes of a Steer? For all his acres, his father was no more than a merchant. There are so many mushroom families in the country nowadays, who can keep track of them all? There are few enough Sir Fredericks hereabouts anymore; he's a rare one for the soil, not like so many of these April-squires."

"And I was made to sit next to Mr. Barclay, but he simply pretended I wasn't there."

"Probably for the best. And what of the conversation?"

"A great deal of it was politics, sir. They spoke of the famine and the war, and after Sir Lucas Pepys arrived, the health of the King, and much more besides. I understood them better when they spoke of local concerns: everyone is very hopeful for the harvest, and someone said Lord Verulam is proposing to cut a goodly quantity of his timber around Anstiebury, and . . . Captain Morris sang a ballad." Harry decided upon consideration to omit any mention of the free-trade; his father's views on the subject were all too well known to him.

"A ballad!" cried Mrs. Steer; "I had not understood it to be a musical evening."

Harry considered his reply. "It wasn't that kind of ballad," he achieved at last. Mr. Steer said "Ha!" again, but forbore to clout Harry this time.

Unfortunately, Mr. Marshall, oblivious to undertones, took up the matter of the song with eagerness. "Was it on a classical subject?" he asked. "Was it in pentameter or dactyls?"

"I should say it more closely resembled dactyls," replied Harry cautiously. "It was like a lyric. And the subject was . . . old age."

"Not a very festive gathering, then," ventured Mrs. Steer.

"There appeared to be high spirits enough," said Harry. And with that his family had to be content.

From this time forward, Harry could not resist examining the rock on the wall every time he was out in the stableyard. It was perhaps a considerable risk to show so much interest in it, for one never knew when Nat or Janey might happen upon him and discover his secret. But he was certain the smuggling would resume at any moment and was determined not to miss any message that might be left by Cursemother Jack.

As days passed without a word, he revolved over and over in his mind his conversation with Milord, wondering whether he had said or done anything to make the master smuggler turn against him. He believed they had parted on terms of amity, but there was no denying that Milord had been at times suspicious and even threatening. Was this a fresh test of his loyalty? Lacking answers, he whiled away his idle hours (and indeed some of the hours devoted to his studies) with weaving scenes in his mind in which the Tilts, father and son, faced perils and Harry came to their rescue; but as each day passed, these tales of derring-do became less and less convincing even to him.

He had been certain that Saint Swithin's Day would see the end to his suspense: that was the night Tomkins was going to carry Mr. Barclay's shipment to the farm near Newdigate. But Saint Swithin's Day came and went, bringing with it only the showers threatened in the saint's curse, and Harry's spirits sank. So he was with astonished on Thursday afternoon when his hand, feeling about the rock atop the stableyard wall, met paper.

As before, he bore it off posthaste to the necessary for reading. Written in charcoal as before, it read simply, "5 Bels. 11."

Harry's escape from the house was conducted without incident; he was becoming an adept in clandestine activity. From there it was only steps to Brimstone Lane and the turn southward to Newdigate. There he found the captain—Mr. James Tilt, as he now knew him to be—again standing boldly in the street opposite the church, directing men and horses. The loading was already well along—it seemed the cellars of the Five Bells had been used this time for storing the casks instead of the church tower—and Harry joined in with a will, carrying some of the smaller burdens and keeping the horses in line.

Catching sight of him, the captain called him over and handed him six guineas—more money than Harry had ever seen in his life. As he gaped at the coins, the captain told him, "Take that over the way and drop it in the poor box."

Proud of being entrusted with such a sum, Harry did as he was asked. Upon his return, he could not resist venturing on a question. "Sir," he began—he was fairly certain that it would be a solecism to reveal the knowledge of his leader's true name—"I'm acquainted with a man named Tomkins—"

The captain suddenly went still, peering closely at Harry's blackened face. "Well well, Monkey," said he at last; "you're menjous high spirity when it comes to poking your nose in everywhere, ain't you? And what about Tomkins?"

"It's just that—I overheard him speaking with a gentleman in Darking last week—"

In a flash, the captain's fist had closed on Harry's arm and was squeezing it in a painful manner. "Sneck up, fool!" he muttered in an undertone, dragging Harry farther away from the working men. Planting Harry firmly in the shadow of a tree, he continued, "Ain't I given you warning afore about your questions? Add eavesdropping to that. I'll wager your parents didn't raise you to go loitering 'round listening in on other people's talk. I don't want to hear another word on *that* subject. If you value your skin, you'll put it out of your mind. Now, get to work!"

Harry scuttled back to the horses and calmed his shaken nerves by stroking their necks; they stared back at him with their patient eyes, and slowly he overcame the urge to cry. But the violence of the captain's reaction had only piqued his curiosity, and he wondered if he might slip away and try to find the house where Tomkins was supposed to lie in wait with his mysterious cargo. He soon realized, however, that since a shipment had come up from the south the day before, it was most likely that Tomkins had already been relieved of his burden and the house would be empty.

And soon enough the pack train was ready to move. The captain gathered the smugglers close around him to give his orders.

"Darking is too hot for us at this present," said he. "As from yesterday, a troop of the Surrey Yeoman Cavalry from Guildford is billeted at the Wheatsheaf Inn and placed at the orders of the Board of Customs. This night we go to Coldharbour, and on across Leith Hill afore turning north. Make for that barn you knows of near Deer Leap Wood. I've made contact with the Leatherhead men, and they'll take the goods on from there. It'll be a long night, and those among you who live 'round here to the south may fall back after Coldharbour. There's men enough in the village ready to take us on through Friday Street and the Tillingbourne Valley. Now, step lively!"

They made their way out of Newdigate, passing south of Harry's home through Beare Green and up by Anstie Farm (another of Milord's properties, he heard one of the men say). Their route took them along well-worn paths, so although there were mud and ruts to be navigated and the clouded night was dark, they made rapid progress, each following the next and the leader marking the way with a narrow beam from a spout lantern.

Despite his rebuff at the hands of the captain, Harry was recovering his spirits. As he swung along at the men's pace, he listened to the now-familiar creak of harness, the men telling their tall tales to one another, and it warmed his heart. He heard the rattle of the nightjar and the cough of a dog fox—the night creatures but little disturbed by the passing men and horses—and thought of his family asleep in their beds, and all the wives and children of these men hoping for an uneventful journey and a safe homecoming.

Soon they were slowed by the steepening way as they climbed the face of Leith Hill. The captain hushed them to silence as they passed Kitlands Farm: the Bax family were Quakers, and no friends to the free-trade. On the higher slopes, glowworms appeared and danced around them by the scores; when Harry looked skyward, the horses' heads appeared to be up in the heavens surrounded by stars. Soon they were skirting the base of the ancient fort at Anstiebury, now planted over with timber by its landlord. Harry had always hoped for an opportunity to explore the fort, but the pack train was maintaining a brisk pace and he could only peer off into the darkness in that direction as they passed by, imagining he could make out the fortifications in the gloom. Horses and men alike blew and strained and slipped on the muddy way, but at last they emerged from the wooded hillside into the village of Coldharbour, tucked into a fold of the hill like a key in a farmwife's capacious pocket.

There the pack train stopped to rest and to water and bait the horses. The old cold harbor for which the village was named still stood on the outskirts, in a small field backed by larch and fir; it was a crumbling, barnlike structure with open walls, promising but a hard bed for travelers, few of whom came this way anymore since the construction of the turnpike. Because the night appeared to be coming on to rain, they brought the horses in under its shelter for a rest after they had drunk from a trough out front.

Coldharbour was a modest settlement, but a line of recently constructed cottages signaled an ambition for growth. There was no church and the only sign of commercial activity was a forge; the settlement bore every sign of being the sort of place, indeed, that no visitor in his right mind ever sought out. What provided employment for the inhabitants, Harry could not begin to guess; but his earlier experience had made him wary of asking questions. He squatted down and watched as a number of men and boys slipped out of the darkness to take the place of those who were turning back.

His cousin Dick found him there and appeared disposed to chat. "You see all those cottages over t'other side the way? All built by Milord, they was, and they're home to his most trusted employees. Just about every man in this village is in his hire. Coldharbour was scarcely a hamlet before he took an interest in it. When my brother inherits the copyhold, I'm minded to move up here; I could build a stable and house a second string of ponies for Milord, suited to scrambling over Leith Hill and the downs. When Milord retires, I aim to become first lieutenant to the captain."

"But who is lord of the manor here?" Harry asked.

"That's the beauty of it," said Dick with enthusiasm. "Some parts are in the demesne of Lord Verulam, and he doesn't even live in the country; some are owned by Mr. Perrin, but he doesn't take an interest in it. The land yields only thinly and when Milord discovered Coldharbour, none of the great men's bailiffs had even troubled themselves to collect rent here for several years. The land hereabouts serves them little purpose, so they have small enough cause to come this way. The village would've gone derelict without Milord; and now its inhabitants live like gentlemen, freemen in all but name. Their wealth is in coin—easy to hide from the tax collector, unlike crops or cattle. Even the vicar of the parish is a permanent absentee. Who's to say what the law be but Milord?"

This intelligence gave Harry much to ponder on. He had never imagined the existence of places that belonged to nobody, where ordinary people could live free of obligation to any overlord, worldly or clerical. And he was astonished anew at the scope of the Tilts' enterprise. Fancy creating an entire community for the convenience of those in their employ! That John Tilt, an illiterate yeoman, should be the promise of home and plenty for dozens, perhaps hundreds of people was an alien and exciting idea.

Suddenly a small boy, his dirty nightshirt flapping about him, came running out of the darkness and made for the captain. "There be an exciseman a-sleeping at the forge, and he's astir!" he cried in a piping voice. "Mum says you mustn't bide!"

CHAPTER THE FIFTEENTH

Everyone was instantly on the alert. The men tightened the horses' girths and lined them up to make their way into the woods behind the village. The captain looked sharply about him and his eyes alit on Dick and Harry, sitting together. "You two!" he hissed. "Get you into the square and make some noise. You're the reason he awakened. If he comes out, fob him off with a tale while we slip away. Monkey, follow your cousin's lead." And in less time than Harry imagined possible, the pack train had vanished into the darkness up Leith Hill to join the track that led north toward the village of Friday Street.

"Do as I bid, mind you," Dick whispered. He sauntered into the center of the village street, hallooing over his shoulder, "Keep up now, Neddy, you gormless clod! If'n you don't mend your pace, we won't be home till sunup." He washed his face at the village pump, then pulled a crudely carved flute out of his pocket and began to tootle a melody.

Harry shambled behind him, doing his best impression of a gormless clod and taking a few awkward dancing steps out of tempo. The door of the cottage next to the forge opened with a bang and a man emerged, pushing his shirt into his breeches. "Oy, there, 'alt!" he cried. Dick stopped walking but continued playing the flute; Harry wandered up and peered vacantly at the man.

"Wotcher business 'ere?" demanded the man, in accents that revealed him to be a denizen of the metropolis, not Surrey-born. "Where's your confederates?"

Harry giggled and said slowly, "Con—fer—e—dats."

Dick gave him a disgusted look before answering the question. "Not certain what it is you mean by 'confederates.' Unless you're meaning my aunt and her family? They live just down over there—third house from the end of the row." He pointed off into the darkness.

"Don't play the innocent with me, cully!" said the man. "I got a tip, see? I knows them smugglers is comin' this way tonight. You the scouts?"

"Smugglers!" cried Dick. "You mean t'say one of *them*'s the dad?"

The man looked at him blankly. "Wotcher mean, the dad?"

"The dad of my aunt's new baby," said Dick. "Mum sent us up for to help when we heard 'twas her time. No girls in our family, so we has to play the girl!" Harry sketched a curtsey and giggled again. "The baby's out now and all's well, so we been having jest a drop or two by way of celebration. You say you knows the dad?"

"No, I know naught of your aunt an' her babe!" cried the exciseman, stamping his foot. "I'm 'ere to happrehend a band of criminals, bringing a load of contraband up from the coast."

"All by your lonesome?" asked Dick. "You ain't afeard?"

"The militiamen wouldna come up 'ere, no matter what I says to 'em!" The man's tone was aggrieved. "They said the odds were the ponies'd come through Darking, and they'd bide in the taproom and wait for 'em. Wot they meant was, they wanted to stay back at the inn acos of the cockfights 'appening in the cellar tonight."

"I'm thinking they had the right of it," said Dick indifferently and turned to go, tugging Harry with him.

"Not so fast, matey!" cried the exciseman. "If you boys ain't in league with th'free-traders, how comes it as this one 'as his face all blackened?" He pointed accusingly at Harry.

"Jest you try and make him wash," Dick warned, eyeing Harry meaningly, "and see what you get! The way he do carry on, it's more than any of us can bear."

The man seized Harry by the arm. Harry immediately went limp in his arms and began to scream in a high, piercing wail, drawing it out till he had to gulp a quick breath before resuming. The man dropped his arm and the sound ceased abruptly.

"We're going home now," said Dick; "our mum'll be eager for tidings. Come on, stop your gooming!" he said to Harry, and they started to walk down the street toward the road.

Not quite prepared to admit defeat, the exciseman called after them, "Where d'you boys live?"

"Ockley," said Dick, and off they went.

Harry could scarcely contain his laughter till they were well out of the town. "How'd you come up with that story?" he demanded.

Dick was not a little pleased with himself. "A few things to remember when you meet up with the Law, Harry. First, they all believe the local folk are stupid, and it does no harm to play up to 'em. I've seen men jump into the village pond and claim they're trying to catch the moon in the water—and those lackwit excisemen believe they're serious! The Excise don't draw the cream of the crop into its ranks, nohow. Second, anything having to do with womenfolk makes 'em nervous, so if you tell 'em you're on business having to do with womenfolk, likely they won't ask too many questions. You did well for your first go."

This encomium filled Harry with a glow that sustained him all the way down into the lowlands, though the rain soon began to fall and he was soaked to the skin before reaching home. The rain troubled Harry not in the least; the only cloud on his horizon was one thing the exciseman had let fall, and which he could not forget—that the officer had received advance word of the smugglers' plans.

The cost of the night's doings was a head cold that had established dominion over Harry by midmorning. He snuffled his way through Virgil, even that worthy's prescriptions for the care of bees proving insufficient to hold his attention. Mr. Marshall was at his wits' end, casting about for a classical subject that could engage Harry's fancy.

During the day no message appeared under the stone on the wall, and Harry's concern grew that the captain had decided to trust him no longer. He was eager to prove his fealty by warning the Tilts about the exciseman's words, but he knew not how to convey a message to them.

He was not the only member of the household to be anxious; it seemed tension pervaded all of Henfold that day. His father was concerned that the rain—which continued and even intensified—would do harm to the corn, coming so close to the harvest as it did. Memories of last year's disaster could not be avoided; and now, when a successful harvest was in view, to see all his labors threatened was dreadful to him. His imprecations against the weather had made the breakfast table so unpleasant that Harry's mother took refuge in the brewhouse and the dairy, preferring the scrubbing of cider tubs and the turning of cheeses to any domestic occupation indoors. And Isabella withdrew to her own chamber to play listlessly with her doll.

By dinnertime the skies were clearing, however, and as Mr. Steer stumped out to see whether the wheat was laid down, Mrs. Steer emerged from her self-imposed exile. She could be heard scolding Isabella for neglecting her sewing basket and Janey for burning the bread. Observing Harry's mind to be everywhere but on the page, Mr. Marshall at last gave over the lesson and released him.

The kitchen, when Harry entered it, proved to be a scene of female distress that nearly drove him out again; but he was hungry enough to brave a situation that would have sent most men into hiding. Janey was tearfully justifying the state of the bread, which upon examination Harry considered not so bad as to prevent his cutting off a sizable portion (but probably too bad to be presented at table under his father's critical eye). Isabella, complaining that nobody ever showed the slightest concern for her pleasure, was whining for a treat. His mother was looking unusually disheveled and harassed, and she found relief for her feelings in whacking Harry lightly on the back of his head with a spoon as he filched a bit of bacon from the hook.

It was as well that he had sought sustenance when he did, however, for his father stayed out surveying the fields until well beyond the customary dinner hour. In the end Mrs. Steer had to send Harry out to find him.

He proved to be far off in the lower fields to the west, which were partly under water; but the wheat and oats appeared to have sustained no lasting harm. The gray pease was flattened, but a few dry days should set the crop to rights. Whether the turnips would sustain damage was a question that depended on the weather going forward. All told, Mr. Steer's spirits were lightened by what he had seen, and he was happy enough to be called in to his dinner. Harry ventured to give him a hint about the conditions prevailing among the womenfolk, which was gratefully received, and they proceeded to the house in amity.

At table, however, Mrs. Steer discovered a new cause for dismay when Harry was unable to conceal the state of his head. "Have you caught cold?" she demanded. "You have been naught but ill all summer!" She placed a hand on his forehead. "You're a trifle fevered, but not greatly so."

"It's nothing," agreed Harry, but promptly undermined his claim with a sneeze.

"Well, it's to bed with you as soon as ever you've eaten."

This injunction suited Harry well enough, since he could watch for a message more easily from his bedchamber. Still nothing had appeared there, and after a few minutes he tired of sitting by the window staring at the stone on the wall. He lay down to rest for a bit and was soon asleep.

He awoke in darkness. Silence reigned in the house, so the remainder of its inhabitants must be abed. He could not say what hour it was, but his instinct claimed it to be still early. There was yet time to warn the Tilts! If only he knew where they were meeting tonight, or whether there was to be a run at all.

He arose and dressed in the dark. Tiptoeing out into the hall, he carefully avoided the boards that creaked the loudest and was several steps down the stairs before he felt a sneeze coming on. In vain did he struggle to suppress it;

no matter how firmly he gripped his nose, it pressed upon him, coming out at last as a strangled bray.

He froze in place on the stairs, listening. He thought he heard a muffled thump from one of the other rooms, he knew not which; but at length when no door opened he felt safe to proceed downstairs. He went into the kitchen and found a cooled corner of the banked fire. Taking up a handful of ash, he smeared his face and the backs of his hands with it.

Once out of doors he discovered the night to be balmy and close, promising more rain in the hours to come; in spite of the heat he shivered and his bones felt heavy, and once he had ascertained that there was still no message for him, he was sorely tempted to return to the embrace of his bed. But concern for the safety of the Tilts and their men, coupled with the desire to redeem his honor in the captain's eyes, drove him onward.

He decided that Newdigate must be his destination. It seemed a safe haven for the free-traders, and in all his limited experience of smuggling runs, it had always been the starting point for goods coming up from the coast. Besides, he was not convinced that he would be able to find the Tilts' farm again in the dark, and it was in any case much farther away. So he took his accustomed course to Brimstone Lane and thence southward.

As he reached the outskirts of the village, intimations of activity told him he had not been mistaken. There was a stir in the town—faint sounds of hoofbeats, a shadow slipping through the darkness of a side alley, a dog that barked inside a house and was quickly hushed. So Harry proceeded boldly to the Five Bells as if invited.

There a familiar scene met his eyes, men scurrying to and fro removing bundles from the church and the inn and packing them onto the backs of the horses. He could see no kegs, however, nor catch a glimpse of the captain. None of the men was recognizable through their blackened faces and disguises, so he hung back against a wall and considered.

At length he began to observe that one or two of the men would from time to time enter and leave the inn empty-handed, so he guessed their leader might be within. He crept around behind to the stableyard and entered by a back door.

The captain was not in the taproom, but Harry located him alone in the front parlor, resting one booted foot on a low windowsill as he watched the activity in the street. "Sir?" said Harry in a tentative voice.

The captain whirled around, and his evident nervousness did nothing to allay Harry's.

"Monkey! What brings you here? You weren't called. After the setter saw your faces yesterday I thought it not safe enough for you."

"No, sir. But last night I heard something—and I thought you should know of it."

"What, then?"

"When Dick and I spoke to the exciseman, he said he had received intelligence that you were going to run the goods through Coldharbour that night. He said the dragoons did not believe him and stayed behind in Darking. But he must have felt his source to be credible—enough that he went up to Coldharbour on his own, to see."

The captain studied him for a moment. "This I knew already, Monkey: your cousin got word to my father afore even I returned home this morning. I thank'ee for wishing to tell it me, though."

Harry hesitated, feeling himself dismissed but yet not

ready to go. Suddenly the captain turned back toward him and bent down to whisper in his ear. "Monkey, there be them as believe *you* are the traitor, and I don't deny we've seen more of the Law than ever we did afore you joined our ranks. It's the real reason you weren't called tonight."

Harry's mind swirled with fear and hurt, but he strove to collect his thoughts. "Sir, how could I betray your intentions to the Excise when I knew nothing of them beforehand? I'd no notion of your father's interest in Coldharbour till we arrived there, and the exciseman was already on the scene. And like the others, I knew naught of your destination till you told us of it, here in Newdigate, after the horses were loaded."

The captain relaxed and almost smiled. "That's how I see it as well, Monkey. So if I do not call upon you to serve for a bit, it's to prove as much to the doubters. If we see trouble and you're not involved, suspicion cannot fall on you. See?"

Harry felt tears of gratitude well up in his eyes, and he covered them with a sneeze.

"You've a sharp eye, Monkey: so what else be in your mind about this problem of a spy?"

Harry bent his thoughts to the problem. "The men in Coldharbour: they had to know in advance to expect us, because they were ready to take over the pack train as soon as we arrived. How early did they get word of the plan? Was there enough time for them to send a note to Darking, and for the exciseman to journey there?"

"There might have been, had the blackguard moved quickly enough. But they all owe the roof over their heads to my father's pleasure; it'ud be against their interest to betray us."

The door of the inn was heard to open and close.

"Quick! Monkey," whispered the captain, "clean this up!" He swept a tankard off the nearest table. Harry dived down and began to scrub at the spill under the chairs.

The man Harry knew as Nasty Face entered the room. "Cap'n, was you wishful that the silks and tea for the Darking shops be kept apart from the rest?" he asked.

"Don't trouble about it now," said the captain, "there'll be time enough for a sorting once we reach the barn."

Nasty Face departed and Harry got to his feet, wiping the ale off his hands onto his breeches. "Not the usual shipment, then?" he asked.

"No, the Sussex boys fell in with an Indiaman hard by Beachy Head and they convinced the crew to give up some of the cargo," said the captain with an arched eyebrow. "There be a barn with a false floor just above Darking, in the Glory Wood, and it's our goal this night; the Darking shopkeepers will find much to their liking in this load! But what of my question, Monkey: why should any of the Coldharbour men give up him who feeds and shelters them?"

"What is the reward for laying information against a smuggler?"

"Forty pound."

"'Tis a large sum but hardly seems enough to tempt a man to take the risk, unless he is prepared to leave the country and start a new life."

"And none of the Coldharbour men has done so," said the captain. "What then?"

Harry thought. "The ones carrying the messages—to Coldharbour, to those who take the goods on to London. A member of your own household."

The captain sighed. "Yes, that's my thought as well. You've a quick mind, Monkey, and I'll miss you for the nonce. Watch for another message: when things are clearer, I'll send for you. Now, get along home."

Harry slipped out the back of the inn and made his way through muddy alleys to the road north. Hearing the sounds of the pack train on the move behind him, he ran a good bit of the way to stay ahead, arriving at Henfold's gate sweating and shivering but with peace in his heart at the confidence the captain had shown in him. He hid in the brake hard by the road, catching his breath, while the horses filed by, and then made for home.

He remembered to wash his face at the pump and scrape his shoes before slipping in through the side door that he had left unlocked. Feeling his way, he grasped the stair rail and lifted a foot—only to trip over something soft in the dark.

CHAPTER THE SIXTEENTH

There was a gasp and a hand gripped Harry's leg. Harry yelped and then sneezed.

"Hush! You don't have to wake the whole house!" his sister whispered, scrambling to her feet.

"What are you doing here?" Harry hissed back, pulling his leg away from her grip.

"Waiting for you to return, of course," she replied. "Come into the kitchen where we won't be overheard."

This was so unexpected that Harry followed tamely after her. Isabella kindled a rush light at the embers of the banked kitchen fire and set it on the shelf in the inglenook before perching on the settle. She was clad only in her nightclothes, and drew her feet up under her gown to keep them warm. Harry watched her warily.

"So—where were you?"

"Taking the air."

Isabella sniffed. "Taking the air in a tavern, it would seem. You reek of ale. Why don't you tell me the truth? Do you *want* me to report you to Papa?"

"I wasn't doing you any harm—why is it any of your affair where I was?"

"Because I know you went out when everyone sup-

182

posed you abed and ailing. You left the door unfastened and we could all have been murdered in our beds! You know what Papa would do to you if he found out. And Mama would be very disappointed in you."

Harry cast about in his mind but was unable to imagine a situation in which he was not in his sister's power and she did not know all his vulnerabilities. Nonetheless, the truth could not be told. "I heard a strange sound and went to see what it was."

"And were gone for hours? Were you being led astray by the fairies?"

Harry had to try to regain the upper hand. "Your tone is unbecoming to a lady," said he loftily. "You have yet to tell me how it's any business of yours where I go and what I do."

"Very well," said Isabella, "if that's your last word, I'll inform our parents in the morning and leave you to take the consequences." She stood and blew out the light.

Harry seized her arm. "Wait!" She remained motionless, and he could feel her smug confidence in the dark. "Isabella, what is it you want?"

She paused, and he realized she really did not know what she wanted; she was simply reveling in holding unaccustomed power over her elder brother. "We shall have to see that, won't we?" she replied at last. "For now, I will require only that you play with me—a game of my choosing—every day after dinner." Harry grimaced but did not dispute this.

"And of course, that won't be all," added Isabella. "Other demands will be made, at a time I alone shall determine."

And so began a period of dual captivity for Harry. His mornings were passed under the eye of Mr. Marshall, whose devotion to his calling only gained urgency as the days before Harry's departure for Winchester grew short. And from dinnertime until nightfall he was Isabella's slave, condemned to spillikins and graces and, worst of all, obedience to her every stated whim and desire.

Mrs. Steer viewed this evidence of seeming comity between her offspring with a skeptical eye, but she could discover no basis for suspecting its cause. The following Tuesday evening, she was observing them as Harry wove a story around Isabella's doll and an old carved soldier from his childhood—a tale that Isabella ruthlessly called to order every time it began to stray away from romance and into the realm of adventure—when a knock fell on the door and a farmwife, Rebecca Grout from Stockriden Farm, northward of them up Brimstone Lane, was admitted to the sitting room.

This was unusual enough: the farms in the neighborhood were widely scattered and their inhabitants generally too hardworking to indulge in idle visits. Mr. Steer was known to be of an unsociable turn, a man who did not encourage his wife to pay or receive calls. But Mrs. Steer rose to the occasion with alacrity, welcoming Mrs. Grout and sending Janey off to hurry the tea.

She inquired after Mr. Grout and the children, but Mrs. Grout could scarce abide the exchange of niceties, so impatient was she to relieve herself of the news she carried. "Oh! Mr. Steer, Mrs. Steer, I suspicioned you might not know what befell last night on the common, being as you are some distance off."

Mrs. Steer confessed their ignorance of any doings on the common. "Was there a disturbance over by the Nag's Head?" she hazarded.

"So ye might imagine, with that Mrs. Wood no better

than she should be and all them rogues what haunt the place," said Mrs. Grout. "I wouldna want to be one of *that* lot when the time come to meet my Maker. But it were closer to the Bottle and Glass, over to the east side."

This drew Harry's notice: the Bottle and Glass was a mean hostelry, catering to a clientele of laborers, which lay very close to Heathfields Farm where the Tilts kept their horses.

"A troop of the Yeoman Cavalry had been riding over the common all the evening and into the night, though the moon were dark. They went up to Swan's Mill nigh on ten o'clock and searched every inch of it, though naught amiss did they find. But later they came slap up against a whole line of ponies, loaded to the ears with cargo what never saw duty paid on't.—Well may you gasp, Harry, for it were a band of smugglers, right here on our own roads!"

"No!" cried Mrs. Steer, but Harry could not speak a word.

"As large as life!" said Mrs. Grout with satisfaction. "And there was a battle like you could hardly credit. The militiamen had their muskets and swords, to be sure, and the smugglers only staves and rakes and a few pistols, but they outnumbered the militia by four to one. They went at it for a good half-hour, and we could hear the shouts and screams something awful, all the way at our house. Like the End of Days, it was. My Jacob went out to see. It were mostly over by the time he came up to 'em; the yeomen was fleeing back to Darking."

"So the smugglers won the day?" said Mr. Steer with disgust. "Sounds like what you might expect from the militia—they're no more than a pack of shopkeepers playing soldier."

"After a manner of speaking, you're in the right of it.

No smuggler was apprehended and their loaded horses was still in the lane when Jacob came upon them. But there was some of 'em wounded, and a man lying lifeless in the road—may his soul be acceptable in the sight of God! Jacob turned right 'round and came home, as you might imagine, and thank the good Lord he did."

Harry at last had to put himself forward, though his voice was hoarse from more than his cold. "Do you know who it was that was killed?"

"They say it were one of the Finch boys—son of the cordwainer, over toward Parkgate. The parents was summoned to Pippbrook House to appear before Sir Nugent today for questioning, and their son not yet in the earth! It would've been kinder had it been Mr. Peters up at Betchworth Castle; he's a rare man for the people, for all he's so new to the country. But Sir Nugent has his face set against all free-trading, and scant mercy could be expected from that quarter."

Harry's mother exclaimed against the cruelty of this, but his father was inclined to believe that the community's interest in stamping out the blight of the free-trade superseded the personal claims of the young man's family. "You say there were four times as many smugglers as militiamen?" he asked. "This is smuggling on a scale I had not imagined! Such activities must be suppressed if we are not to find ourselves at the mercy of gangs like those in Sussex."

"You're farther from the road than us," said Mrs. Grout, "so it may be as how you don't hear 'em so much. Night after night there's the sound of horses in the lane, and the men talking among theyselves; but we keep close and they pass us by. They minds their own business and we minds ours. It's bin oftener since last year, now that folk have no work anywheres and not even a penny to buy a crust of bread. We had good stores and the duke reduced the rent, or Jacob mighta gone with 'em too, though he knows he didn't ought to do it, if only to put food on the table—irregardless of the wickedness of it."

Mrs. Steer agreed diplomatically that last year had been a dreadful year for everyone, and small wonder the laborers were desperate. "We are in a very quiet situation here and are grateful to you for bringing us word. Perhaps we should put a lock on the gate so they can't use our barn to store their tubs."

Harry could have told her of the many alternatives the smugglers had for concealing their goods and how unlikely it was that they would select a hiding place on his father's property; but he was chiefly concerned about the battle outside the Bottle and Glass. He wanted to ask about the number and identities of the wounded but feared arousing suspicion by displaying too much curiosity on the subject. And as Mrs. Grout soon departed to spread the word elsewhere, he was compelled to stifle his remaining questions. He had entirely lost the thread of the story he had been telling to Isabella, who complained loudly about his inattention until recalled to decorum by her mother.

This state of suspense had to be endured, but the promise of relief arrived the very next day in the form of a note from his cousin Dick's mother. It seemed she was behindhand with her jellies and, with Dick laid up by a fall from a ladder, she wished to borrow Harry for a few days to comb the hedgerows and the water meadows for whorts and currants. With the crops so beforehand, the harvest was soon to be upon them, and she had to finish her preserves now or go without. She hoped Mrs. Steer might bring Harry in to Darking on Thursday for the market day and allow him to stay with them till Saturday, when he would be returned home.

This proposal of course provoked argument, with Mr. Steer objecting to the time taken away from Harry's studies and Mrs. Steer supporting the claims of kin to assistance when required. Harry listened to little of it, for the intelligence that Dick was ailing superseded all other concerns. Not for a moment did he believe the story of falling from a ladder. Was he one of the wounded from the battle? He must have suffered more than a few bruises if he was unable to pick berries! Harry knew better than to express a wish in opposition to his father's, but he prayed with all his heart that his mother might prevail. She was dwelling with energy on the many kindnesses extended by Dick's family—the cherries, most recently—and the necessity she would be under to supply the deficiency should their kinswoman be unable to put up her preserves for the winter. Mr. Steer did not think it so very bad for his cousins to do without, and if Harry were to leave off his books, why should it not be to help his father in the harvest, now hard upon them? How were the claims of mere cousins more pressing than his own domestic concerns? Appearances were not in Harry's favor until Mr. Marshall ventured timidly to enter the affray.

"Sir, I received a letter yesterday from my sister informing me that my mother is ill, and the entire household is alarmed for her. If I might beg leave to go home for a day or two, I am certain it will bring them comfort. I should not have ventured to ask permission before, but now that there is some question about whether Master Harry will even be home, perhaps it might be a convenient time?"

Mrs. Steer was quick with her exclamations of dismay

and sympathy, and Mr. Steer was fairly cornered, though loth to admit as much. "And what is your view of the state of Harry's preparation?" he asked.

Mr. Marshall struggled with his conscience, but his familial ties triumphed. "I would say, sir, that Master Harry is almost as well prepared for Winchester as most students who have been schooled at home," he said with a blush.

With the household thus united against him, Mr. Steer retired from the field of battle, granting his permission with only a parting shot that "there are to be no further holidays in August!"

Harry endured yet another sleepless night, his fears for Dick pressing hard upon his thoughts, and the morning could not come too soon. His mother, tiptoeing into the room to awaken him before first light, discovered him already dressed. They ate quickly before the remainder of the household was awake while Nat grumbled as he moved about the farmyard, poling up Parsifal and loading onto the cart the crates of chickens and damp baskets of cheese.

They departed in the freshness of the day, directing their way toward the turnpike. Harry asked if they might take the road that ran along the eastern side of the common, hoping to catch a glimpse of the scene of the battle; but his mother, knowing the recent rain would have flooded the lanes in that direction, preferred the safer route. As they set out, the dawn chorus was already begun in anticipation of the sunrise. Amid the competing voices Harry made out the blackcap's rich warble, the plaintive call of the willow-wren in the bramble; and, as they passed by the stubble of a hay-meadow, the green-finch's "breeze—breeze—breeze" could be heard, though the singer remained invisible. In the lightening sky over the treetops, swallows were already hawking for insects, chasing a tardy flutter-mouse to its rest.

They rode quietly at first, listening to the music, but as the sun rose and the air grew warm, Mrs. Steer commenced a song of her own, Harry joining on the refrains. His mother seemed lighthearted in a way rarely seen at home—market day was an interval of release from her ordinary duties, and she had the company of her son besides. As the road became busy with traffic, Harry was charmed to observe this newly lively version of his mother, as she chaffed her friends and entered into the concerns of their lives with goodwill. Seeing her thus freed from care left him wondering about his own home, and what circumstances prevailed there to make her such a different person most of the time. He had always taken his family life for granted, and this new perspective was not a little discomfiting.

Soon enough they were approaching the edge of the town, heralded by the turnpike gate with Mr. Feachem's new vicarage hard by. A sharp tang in the air signaled that work was already under way at the brewery opposite the chalk plat; then came the workhouse, downslope to the left of the road. Out front the Cage (as the jail was known) was evidently occupied by some unlucky miscreant: Harry could hear him pleading for his release, but he was ignored by the workhouse's governor, Mr. Boyce, stumping past on his wooden leg.

As they came abreast of the Hole in the Wall, the cottage that had been the Walking Dunghill's late habitation, they were held up for a time. A herd of goats, startled by all the unaccustomed noise and activity, had broken away from supervision and were milling about in the roadway. Harry sat idly in the cart more relaxed than he had felt for weeks, smiling on the scene as he called to mind the Dunghill's words from one of his sermons: "The presence of God calms the mind, gives sweet repose and quiet, even in the midst of our daily labors." In his mother's company, the cares of the world, even concern for Dick's well-being, felt reduced to insignificance. At last a good-natured farmer sacrificed a few of the cabbages from his cart for the herdsman to use in enticing the goats to obedience, and in due course they were brought under regulation.

As Harry and his mother passed the pound, Harry stood up in the cart to peer over the fence, hoping to catch a glimpse of the dray that Dick and his compatriots had planned to disassemble and reassemble inside. But all he could see was a lone skinny cow that had been brought in from the common, lowing mournfully to its fellows as they paraded by on their way to be sold. He sat down again, his impatience returning to see his aunt and hear how his cousin did.

The High Street was already alive with a cacophony of sound, animal and human. Although the pitching of grain was not to reach its peak for some weeks to come there was hay aplenty on offer, and the air was alive with voices calling their wares—fish, livestock living and butchered, brooms, tools, soap and candles and muslins, tobacco and tea. Harry could not hide a smile at the sight of several shopkeepers opening stalls adorned with beautiful shawls from India: the Tilts had wasted not a moment distributing their bounty from the intercepted East India Company vessel.

Mrs. Steer made her way to the poultry area and set up the crates, lining up her cheeses on the mudguard of the cart. Evidently she was well known to the buyers for the London trade, because soon she had gathered about her a cluster of Lambeth men, hard of visage and speaking in sharp, whining tones as they weighed her Darking fowl and turkeys with their eyes. Her cheeses were more popular for the local trade, going to one or another landlady of the many inns that lined the thoroughfare.

Harry stayed out of the haggling, instead watching the peddlers and bagmen as they moved along the street buying here handkerchiefs, here tea, here tinware, at another stop thread and needles, all to sell at the remote villages and farms. As Mrs. Steer's stock became depleted, she sent Harry off to buy them both meat pasties, which they ate companionably together on the seat of the cart. Then, leaving Harry in charge of what remained, she took her profits off to the shops in search of a block of sugar, a bag of currants, more cheroots for her husband, and a new ribbon for Isabella's pleasure.

While she was away, Harry's aunt Steer arrived, fat and panting in the heat, carrying an assortment of baskets and parcels. He relieved her of her burdens and offered her the last of the meat pasties.

"Thank'ee, Harry, don't mind if I do! I'm that glad your parents gave leave for you to come."

Glancing about to be certain no one was in earshot, Harry asked, "How is Dick? Was he injured in the battle?"

"That he was. I made certain you wouldn't think I really needed you for berry-picking. Why, haven't I the two girls well able to help with such tasks? Dick caught a slash on his leg from one of the soldiers' swords. He was able to limp into a coppice hard by and laid up there till morning afore making his way home. Thanks to Providence it was not far! And the cut is not deep but he had hours to bleed and was weak as a kitten yesterday. He'll be right again soon enough. But he was wanted for a run tonight, and he thought you'd do as well in his stead."

Harry, blushing, assured her he would do his best; but there was no time to say more as his mother was upon them again.

Impatient to be off to see Dick, he scarcely heeded the two women as they exchanged their pleasantries. It was necessary, however, to endure many admonitions and adjurations from his mother before she released him into his aunt's care. He promised to work hard and stay clean and be respectful to his aunt and uncle, and would have promised to do all this while standing on his head and reciting in Latin had it been required of him—anything to be away on the Tilts' business.

Aunt Steer had no conveyance at her disposal, so Harry shouldered her burdens and they walked. Their way lay alongside Cotmandene, where he hoped for a sight of the Darking cricketers but was disappointed, everyone being engaged with the market day. They passed The Deepdene and Chart Park, after which Aunt Steer paused to attach pattens to her shoes for the lane was awash in mud, just as Harry's mother had predicted it would be. Harry found it onerous having to keep pace with the mincing steps she was required to take, so he amused himself with running a few paces and then attempting to slide atop the surface of the road. His efforts were met with the foreseeable results, and by the time they arrived at Stumblehole, the Steers' farm, he was considerably dirty and disheveled.

Uncle Steer, hard at work cleaning an ox's hooves in the stableyard, greeted him with "Well, and who is this shag-rag you've brought home to us, Maggie? He's too tall to be our Harry!"

Harry bashfully apologized for his appearance, offering up his hand to shake. Uncle Steer brushed the hand aside and gave him a friendly cuff instead. "Ain't we becoming the fine gentleman? You ain't been spoiled by that grand school afore even getting there, I hope." Relieving Harry of the parcels, he added, "Mind you clean off at the pump before coming inside—Maggie won't thank you for bringing all that dirt into her kitchen."

Harry did as he was bid and then ventured indoors. The house was not a large one, though it had grown over the centuries from one even smaller. Oak-framed with brick added between the timbers, like so many of the houses in the district, it had few rooms on the ground level, the large kitchen sufficing for most purposes of daily life. One of Harry's young cousins, Jane, was in the chimney corner playing with a litter of puppies, while her older sister Eliza, on the settle under the bacon loft, hunched over a shirt she was sewing. Dick was slouched in a chair nearby, one leg propped up on a stool. When Harry entered, however, he got to his feet and hobbled over.

"Harry, I made sure you'd not fail me! I was at my wits' end over what to do, but the cap'n said you knew something of the business already, and he suggested you'd do as well in my place. More of that later, though," he added hastily, seeing Jane's alert eyes turned toward him, "there's no hurry to get into it."

The kitchenmaid was already chopping potatoes for their dinner, so Eliza set down her sewing and helped to lay the table while Aunt Steer took her place on the settle. "My word, but it's hot out there, and I'm fair beazled from wading through all that dirt! Harry's mum says they're to start the harvest next week, Daniel, they're that forrards on the lighter fields—though the corn wants yet a week or two on the clay." She directed Jane to unpack the parcels and baskets and stow her purchases, which she did with a running commentary on the items her mother had selected. "Ma! This butter is none so fine as what I can make!"

"Then you should take up the churn more often, girl! Do I have the time for't, chasing after you all as I do?"

"I thought you were going to get a new packet of needles!"

"And so I did! Ain't they just here, in my pocket?"

The banter continued at table and brought a smile to Harry's face, though he said but little; he always took pleasure in the family's cheery quarreling, in witnessing a type of running warfare that conveyed no malice. Dick's younger brother James came in late to the meal, deflecting attention from his dirty hands with a complaint against his elder brother for finding a way to shirk his chores. "I make no doubt you'd be fit enough to work if 't weren't the day for mucking out the stables," he said.

"I'm surely well enough to teach you respect for your betters, Jimmy," retorted Dick, struggling to his feet.

James danced out of his reach and took a seat on the other side of the table, greeting Harry with a clap on the back. "Always turning over his work to others—mind you don't let him take advantage, or you'll never see the end on it."

"I'm happy to help!" protested Harry.

"Then God help'ee,' said his uncle, chuckling; "I'm sure you'll be hearing from us when it's time to spread the midden on the fields."

Harry pretended to stiffen up with offense. "I should be honored to be of assistance to my kin in any manner called for," said he in his most affected accent, making a bow.

This brought a roar of laughter from all around the table. "It's a wonder to hear you speak, Harry," said Mr. Steer. "I'd never know you hailed from Surrey! I'm certain your ma don't speak so fine, nor even your pa half the time."

Harry protested, "I'd speak plain but my dad insists on what he calls proper English from me, and from Isabella too. He's certain I'll be laughed at once I go to school if I don't talk that way."

"He's in the right of that, no doubt—the other boys'd make your hide smart for sure. Well well, it matters but little how you speak so long as you show yourself pleased with your company, whoever they be."

"I'm by far more suited by the company of other farmers than by going among the high and mighty," Harry replied. "A fortnight ago our cousin from Jayes took me to a meeting of the Gentlemen's Darking Club, and it seemed to me every man there was bent on exalting his own position by belittling someone else. It was all veiled insult and innuendo; I couldn't even make out the half of it. For the life of me I couldn't understand why they troubled themselves to meet: I never met a set of people less interested in each other's well-being."

"But it was kind in Mr. Lee Steere to take you up in that way, Harry," his aunt reminded him (his uncle muttered "Lee Steere *Steere*," with a guffaw), "for you can't but gain from being known to the carriage folk."

"So I'm told," said Harry with a doleful face, "but perhaps I'll lose just as much if I'm seen to be holding myself above my neighbors. I'm afraid I'll learn only how to be a gentleman, without having the means to support such a life."

After the meal, Dick called for the support of Harry's shoulder and they hobbled outside to take a bench in the orchard under an apple tree. As soon as they were out of earshot of the others, Harry could keep his peace no longer. "I wish I had been there for the set-to with the militia!" he cried. "It seems a most cruel chance that I was not."

"To me it seems a most *happy* chance that you were not," retorted Dick. "How could you wish for it?"

Harry was mystified. "Why, for the honor of fighting alongside my comrades. How else is one to prove himself a loyal man?"

"You'd be more likely to be laid out upon the road like Jemmy Finch! Would that prove you a man? Even thinking so much proves you nobbut a babe, with your head turned by stories of knights and heroes. If that sword had caught me an inch deeper or six higher, I'd have been either dead or a burden on my family for the rest of my days, instead of helping to provide for 'em! Is that what you want *your* future to be?"

Harry hung his head and remained silent, thinking only that Dick was to be pitied for his loss of courage and trying to make allowances for the shock of his injury and loss of blood. Perceiving as much, Dick continued in bitter tones, "Who d'you think we was fighting, idiot? It weren't a proper enemy like the French. The Yeoman Cavalry be no more than extra boys from Darking and Guildford with no employment. Boys like Charles Attlee—his dad buys my dad's spare hay to sell. Or the middle Cheesman boy, I don't recall his name. They're our neighbors—the sons of the shopkeepers who buy their goods from Milord. They're ordered to fight by the great and mighty who care not a whit for any of us. Mum and Dad are just like you: they think this all a game of cat-and-mouse, with a fat prize of shillings as a reward. But it ain't all play, and you can't simply quit the field when you tire of it."

He frowned at Harry. "You're too young to be mixed up in this, and that you can't see it only proves as much. I could wish you'd failed to show today."

Harry held his uncomprehending peace. Seeing the

cause hopeless, Dick shook off his ill-humor. "Well, no remedy for it now. All I can do for you is prepare you the best I can for this night's doings." He fetched a deep breath. "The cap'n tells me you're acquainted with a man named Tomkins." Harry's heart began to beat faster—here might be answers at last! "It's him you're working with tonight."

"So we'll be traveling from north to south?"

"It queers me how you know that!" Dick was plainly impressed. "Where you learned it I can't think."

"I don't know what the cargo is, though."

"No more do I. But there'll be two brace of batmen alongside, so I'll wager it's important. Here's your part in the task: Soon now, you'll go to Heathfields afoot and collect a string of ten horses. Old Joll is there, he'll get you what you need. You'll be walking 'em north in daylight, that way you'll arouse no suspicions. Have you been to the meadows alongside the Mole to the north of Darking, hard by the Leatherhead road?"

"Only so far as the footbridge over the river—the one you took apart the day of the Dunghill's funeral."

"Just a little north of there, then. When you get into Darking High Street, go east as if making for that bridge, but then take the first road northward. Keep to the road past the turnoff for Pixham Mill and the tollgate. When you can see a fine house just ahead to the left—they call it The Grove—step aside on a footpath on your right. If you get to Burford Lodge, it's too far. This is the tricksy part! Nobody must see you leave the road. Make your way down the path and find cover for the horses at the point where you can see the Whites on t'other side of the river."

"What are the Whites?"

"It's the name for the cliffs on the east side of the Mole,

where the chalk is exposed. You'll lie up there some hours; Mum'll send you with some food, and perhaps you can con your Latin while you wait!" Harry gave Dick's arm a cuff in protest against this objectionable slur. "Water the horses and let 'em graze, but only where they're out of sight of the road. If anyone sees you and asks, you're from Norbury Park and the horses have got loose."

"Norbury Park," repeated Harry, committing it to memory.

"And try to speak like a Surrey lad, not so fine," said Dick impatiently. "Tomkins and the batmen should be there sometime after nightfall. His signal is three whistles in descending notes, like this—" he demonstrated the sound, which was to Harry's ear a bit like the call of a curlew, and made Harry imitate it until he was satisfied. "You'll bide there till the shipment arrives. Transfer it to your horses and do as Tomkins bids. You'll stay with the goods till they're handed off somewhere near Newdigate—" Harry knew it would be the house with the secret chamber behind the hearth—"which is why you won't return home till Saturday." Dick made Harry repeat all the details several times, especially the way to the meeting place where he was to hide. "And it won't do to be hovering about in the road, looking for the footpath—you'll only draw notice."

Harry was eager to set forth immediately but Dick did not want him to arrive too early at the rendezvous and court discovery. "The road will be busy till close to nightfall with people making their way home from the market. The timing must be right." So he insisted that Harry stay on for an hour before setting out for Heathfields.

Harry tried to lay aside his nervousness and enjoy his remaining time with his cousins, but it was with the sensation of a dog let off his rope that he at last escaped his aunt and uncle, sent on his way with a packet of bread and cheese in his pocket. Perhaps Dick's fears had had their effect, for his aunt and uncle's smiling calm now seemed vaguely unnatural to him—with their eldest son recently wounded in a battle in the Tilts' service, how could they have so little apprehension about their nephew's welfare? Harry was ashamed to be harboring doubts, but they could not altogether be banished.

As he walked, he tried to rehearse the instructions again in his mind, but the road was crowded with people homeward bound from the market day, including, it seemed, an inordinate number of his acquaintance. He was forever being jolted out of his brown study by the necessity of responding to greetings—and this raised a fresh area of uncertainty. What if he were recognized on his way back toward Darking—how could he explain leading ten horses? Anyone familiar with his father would know he had never owned so many in his life; and even if he had, why would Harry be leading them away from their stable at close of day? He felt his guilt must be a large stain visible on his countenance to all he met as he tried to go about his underhanded business.

Upon arrival at Heathfields, he was greeted by Old Joll, recognizable only by his rolling gait, so different was his appearance without soot smeared over his face. The captain had thoughtfully sent Joll a message that Harry would be taking Dick's place, so Harry at least had no convincing to do before receiving his horses.

"I never reckoned you was no snitch—not like the others," Joll confided. He was not the most articulate of the smugglers, but his words were eloquent enough; Harry repressed a shiver and reflected that he might learn to be grateful for having been outside the circle of trust on the night of the battle.

As they were selecting the horses and tying them in a string, Harry ventured to divulge his concern about being recognized on the road by homeward-bound neighbors. "Walk on t'other side, then!" said Joll, hissing through his two remaining teeth; then he chortled and removed the plaited hat from his own head, settling it ungently over Harry's ears. It was a great deal too large and forced Harry to keep pushing it up away from his eyes, as well as being greasy and steeped in Joll's sweat, but Harry had to acknowledge its effectiveness in frustrating undesirable scrutiny. No one could find his face under such a covering.

The horses were none too pleased with the prospect of their outing, and the ones at the back of the string were disposed to consider themselves too far removed from authority for obedience to be required. But at last Harry got them under way, chased from the Heathfields gate by Old Joll's derision. At least on the Stonebridge road he need not fear that they would be startled by passing carriages, the road conditions being too poor as usual to allow for narrow wheels. Most of the traffic was afoot, with only the occasional cart being laboriously hauled through the mud by men whose farms lay too far east of the common for the turnpike to serve as their route home.

And so Harry returned to Darking without mishap. The crowd was already much thinned, and to his left on the High Street he could see the remaining vendors packing up their wares in the slanting light of the setting sun. He was certain his mother was long since departed, so he set his nose to the east and left the town behind, passing the Royal Oak and Shrub Hill House before turning northward at the smithy, hard by the nursery ground.

There were still some travelers on the Leatherhead road, including carriage traffic, and Harry had to keep his mind on maintaining order among the horses. He passed the chalk pits and the turnoff for the Pixham Mill without untoward incident, only to be confronted with an unforeseen dilemma: he had forgotten about the tollgate at Giles Green and had not been provided with so much as a shilling to pay his way! He would need a penny per horse to pass the gate. He had no desire to attract attention to his activities by arguing with the keeper of the gate or making an attempt to evade the toll. Uncertain how to proceed, he came to a halt in the roadway.

His very indecision proved an unfortunate choice. The horses at the end of the string, tractably moving along behind their fellows so long as the ropes were taut, no sooner felt them go slack than they took new ideas into their heads. One decided the grass on the verge opposite was worth sampling while another tried to turn for home; and a third, pulled between them, jerked up his head and neighed a protest. It seemed only a moment before all was in a tangle, with Harry unable to let go of the lead horse to restore order.

The only solution he could devise was to lead the horses in a wide circle so that he could sort out the rearguard horses while still maintaining control over those in front. Unfortunately, the road narrowed at this point for the tollgate: when he attempted to put his plan into execution, he soon blocked the way for all travelers—and just at that moment, he heard behind him the blast from a yard of tin as a gentleman's coach, drawn by four matched high-steppers, bore down upon the tollgate.

Chapter the Eighteenth

The coachman, finding Harry's horses strung out across the road, hauled on the ribbons and managed to stop his team just in time, but the near miss so startled Harry's already bewildered charges that they shied and plunged, driving the entire string into chaos. The coachman vented his wrath in a flood of personalities about Harry and his parentage that would have sparked Harry's ire had he leisure to attend to them. But he was too busily engaged with the horses to take offense, much less respond in kind.

After a few moments the passenger in the coach, a portly gentleman, put his head out the window, shouting, "Damn you, Parton, what is the cause of this curst delay?"

The coachman cringed and his tone turned servile. "It's some boy, my lord, with a long string of horses he's scattered all across the road. He's blocked our way to the tollgate."

"And this is beyond your powers to remedy, dullard? Each of my servants is stupider than the last! Remove the boy and his damned horses, and move along. Am I to reach home at midnight?"

Parton and one of the postboys scrambled down to help Harry sort out the horses, the coachman delivering all the while a string of vulgar threats that made Harry cringe and the postboy snigger. But the fear trembling behind the coachman's harsh words gave Harry a sudden idea.

"Even once the horses are back in order, they will still be in your path," he said, taking care to stand well away from Parton's reach. "If you would step up and pay the tolls, I can lead the horses through and off to the side while you return to the coach, and then you'll be on your way sooner. I shouldn't wish that fine gentleman of yours to be angry with you."

Parton had to agree that this was sensible, though he did so with a poor grace. "Very well, you impudent jack-anapes, give me the money for your toll and I'll pay 'em both," said he, watching the door to the carriage with a wary eye.

"I regret to have to tell you that I cannot," said Harry. "You see, I have no money for the toll."

Parton puffed up in outrage. "After all the trouble you've caused, demon-seed, you demand we pay your toll for you?"

"Well, here I stand in your path," said Harry, "and I don't rightly see how I can move out of it without being on the other side of that gate. It's up to you, but I don't believe your master will object to tenpence gone astray half as much as he'll object to being held up here any longer than necessary. But of course you know his mind better than I."

Parton glared at him in silence for a moment and then stamped off to pay the toll. Harry set his horses in motion and marched past the gate, keeping his eyes averted so as not to observe the eloquent hand gesture the coachman offered as Harry passed him by. Harry obligingly moved the string of horses to the verge of the road on the other side and waited till the coach had rattled past.

On this side of the tollgate the road was nearly deserted, so Harry had little difficulty in turning off onto the footpath described by his cousin once he had located it. The horses seemed to know the way; as the sliver of a moon, just past the new, hung low in the sky behind them, they moved eagerly into a meadow beside the Mole and dropped their heads to drink. Harry looked about him and seeing the white cliffs across the river, overhung with box, knew he was in the right place for the rendezvous. Once the horses were satisfied he staked them down, leaving them to crop the grass while he found a fallen tree that was well hidden by a tangle of hazel and alder and settled down on its trunk to wait.

To his mind there could scarcely be a pleasanter spot to pass the time. The river was sluggish here, its surface broken only by an occasional splash as a perch rose to seize an unfortunate beetle that had fallen from a reed. Across the river lay a well-tended orchard with the Whites behind, blazing brightly just now as they reflected the setting sun. A thick tangle of rushes, willow-herb, sneezewort, loosestrife, and meadow-sweet along the riverbank offered haven to a family of sedge-warblers, chucking and twittering as they disputed the encroachment of dusk. After Harry had remained still for a while, rabbits emerged from hiding to join the horses in their meal; a light mist settled over the water, dispersed in a puff of breeze, and settled more firmly as the light failed. Harry gazed up at the sky and watched the bats emerge for their evening's hunt.

He had already consumed half the provisions supplied by his aunt by the time he was startled to alertness by a sound more human than equine. He peered out through the branches that shielded his hiding place and presently made out a figure advancing on the footpath through the gloom. Upon becoming aware of the presence of horses, this person halted and whistled the three descending notes Dick had taught Harry to expect. Harry responded in kind and then dropped down from his perch to meet Tomkins.

The sight of Harry where Dick was expected startled Tomkins into a yelp. Harry hushed him and explained what had befallen his cousin.

"Aye, I was laying up at the Nag's Head that night and we heard all the to-ing and fro-ing on the common," whispered Tomkins, "though the battle itself was too far distant. Bothered if the Excise and the Cavalry ain't getting too close for comfort hereabouts! A man can't earn a wage without risk of transportation—or worse. I has my pay reg'lar, or I'd be off back to Hampshire to try my fortunes there. It do seem as they has their sources of information."

Harry agreed to this.

"Well, and I'd as lief have you along this night as your cousin; you're smaller, and you've a good head on those little shoulders. I won't deny I've had a kindness for you since that day we met. Stick by me and we'll come off scatheless."

With such goodwill in this quarter, Harry could not forbear attempting to extract further information. "What is the cargo we're running tonight?"

Tomkins stiffened. "I don't rightly know as I should speak on that, for all you're helping me. Our betters' business is their business, if you ken my meaning. Ours is to follow orders, and if we earn our pay then they pays us."

"But you know what it is, don't you?"

"If it be the same as last time, I'd say I knows a thing or two," admitted Tomkins cautiously. "But the whys of the matter—no."

"By the last time, do you mean Saint Swithin's night?" persisted Harry.

Tomkins was startled afresh. "What d'ye ken about that?"

"If you recall, my kinsman and I helped you on your way in to Darking on the day of your errand there, when you were—ah—traveling incognito. Later I saw you in the stableyard of the Red Lion, in converse with Mr. Barclay. I heard him speak of this place, and of a house in Newdigate where you were to lay up, and of Saint Swithin's night."

Even in the darkness Tomkins's agitation could be felt. "You heard all that, did you? Was anyone else by?"

"No, I was alone."

"I'd rather have been seen by no one that day." Tomkins ran a shaky hand over his whiskers.

"So I can imagine," said Harry with a smile. "It was a most extraordinary disguise."

"'Twas all I could think of!" protested Tomkins. "I'm not a long man, and so it seemed the best I could do. Folks see what they be expecting to see half the time."

"You made a very pretty female—but did you not think to shave?"

"Well, as to that, I hoped the bonnet would hide my face, and shaving seemed a large sacrifice for a small purpose."

"In any case, I am glad you did not consider a disguise necessary tonight."

"Not like yourself, Harry—that hat do make you a figure! It's half as big as you are. And speaking of this night," said Tomkins, attempting to seize back the reins of the conversation, "if we be stopped by the militia, you're my son, and we're making for Chichester on the business of a shopkeeper there."

"What of the batmen?"

"No doubt they'll be here soon."

"I meant, how will we account for their presence?"

"They'll conceal themselves if we hear horses a-coming. They'll defend us if it's lawless men—it wouldn't do to have *this* cargo stolen—but they'll stay in hiding if it's the Law."

Suddenly Harry froze, clapping a hand over Tomkins's mouth. Through the gloom he had espied a light, flickering in the near distance to the north of their position. He pointed silently to it.

Tomkins extricated himself from Harry's grip. "Lord bless you, nipperkin, *that's* naught to trouble yourself over. That there's a light from Burford Lodge. It's just there, on t'other side of the trees."

Harry was startled. "There's a house so close by? I had no notion of it."

"But it were there just the same. It didn't walk here while your back was turned. You've no cause to fret—that be Mr. Barclay's house."

Harry was ashamed that in all the flurry of introductions at the Gentlemen's Darking Club, he had forgotten the name of Mr. Barclay's abode. He was also embarrassed to have omitted reconnoitering his position before settling in to wait for Tomkins. "So we are on his own land, then? He's a man who enjoys taking risks, I take it."

"I do believe you're in the right of it, but if we're caught here, we're to deny all knowledge of him."

"And say we're from Norbury Park, yes, I was told as much. But all the same—"

"Whisht!" hissed Tomkins, and, seizing Harry in his turn, dragged him back under the cover of the trees. But it was only the first of the batmen, whistling the three descending notes of the signal as he came down the path.

Harry soon recognized him as Dick's friend Slug, and made free of the name. Slug, however, felt equally privileged by virtue of his superior size and weight, and a silent tussle ensued, from which Harry emerged bereft of the knapsack with the last of his food, and with Old Joll's hat crammed down about his ears. "Thanks, Monkey," said his assailant through a mouthful of cheese.

"Hedgebird," retorted Harry bitterly, restoring the hat to its intended position.

The other three batmen appeared in short order, and Harry took care to greet each one with greater circumspection. One he recognized as a young blacksmith from Beare Green, but the others were strangers to him. Mayhap he had been on runs with them before, but this time no one had a blackened face. They seemed a confident lot and passed the time cheerfully in exchanging boasts about their performance in the Battle of the Bottle and Glass. Harry listened with open respect to their revelations about the skirmish, regretting again that he had been absent.

A few hours passed in this manner, and even the tales of derring-do began to pall. Harry was feeling quite sleepy, though as the junior member of the party he was loth to confess it, when Tomkins, who had held aloof from the banter, hushed them sharply.

They could all hear what had caught his attention: a cart was moving along the road, not half a furlong off. They all stretched their ears into the darkness until they heard the horses pull up, hard by the entrance to the footpath.

"This is it," whispered Tomkins, and he began to move silently back up toward the road. The rest followed suit.

About thirty feet from the 'pike, Tomkins gestured to them to stop, and he proceeded alone. He stepped boldly up to the cart and bade the driver a fair evening. The man merely grunted, and Tomkins added, "What brings you out on this fine night—you after taking *the King's shilling?*"

"Aye," said the driver, "'tis for the sea I'm bound." He did not suit action to word, however, but instead descended from the cart and drew off a heavy cloth covering its load.

"All well on your journey? Were the road busy?" inquired Tomkins, gesturing his confederates to his side.

As they scrambled up, the driver replied briefly, "Didn't take no road; I comes up over t'downs on t'Pebble Lane."

"Hard work, that," said Tomkins with ready sympathy, but the driver had used his store of words and had no more to offer. So they all began to unload the cart. Its cargo appeared to consist of only a number of bags of middling size, larger than a purse, smaller than a sack of grain. When one was dropped into Harry's arms, however, it proved to be astonishingly heavy. He gripped it more tightly and heard the chink of metal; it felt for all the world like a bag of coin.

Harry looked sharply at Tomkins, only to find himself being scrutinized already. "Take it down to the meadow and prepare the horses, Harry," said Tomkins, his tone forbidding comment.

Harry did as he was told, his thoughts in a whirl. Even if the contents of the sack were no more than coachwheels, this single bag represented more money than he had seen in his lifetime. And it was only one of at least a score of sacks he had seen sitting in the back of the cart. Here were riches beyond his imagination! No wonder a small pack train only was required, but an unusual number of guards needed to escort it. And to what use might this fortune be put? Was Milord needing to replenish his capital for paying his workmen? The thought occurred only to be rejected: Milord's team were merely bringing the cargo south to the Sussex border, where others would take charge of it and deliver it to its destination.

As he brought the horses back to the footpath and tightened their girths—a tricky maneuver since he was unwilling to relinquish his hold on the bag while performing it—Harry thought further and concluded that the money must be coming from the receiver of a smuggled load in London, who was returning payment to the seafaring men who had brought it in; or perhaps it was payment for the purchase of the next shipment. Though he had never before considered the question, it seemed implausible that the free-traders would employ letters of credit in the conduct of their illicit activity; what reputable banker would do business with them? So perhaps it was a regular thing to transport large quantities of coin to England's southern shores. He only wondered why Mr. Barclay had a hand in the business: he was not even a banker but merely a merchant and director of the Royal Exchange Assurance Corporation. He trafficked in guaranteeing naval and merchant vessels and other property—though in a position such as his, a considerable amount of money must pass through his hands. Why could Milord not deal directly with the receivers?

All the while he puzzled over these questions, the batmen were staggering to and fro with the sacks, grunting and cursing at their weight, loading four onto each horse. Forty sacks of money! It was a thought to make Harry's heart beat uncomfortably fast. Who might not seek to seize it from them, should knowledge of its existence reach their ears? All of a sudden, four batmen seemed woefully insufficient for the task at hand.

Then Tomkins was back and they were ready to set off. Two of the batmen remained close to the horses while the others walked one ahead and one behind. At the tollgate the one ahead paid the sleepy gatekeeper, who lost no time in returning to his lodging, almost before the horses were through. Harry thought he had seen the batman slip him a bottle along with the pennies, but in the darkness he could not be certain. Their party moved on, leading the horses off the turnpike and down Punchbowl Lane. The network of paths and lanes they used to skirt Darking was unfamiliar; it was some time before Harry was able to recognize any landmarks, not until they joined the road he had walked earlier in the day with his aunt.

He felt no inclination to play in the mud puddles now, however. The burden of those sacks of money, though it was borne by the horses, nevertheless weighed him down and he plodded heavily in silence, his ears on the prick for trouble.

His fellows appeared to feel the same. There was no banter among the batmen now—a far cry from his ordinary experience of smuggling runs. The way seemed very long, the unrelieved darkness of the moonless night offering no assistance in marking the passage of time. Eventually they came to Heathfields, however, and Harry darted off to the barn to leave behind Old Joll's hat, which had proved more of a liability than an asset. Soon they encountered the Bottle and Glass, shuttered and quiet. With one accord they paused, doffed their hats to the memory of Jemmy Finch, and moved soberly on.

Not long after, the pack train left Brimstone Lane and followed a road angling off to the eastward that Harry had never before traveled. He ventured to protest that this was not the way to Newdigate but was cut short by Tomkins. "The house we're to lay up in ain't in the town. It makes no matter of mind to you where we're bound." Harry could not agree but ventured no further dispute; he kept his mouth shut but his eyes open.

There was little enough to see. The night must have been nearly spent but still darkness reigned; overcast skies promised the continued fulfillment of Saint Swithin's curse, and their way led through a series of copses. Here and there a hedge or wall implied habitation, but nary a light nor a soul was to be seen—for which Harry could only be grateful. If he had been apprehensive on familiar ground, now he was frankly terrified of discovery. The bags of coin seemed ever more sinister; if he and his companions were to be taken up by the authorities in an unfamiliar parish, how would his parents even learn of his plight? And which would be worse—their ignorance or their knowledge?

These ideas began to show his illicit activities in service to Milord and the captain in a new light. What had previously appeared in the guise of adventure—forbidden of course, yet still harmless—now assumed more threatening dimensions. If he were caught, what might be the penalty? Floundering along muddy tracks in the dark, he was suddenly assailed with visions of losing not just his admission to Winchester College but also possibly his family, his home, even perhaps his life. Why the sacks of money should be so much more frightening than kegs of brandy or bolts of silk he could not say, but in his heart he knew they were. More than the long day and night of activity, the burden of his thoughts dragged him down into exhaustion.

Just as the sky was lightening, the little pack train arrived at a crossroads clustered 'round with cottages. And as they passed by one—a tidy, new-built structure of brick with tile-hanging above—a man emerged from the door carrying a bucket. He walked a few steps toward his pump but suddenly caught sight of their procession, halting in his tracks to gape.

Slug, in the lead, gasped and paused as well, but then marched on, staring straight ahead, so the rest of them—Harry, Tomkins, the other batmen, and the horses—perforce followed suit. Harry could see that Tomkins and the others were averting their gaze, though the man continued to watch them.

Harry could not understand it. Surely it made sense to acknowledge the man, to clothe their travels abroad at such an untoward hour with some pretense of normalcy? It appeared to him that his fellows' behavior was calculated to arouse suspicion rather than dispel it. So he smiled at the man and offered a nod of greeting.

The man did not twitch or blink, he only continued to stare. Harry felt that gaze pierce his skin and penetrate deep into his guilty soul; he blushed, then paled as the glare continued to hold him captive.

After an eternity he was past the house and had left the man behind, but still he could feel the eyes on their backs as they walked on.

When at length they were out of earshot, he whispered to Tomkins, "That man back there—he appeared hostile to us. Do you think we have anything to fear from him? Might he lay information against us?"

Tomkins sighed. "He may or he may not, bantling, but if he do it'd be no great wonder. That were William Finch—the father of Jemmy what died t'other night by the Bottle and Glass."

Chapter the Nineteenth

It was a solemn procession that continued forward, passing a long, dilapidated building evidently constructed in the time of the Virgin Queen. Perhaps wishing to relieve the tension, Tomkins commenced chattering to Harry about it: it was called Cheesmans, having in the past been the property of the family that had so much to do with the making and selling of beer and ale in these parts, and now served as the workhouse for Newdigate parish. "Don't never go and seek poor relief in Newdigate," he added. "They work the indigent—man, woman, and child—at weaving, day and night the same, every day 'cept the Lord's. I'd rather dig a ditch or spread offal on the fields than be penned up indoors like a sow my every waking hour."

Harry was in fervent agreement, reflecting that the fate of Newdigate's poor was not unlike his own, bound every day to his books and his tutor. At least at this moment he was out in the world, moving freely and being his own man. The thought helped to dispel some of the fears that had held him captive throughout the night. And now, just over a bridge—a disgraceful structure, which seemed as likely to pitch them into the brook as not—they came to their destination; and not a moment too soon, for the swallows were plying the air above the water and full daylight could not be far off.

The house sat amid the fields of a small farm, its few acres lying fallow, the garden raising only weeds and a few stubborn cabbages that refused to be choked out. Tomkins unlocked the door and the batmen began swiftly to unload the sacks. Harry found a trough around the side of the house and pumped water into it; as the horses were relieved of their burdens, he led them off to refresh themselves. Then Slug took the string in charge and, mounting on the lead horse, returned the way they had come.

Harry entered the house and looked about him. It was a simple structure in the old style, with a sunken dirt floor and a wide inglenook hearth. A narrow stair rose precipitously in the corner, promising a broken leg to anyone so rash as to use it. The five of them remaining were a crowd in the space.

Tomkins approached the cold fireplace and groped into a small salt hole at the side. There was a click and then, as he pressed against the wall below the hole, a grinding sound and the wall rotated in place, showing a dark opening behind. He turned to Harry. "Well then, in you get," he said.

Harry stared at the hole and then eyed Tomkins suspiciously. Had he been wrong to think that the captain trusted him? Perhaps he had been led on to believe so, while all along an elaborate scheme was growing about him, intended to culminate in his being immured in the walls of this hovel and left to die.

"Step lively, Harry!" said Tomkins. "Why d'you think we needed a boy? The rest of us be too big to squeeze in. Get you inside, and when all the bags is stored in there, none the wiser!"

"And I'll be allowed to come out again once the bags are in?"

Tomkins laughed. "So *that's* your worry? I'll not shut you up in that hole, bantling. Look, I'll stand well away from the spring while the others hand you in the sacks."

With this assurance Harry had to be content, so he got on his knees amid the remains of ash on the hearth and crawled through the opening. He was in a small, airless chamber, scarcely more than a cupboard, which had evidently been formed from a gap left behind when an earlier stairway was removed. The space was dusty and the only light came from the opening into the fireplace, but he could faintly see the marks of recent use—presumably from the run on Saint Swithin's night. He had little time to develop a sense of dread, though, for the bags of coin soon began to be slammed down in front of the opening, faster even than he could haul them in and dispose them in the corners.

About half of them were in when a small accident occurred. The blacksmith clumsily snagged the canvas of a sack on the old spit that projected over the hearth. There was a tearing sound, and a single coin fell out of a small rent in the bag. It dropped to the stone, landing with a ringing sound that appeared loud in the sudden silence that fell—for the coin was gold.

The moment stretched out as everyone stared at it—Tomkins, all the batmen, Harry inside the hole. It had been sobering enough to imagine themselves responsible for forty sacks of shillings or half-crowns. But *guineas*? Here was a burden of an entirely different order.

And then the blacksmith dived for the coin, only to find his arm pinned to the floor by Tomkins's boot. Harry shrank back into his hole, uncertain whether to be grateful for its protection or more frightened than ever.

"Leave it be!" muttered Tomkins in a growl. "We'll poke it back into the bag and close the hole somehow."

"But why?" protested the blacksmith. "A single coin's not like to be missed."

"Ye're thinking too small," said another of the batmen. "Each of these bags holds a fortune. Here we be, risking our skins for Milord and getting paid a pittance for our trouble. If we divvy up the bags and scarper now, we'll be beyond his ken afore he knows we're gone. With brass like this, we could go anywhere and do anything! Me, I'm for taking ship to Santo Domingo. I'm told a man with brass can live like a lord there, no matter who his parents might be."

"You're thinking like a gormless clod, more like," said Tomkins, still pinning down the blacksmith's arm. "It's not Milord you need to be escaping, it's my master—and his master, and his, no doubt, right up to some very powerful men. Them that commands riches like these ain't likely to shrug and settle for a loss. I dunno who they might be and nor do you, but I'll wager they're not the sort you want hunting you down. Do you reckon they'll set the Law arter us? The militia, haply, or the Bow Street Runners? It's not law-abiding men that sends forty sacks of gold jauntering about the countryside in the dead of night. These be dangerous men we're serving—hard men—and if we value our skins, we'll serve 'em as they wants to be served and then be done with it. We deliver every last guinea to the Sussex boys and we walks away alive."

His words gave Harry pause. In the first moments he'd shared the blacksmith's phantasm of wealth unimaginable: his parents able to increase their land, to hire all the servants they might wish; his sister well dowered; relief for all the workingmen in the parish struggling to fend off starvation, for the widows and the sick. Himself a man of substance, respected by all. But if he took his share, he would never be suffered to go home with it—never be able to go home at all. His family could never know a thing about it, or their lives would be forfeit; the parish would be left to struggle on as before, and his entire world lost to him forever.

He tried to imagine how Milord and the captain had ever found the stomach to entrust such a fearsome cargo to a highwayman, a boy, and a handful of young men more noted for their brawn than their brains: surely it was a reckless folly. How could they have taken such a risk? Why was the captain not on this run, ensuring personally that all went as planned?

And yet in the end, the Tilts' confidence proved to be well placed. The blacksmith surrendered the guinea to Tomkins, it was poked back into the sack, and Tomkins set about repairing the rent while the remaining sacks were silently pushed toward Harry and stowed in the secret chamber. He crawled out, Tomkins closed the wall, and they lit a fire on the hearth as instructed.

Harry had been feeling the pangs of hunger when they first arrived, but that was all done with now. He sat on the dirt floor staring at the flames, a sensation both heavy and giddy in his stomach. He was thinking, trying to construct a meaningful picture of events and imagine his way into Milord's skin. Mr. Barclay had approached the Tilts with a proposition: make a series of runs (for this was at least the second) carrying gold from, presumably, London toward the south coast of England. Use as few men as possible in the transport, a number calculated to draw the least attention and yet to defend the cargo effectively if called upon to do so.

There must have been a powerful inducement for the Tilts to undertake a commission of this nature. If they were caught there must be an inquiry into the source and the destination of the money. No stone would be left unturned in the examination of every aspect of this affair. The Tilts had a profitable enterprise in their ordinary smuggling business, and they stood to lose all should this project go awry. Perhaps that was why the captain absented himself in the matter: he would be hoping that the crime could not be traceable to his family. But that seemed a vain hope, to Harry's way of thinking; would none of the men gathered 'round him give way under such pressures as must be brought to bear on the perpetrators of such an act? It could scarcely be imagined that one or more would not be happy to tell all he knew in exchange for escape from—what, precisely? Surely the penalty must be hanging, at the very least.

And exactly what was it they were doing? Harry could not even give a name to their crime. They were carrying a large sum of money—an unimaginable sum—from one place to another. No doubt men in the employ of banks, and even of wealthy lords, did as much every day. To what use was the money now residing behind the wall intended to be put? Harry could find no answer.

He became aware that Tomkins was watching him, as if reading his thoughts. "It's been a long night, boy, and bound to be a longer day," he said with something approaching a rough tenderness. "Lay yourself down and close your eyes; I'll find you something to eat by and by."

Harry realized he was indeed very tired, with a fatigue that weighed on both his bones and his spirit. He lay down and attempted not to think any more. Sooner than might be imagined, he was asleep—only to be racked by dreams of trying to run through deep mud down a lonely road with King George pursuing him in his state carriage; the Walking Dunghill was driving the carriage, waving his whip and shouting, "Truth is mighty and will prevail!" as he came. And William Finch stood by the side of the road watching it all with his unblinking stare.

Harry awoke, his limbs aching, to find that it was late in the forenoon. Tomkins had obtained a chicken from somewhere and was roasting it on the spit, raindrops still beaded on his smock, while the three remaining batmen divided up a loaf of bread one had brought with him. The resolution of earlier differences had induced a state of wary camaraderie, and the food was shared without competition or dispute.

With food in his belly, however, the blacksmith appeared heartened to reopen the debate over the guineas. "I'm not so well suited to how we've left things," he said to Tomkins, with a glance around at the others to assess his support. "The folk whose brass this is, whoever they be, ain't folk as can act in the open. If their brass goes missing, they canna shout about it or make a stir."

"But they knows who *we* be," objected another. "They knows where to start their hunt. Milord won't protect us if we betray him. It'd be right fine to buy meself a farm and hand out a guinea to every soul in the district—but I'd only be suffered to do it the onct. Then we'd be dead and the money all spent and no more to follow. The way I sees it, we every one of us has a stake in Milord's business; half the county lives off the income earned in the free-trade, or can buy what is needful accos of the low prices. We fail Milord now, all that stops."

And the dispute went around and around, but still the sacks remained in their hiding place. Harry had long since settled in his mind the impossibility of absconding with the guineas, but to his other concerns he was loth to give voice: Whither was the money bound? For what purpose? It seemed impossible that there could be any legitimate use for it—but if not, what illicit activity might require such a vast fortune as this? His perturbation could not entirely be concealed, and at last he ventured in an undervoice to put a question to Tomkins.

"If we should be taken up—by the militia under direction of the Excise, even by a constable—what would be the penalty?"

Tomkins was inclined to dismiss the hazards. "The risk of capture by the militia or the Excise was all but done away once we got ourselves safely off the roads. And Newdigate parish has no constable at present."

"But does Mr. Finch know of this house?"

"You're thinking he'll send the Law our way? I misdoubt he knows enough to do us harm—they say he never took part in the runs, and from all I'm told, this house weren't in use afore now, so even if his son was to have talked, he wouldn't of known to talk of this place."

"But if we were caught—if, for instance, a neighbor thought it odd to see smoke rising from the chimney of an abandoned house and reported it—what would be the charge laid against us?"

"Bless you, what worse can they do than if they took you up for smuggling? The price for getting caught with your face blackened at night is hanging. Dead is dead, boy, no matter the charge. You knows what they say—as best be hanged for a sheep as a goat."

Harry rose without another word and went outside to wash his face at the pump. But the shock of cold water on his skin was insufficient to ease the sick feeling in his gut.

He looked about him at the neglected garden, the wasted fields dripping in the rain. Could he simply walk away, attempt to retrace his steps till he arrived at Brimstone Lane and could make his way home? He longed to make the attempt but knew the others would not risk letting him go; if he disappeared now they would presume he was bent on betraying them. They had traveled beyond all that was familiar to him, and he would be casting about to find his way while the batmen ran him down. Harry returned to the house.

The day was long and it seemed night would never fall, but at last they were left with nothing but the firelight. Still they waited, but it was not till after the waxing crescent had set that they heard a signal: three descending whistles. Tomkins bolted to his feet and opened the door to return the signal. Steps were heard approaching the cottage, and "the King's shilling" was named.

In came the Sussex men, eight rough coves who smelled like the sea. The fire was doused and the ashes scraped aside; Tomkins reopened the hidden chamber and Harry crawled back in. He dragged the sacks one by one to the opening and they were snatched away. The Sussex men exchanged no pleasantries with their Surrey counterparts; they simply seized the bags and bore them out to a cart waiting in the lane, and then they were gone.

With the departure of the guineas, the mood lightened. The blacksmith proposed that they all return to the Bottle and Glass and hoist a pint; Harry said nothing for or against this plan, but he was determined to put himself at a safe distance from the company as soon as he could. He wanted desperately to return home, but his arrival at a late hour of the night would prompt too many unanswerable questions. He felt unequal to the invention of a plausible lie, and the very idea of lying any more to his family only increased his exhaustion. Yet the truth was unspeakable— so home was out of the question.

As they at last approached the Bottle and Glass, Tomkins paused and meted out to them all their pay, four shillings apiece instead of the usual two. Harry, casting about for a way to separate from the party, remembered that Heathfields was hard by, and he contemplated curling up in the hay with the horses there. But after making his farewells to Tomkins and the batmen, it occurred to him that he had other connections close at hand, people who knew something of his situation and might be counted on to offer him comfort. So it was that scarcely a half-hour later, Harry made his way to the door of Stumblehole Farm.

After he had knocked for several minutes, a sleepy Uncle Steer opened the door, and he was welcomed in. The kitchen fire was long since banked, but whatever of cold food that might be found in the pantry was offered to him, and he when he had eaten his fill he was taken to his cousin's bedchamber. Uncle Steer adjured Dick to roll over and make room, and Harry curled up against his cousin's back and knew no more.

CHAPTER THE TWENTY-FIRST

The night's sleep restored a measure of Harry's optimism, and the warmth of Dick's welcome, after he awoke to find Harry there, sent some of Harry's terrors into hiding. His activities over the previous day and a half could not be canvassed openly before Dick's sisters, but Aunt Steer was voluble in her expressions of pleasure at his safety, and Dick whispered that he was glad Harry had come to no harm.

After their breakfast, Aunt Steer loaded Harry with baskets of plums from the orchard and strawberries from the garden and sent him on his way home to Henfold. With every step he took past Heathfields he felt a little lighter in his heart, despite his burdens, and he was almost skipping by the time he arrived at his own gate. He heard his mother humming in the dairy and turned aside from the door to greet her.

Mrs. Steer paused in her churning. "Harry! You're home already! I had not thought to see you for hours. And look at all you've brought us—your aunt is too generous. Strawberries! Isabella will be overjoyed."

"My aunt was very grateful for the cheese you sent."

"Well, we must all share what we have aplenty of. And

look at you! Your hands are not stained at all from the berry-picking. I must ask your aunt how she managed to keep you clean; the Lord knows I cannot. How is Dick going along?"

"He is on the mend, Mama."

"That will be a comfort to your aunt and uncle. Mr. Marshall is not yet returned, so here's a free day for you by way of reward for your goodness in helping your cousins. How shall you spend it?"

Over the past twenty-four hours Harry had come to see himself as involved in such wickedness that the idea of having earned a reward left him nonplussed. What he longed for more than anything was to be restored to normality, to belonging within his own family, to an end to secrets, but forty sacks of gold were piled between them, raising an insuperable barrier. He hesitated, and knew he was hesitating too long to offer a simple answer to a simple question. At last he blurted, "I should like to help on the farm. What can I do for you, or for Papa?"

Mrs. Steer laughed and ruffled his hair. "Have you been tied to your lessons for so long you've forgot how to amuse yourself? This is not the adventuresome Harry I know. Who has stolen off with him, and replaced him with this pillar of rectitude?"

The notion of seeking adventure was anathema to Harry in his present state of mind, but he could not explain that to his mother. He merely said, "There were further stands of blackcurrants and gooseberries I saw in the hedgerows but had not time to pick, and besides Aunt Steer said she had enough. Would you like me to gather some for you?"

Mrs. Steer eyed him speculatively. "Might I ask—or is it too great a tax on your newfound saintliness—that you take your sister with you and show her where the best berries are? Next year you won't be here to gather them." The thought of his banishment to school struck him to the heart, and so great was Harry's lately acquired attachment to home and hearth that he agreed.

They set out under skies still overhung with cloud. Isabella, secretly delighted by her promotion to the status of companion to her brother, was on her best behavior, and she withheld her sharper comments even when they discovered that birds or other children had gone ahead of them and stripped some of the most flourishing hedgerows of their fruit. She attended solemnly to his instructions, well knowing that boys derive pleasure from explaining matters to girls, and promised to remember how to find the best spots next year. Thus encouraged, Harry also showed her where the sweet chestnuts and filberts were ripening. She even withheld complaint when they were interrupted by a passing shower, and joined him in waiting it out under a giant oak.

They were not the only children abroad on this Saturday; it seemed the woods and lanes were alive with the ragged offspring of poor families, all bent on gleaning sustenance off the common lands and roadsides. Harry was acquainted with many of them: during past harvests they had been his playmates among the stooks, and for a few moments he could deceive himself that he was still one of their number. But a chasm had opened between them as soon as his father had set him to preparing for Winchester, and it had only widened when he acquired experiences he could never divulge. His impulsive offer to go berrying for his mother, far from marking a return to his old life, only laid bare how great a distance he had traveled during the course of one summer, and how impossible it was to find his way back. The loneliness of it stabbed at his heart.

At length he and Isabella did fill their baskets, but they were both footsore and hungry by the time they turned their steps homeward. Mr. Marshall had returned with tidings that his mother was on the mend, and dinner was waiting for them; Harry's interval of liberty was over.

Mr. Steer, who had spent the day assessing his fields and visiting the cottages of his laborers to warn them that they must stand in readiness, was alight with hope for the harvest. "If the weather is fair on the morrow, the black oats shall be ready for the start of reaping on Monday," he said, helping himself to another slice of mutton on the strength of this prospect. "I do believe that by the time the wheat and the beans are in, we shall be hard put to find space enough for it all. I must be speedy in getting the surplus corn to market before the prices begin to drop. If only the weather should favor us for the next fortnight, we shall see well over four quarters to the acre for the corn. I am glad I thought to plant so much of the white Dantzic; it should fetch a pretty penny."

"That is excellent news," said Mrs. Steer; "perhaps then I shall be able to purchase carrots to replace those eaten by the rabbits in the garden."

"Carrots, ay, and what about muslin for new dresses for you and Isabella?" said Mr. Steer, his optimistic humor expanding to embrace the entire family.

Isabella was elated, but Mrs. Steer was more cautious. "Perhaps we might rebuild the henhouse first and then see where we find ourselves. There are Harry's school fees to be paid, after all."

"I am counting on the beans for that. I have read that beans are much in demand for feeding the slaves in the West Indies, so I shall try if I can locate an export agent who will market them for me."

"Do you intend to bag the corn or cut it with the sickle?" asked Harry.

"There is little to be gained, I believe, by putting the men to the extra labor of bagging. We have an ample supply of hay from the clover harvest; and in a year like this one, I won't begrudge the gleaners their full share."

Mr. Marshall then betrayed his ignorance by inquiring when the hops were to be cut. After general laughter, Mr. Steer informed him that his plantation was no more than an early experiment, on the only one of his fields that offered suitable conditions, and Mr. Marshall was welcome to return for a visit after another fourteen months had passed to observe the first harvest.

Harry smiled as he looked about him at the happy faces; in that moment, his life appeared almost ordinary and the Tilts' enterprises belonged to another world. He continued in lighter spirits through their attendance at church the next day, when—having learned his lesson—Mr. Steer decreed that the entire family should walk this time, and allowed his wife a few minutes to visit with neighbors in the churchyard afterward. Even when Harry's studies resumed on Monday, he was able to meet them with equanimity; it is possible even to say he had learned to feel that concentrating his attention on declensions and the tortuous syntax of the Latin tongue afforded his mind a measure of peace, or at least a distraction from the things he would much prefer not to think about.

At night, however—when he was alone in his bed, waiting for the cool breezes of midnight to relieve the heat of the day—his thoughts reverted to the captain and Milord and the puzzle of the guineas. Night after night passed and the moon waxed to the full without his being called to take part in another run. Once more doubts began to press on him. Had Tomkins divined Harry's discomfort with the task and reported it to the captain, placing Harry once more under suspicion? Were the Tilts themselves lying low after the Battle of the Bottle and Glass, hoping the Excise would lose interest and send the Yeoman Cavalry elsewhere? Isolated as he was at Henfold, Harry could obtain no reliable intelligence to feed or starve his speculations. And the gold sat on his heart like a malignancy.

In the meantime, his father was absent from first light until dusk, overseeing the progress of the harvest. Mrs. Steer and even little Isabella were kept on the hop bearing sustenance and refreshment to the laboring men, organizing the women in tying up the sheaves, and watching over the gleaners. Even Nat and Janey were rarely at home, for everyone except Harry and Mr. Marshall had a role to play in the effort. The hot, dry weather held, so it was no more than five days before the precious white Dantzic wheat began to be brought under cover, and Harry was forever being distracted by the sound of bells on the draft horses' harness as the wagons turned in at the farmyard gate, the men singing as the bounty was brought under shelter. Even so, he made greater progress in his studies during these weeks than he had done all summer long, and he began to feel some small portion of the satisfaction Mr. Marshall derived from reading the classics. Perhaps the advantage lay only in their capacity for diverting him from his worries, but that was a benefit not to be held cheap.

Harry's fears, however, had their own notion of their claims upon him and asserted themselves abruptly again when he heard a knock on the door. There being nary a soul in the house but himself and his tutor, it was Harry who went down to answer it.

Before him on the doorstep stood Mr. Rose, the constable of Capel parish, mopping his brow. "Is your father within?" he inquired.

His mind racing to discovery and capture, Harry replied in a shaky voice, "No, he is in the fields with the harvest; my mother as well."

"Perhaps he might be sent for?" asked Mr. Rose, eyeing the cool interior of the house hopefully.

Harry strove to overcome the disorder of his thoughts and present an appearance of normalcy. Taking the hint so broadly offered by the constable, he said, "Won't you come in?" He conducted Mr. Rose to the parlor, instead of the kitchen where he more properly belonged, and offered him refreshment with mechanical civility. The appearance of the constable on Henfold's doorstep was an unprecedented event, and Harry's guilty conscience could imagine only one thing: that he must be found out.

By the time he had Mr. Rose settled with a mug of porter, Harry had come up with the rudiments of a strategy. "I believe it may be difficult for my father to leave his duties at just this present. Would you be able to state your errand to me, that I might carry the message to him and return with his reply?"

To Harry's immense relief, Mr. Rose saw no difficulty with this proposal. "That'd be mighty helpful, Master Steer," he said, settling more comfortably into his seat. "It's like this, you see: the captain of the Yeoman Cavalry what's stationed at Darking has heard a report of an illicit cargo of a particular kind what's said to be passing through Darking Hundred. While the militiamen are looking into the inns and taverns and other suchlike places, all the constables as can be spared is sent out to search every outbuilding and cottage on all the farms. Your barns and granaries might be being used without your knowing it."

"How very exciting—and how exhausting such a task must be for you," said Harry with spurious sympathy. "What does this cargo look like? And how may we help you in this search?"

Mr. Rose sighed. "I wish I was allowed to recruit assistance, but orders is that I do it all meself. This ain't the usual stuff, casks of brandy or bolts of silk."

"I understand," said Harry, understanding far more than the constable could know. "I have no doubt my father will readily grant his consent. Do us the honor of resting here for a time while I seek him out." And after refilling Mr. Rose's tankard, Harry sped on his way.

The harvesters, he knew, had finished with the upper, drier fields and were now working among the heavy soils of the Wealden acres, so he was not long in locating his father. Mr. Steer, too busy to be curious about the constable's unusual request, agreed to it immediately, stipulating only that Harry accompany Mr. Rose to ensure that his activities did no harm to corn or cattle. Well pleased with this mandate, Harry returned to Mr. Rose, now much refreshed by Henfold's hospitality.

The constable baulked at first over the requirement that Harry shadow him, but the promise of one of Mrs. Steer's cheeses at the end reconciled him to this minor divergence from his accustomed practice. So Harry graciously conducted him through the stable, the granaries, the barn, the wash-house, the poultry-house, and the dairy, watching with growing amusement as Mr. Rose stabbed a rake handle into every pile of hay, turned over tubs, and peered into barrels. He occasionally asked helpful questions: "Are the objects you seek small enough to fit into a bucket, or may we overlook those?" or "Might they have been put down the coal hole?"—which in time informed him that the dimensions of the contraband being sought were not incompatible with the sacks of guineas.

At the end he dismissed Mr. Rose to the tenants' cottages with the cheese and a note signed on behalf of his father granting authority to search their premises, and he was left to his own thoughts.

These were not of a happy order, even though he was certain that the gold he had been responsible for was long gone and he doubted more had passed through since, there having been too much moon for the pursuit of such activities. It was evident the authorities had developed remarkably reliable sources of intelligence; exposure was altogether too close for comfort. Not only were they able to track the smugglers during the ordinary course of their journeys, as the late battle had proved, but they also knew some part at least of the other business. Once again he wished he had some means of communicating his alarm to the captain and Milord, but taking even a boy away from the fields at this moment to run an errand would attract unwelcome notice. And what could he say in such a message? How could he possibly raise the alarm without using words that would be incriminating if intercepted?

It must also be acknowledged that a corner of Harry's heart was now unsure whether sending a warning to the Tilts was the right thing to do. Try as he might, he could imagine no licit use for those damnable guineas. If the government were transporting the money from one place to the next, it would be accompanied by a force of armed outriders and would travel by daylight. The secrecy—the very use of free-traders for the task—implied the reverse of legitimate intent. And the illegitimacy of the enterprise imposed certain duties on the part of an upstanding citizen. Yet Harry felt very much too small to put his finger

on the scale of justice in the matter; the best he could hope
was that the Tilts might summon him no more.

With these reflections he made his way slowly back to
his tutor, but this time his lessons were powerless to hold
his attention.

And so the moonlit weeks passed and the nights began to
be darker again. No word came to Harry from the outside
world until his mother returned from the Darking market
day, one Thursday early in August, with a full budget of
news. As the family sat over their tea, she repeated the
salient events that Mr. Steer would later read about in
greater detail in the newspapers she had brought home—
the Acts of Union were agreed to by the Irish Parliament;
there were rumors of an armistice with France but nothing
was confirmed; the House of Lords had proposed the cre-
ation of a Flour and Bread Company, which was believed
bound to distort yet further the price of wheat and compel
ordinary folk to buy only dark bread.

"Then I must see to it that my excess wheat is sold
before they can act," said Mr. Steer with determination.
"How do the lords up in London imagine we are all to
survive, here in the countryside, while they continue to
consider only the needs of the Crown and the army? Will
they never leave off bleeding the calf that is raised to
feed them?"

"Perhaps it will come to naught," said Mrs. Steer. "But
that was not the subject of all the talk in the High today.
A man was grossly mutilated! And the circumstances are
most peculiar."

Politics and world affairs were all forgot; here was
real, local news, and her audience was rapt. "It seems no
effort was made to conceal the deed," she continued. "His

tongue was cut out and he was left in the stocks, although it is believed, from the absence of blood at the scene, that the mutilation happened elsewhere. The poor soul is unlettered, so he is unable to tell who committed the crime. But the most peculiar aspect of the affair was that when he was discovered, thirty shillings were laid out in rows on the earth beside his feet."

Isabella listened to the news with a mixture of horror and excitement that was most delightful to her sensibilities, but Harry, whose mind was racing to connect this dreadful act to the burden of secrets he bore, was paralyzed with terror. He must learn more but could not find courage to speak.

His father, for whom the event was little more than a curiosity, was answering his mother. "Thirty shillings! A not inconsiderable sum to leave behind, simply to make a point. So it was intended that people should learn of the deed and should understand him to be a Judas. It sounds very much like a falling-out among thieves."

Harry finally managed to force out a question. "Has the unfortunate victim been named?"

"I do not know his name, but it is said he is a servant in the household of Redlands Farm."

A part of Harry had been certain of the answer even before hearing it, but the confirmation was dreadful to him. So the captain and Milord had identified the spy who was betraying them to the Excise as a member of their own household, and had made certain that anyone else tempted to play them false would be warned of the consequences. He sat, his tea forgotten, hearing nothing as his parents continued to examine every detail of the event. He could not escape the image in his mind of a mutilated man trapped in the stocks, wild-eyed, struggling to escape, struggling to name his assailant. His own tongue felt huge in his mouth as he felt what it must be like to be seized and held down, the knife coming closer to one's face, the terror and the agony, the choking on one's own blood.

Harry attempted to reconcile in his mind the brutal fact of the mutilation, and the man who could order it done, with the captain, the man he had come to admire and trust; but the two were resolutely incompatible. One must be real and the other imaginary—and he could not escape concluding which was which.

Aided by Milord's representations to him, Harry had construed in his mind a justification for the free-trade that appeared seamlessly reasonable. And if he were to be truthful, the very lawlessness of the enterprise had appealed to Harry; it was thrilling to loosen the bonds of his daily life and join a band of men taking their fate into their own hands.

But the presence of the man in the stocks made a mockery of it all. The very memory of his prior views was now mortifying to Harry; he suffered from the contemplation of them. Instead of a united cohort working together toward a common end of bringing plenty to the land, the smugglers now appeared as prisoners to a brutal master who would go to any lengths to prevent exposure. Milord, the elder Mr. Tilt, had been a formidable enough figure when met face to face, but now he loomed as a veritable monster in Harry's imagination, a Cyclops whose eye was always upon them all and never slept. With greater ease could he imagine Milord attacking his servant than the captain, but Milord was after all an old man, and Harry had seen enough to understand that while he might be the master-mind of the business, the captain was its hands. It was a crushing blow.

CHAPTER THE TWENTY-SECOND

The stone on the stableyard wall now became an object of dread. Every time Harry passed a window that overlooked it, his eye was drawn toward it and his breath suspended till he could see no paper visible beneath it. Every night he prayed that no summons would be delivered—that the Tilts had forgotten him, or no longer found him useful, or were under too imminent a threat from the authorities to ply their trade. It was now hardly more than a fortnight before he was to be sent away to school, and this banishment, which had always appeared so cruel, was all he longed for. His mother had sewn his supply of shirts and Mr. Marshall was testing him daily on all he had learned; there was nothing further to hold him here.

And yet such was the stubbornness of Harry's temper that he clung to his desire to remain at home—albeit a home freed by a miracle from the encroachments of terror. He longed to be told how to unravel his involvement, longed for someone who could step in and make everything right again. His father continued to be absent every waking hour about the harvest or in the granaries, seeing to the stacking and the turning; Harry saw little of him from one day to the next. Had he been more present, however, what could Harry have asked of him? To confess his nocturnal adventures was impossible—and without a full confession, no advice could be sought. Nor could his mother ever be asked to assume such a burden of knowledge and the risk that came with it. Mr. Marshall, though a man grown, had always appeared somehow childlike in his single-minded devotion to the world of his classical texts. There was no wisdom to be sought in that quarter. After every hour of fruitless reflection on the subject, Harry was obliged to conclude that the burden was his and his alone. And each night the moon continued to wane.

The following Thursday came around and both of his parents were up at dawn with Nat, loading the precious white Dantzic wheat onto hired wagons to carry it in to the corn market in Darking. This was the day the family's fortunes were to be made—at least for the year to come. Isabella rode with them, excited at the promise of new clothes and shoes. Mr. Marshall drilled Harry in his Greek grammar all the morning, but in the afternoon the fineness of the day enticed them out of doors, where the tutor told Harry tales of the Grecian gods and goddesses, their noble deeds and their petty quarrels. The sun and the heat made them both a little sleepy, and after dining tête-à-tête, both felt impelled to retire to their rooms for a nap until the rest of the household returned. Harry, as was his habit, glanced out his window toward the wall—and froze. There was a paper under the stone.

He considered simply going to sleep. It seemed the easiest thing to do, to pretend he had seen nothing. And yet—there was the man in the stocks with no tongue. If Harry did not appear when summoned, what would the captain and Milord think? Surely the worst; and then not only Harry but also his family would be in peril. He could not be responsible for bringing the wrath of the Tilts down upon them. Perhaps it would be easier to comply for now, until it came time for him to go to school. When he saw the captain he would explain that he was being sent away; perhaps he might even lie a little and say his day of departure came sooner than it really did. If he did so, this might be his last night in the smuggling trade! To protect his family and to extricate himself without evil consequence, he must follow orders one last time.

He descended the stair, sick in the pit of his stomach, and stumbled outside. Knowing the place to be deserted, he went straight to the wall and plucked down the note. He did not even retreat to the necessary for secrecy but read it on the spot.

What he saw filled him with cold horror. It read, "Ten horses from the stable. The Whites at sundown." The hand was not the rough one of Cursemother Jack; it was better formed, and spelled correctly, and Harry was certain it must have come straight from the captain.

He sat down on the back step, staring at the words till they blurred. Perhaps he could will the letters to split apart and form themselves into a different message. He had been hardening his courage to read "Five Bells" or "Swan's Mill," but this—! How could he possibly summon the fortitude to collect another fortune in guineas and transport it to the deserted farm beyond Newdigate? Of a certainty it would be wrong to do so; and the Yeoman Cavalry and the constables were all on the watch.

As if such considerations were not dire enough, as a purely practical matter he could not see how the task was to be achieved. Should the venture prosper, he would be gone for all the next day and into the evening. What excuse could he possibly make for such a disappearance? Obeying this summons would mean certain discovery.

But to disobey—the consequences were too horrible to contemplate. He sat on, so possessed by fear that he could neither move nor think. His eyes darted about yet he was unable to recognize the old familiar walls, the cobbles of the courtyard, the dairy, the stable, the pump.

At last a kind of desperation took hold of him. Every moment he delayed, the retribution of the captain and Milord drew closer to his family, to their farm, their cattle and sheep, their house, their prosperity, their respectability, their very lives. Harry must not be the one to invite their destruction. That could never happen, and he knew only one way to prevent it. He got to his feet, climbed back up to his room to retrieve some shillings, and walked away, putting one foot before the other as he made for Brimstone Lane on his road to Heathfields. He left no message for his parents.

The journey seemed short, reluctant as he was to reach his destination. Old Joll met him as before and offered his hat again, but Harry declined it. It seemed to him that even if he met neighbors or friends along the way, they would never recognize him, so altered as he felt himself to be. His movements were deliberate but his thoughts were wild, racing from panic to determination and from sacrifice to resentment all in a moment. The horses felt his unease and moved about restlessly, at cross-purposes with one another. After the second time they became entangled, Harry knew he had to calm his mind so their unruliness would not draw unwonted attention; he achieved a measure of peace at last by concentrating on detail—keep the horses' leads taut, move them forward with purpose, keep to the greensward where possible, stay on the side away from the other travelers on the road. Every step away from Henfold separated him more securely from his family, improving their chances of safety but also severing him from them forever.

He approached the Giles Green tollgate on the northern side of Darking without hesitation this time and presented his payment, but came under scrutiny from the gatekeeper. "You got far to go with them prads?" the man inquired; "'Tis near on nightfall."

"Jest up by Norbury Park," replied Harry, remembering to speak like a stableboy.

The man grunted and let him pass; but even as the horses were moving through the gate, he was scrawling out a note and handing it to his son, who made off at a run for Darking. Harry caught a glimpse of the boy but thought little of it: even had he aroused suspicion, those seeking him around Norbury Park would seek in vain.

This time, he had to loiter a bit on the road before the way was deserted enough for him to lead his string undetected onto the path to the meadows beside the Mole. Although the shadows were gathering, he took extra care in concealing the horses before seeking his familiar seat on the fallen trunk. He commenced to wait there, reclining in a caricature of ease, till night and his companions should arrive.

It was the batmen who appeared first, Slug and the blacksmith and the others, all in a group. It was clear to see that they were almost as nervous as Harry; this night there was no banter. "Tomkins ain't here?" asked Slug, and after Harry whispered that he wasn't, no one spoke further.

In the silence the night sounds became intrusive. The treetops swayed, uttering the gentlest of sighs; something, perhaps an eel, slipped across the river's surface with a prolonged hiss; small animals agitated the tangle. Each new sound was felt by the watchers to promise a threat, till its source could be identified and they might relax for a moment before startling again.

At last there came sounds identifiably human as someone blundered along the path toward them. They started up, only to hear the three descending notes of the signal; they replied and Tomkins joined them, breathless.

"The Yeoman Cavalry be on the road tonight," he said on a wheezing breath. "They passed me twice, once northbound by the nursery-ground in Darking and again southbound, hard by this spot. Seems they're riding back and forth along this very stretch of road."

"Between here and Norbury, I'll wager," whispered Harry. "The gatekeeper questioned me about where I was going with the horses, and I told him Norbury Park."

"This'll be a chancy business tonight," said Tomkins. "We must hope the cart don't come off the downs and straight into their arms. If the carter makes it this far, we'll unload as fast as we can and take the horses down along the river till we're south of Darking, then find a track or a ride that puts us back on course."

"And if the carter doesn't make it this far?" asked one of the batmen.

"Then we lie up here till morning and each of us takes a couple of horses to lead back to Heathfields, by separate ways."

With this semblance of a plan they had to be content. The night advanced and the moon set, extinguishing the brilliance of the chalk cliffs across the river and reducing them to hulking shadows. There was no joking or story-telling tonight: the watchers sat quietly, waving off the assault of insects, ears on the stretch for sounds from the road. At last they heard the rumble of a cart, and with one accord they crept closer, keeping to whatever cover they could find.

One of their concealed horses whinnied to its fellow on the road and Slug turned aside to quiet it. The cart slowed and halted, and they heard the signal; Tomkins and the others set off at a run, stumbling over the uneven ground and bursting onto the verge in a group. The carter raised a pistol before Tomkins remembered to answer the signal and deliver the password.

"We must be quick—the militia are on the road tonight!" he told the carter. By way of answer the man leaped off his seat and set about hurling his load of sacks onto the turf beside the opening of the path. The batmen and Tomkins hastened to snatch them up and haul them out of sight; time enough to carry them down to the horses when all was clear on the roadway.

Harry hovered by the cart, anxious and uncertain. Because he was only strong enough to drag one sack at a time he was of little use to the party at this juncture, so he appointed himself a watchman and peered up and down the road in the gloom. When the carter had finished unloading, he suddenly clapped his hand to his coat. "Bless me if I hadn't forgot! These are to travel with the cargo." He pulled out a thick sheaf of papers, tied up with string, and thrust the packet at Harry before mounting up on his cart and turning the horse around.

Harry stowed the papers inside his shirt, returned to the path, and picked up one of the sacks still waiting there. He had carried it no more than a dozen steps, staggering under its weight, before he heard what they all dreaded: a group of horses cantering up the road from the south.

"Halt!" cried a voice, and Harry, looking back, could see the carter drawing up to obey. Harry dropped the sack of gold and fell to his knees, crawling in under the cover of a hazel. Slowly he began to retreat from the road on all fours, down toward the river, shaking and panting with the pound of his heart. Twigs snagged his clothing and scratched his face. It was everything he had most dreaded come to life; all he wanted to do was sink into the earth, but he had to try to think through his panic.

He could hear the militiamen questioning the carter, who was whining out a tale about having had to wait in Darking till nightfall for a farmer who had promised to buy his pig but was late returning to him with the payment. They did not believe him, however, for although his cart was empty of any incriminating objects, the militiamen commenced searching about the verges for any signs of an abandoned load. It did not take them long to discover the existence of the path. One man shouted for a light; they seized the carter's lantern and aimed it in Harry's direction.

Panic seized him till he realized he was by now far enough away to avoid being caught in its beams, but the remaining sacks of gold were plain enough to see. The militiamen fell upon them with a shout; the carter attempted to flee, but was seized. Harry couldn't stand it any longer: he took to his heels.

Amid the noise and excitement by the side of the road, one boy running might have passed unnoticed. But the shouts of the militiamen had driven the rest of Harry's party to desperate measures, and suddenly the meadows were alive with the trampling of horses, a few unburdened, others running free with sacks tied to their backs, and some bearing the batmen and Tomkins, riding in every direction for their lives. Harry tried to snatch the lead of one horse as it stampeded past him but was unable to hang on; it snapped through his fingers, leaving him with a wrenched shoulder and a welt on his palm. He ran back toward the river, pushed his way into a bramble, crawled under the hanging branches of a willow at the water's edge, and fetched up against its trunk, well-hidden on the landward side—or so he hoped—behind the curtain of leaves.

For a long time there was pandemonium, men and horses racing about, shouts and the flickering of the lantern making all confusion. He could not say whether any of his companions had been captured, but at the very least the militiamen must be unconvinced of their success, for after a while they regrouped, sent two of their number off to the tollgate for more lanterns, and began a systematic search.

Harry slid to the earth and leaned against the comforting solidity of the willow's trunk, shivering as the perspiration dried on his neck. He waited breathless for what seemed like hours, unmoving as insects attacked his neck and hands, while the militiamen combed the area, moving in a phalanx from a point well to the south and all the way up to the pleasure-gardens of Burford Lodge. Harry wondered what Mr. Barclay must be thinking of the disturbance—did he understand that his plan had gone awry? Was he cowering in fear of discovery? But he of course enjoyed the protections of a gentleman, so he remained within his own walls with all the appearance of blamelessness. Harry both envied and resented him.

The terror of discovery gripped Harry in the chest and he was certain it was only a matter of time before some man pushed through the willow branches to pin him down. He stayed curled up, cornered like an animal, when the lights flickered on the leaves above his head as they approached his hiding place. And yet, for all their care in searching, the militiamen failed to fight past the brambles and discover Harry. At long last he saw no more lights and heard no more voices and was able to relax a little, believing he was alone.

Chapter the Twenty-third

Although the militiamen were gone Harry remained where he was, unmoving and wakeful. By the very deprivation of his visual senses, every sound of the night creatures, every brush of wind startled him and his overanxious mind had to examine it before he might dismiss it as harmless. The willow branches brushed slyly against one another with each puff of breeze, sounding like stealthy footsteps. The fears of the night piled atop desperation until he was seized by blind terror, frozen in place with a mind closed off to all reason. His heart galloped in panic; all he knew or believed dropped away; he was turned inside out and presented to his stunned mind a stranger.

Thinking was impossible, reasoning beyond him. He crouched behind the tree, shaking and too terrified even to cry. And thus he stayed until the darkness began to ebb, and in the gray foredawn he was able once again to look about him and find comfort in familiar landmarks, settling back by gradual degrees into his own mind.

There was a small sandy shoal at the foot of the willow. Where it was a little submerged, gudgeon were swimming to and fro, wriggling into the open only to dart back under the roots of the tree when startled. The faintest of rustles sounded in the water tangle around Harry's hideout and a hedgehog crept out, snuffled at the toe of his shoe, murmured quietly, and moved on. With a whistle of pinions, two ducks flew in from somewhere, landed on the river, and commenced dabbling in the shallows. With a shock Harry became aware that all along, a kingfisher had been perched on a low branch just beside him, glaring down its beak at the water. If he had missed such a brilliantly plumaged bird, what else had he failed to observe? It was a humbling and unsettling idea.

The gudgeon fled again and a moment later an otter swam upstream, only its head glistening above the surface of the water; just after it passed beyond Harry's sight, he heard its whistling call, answered by another farther off. Overhead and among the rushes the birds began one by one to sing, until the dawn chorus filled the air and Harry sat enraptured in a cathedral of sound. It was impossible to cling to his terrors with such beauty surrounding him; the splendor lifted his spirit as if cradling him in the hand of Providence. But the ebbing panic only made space for despair as the truth struck him in the face—all this treasure of the world he loved, so gloriously spread out around him, was now most likely lost to him forever.

With the advance of the light, however, other thoughts slowly began to supplant the miseries that fed upon his spirit. The assurance of the wild creatures told him there were no other people about and he began to entertain a tiny measure of hope. Perhaps it might be possible for him simply to walk away and return home, inventing some excuse for his overnight absence. If any of the other smugglers had escaped, the captain and Milord would soon be aware that Harry had turned up at the appointed time and done as he was told. And surely, after the past night's debacle, all smuggling would be suspended until after Harry was safely away at school.

He stirred, stretching to ease the ache in sinews too long motionless, and felt the papers inside his shirt rustle and prickle at his skin. They had been forgotten in the horrors of the night. He tried to puzzle over what they might portend and whether he should discard them or try to deliver them to the Tilts, but hunger and fatigue were dulling his mind and his thoughts drifted away from speculation. Perhaps he could look in on his cousins at Stumblehole and beg a meal. The idea gave him comfort, and as the light grew and the river slipped gently past him he drowsed for a time, not fully asleep but not yet willing to rise and face what was to come.

Soon, however, the sound of wagons and carriages on the road informed him that the world was abroad, and he crawled to his feet, moving awkwardly on prickling feet as he climbed out of the thicket. A hare stood up in the meadow and then lolloped away, but there were no shouts; no heavy hand fell upon his shoulder. He moved slowly up the path, reentered the roadway in the shadow of a heavy wagon bearing casks for delivery to the inns of Darking, and set his face southward. He even indulged a secret smile at the thought that his escort into the town was to be an innocent load of legal spirits.

He came up to the tollgate and paused with the wagon as if he belonged to it, awaiting the gatekeeper's emergence. The man came out of his house, holding a tankard he was polishing with a rag, a word of greeting on his lips for the driver; but no sooner had he caught sight of Harry than he gave a shout, dropped the tankard, and dived to seize him.

Harry tried to whisk around to the other side of the draft horses, but his exhaustion made him sluggish and the gatekeeper got a firm hold on his arm. "Here's one of 'em!" he cried; "I have the one as brought the horses!" There was a clatter and three militiamen rushed out of the gatekeeper's cottage. They surrounded Harry and flung him to the ground, pinning him with their knees.

His breath knocked out of him, Harry struggled but could not move. The driver gaped at him until ordered by the gatekeeper to move along and not block the way. The men searched Harry roughly and found the sheaf of papers.

"What be these?" one demanded.

"I don't know," gasped Harry as the pressure on his chest eased slightly. This earned him a clout to the side of his head, and he added, still breathless, "A man gave them to me—told me to keep them safe. I never met him— before." It sounded implausible even to his own ears. Why hadn't he dropped them in the river?

The gatekeeper, evidently believing he had a role to play in the drama unfolding on his doorstep, now demanded, "Where be them horses you was leading?"

"I took 'em to Norbury, like I said," replied Harry, remembering belatedly to speak like a groom.

"That you didn't, young good-for-naught," said the gatekeeper. "I told the sergeant I suspicioned you, a-leading of all them horses about jest afore nightfall. I told him you said you was making for Norbury, and he went there and asked. There was no horses delivered there, nor none expected, neither."

One of the militiamen then thanked the gatekeeper for his assistance and told him to hold his tongue about the business. To his comrades he muttered, "We need to get him to the sergeant right quick." So they hauled Harry to his feet and marched him along the road to Darking. Through tears he was dimly aware of people staring and the mutterings of speculation, but he kept his head down and concentrated on putting one foot before the other. Humiliated and defeated, his mind a jumble of formless terrors, he could do no more than remain upright and move at the pace set by his captors.

They bore him off to the Wheatsheaf Inn and thrust him down upon a bench, right under the nose of the giant stuffed hog that made the hostelry so famous—but Harry was in no humor to admire this wonder of nature. Two guards remained by his side while the sergeant was sought for consultation. In due course he came, a burly man who might have been a butcher or a blacksmith in his civilian life. Word had reached Darking's constable there had been an arrest, and he came puffing up as well, dressed all by guess. They examined Harry, unimpressed till one of the men handed over the packet of papers. The sergeant turned them over and over in his hands, his face grave, as the militiamen began their report. Harry, numb with exhaustion, listened as if they were speaking about someone else.

"You've not so much to go on," interrupted the constable after a moment, eager to assert his authority. "The horses are suspicious, I grant you, but you never seen him with them. He don't look like much of a ruffian to me. He's but a slip of a boy. And he don't have no run goods in his possession, so what could you charge him with? What are these papers about?"

The sergeant seized on this opening. "Our orders from the Lord Lieutenant, Lord Onslow, says we was to look for papers, but not to look *at* 'em. Privy secrets, they be. If papers was found, we was to bring 'em to Lord Onslow as fast as may be."

"We did also recover some sacks of gold last night as well, hard by where we came across this imp of Satan," added one of the men.

The constable gasped. "Sacks of *gold?*"

"Ay, this ain't no ordinary smuggling case," said the sergeant with satisfaction. "And this boy prob'ly knows where the rest of the loot is hid. We needs to get truth out of him as soon as may be. This be a right serious business."

"And how do you plan to do that?" scoffed the constable. "Do you mean to drag him halfway across the county to meet my lord Onslow, in the hope he's at home just waiting to receive you? Better the boy stay right here in Darking and be brought up before the nearest magistrate, I'd swear. That'd be Sir Nugent Lumley-Dacre-Prudhoe. He lives at Pippbrook House, just past the eastern end of High Street."

"But these papers is too important to be handed to just anyone! I has my orders, and they said naught about no magistrate."

"Well, if you have all the time in the world, I suppose you could haul this boy about the countryside in a cart. But I am commissioned with keeping the peace here, and if this boy is thick with smugglers in *my* borough—smugglers of gold no less!—then my duty is clear: to present him to the magistrate."

The sergeant wavered. As little as the constable wished it did he look forward to chasing down Lord Onslow. Too much could go wrong. Partridge shooting began in a few days, after all, and his lordship might have gone off who knows where with a party of friends in pursuit of sport. How were they to keep the sacks of gold secure in the meanwhile?

"I'll have a messenger carry a report to the Lord Lieutenant," he said at last, "and we'll present the boy to Sir Nugent without delay."

Having won his point, however, the constable now began to vacillate. "It's right early in the day to be disturbing Sir Nugent: he's the sort of gentleman as keeps to himself till midday, if you take my meaning. Mayhap we should lock up the boy till later, and then you can make your case."

The constable's reluctance only steeled the sergeant's spine in opposition, as the vision of no longer being obliged to defend a fortune in gold grew in appeal. "This affair's too important for us to kick our heels," he declared. "I say we present the case to Sir Nugent straight away."

"On your head be it, then," said the constable, no more capable than his adversary of coming to agreement. They hauled Harry to his feet again and ventured forth, several militiamen following with the retrieved sacks of gold. With a proprietary air the constable escorted them up the street to Sir Nugent's house.

Pippbrook House proved to be a modern structure of neoclassical design, set in a pretty pleasure-ground. The group marched smartly up the sweep and the sergeant rapped at the door with confidence. It was opened in due course by a butler, astonished to be receiving a summons at so untoward an hour of the day, and all outrage at the sight that met his eyes.

"We're here on the King's business," said the sergeant. "We have a prisoner who must be seen without loss of time."

The butler cast a glance over Harry in a way that made him painfully aware of his dirt and dishevelment, and remained unmoved. "You'd roust my master out of bed over some pickpocket?"

The sergeant puffed out his chest. "The charge is treason, I'd have you know."

Harry's legs began to shake under him. *What on earth? How had it come to this?* Surely he had misheard.

The butler was similarly skeptical. "This shag-rag committed *treason*?" he cried. He made as if to slam the door but was forestalled by the sergeant's heavy boot.

"Our orders come from the Admiralty direct to the Lord Lieutenant," replied the sergeant. "We was told what to look for, and we found it in this boy's possession. The rest ain't for you to know."

The butler still appeared inclined to doubt, but the sergeant observed a stony silence and stared him down. Harry was so faint that he was even a little grateful when at last they were admitted to the hall and he was pushed into a seat under an enormous portrait of Sir Nugent as a young man being adored by a spaniel. The constable, all too familiar with Sir Nugent's temper, slipped cravenly away as they entered, leaving the administration of justice to the militiamen.

There they were left for a considerable time; it appeared that not even a charge of treason sufficed to hasten Sir Nugent's toilet. Neither did the butler offer any refreshment, not even to the sergeant.

Harry's mouth was dry with thirst, and in his hunger and his fear he could not stop shaking, though his stomach churned at the thought of food. He could not even muster the curiosity to examine the portrait to see whether it depicted Sir Nugent's maimed hand.

Harry's benumbed mind strove in vain to connect that dire word—*treason*—to himself. It echoed about his head but attached to nothing in his experience. The charge made no sense, and the persuasion that he was inhabiting a nightmare possessed him. Still he could not help wondering about it: What on earth could it be about? What could he possibly have done that merited such a calumny? What had the captain and Milord involved him in, and then left him to face alone? He prayed they would learn of his plight and discover a means of rescuing him. But in his heart he knew this was no more than a boy's meedless wish.

They sat on, the militiamen stolid and confident with sacks of gold on the floor at their feet, Harry atremble and miserably aware of all his aches. Nobody looked at him. The sergeant was whispering; from the few words Harry could make out, it appeared he was rehearsing what he should say to the magistrate when it came time to make his case.

At long last Sir Nugent put in an appearance, garbed not in silk and satin this time but nevertheless with a degree of elegance not ordinarily to be met with in the country; it was as if his dress were selected to lay emphasis on the gulf between himself and his lowly visitors. His very doeskin breeches mocked their pretensions to his notice. He paused for a moment before them—they had all stood up when he descended the stair—uttered a single syllable: "Pho!"—and passed on into the breakfast parlor. Everyone sat down again.

He was soon followed by a lady, presumed to be his wife, and several children, those old enough not to be eating in the nursery. For the next half hour the party assembled in the hall was privileged to listen to the sounds of Sir Nugent and his family addressing their breakfast, which he at least did with every sign of enjoyment. No more than Harry had the sergeant eaten that day, and their bellies rumbled in counterpoint. At last, after Sir Nugent's wife and children had departed, they were called into the room.

They were brought to stand in a row at the foot of the table, Harry in the center flanked by his captors, facing Sir Nugent at the head. Sir Nugent said merely, "Yes?"

"Your Honor," the sergeant began, "I bring before you a person tender in years but hardened in infamy. We have this day captured him in possession of secret documents that we was ordered by the Lord Lieutenant to search for."

"What are these documents?"

"That I cannot say, Your Honor. We was not granted the authority to examine them. Our orders was to bring them immediately, if found, to Lord Onslow, and we have sent a messenger to find him, but in the meantime we have brung you the boy."

Sir Nugent stretched out his left hand. "I will examine these papers first."

"Sir Nugent! They be for Lord Onslow's eyes only!"

Sir Nugent's outstretched hand gestured imperiously. "How am I to know what the boy's offence is if I don't know what the papers are about?" he demanded. "I am the Lord Lieutenant's designated representative in this district. You are present in my jurisdiction at my sufferance and I *will* understand this business! It must be by some oversight that the Lord Lieutenant failed to brief me. Bring them here!"

The sergeant looked miserable, but Sir Nugent's hand remained outstretched. At last the sergeant scurried to the other end of the table, presented the sheaf of papers, and bowed his way back to his assigned position. Sir Nugent fumbled in an attempt to untie them, affording them for the first time a glimpse of his right hand, bereft of fingers. Harry at last had the satisfaction of glimpsing the interesting injury his cousin had described, caused by Sir Nugent's angry horse. How desperate he had been to catch sight of this member! And now he was only frustrated that Sir Nugent's injury delayed the discovery of the mysterious papers' significance.

With an exclamation of impatience, Sir Nugent tossed the papers aside and glared at the sergeant. Bowing and murmuring "By your permission," the sergeant approached again, untied the packet, and retreated. Sir Nugent picked up the first sheet and began to read.

In a moment he had dropped it as if it burned his fingers. He picked up and dropped another, then another. He turned pale and then red. "How did you come by these?" he roared at Harry.

Harry knew he was supposed to answer but was lost in an agony of confusion. It was impossible to lay information against the Tilts, of that he was certain; and he had no desire to identify any of the free-traders to this ogre of a man. Yet to defy authority was equally unthinkable: how could he remain entirely silent after being caught in possession of the papers, whatever dreadful secrets they held? He tried frantically to parse what knowledge he had: How much could be told without betraying individuals? Could he possibly appear to cooperate without betraying any particulars? What would reveal too much, and what too little? In a shaky murmur, Harry said at last, "A man gave them to me last night and told me to keep them safe."

"Just that? Keep them safe? And do *what* with them? Pass them on to whom? Who was this man you speak of?"

"I don't know his name," said Harry miserably. "The papers were to travel with the sacks."

The sergeant interposed. "If I may, Your Honor, he is referring to the sacks we have here. There is more to this story than just the papers."

"More than *these* papers?" cried Sir Nugent. "These

papers are copies of orders from the Admiralty to the commanders of the fleet all the world over. Even *I* lack the authority to read them. How came they into the hands of this—this street urchin?"

"Well, Your Honor, it's like this. I expect you know we've been posted here to pursue the smugglers hereabouts. We'd received intelligence of a large illicit enterprise being conducted through Darking. We've made some gains in bubbling their lay but haven't till now captured one of their number. Then we got our orders—the Lord Lieutenant met me personal—to watch for these papers, which was moving south toward the coast, through an unknown network. And we thinks the smugglers might be involved.

"So we tells the keepers of all the tollgates to be on the watch, and we offers a reward for reports of suspicious activity. We get a tip about a boy—this boy—leading a string of packhorses northward out of Darking at nightfall. I thinks to myself, 'Why would the smugglers be moving unloaded horses to the north, when the goods they run come from the south?' So we mounted up the whole squad and rode up and down the Leatherhead Road, looking for aught suspicious. The gatekeeper had said the boy claimed to be going to Norbury Park, but we asked there and no one was expecting no horses.

"After midnight we come acrost a carter with an empty cart. He tells us some inching tale about a deal to sell a pig at the Darking market that kept him late in town, and he was now going home. We was about to let him go when one of my men, who was looking sharp about the area, discovered the gold."

"The *gold*? What gold?"

The men stepped forward with their sacks and placed them one by one on the table—in all, six bags, which

Harry recognized as identical to the ones he had transported three weeks previously. There was a pause before the sergeant realized that Sir Nugent would be unable to open them either, so he bowed again, stepped forward, and untied one. Sir Nugent reached in with his good hand and brought out a fistful of guineas. They chimed sweetly as he turned them in his fingers, and then he dropped them back into the bag. The sergeant bowed once more, retied the sack, and retreated into the silence.

Sir Nugent rounded on Harry. "You—what is your name, boy?"

This was the moment Harry had been dreading most of all. Should he invent a name? He was persuaded the Tilts would wish him at most to offer up his moniker, Monkey. But Sir Nugent did not seem like the sort of man to find such a response amusing. Did he owe it to the Tilts to keep silent on all points, and thereby incur even greater wrath from Sir Nugent, even more severe punishment? If Milord and the captain found themselves in these straits, would they protect Harry as no doubt they expected him to protect them? Harry floundered and drowned in his confusion.

"Speak up, boy! What is your name?"

There was no time to think, but Harry was conscious of having reached a point of decision. "My name is Harry Steer, sir," he said in a faint squeak.

"Well, Steer—hold! Are you claiming kinship with Mr. Lee Steere Steere of Jayes?"

Harry weighed the possibilities. "Our families are connected," he admitted.

"Where do you live?"

Another Rubicon to cross. "At Henfold, sir."

"And where is that?"

The sergeant looked on Harry with fresh suspicion as

he answered for the prisoner. "It is south of here, along the road to Newdigate. Are you telling us you are a servant there, or that your father is a tenant?"

Harry cleared his dry throat. "No, sir, my father is the owner of Henfold."

"Stop—I've seen you before!" cried Sir Nugent. "Your connection from Jayes brought you with him to a meeting of the Gentlemen's Darking Club! You sat at table like an equal with the first gentlemen of the county—you shared bread with members of parliament and the Duke of Norfolk! And all the while you were a smuggler—a felon—a traitor to your king!"

Harry said nothing.

"Explain this to me!" demanded Sir Nugent, waving his fingerless hand at the table, the papers, the sacks of gold.

Harry was trembling so hard it was all he could do to remain standing. He must say something, but perhaps by keeping his focus on what he did *not* know, he might divert attention away from what he did. "I was told to bring horses to the place where the militiamen found the gold."

"Who told you?"

"I do not know. I received a note, unsigned, in a hand unfamiliar to me."

"And yet you did as the note said, coming from nobody you were acquainted with?"

"Yes, sir," said Harry miserably. "I was afraid not to." He moved on quickly; it was impossible to explain the threat hanging over him without giving away all. "The sacks were to be loaded on the horses and then taken south, to a house—I don't know precisely where it is, one of the others knew—and we were to wait there till men from Sussex came to take the gold along. I know nothing of the papers; the man who brought the gold to us remembered them at the last moment and gave them to me, saying they were to travel with the gold. The others were loading the sacks onto the horses when the militia overtook us. We were all separated, and I hid till morning and then tried to go home."

"A pretty tale, from a gentleman's son! Or is your father a gentleman? *I've* never met him. Regardless, you have not even the excuse of ignorance or poverty—not that any level of stupidity or need could justify the betrayal of King and country. How came you to be embroiled in this affair? You say you were told to do these things: told by whom? Is your father the author of this plot? Or perhaps your kinsman at Jayes? I know *his* birth is low, and he came into the estate by the merest chance. His father was a shopkeeper in a country town, was he not?"

"No, no!" cried Harry, sorry now that he had given his name. "They know nothing of this. It was all my doing." The need to satisfy Sir Nugent of his family's innocence drove him to say more. "I became a free-trader in secret, weeks ago. I heard them moving through the woods one night, and I followed them, and—and they allowed me to join them. On the dark nights, someone would leave me a note telling me where to go. I would help with the horses, and loading and unloading. It—it seemed like a lark," he ended, inadequately. The gulf between what he had believed and the reality he now understood appeared infinite even to his ear.

"A *lark*," pronounced Sir Nugent in disgust. "Just a boy out on the spree. The free-trade undermines Britain's security! If we have not the funds to support the army and the navy, how are we to defend ourselves against the threat from France? That devil Bonaparte is building an invasion force on his northern shores—and you, Harry Steer, are abetting him in his designs!"

"That was never my intention, sir."

"Never your intention? And to what purpose did you *intend* that this gold should be put? For whose benefit were these papers stolen and smuggled out of London?"

"I did not know anything about the gold until very recently, or about the papers till last night. I didn't even know what the papers were until you examined them just now."

"But you did know of the gold before last night?"

"Yes, I—I helped to transport another shipment a few weeks ago."

"There have been other shipments of gold? And you said nothing to the authorities? You were well suited, I gather, to take part in an enterprise that was clearly criminal in its nature. Never in my life have I seen anyone so hardened in depravity at such a tender age!"

"I was *not* well suited," protested Harry, goaded into unwariness. "I was afraid. The usual runs, of brandy and tobacco and the like, were one thing, but the gold—it was different. Even so, all I thought was that perhaps it was intended to pay for the purchase of more goods to run, or for the costs of transport."

"A fortune like *this*?" Sir Nugent waved his stump in agitation at the sacks on the table. "And why were you afraid? You had been working with these criminals for a considerable time, had you not?"

Harry paused. Mentioning the Tilts' mutilated servant would lead to revelations he was not prepared to make. He had no doubt that vengeance for his betrayal would come swiftly, and not only to himself. He had no wish to draw further attention to his family. "The free-traders make it clear that retribution will fall on anyone who reveals their secrets," he said at last. "I felt I had to comply."

"It did not occur to you that the authorities could safe-guard you if you laid information against the rogues?"

"No, sir. I hoped that, with all the pressure being brought to bear by the Excise and the militia, the runs would stop. I am supposed to go away to school in a fortnight, and I believed I should escape them that way, without consequences to my kin."

Sir Nugent goggled at him. "You had a clear duty to report these criminals, no matter the cost to yourself! Even if you did not realize you were providing support to Britain's enemies, you knew their activities were against the law."

Harry held his peace; he had just enough commonsense to understand that this was not the forum in which to debate the merits of obeying unjust laws.

And Sir Nugent was not done. "You thought only about protecting yourself, not about your duty to your nation! You believed that the reward for your iniquities should be to go off to school—leaving behind who knows what lawlessness and vice in your own parish! What does it matter the evil being done here, while you are off to—where? Guildford? Cheam?"

"I am to go to Winchester, sir."

Sir Nugent leaped to his feet. "*Winchester?* Unlucky for you then, young Jack-at-warts, for I am myself an Old Wykehamist, and you shall never, while I draw breath, pollute the shades of my alma mater. It shall be my per-sonal honor and pleasure to see you hanged first. I have a great deal of interest there, both in the town and at the college, and I shall write this very day to the headmaster, Dr. Goddard, to expose you—as soon as I see you clapped into jail. You shall never be educated at *my* school." He rounded on the sergeant. "This—this—*prisoner* is to be held in custody until the Quarter Sessions, when the bench shall consider all the evidence against him. In the meantime, I shall require an escort of your men this afternoon as I return the papers to the Admiralty and deliver the gold to the proper authorities at the Treasury."

"Yes, sir," said the sergeant, grateful at the prospect of being relieved of his burdens. "I should mention to you that we also have in custody the carter we apprehended at the scene where the gold was discovered. The boy mentioned that he was there with 'others'; and we heard men fleeing the scene on horseback, though we were unable to catch any of them. Your Honor can rest assured we will continue to pursue the remaining malefactors."

"Of course, of course, and I shall interview the carter when I have the time," said Sir Nugent; "but for now, remove this boy from my sight!"

So Harry was seized and dragged back through the town. The militiamen bypassed the old cells in the Market House and took him down South Street. It felt as if every citizen of Darking had come out into the streets to stare at him; and he knew that once the charges against him became known, he would face greater insults to his dignity than their censorious eyes. He was banished forever from the only society he had ever known. Never again would he be suffered to ride in to the town to perform an errand for his father, or accompany his mother to market.

The militiamen paused in front of the workhouse, where stood the small but sturdy brick structure known as the Cage. It was divided into two compartments; they opened the door to one of these and thrust Harry inside. He thought of his mother and what she must be feeling, and the idea was too much for him: he cast himself down into the straw covering the floor and wept.

Chapter the Twenty-fourth

Not even a boy who has been charged with treason can cry forever, though, and after a time Harry dried his eyes and looked about him. The chamber was dark, the only light coming from a small opening set high in the wall, an unglazed window crossed with bars. It provided only sufficient illumination to reveal the dust motes floating in the air and the patches of damp in the ceiling. A bench against the wall under the window was the sole furnishing. The place smelled of previous inhabitants and of Cheesman's brewery nearby. The Walking Dunghill's home, the Hole in the Wall cottage, was just across the way and a memory arose in Harry's mind of the major shouting, "Liberty must be God's work, not man's!" Would God have mercy on him and deliver him from his prison? Harry could think of not a single reason why he might deserve such favor. To the contrary, he felt he had all unwittingly become a patriot in the kingdom of Satan, which the Dunghill had described as "the reign of disorder and darkness." Certainly, his cell fitted that description.

Harry climbed up out of the straw, mounted upon the bench, and stood on tiptoe. He could not quite stretch high enough to obtain a view through the window at ground level, but he could see the upper branches of a tree not far off. He could hear no birdsong, however, only the rattle and bustle of traffic on South Street on the other side of the door, the bawling of a muffin man and the sharp voice of a boy hawking spruce beer. He sat down on the bench to consider.

His case was unquestionably dire. He was without a doubt guilty, however unknowingly; he had been captured with secret documents on his person. He had earned the personal opprobrium of the magistrate into whose charge he had been delivered, not only as a gently born boy who had turned willingly to a low crime but also as an aspirant to that magistrate's alma mater. He could imagine no future but the gallows—and very soon his parents would be informed of his iniquity. It would mean the death of all their hopes to rise above their present station in life; in fact, they would indubitably be shunned by all who had hitherto claimed acquaintance with them. No doubt they would cast him off forever—or at least his father would, and his mother would be forbidden to see him. He knew the disappointment they would experience and felt it acutely. His cousin Steere, too, surely would never notice him again. He hoped he had not said too much but feared he had dropped some clue that would lead to the Tilts; he saw himself lying helpless in this cell while vengeance was wrought against those he loved.

At the same time, in his imprisonment he was to a degree safe. It was strange to look around the walls that hemmed him in and think of them as his only refuge; outside lay nothing he could envision that was not worse.

Harry tried to discipline his mind to resolution, but in the face of so much peril and humiliation it was impossible to maintain his equanimity. Over and over he began to shake and tears started to his eyes, and altogether he remained for the entire afternoon a very miserable little boy. When some bread and ale were delivered to him, late in the day, by a silent jailer, the nourishment helped him a little, but not enough to make him sanguine about his future. Night fell and the sun rose, and still no one came near enough to Harry to speak with him.

His solitude was interrupted about midmorning when three of the militiamen appeared and removed him from his cell. He was by this time in a disgraceful condition of dirt and the odors about his person were offensive even to him; the men seemed to feel the same, for they bore him off to their stronghold at the Wheatsheaf Inn and gave him a good washing at the stableyard pump. Throughout these proceedings, the men said nothing to Harry; neither did any passersby, though stares were plentiful. Leaving him and his clothes to dry as they might, the men next marched him back up the road to Pippbrook House. Harry steeled his nerves for further questioning.

This time the party was conducted into the library, where Harry was confronted with not only Sir Nugent but an entire bench of magistrates: Mr. Peters sat to his left, his countenance watchful, and Sir Frederick Evelyn, dressed for riding and with his eyebrows cocked as ever in an attitude of astonishment, to his right. A clerk sat at a desk to one side, his quill poised. Harry drew his damp jacket about him and waited.

Sir Nugent began. "Owing to the serious nature of the principal charge laid against the defendant, Harry Steer, the justices of the peace for Darking Hundred have agreed that a formal hearing is required before the prisoner is remanded into custody at the Guildford Bridewell, pending a trial at the assizes. This case is a complex one, with many questions yet unanswered, and certain aspects of it require timely elucidation if further harm to the Crown is to be averted.

"What do we know at present? First, we know that a carter, one Ezekiel Dardy, did on the night of Thursday last, August the fourteenth, transport from London thirty bags of guineas and a packet of papers containing copies of orders from the Admiralty to the ships of the fleet in all corners of the seas. Those copies, had they reached their intended destination, would have exposed the entirety of British naval power to the gravest danger: the whole foundation of British power across the globe might have been destroyed. As to the means by which those papers came to be copied and smuggled out of the Admiralty, we have no information as yet."

"And," interposed Mr. Peters, "it might be argued that the investigation into that aspect of the case lies in other hands than ours. Perhaps the Admiralty might not thank us for inquiring too deeply, and we ought to limit the scope of our questions to local matters." He directed toward Harry an unsmiling stare.

Sir Nugent did not appreciate the interruption, nor was he pleased by a reminder that his role in the discovery of a large-scale treasonous plot was destined to be a small one. "I am not prepared to concede that our concern here today is entirely with the misdeeds that took place in our neighborhood. We are in possession of the only two known co-conspirators, so it stands to reason that we alone are capable of shedding light on all aspects of the plot."

Sir Frederick appeared even more surprised than ever. "What, an ignorant London carter and a stripling? If your only hope of unmasking treason on a massive scale rests upon their shoulders, it seems a hopeless business."

Sir Nugent puffed out his cheeks and sat up higher in his chair. "If neither of you is prepared to take this inquiry seriously, I would be just as pleased to pursue it on my own. I am convinced that the prisoners, particularly this one"—he thrust out the stump of his hand in Harry's direction—"are in a position to provide material evidence that will shed light on this wicked plot. Do not be deceived by this boy's age or his air of harmlessness. He is hardened in infamy beyond his years. He has admitted to being willingly in league with smugglers, the so-called free-traders, the 'gentlemen' as they are pleased to style themselves, who have been conducting their trade with impunity all 'round this part of the country. He must know their methods and their leaders, their routes and places of concealment. Perhaps he even knows something of the men who employed the smuggling gang in the furtherance of their treasonous intent."

"Very well," said Sir Frederick, "get on with it then. I'm certain I speak for all of us when I say we are determined to learn all we may about the matter."

"So I may return then to my summary?" inquired Sir Nugent with elaborate civility. "Very well," he added when no one spoke. "There is also the matter of the gold. The Treasury assured me yesterday, when I brought it to them, that they have heard nothing of any bank in the City being robbed of such a sum as thirty sacks of guineas represents. A theft of that magnitude would have been speedily reported. They have promised to pursue inquiries, but we may perhaps conclude that a personage of enormous wealth—or a group of such persons—is willfully shipping British gold out of the country, for a purpose yet to be determined. The fact of its being accompanied by the Admiralty papers, however, strongly implies that the intent was to aid the French in their aggressions. That any British subject should knowingly offer support to the godless revolutionaries of France, who are plainly bent on expanding their empire to all corners of the globe, is unthinkable! Yet such is the loose talk we hear on all sides about 'liberty' and 'the natural rights of man' and such poppycock—talk that has not been suppressed, despite the government's efforts to control the seditious element—that someone, despite the wealth that our British way of life has permitted him to amass, has become so deluded as to believe that French tyranny, French anarchy, French atheism would be better for us all—! Why, we have heard even our own lord of the manor, the Duke of Norfolk—"

"That's enough!" snapped Sir Frederick. "You take your outrage too far. Are you suggesting that my friend Norfolk is the traitor? On what sliver of evidence, pray? Take care before you make such an enemy."

"I made no accusation of the kind!" replied Sir Nugent sulkily, his flight of eloquence interrupted. "I merely alluded to loose talk, and you cannot deny that the duke's tongue is among the loosest. Did he not publicly toast the Majesty of the People, the rallying cry of the revolutionaries?"

"But as Sir Frederick pointed out, we have no evidence whatever that would allow us to point the—ah—finger at the duke, or any other individual," said Mr. Peters, averting his gaze from Sir Nugent's maimed hand. "Let us not run ahead of ourselves, but return to the matter at hand. A person or persons unknown supplied a very large sum of money to be transported in the dead of night from town toward Sussex. Perhaps you might continue your summary from there."

Sir Nugent glared sullenly at the table but at last complied. "We have recovered six of the sacks of guineas, but we know from questioning the carter they numbered thirty. Where did the remainder go? Also, we know that local smugglers were employed in the business. Who are these men? Where are their storage depots? If we can disrupt the Surrey link in the chain of transport, we shall make any repetition of this crime more difficult. And before us stands a member of that local gang of malefactors."

All eyes turned to Harry. His slight frame appeared too frail to carry such a weight of infamy, and indeed he quailed before the full disclosure of the plot in which he had become embroiled. There was a roaring in his head and he felt faint. The men confronting him appeared determined to learn all he knew; and now that he understood the scope of the crime, his own conscience urged disclosure. He was crushed by the knowledge that he had abetted treason against king and country. Harry had never thought much about patriotic duty or the defense of his homeland; any aspirations he might have entertained of that nature had centered on the glory of doing battle with an enemy and the honor of stirring deeds as described in children's stories. He had seen his forays with the free-traders as no more than a different kind of adventure, the only way of being a hero that lay open to him in this uneventful corner of Surrey.

But now, in how different a light did his actions appear! He perceived, in an agony of shame, that he had shown disregard for the laws of his country and associated himself with those who pursued their own gain at the expense of the commonweal. Why had he not paused to consider that the smugglers must be trading with Britain's enemies? The ankers and tobacco, after all, had to have come from France. He was still rather muddled in his mind about how the ankers of brandy and gin, the gold, and the secret documents were all connected, but he could see that all this time he had been fumbling about in darkness both literal and ethical. It was a humiliating realization and he was overwhelmed by the desire to offer whatever atonement lay in his power.

And yet—there were also the representations made to him by John Tilt. There were all the impoverished families of the parish who could not afford the necessities of life because of duties the government levied on the import of everyday goods so it could afford to wage its wars. There were still the uncaring landlords who evicted hardworking farmers if they had not the means to pay their rents—and how were those farmers to come up with the money by legitimate labor, if the harvest failed? How was Harry to understand right and wrong in such a world?

But he had no time to ponder, for Sir Nugent was ready to open the questioning. "Tell me about the gold: where is the remainder now?"

"I cannot say," replied Harry, "since I was captured yesterday morning. If none of the others or their horses was apprehended, I must presume it to be moving through Sussex by now—assuming of course that this shipment went the way of the last."

"*The last?*" cried Mr. Peters. "Do you mean to tell us that there have been other shipments of gold?"

"Yes," said Harry. "As I said yesterday to Sir Nugent, I took part in a previous run of guineas. Forty bags it was, that time. And I heard tell of an earlier one but was not involved."

There was a momentary hush as the magistrates strove to calculate the sum of money involved, and failed. And into the silence came the sound of voices outside the room; someone was seeking admittance and was encountering opposition. Apparently the visitor won his point, for the butler appeared and whispered in Sir Nugent's ear.

"Well well," said he, rubbing hand and stump together, "this may prove interesting. You told me yesterday, boy, that neither your father nor your kinsman from Jayes was implicated. And yet here is Mr. Lee Steere Steere, bent on interrupting these proceedings. Send him in!"

Harry turned a bewildered face to the door as his cousin strode in. Mr. Steere came to stand by Harry, placing a hand on his shoulder and giving it a little squeeze.

"Good day, sir," said Sir Frederick. "To what do we owe the honor of your visit?"

Mr. Steere bowed to the magistrates but did not quail under their gazes. "Sir Frederick, Sir Nugent, Mr. Peters, your servant. It came to my ears that my cousin had been detained on a most serious charge. I immediately went to his father at Henfold and learned that he had already been questioned in the matter, and what the charges entailed. His father being much occupied with business about the harvest"—he cast Harry an apologetic glance—"I undertook to come here in his stead on my cousin's behalf. Harry is but a child, as you know—he is but twelve years of age—and it does not seem appropriate for him to be interrogated without an adult family member here to represent his interests."

Harry understood him: his father was so angry that he had cast Harry off and would not lend him any aid. It was no more than he deserved; but the undeserved kindness of his kinsman brought tears to his eyes.

"What 'interests' do you believe a traitor to possess?" asked Sir Nugent with awful sarcasm. "He is a confessed smuggler. He was caught with state secrets in his possession. He admits to transporting a fortune in guineas in the dead of night—gold intended, we must presume, like the secret papers, to succor our enemies. I must ask myself why you, to all appearances a respectable man of substance in our community, should come running to the aid of such a person. Do you perhaps have an undisclosed interest in his activities that you wish to protect?"

Mr. Peters uttered a protest, but Mr. Steere was undismayed. "This is a dramatic manner of speaking about an event that may be seen in a very different light. I ask you to recollect the age of your prisoner. When you were twelve years of age, were you capable of collaborating in a grand scheme of treason? Had you even formed political beliefs worthy of the name? It seems more likely to me that the real villains duped my cousin and made use of him, that they trespassed on his innocence to embroil him in an affair he did not even understand."

"As the father of two boys, I must say I lean toward your view," said Mr. Peters. "How *did* you become involved, Harry?"

Sir Nugent broke in. "He had the effrontery to inform me yesterday that he thought it a lark—a lark, to betray his sovereign!"

"That's not what I said!" protested Harry. "I said I thought going on runs with the smugglers would be a lark. You know," he turned to beseech his cousin, "like being a pirate or something. It was an adventure. I spent all day shut up with my tutor and never did anything. But then this other thing happened—with the gold. I didn't know what the guineas were for, but I didn't like it. It felt all wrong. But by then I was frightened of the smugglers, and I didn't dare stop. I thought they would come and hurt my family."

Mr. Steere looked ruefully down at him. "You got that notion from me, did you not?" He turned to face the magistrates. "I recall a conversation I had recently with Harry and his father. We were speaking of the free-trade, and I said it didn't pay to inform on the smugglers because they would steal my horses or burn my hay ricks if I did. I would wager my life that Harry was simply a boy looking for excitement, who was drawn into a scheme he was too frightened to escape."

Mr. Peters and Sir Frederick nodded; the picture he painted seemed reasonable enough. Sir Nugent looked black but had for the moment nothing to offer, so Mr. Steere pressed his advantage.

"That being the case, perhaps we may examine how to achieve a happy resolution for all. I am persuaded that none of you wishes to attract the kind of scandal that would attach to your names were you to hang a misguided young boy on a charge of treason. What the newspapers would do with such a story does not bear contemplation. On the other hand, a most serious crime has been committed—and there, perhaps, my scapegrace cousin is in a position to help you. Nay, I have no doubt he would be eager to assist by providing whatever information he may possess that would put you on the scent of the real criminals—perhaps in exchange for the dropping of charges that will benefit no one, and only prove an embarrassment in the end? And I should be honored to offer something to defray the expenses you have been put to in this matter. . . ."

"I am by no means ready to concede to your representations, sir, nor to come to any terms with this boy," said Sir Nugent. "Drop the charges? From treason to 'go your merry way'? I think not! He will tell all, certainly—and we were about to get a round tale out of him when you interrupted us. But I cannot take his crimes as lightly as you do, nor countenance his walking free."

Sir Frederick, meanwhile, gave every sign of being relieved by Mr. Steere's proposals, and Mr. Peters even ventured to expostulate with Sir Nugent. "He's only a child. What he did was foolish, but I'm certain he regrets his actions and is prepared to make amends."

But Sir Nugent was adamant. "He shall tell us all he knows *and* take the consequences!"

Harry could feel his cousin's hand on his shoulder begin to tremble, but Mr. Steere spoke calmly enough. "Then I shall have to advise my cousin to say nothing at all. Until we have received assurances of his safety from prosecution, he is regrettably unable to cooperate with your investigation."

"The law *does* allow for the pardon of a smuggler who reveals the identities of his confederates," Mr. Peters pointed out.

"Ay, and a reward of forty pounds!" cried Sir Nugent. "Would you have me send this wicked creature away with a pocket full of silver? So that it might go the way of the gold, no doubt!"

Mr. Steere hastily denied a desire for reward of any kind.

Sir Frederick, meanwhile, had been thinking, and now he spoke up. "Perhaps we should not decide anything in a hurry. This hearing has given us all considerable food for thought, and I should prefer to have a little time to weigh the matter. The young man is in custody, and there he shall remain. I have no desire to rush into a public airing of a delicate matter—nor, I imagine, would the Admiralty welcome a public trial. They have their own house to clean, evidently, and would no doubt prefer to do it in their own way and with as little attention as possible drawn to the breach they have suffered. We can best please them by providing useful information through channels, not by dragging their failure to secure their secrets through the public courts and strewing speculation about it across the pages of newspapers. Let us all think about the most discreet way to proceed, and then we may reconvene next week." And without further ado he rose and left the room.

Sir Nugent, thus outflanked in his own home, impatiently signed to the clerk to cease writing and turned to Mr. Peters, only to discover him also in the act of rising. Mr. Peters took a more conciliatory tone, however, merely saying, "I confess I too would be grateful for the opportunity to consider the implications further before taking any action. As Sir Frederick has reminded us, it is a delicate matter—a very delicate matter indeed." He bowed first to Sir Nugent and then to Mr. Steere, and departed.

Mr. Steere tried to speak reassuringly to Harry but was cut short. "You have done quite enough this day, Mr. Steere, and I would thank you to leave my house," cried Sir Nugent. "The next time, I should be grateful to you if you would wait to be invited." And to the guards, "Take the prisoner away!" So Harry was marched back through the town and returned to his cell.

CHAPTER THE TWENTY-FIFTH

Hope and fear warred in Harry's breast, gratitude to his kinsman for championing him, misery over his father's abandonment, and altogether such a confusion of emotions that he was unable to think clearly. His cousin's proposal that he lay information offered him the first hint of promise that he might escape the gallows. But just as his spirits rose he recalled his vow to John Tilt that he would never betray the free-traders, and he was left wondering whether the price of his freedom were too steep.

And so he wore out the day in a state of uncertainty and bafflement that fevered his exhausted brain. He was given little food or drink, and the discomforts of his cell were compounded by a host of insects evidently persuaded that he was placed there expressly for them to feast upon. Between the miseries of the flesh and those of the spirit, it was a very unhappy boy who fell at last into an uneasy sleep.

He could not say how long he had been lost to consciousness before a hissing voice roused him. It whispered, over and over, "Whisht! Monkey."

Harry unfolded his stiff limbs and climbed upon the bench. "Who's there?"

"I've a message from Milord," responded the voice; it might have been Cursemother Jack but Harry could not be certain. "Milord says, he finds your mother Jenny and your sister Isabella well for now, and is sartin you knows how to hold your tongue." Without waiting for a response, the person padded away into the darkness.

And there it was. At the moment when Harry had finally relinquished all the respect and partisanship he had felt for the free-traders, he also lost all possibility of saving his own skin. If he informed on the smugglers, his family would pay the price he evaded. To protect those he loved he would have to forfeit them, forfeit also the goodwill of his cousin who had tried to help him. Harry threw himself down in the straw, sick with the horror of his situation.

A young boy's frame is not made for such rigors, and despite everything he fell asleep again. But it was a shallow, restless repose in which part of him remained aware of his surroundings while another part broke free from reason. He dreamed the ghost of the Walking Dunghill was emerging from the cottage across the way and pacing in the street outside, preaching as Harry had so often heard him do in the past. Fragments of his sermons lit up Harry's memory one by one, exhorting him to attend to them.

"It is said in Isaiah, 'Yea, when ye make many prayers, I will not hear, your hands are full of blood.' But Isaiah also tells us, 'Come now, and let us reason together, saith the Lord: though your sins be scarlet, they shall be as white as snow.'" . . .

Now it seemed the ghost of the Dunghill was sitting in the Cage beside Harry's sleeping form. Harry's mind shied away but his body could not move. The reek of decay mingled with the smells in the noisome chamber. The wraith said, "Wisdom exalteth her children, and layeth hold of them that seek her. At the first she will walk with him by crooked ways, and bring fear and dread upon him, until she may trust his soul, and try him by her laws. Then will she return the straight way unto him, and comfort him, and shew him her secrets." Harry tried to speak but his mouth was gagged, and the specter kept speaking: ". . . Liberty is that power which belongs to a man, of doing everything that does not harm the rights of others. Its moral limits are confined by this maxim: 'Do not to another what you would not wish done to yourself.'" . . .

And drifting gently out through the barred window, the ghost uttered its parting words: "Act well your part, for there the honor lies. . . . Here are glorious tidings of forgiveness for a thoughtless world—if they will consider and return, like the Prodigal." The voice faded into the distance.

The words revolved in Harry's sleeping brain and he understood that somewhere in the madman's declamations lay ideas that could show him a path forward—if only he could determine which words were the useful ones; if only he could recall them when he awoke.

But of course, when he opened his eyes to the morning they had slipped away.

The day being Sunday, Harry could not expect any events to relieve his tedium: all he had was time, time to fret over his insoluble problem and dwell in the vain hope of miracles. He thought the prudent course would be to pray, and this he did most earnestly. But he heard no reply; his path remained occluded. He had half a hope that his cousin might come to relieve his solitude, but this did not happen. So after praying for a time and then praying again as new prayers occurred to him, he sat in his hot cell, scratching and listless.

Late in the day, however, there came the sound of the key grating in the lock, and the warder opened the door to a stranger. The man—a person of middling height and years, dressed in an old-fashioned style with buckled shoes and a powdered wig—stood politely in the doorway as if seeking admission to Harry's parlor.

"May I come in?"

"If you please, sir," said Harry, instinctively returning courtesy for courtesy, "and be so good as to be seated." He gestured toward the plain bench. "I regret that I can offer you no refreshment—and should warn you that there are fleas."

The man turned on him a kindly gaze; he smiled and sat down. "I am prepared to brave the fleas but not the lack of refreshment. So I have asked for tea to be brought in."

A servant then appeared with a tray bearing a teapot, cups, and a plate of cakes, which he set down on the bench before bowing and withdrawing. Harry gazed astonished upon this evidence of his visitor's power and influence—he could scarcely imagine what persuasions might have made this indulgence possible. But the man merely thanked the jailer and said, "You may return in an hour to let me out."

"I'll stand outside," said the jailer.

"No, I think not," replied the stranger gently. "I require privacy with my student."

The jailer locked the door but continued to stand outside, shifting from one foot to the other and coughing from time to time. The stranger poured the tea and offered Harry the plate of cakes, but did not speak further until finally, with hesitant steps, the jailer walked away.

"How do you do, Master Steer?" said the man at last. "My name is Goddard, and I am the headmaster of Winchester College."

Harry crushed the cake in his hand in his astonishment. "How do you do, sir? I—I did not expect to meet you."

"Whyever not? You are one of my new students. The description that your kinsman, Mr. Steere, gave me of you several months ago left me eager to make your acquaintance, and I should certainly have sought you out in a fortnight when you arrived for the first half. But then yesterday I received a most extraordinary letter from a former student, who appeared to be laboring under the delusion that he had only to mention the matter and I would rescind your admission at Winchester. From some—ah—hints he dropped it became apparent to me that you might require some extra assistance in making your way to school. I therefore journeyed here to see what might be done in the case."

Harry stared. "You intend to say, I must suppose, that Sir Nugent Lumley-Dacre-Prudhoe wrote to you. If that is so, Dr. Goddard, I own I am surprised that you should wish to meet me at all."

Dr. Goddard chortled. "On the contrary, Steer, his letter gave me the liveliest curiosity to meet you, a curiosity that would not be satisfied by tamely awaiting your arrival at school. To judge by the flights of his prose, I was led to expect an ogre, a very demon of iniquity. Having never met such a monster in the body of a youth of twelve, I set out at once to see this fearsome creature for myself. And yet here I find—nothing more than a well-mannered young man. Picture my disappointment!"

Harry quelled a nervous urge to laugh and said in all seriousness, "But sir, the truth is bad enough. I have done the things I am accused of."

"You are a person of courage, I see," replied Dr. Goddard, unruffled by this disclosure. "I might have guessed as much about a child who took up with smugglers—though you may not, perhaps, at this stage of your life be a person of wisdom."

Harry hung his head.

"I have just come from Sir Nugent's house, where I heard the particulars of the case. He appears adamant that you should be held to account. Yet he gave me to understand that there are other justices of the peace who have interested themselves in the case."

"Yes, sir, Sir Frederick Evelyn and Mr. Peters."

"And what, would you say, are their views?"

"Well, sir, my kinsman interceded on my behalf and proposed that I might lay information in exchange for—I am not certain what. My liberty, I think he hoped to achieve. Sir Frederick called it a delicate matter and appeared concerned that the Admiralty might not want it publicly known that sensitive papers had been stolen. Mr. Peters said only that he wished to consider further."

"A careful response, Steer: you hesitate to ascribe to them positions they have not explicitly stated. Very wise. But I shall be less wise and hazard the guess that it is only Sir Nugent who has an appetite for your prosecution. The resentment he expressed over his colleagues' lack of cooperation leads me to surmise as much. Of course, since you were first brought up before him, it is his decision that matters. Tell me: what do you think about laying information?"

Despite all the time he had been given to consider the question, Harry was yet unprepared with an answer. "I—I wish I could, but I cannot."

"I find that a curious answer, Steer: why can you not inform against criminals and traitors? Have you sympathy for them personally? Are they your friends? Do you endorse their actions, and wish their cause well? Wherein lies your hesitation?"

"I do *not* endorse the sending of British gold and secrets to France!" cried Harry. "I did not know that was what I was doing. And no, they are not my friends."

"More careful speaking, I observe, Steer, for all the heat of your response: you did not answer my questions in full. So you oppose treason, but you did not say you oppose smuggling. And you said your associates are not your friends, but you did not say you lacked sympathy for them. Explain."

Harry strove to assemble his ideas; evidently this odd man expected it. "I encountered the free-traders by chance a few months past," he said. "I saw lights in the woods and followed them. They made as if to kill me for discovering them, so I said I would like to join them."

"Did you in fact wish to join them?"

"Yes, sir. It seemed exciting, to be a smuggler; and I was so very bored. My tutor—"

"Ah! Now we come to it. Your tutor kept your nose to the grindstone all the while you wished you could be out in the world, doing deeds. Very proper."

Harry looked skeptical.

"No, indeed, you must believe that I do not hold with tying young men to their books every hour of the day," continued Dr. Goddard. "It is one of my educational innovations: I have proved through experimentation that students perform better in their studies when there is a balance between mental and physical activity. You have provided further evidence in support of my theories. But continue. You became a smuggler—"

"Yes, on the dark nights. I would receive a note telling me where to go, and then we would receive our orders once we got there."

"And did you become friendly with these men?"

Harry considered this. "In a sense, perhaps. The captain, the man who led the runs, was kind to me and answered most of my questions. And we all needed to work together to complete the task; when there was danger, we had to trust one another. But we blackened our faces and some wore kerchiefs to conceal their features, so we did not really know one another; and we never used our real names."

"How then did you address one another?"

"The captain gave us names. There was Old Joll and Slug and Nasty Face and Thirsty Chub and Cursemother Jack, and I was Monkey."

Dr. Goddard uttered something perilously like a giggle. "You make me wish I were younger. So you participated in these activities all the summer, and you developed sympathy for the free-traders' cause: why?"

"Times have been very hard around here the past two years, sir. With failed harvests and the prices for everything so high, people have been losing their farms and their livelihoods. The laboring poor couldn't afford coals to cook their food—if they even had food to cook. The landlords mostly live far away; they aren't here to see the misery. The Poor Rates are so high they drive people who are just getting by into poverty, and even so there's not enough to go around for the destitute. The smugglers, they pay as much in a night as a laborer can earn in a week of regular employment on a farm. And by distributing run goods they reduce prices so more people can buy what they need."

Warming to his subject, Harry continued. "People hereabouts know little and care less about France and waging war. They only know they want to eat, and feed their children, and they believe all the taxes and the scarcity of bread and meat exist because of the government having to pay for the war."

"A glib defense indeed, Steer. But I can see several flaws in your reasoning. Flaw the first: Britain is a nation under law, and the individual subject with his particular concerns cannot simply decide which laws are to be followed and which ignored. That road leads to anarchy, does it not?"

"I suppose—yes."

"Flaw the second: those in a position to know the most about it tell us that First Consul Napoleon has ordered an invasion fleet to be built along the northern shores of France. Have you heard of this?"

Harry admitted that he had.

"We also know that the French have conscripted their entire population of young men into the army—creating a fighting force of unimaginable size, such as the world has never seen. They cannot raise such an army and then leave it standing idle. So: if the British government does not increase its revenues, it cannot raise its own army or build the ships necessary to defend itself. The French may or may not attack us, but would you agree that they are more likely to do so if we are not seen to be building defenses to match their offensive capacity?"

"Yes."

"Very well. Here we come to examine where your heart truly lies. Do you wish for France to invade our island? Are you, in fact, a Jacobin, yearning for liberty—however it may be defined by the First Consul of France?"

"No, sir," said Harry stoutly. "The British must govern themselves."

"And if the government is prevented from raising revenues as it sees best, by individuals who dislike the price of their tobacco or their tea, how is our nation to defend itself?"

Harry admitted that he did not know.

"Nor does anyone else know, sad to say. Some would tell us that the Prince of Wales should be less extravagant, and no doubt they are correct. Yet the extravagance of one man, however excessive, will not suffice to feed an army. So individuals are asked to make sacrifices for the safety of all. We might dispute around the margins of this expenditure or that, but if, as you say, the British people must govern themselves, then it follows that you cannot lend support to smuggling. This is not blind obedience. It is a rational choice made by an entire society to safeguard its own survival.

"And there is, of course, yet another flaw to be examined. We have been speaking of the running of ordinary household goods. But you became involved in another kind of activity, did you not?"

Harry's cheeks burned hot, and the cake sat like a stone in his belly. "Yes, sir. I was sent to help move a shipment of sacks from north of Darking down to close by the Sussex border. I could tell the sacks held coins, and when one sack was cut open I learned they held guineas."

"What did you think those guineas were intended to be used for?"

"I wondered. Purchasing more goods to be smuggled, perhaps. But it seemed like such a lot of money. And the man who usually led us was not there. He had always explained things to me—and I could not understand why he was missing from a run of such importance."

Dr. Goddard studied him thoughtfully. "The seamless rationale, in short, began to show fissures. So when the stakes were high, this man who had always been there, who had always made sense of things for you, was absent. He left you to succeed or fail on your own." If he observed the tears in Harry's eyes, he gave no sign of it.

"And so you did as you were told. You took the sacks where they were supposed to go; you did not, I observe, take any of the guineas to give to the poor whose plight you feel so acutely."

"We discussed doing that, but concluded it would not serve."

"We?"

"There was a man leading the run, and batmen to protect it."

"Why would it not serve?"

"Because if we betrayed Milord—"

"Who is Milord?"

Harry paused. "That's what they call the leader of the smugglers. If we betrayed him in such an important matter, we would certainly be hunted down. We might be able to deliver some money to our family and others, but only the once. There would never be any more runs. We might leave our homes and flee, but we would be pursued. What use would the money be to us, at that price?"

Dr. Goddard studied him intently. "You are afraid of Milord."

"Yes."

"But if you said his name—his real name—he would be apprehended and you would be safe from him."

"I cannot do so," said Harry in a whisper. "His punishments of those who betray him are severe. Recently, there was a man found in the stocks with his tongue cut out—"

"And this was the work of the man called Milord? Have you proof?"

"I do not, though the circumstances make it appear likely. There was someone who was giving the Excise intelligence about the smugglers' movements, and the man in the stocks had thirty pieces of silver left at his feet."

"Intended to be understood as a Judas, then. I see why you might be frightened."

"Yes, sir. And Milord has also implicitly threatened my family. Even if he had not, though, I swore an oath never to betray him."

To Harry's astonishment, Dr. Goddard appeared pleased by this. "You are lending support to my theories again, Steer," he said. "I govern all my students by relying on a boy's innate sense of honor. And here is yet another example of why my faith is not misplaced. You gave your word, and you do not wish to go back on it. That is precisely why, Steer, you are worth saving."

Harry's lip trembled and he was unable to speak. Dr. Goddard proceeded serenely, regardless.

"Now we come to the nub of it, do we not? You followed your orders, you delivered the shipment of gold, you went home, you said nothing. What a burden for such slight shoulders to bear! And then you were summoned again. You obeyed again. Once more there were sacks of gold, and then there were the papers. Did you know what they were?"

"No! They were tied up, and it was dark and there was no time. I was given them, and then the militiamen rode up, and I hid; and when it got light and I came out, I tried to go home. But I was captured at the tollgate."

"Very well, you did not know what you were carrying. Did the others of your party know?"

"I don't think they could have. They were already loading the sacks onto the horses when the carter gave me the papers as an afterthought. I never saw any of them again. Tom—the man who was leading the run—he might have had suspicions, but I think he did not wish to know any more than he had to. He had lost his farm in Hampshire and tried to be a highwayman but he was no good at it, so he took this job because the pay was good and he hoped to be able to get his farm back."

"In short, none of you knew more than did the horses carrying the gold: you were tools of more wicked men. But the chief smuggler—this Milord—must have known, don't you imagine?"

"I'm not certain. He might have asked why his men were being hired for such an unusual run—"

"Why his men were *hired*? So he was not the instigator of the affair?"

"No, sir. The man responsible for the runs with the gold most likely went to Milord in person, or else sent his agent—"

"Tom, the incompetent highwayman, in short."

"Yes, perhaps. One of them went to Milord and asked to hire men and horses."

Dr. Goddard sat in silence for a considerable time. At last he said, "Help me to understand this, Steer. I gather from your words that you are not the imp of Satan Sir Nugent represented to me; I am of the opinion that you believe in the existence of right and wrong."

"Yes, sir."

"I think you may be somewhat bewildered, however, as to where the right and the wrong may lie in all this tangle. Another question: do you believe right and wrong to be absolute?"

Harry frowned. "I'm not certain I understand you, sir."

"When do you know if something is wrong? When you have been told that it is? Or when that boy's sense of honor tells you that it is?"

"Mostly the latter, sir, I think. If I see that a thing causes harm, I know it is wrong. But sometimes people will say a thing is wrong, but it doesn't seem so very bad to me. Or doing what they call right causes harm in a different way."

"Very well—although as a very young person, you must acknowledge that at times you may not know all you need to know in order to determine where the greater harm lies. I am not prepared to cede the discipline of obedience so easily, you see! But speak to me a little of where the greater harm appears to be located in this case."

"Well, the smuggling was wrong, and you have explained to me the harm it does, but it also helped people. Men fed their families as a result of it. I cannot truly blame them for doing whatever they could to sustain life. Milord assembled a criminal enterprise, and he may have cut a man's tongue out of his head or ordered it done, but he also built cottages for those in his employ to live in, and cared for them when their own landlords would not."

"Did he so? A most interesting person, this Milord of yours—in effect a self-appointed lord of the manor, a natural gentleman. We've come to a pretty pass when such an act can even be contemplated! I confess I should wish to sit with him one day as I am sitting with you now, and converse. But next we come to this 'Tom' fellow—what of him?"

"I feel sorry for him. He was cast out of his home for no fault of his own—it was the weather that ruined the harvest, he could not help being unable to pay his rent. He was doing whatever work came to hand, trying to get home again." Harry's voice became suspended as he thought of his own home, now so far away, perhaps never to be seen again if his father would not forgive him.

"This brings us to another figure in your story—the man who hired this Tom fellow. Where do right and wrong come into his part of the tale?"

Harry sat up straight, his heart beating faster. "I can see no mixture of good in his character. He is a wealthy man; he is not in want. He has a home and a livelihood. He reaps the benefits of being a British citizen, yet he traffics in gold and secrets with our enemy. To me, he is the real villain."

Dr. Goddard exhaled a long breath. "Your words imply that you know his identity."

Harry for the first time looked the headmaster in the eye. "I do."

"It seems to me, Steer, that you need very little help to find your way through this tangle. You have described to me a number of men with ordinary human frailties and needs, an admixture of good and bad, stumbling through their lives. You have described a man who is a shade blacker: in addition to having these ordinary human frailties, he may or may not have punished another man in a brutal, but not fatal, manner. He might be subject to criminal prosecution for that, were it not for the absence of proof. But the law states that neither he nor any of the smugglers can be prosecuted simply based on report: they must be caught with the goods in their possession. And since they have not been so found, it is useless to accuse any of them. Were you to stoop to naming them, they would still have to be stalked and caught in the act—more easily said than done, I should think."

"I didn't know that!"

"I imagine it did not serve Sir Nugent's interests to acquaint you with the minutiae of the law. So perhaps you need not violate your oath to your smuggling acquaintances after all. It seems likely in any case that they may be daunted by all the attention that has been attracted to their activities, and cease to do wrong—at least for a time.

And we shall not forget that, as you suggest, their activities have done as much good as harm.

"But after we dismiss all of these people from consideration, we are left—are we not?—with one man who is unquestionably a monster. What of him?"

Hope rose and expanded in Harry's breast; he could have no qualms about naming Mr. Barclay. But still he doubted. "I am prepared to tell all I know about that man. But will it be enough to satisfy Sir Nugent?"

Dr. Goddard patted his knee. "It will be your task to see to it that he is satisfied. I will apprise Sir Nugent and, I believe, Sir Frederick and Mr. Peters as well, of your willingness to speak about this man. The rest must lie with your persuasive powers. This is your monster to slay, Harry Steer.

"I look forward to making your better acquaintance in a fortnight," he concluded, rising to his feet. "But in the meantime, I find that you were absolutely right about the fleas, and must beg leave to part company for now."

Chapter the Twenty-sixth

Harry remained immured all through the evening and on into the next day. He passed the time in pacing to and fro, rehearsing his arguments though he could not know what he would be asked or what was to be expected of him. He vied continually against the seeming hopelessness of his task: Sir Nugent did not appear the sort of man to yield to persuasion, and Harry placed little faith in his inclination to mercy. What could he do if Sir Nugent were not satisfied with Mr. Barclay, if he wanted the Tilts as well?

After the morning was well advanced, however, an escort of the militia finally appeared to return him to Pippbrook House. Harry tried to hold his ideas together, but they scattered and fled as he drew near to the spot where he would meet his fate. How could he possibly stand up to the Law and steer the proceedings from down in the pit of his guilt? It seemed impossible to climb out.

Admitted once again to Sir Nugent's library, he knew a moment's disappointment upon seeing that neither Dr. Goddard nor his cousin was present. Yet Sir Frederick and Mr. Peters were in attendance, and he drew at least a small consolation from this circumstance.

Sir Nugent was fearsome enough, however, as he opened the proceedings with a scowl. "I am given to understand that you are repentant and prepared to reveal your secrets to us, Steer."

Harry was startled by the sweeping nature of this opening. "I am prepared to tell you what I know in the matter of the treason, sir," he replied cautiously.

"You shall tell us all we ask of you, Imp, or you will be made to pay dearly!" cried Sir Nugent, pounding his stump on the table. "Do not deceive yourself that you have a choice in the matter."

Mr. Peters looked as if he had a thought of interceding, but reconsidered, saying only, "Let us hear what the young man has to say."

Harry took a deep breath and got straight to the point. "The man who had the direction of the shipments of gold was Mr. Barclay of Burford Lodge."

"Nonsense!" exclaimed Sir Nugent. "How dare you impugn a gentleman with such an accusation? What could he have to do with smuggling? Don't serve me up any of your effrontery, boy."

Sir Frederick, however, leaned forward. "I am unpersuaded by Mr. Barclay's claims to the title of gentleman," said he. "It was with the greatest reluctance that I agreed to admit him to the Gentlemen's Darking Club. He carries himself like a rogue, and his parentage is certainly questionable. And we cannot dispute that his position in life offers him access to much that would be needful to carry out this plot. Speak up, boy! What leads you to fix on him as the man responsible for this crime?"

"Well, sir, it's this way: I had some prior acquaintance with a man who came into the neighborhood not long ago and was living here by his wits. A few months past he held me up on the turnpike—though I had nothing to give him, and he did me no harm. The night I attended the meeting of the club, I saw this man again at the Red Lion—in a disguise. He was in the stableyard, and speaking with a gentleman. The gentleman was giving him orders: to wait after nightfall at a place along the River Mole, north of Darking opposite the Whites, on Saint Swithin's night. There he was to stay till someone brought a cargo, and with some of the smugglers' men and horses he was to carry the cargo to a house down south near Newdigate. The gentleman gave instructions for how the cargo was to be concealed in the house, and that the men should wait there till other men from Sussex should come to take the cargo on. All of these circumstances were identical to what happened more than a week later, when I was sent on just such a run; and that was when I saw the gold."

"You say the man in disguise was speaking with a gentleman. How did you know he was a gentleman?" asked Mr. Peters. "And why do you identify the gentleman as Mr. Barclay?"

Harry puzzled over the first part of this. "When I caught sight of the man in disguise in the stableyard, I was curious to discover what he was up to, knowing him for a scoundrel. His wearing of a disguise appeared suspicious. So I hid, and listened to what went forward. The man he was talking to spoke in educated accents, not like a common Surrey man. And when they had finished their conversation, the gentleman walked straight up to where I was concealed. That's when I saw him to be Mr. Barclay. He spoke to me, and I had sat next him at dinner so there was no mistaking him. It was he giving the orders for the transport of the gold. And the place where we met the cargo is on his property, or immediately beside it. We could see the lights in his windows from where we lay concealed."

Mr. Peters spoke. "It is difficult to doubt your conclusion that Barclay is the man responsible. But why would he engage in such a nefarious enterprise?"

"I have no knowledge of his motive," replied Harry.

"And it is unlikely that he would possess a fortune great enough to supply guineas in the quantity involved," mused Sir Frederick. "Nor is he an official at the Admiralty, though no doubt he visits there regularly in the course of his business with the Royal Exchange Assurance Corporation. If he is indeed the author of this plot, he must have confederates. What of them?"

Again Harry denied having any information.

Sir Nugent uttered an exclamation of impatience. "I am by no means persuaded that this boy is telling us the truth. But if he is, what can be done with such partial intelligence? We must locate the man in disguise—what is his name? Where is he to be found?"

Harry had been dreading these questions ever since he had been obliged to reveal the existence of Tomkins. "I doubt he remains in the neighborhood, sir," said he after a little hesitation. "And I believe it likely that he knew very little of the larger plot, or any coconspirators Mr. Barclay might have had. He was in the way of being a servant to Mr. Barclay—he was a simple man, a displaced farmer from Hampshire. I suspect that when the third shipment was disrupted he would have fled the county at his earliest opportunity."

"Very likely," said Mr. Peters. "And I would imagine the smugglers who took part in the transport of the gold would be even less likely to have useful information." Harry nodded.

"But we should interview them anyway," said Sir Nugent. "Provide their names, if you please."

Harry said with secret relief that he could not. "We never used our real names, so how could I know their identities?" He hoped desperately that this little evasion would pass unnoticed.

Sir Nugent glared at him and champed his jaws in annoyance, but Sir Frederick redirected his attention. "It appears likely that only Mr. Barclay would be in a position to reveal the names of his confederates. And although I am certain we would all be happy to provide a complete picture of this plot to the Admiralty and the government," he bent his bulky frame politely toward Sir Nugent, "I fear it must remain beyond our powers to do so. This very morning I received no fewer than three communications from high officials on the subject—one an express from the prime minister himself. They all say much the same thing: if we can provide any insight into the architect of the plot they will be obliged to us, but they say quite plainly they do not wish us to inquire too deeply into the details. I believe our duty lies in passing on the name young Steer has provided, and then endeavoring to forget that anything ever happened here." He pursed his fat lips and folded his hands over his belly.

"Forget it ever happened!" cried Sir Nugent in outrage. "I never heard such nonsense. Are we to look the other way at treason? All the orders for the navy! Fortunes in gold smuggled under our very noses!"

Sir Frederick raised his chin and looked down his nose, the natural arch of his eyebrows increasing the hauteur of his expression. "I believe it to be our duty *not* to pry into affairs of state, simply because they happened to cross our path. We have been warned off from indulging our curiosity too far. I for one have no intention of offending half the ministers in the government by raising a dust about matters they clearly wish to keep secret."

Sir Nugent's attention was diverted to a fresh outrage. "Why did the ministers write to you instead of to me? *I* am the magistrate in charge of this case!"

"Recognizing the situation as one that demanded a measure of delicacy, I wrote to them to seek advice on how we might best proceed," said Sir Frederick. "They did me the honor of replying."

Mr. Peters interposed. "There is more to consider than even the Admiralty papers. Think for a moment about where the gold must have come from: it seems impossible that one individual could possess so much, or would pass it off to the French if he did. I should not be surprised if there were not a director of the Bank of England involved; and if so, it might be possible to trace letters of exchange back to the French government. The prime minister may be able to make discreet inquiries of this nature, but he surely would not thank us for making it known that a massive sum of English gold is being diverted to benefit our enemy. Can you imagine the panic that would ensue? If we precipitated a financial crisis, surely we would be doing as much harm to our country as the traitors! I am with Sir Frederick: we provide the name of Mr. Barclay and allow wiser heads to decide what to do with it."

Sir Nugent sullenly agreed that this was the course of prudence, but he was not prepared to drop the matter entirely. "What of the smugglers in our midst? This incident has revealed that we have a criminal enterprise flagrantly operating in Darking! This miscreant before us has far more to reveal about the responsible parties there. We can at least stamp out the lawlessness in our own neighborhood. Speak up, boy!"

For a time Harry stood silent. Though the chamber was a commodious one, he felt its walls closing in around him, his plan of escaping consequences crumbling around him. All his hopes for mercy blew away like dust in the gales of Sir Nugent's obduracy. There was no escape: he had to make his choice.

At last he spoke in a bare whisper: "I cannot tell you anything about the smugglers."

"Nonsense! Tell us all you know."

"I am sorry, sir," said Harry, trembling, "but I must refuse. They have threatened to harm my family, and I cannot do anything to bring calamity down upon the innocent. God knows I've brought them enough misery as it is, by my actions."

"*Speak!*" roared Sir Nugent, enraged. "You dare to defy me, boy?"

But Mr. Peters intervened. "You cannot ask a child to send his parents to their deaths," he said. "Steer has been open with us about the greater crime. I'm positive you, like all of us, have drunk brandy and port that never had duty paid on it at many a house in the neighborhood, and the fabric of society has not come unraveled. No doubt most of the contraband merely passes through on its way to London; surely it's for the Excise to pursue the matter, now they have been given authority to command the dragoons. What could the boy even tell us? He has said no names were used."

"But he must know of the route they travel, and their places of concealment, at the very least. You may choose to wink at the free-trade, but I do not consider it an innocuous activity. Just look at what these blackguards were willing to lend their resources to! I won't stand idly by when there are criminals among us who are prepared to abet treason for profit."

Sir Frederick turned to Harry. "Do you indeed have intelligence to offer about the smugglers' methods and habits? I own I should sleep better at night if we could disrupt such lawlessness—smuggling may seem a minor offense, but once people become hardened to criminality, who knows what they may do?"

Harry looked to Mr. Peters as his final hope. "I could tell you of the ways I took with the pack trains, but it would do you little good, I believe. Each run was different, and knowing that I was captured, they will now be sure to use new ways going forward. In any case, the Excise was getting very close to catching up with them—they appear to have good sources of information—so it's my belief the smugglers will suspend their activities. I have been told they must be caught with the goods in their possession in order to be prosecuted, is that not so?"

Mr. Peters was inclined to be amused by this outbreak of lawyerliness, but Sir Nugent was not. "I can tell you of one smuggler who was caught red-handed, scapegrace, and that's yourself! You're scarcely advancing your cause with this effrontery. You will tell what you know or suffer the maximum punishment for your crimes."

To his mortification, Harry felt tears press against his eyelids, and he was powerless to stop them from trickling down his cheeks. "Sir, nothing I can tell you would be of use to you; it would only serve to condemn my family. Surely you don't wish to incite a more serious crime in your desire to prosecute a lesser one! How can smuggling be weighed against murder?" He had done his best, and now there was naught remaining to him but surrender. "You must do with me what you choose," he whispered, "but I cannot send my family to their destruction."

Mr. Peters looked his approbation, and even Sir Frederick seemed moved by Harry's plight. Sir Nugent opened his mouth wide to roar, but Sir Frederick cut him off. "Young Steer has freely given us all he knows about the most serious crime. This shows him to have a cooperative spirit, and I believe him when he says he fears retaliation from the smugglers. Let us not forget that he is a mere boy. He has made a serious mistake, but I believe him to be genuinely repentant and unlikely to repeat it. Is that not so?"

Harry agreed fervently that it was.

"In that case," Sir Frederick continued, "it's my view that he has paid his debt with his candor and should be excused from further disclosures. Furthermore, his youth argues for our offering him the opportunity to choose a better path: he should be set free and left to return to his home."

"I concur," said Mr. Peters swiftly, before Sir Nugent could object.

Yet object he did; yielding to persuasion was never easy for a man so enamored of his own dignity, and it did not sit well with him to be overruled in his own case and in his own home. He still had not recovered from his pique over Sir Frederick's presumption in approaching the ministers behind his back, and was determined to reassert his authority. The others attempted to flatter and soothe him, but in the end he sent Harry back to his cell.

Harry and his guards had not gone far toward the Cage before Mr. Peters caught up to them. He strolled alongside Harry, loftily ignoring the presence of the guards. "You have been through your share of tribulations, young man," said he, to Harry's surprise, "and have acquitted yourself throughout with honor. I am determined to see to it that neither you nor your family suffers further in this matter. Don't be downcast—I have a few ideas about how to work on Sir Nugent."

He walked a few more paces by Harry's side and then added inconsequently, "Old Tilt is an impressive fellow, is he not?" At Harry's stricken look he laughed and said, "I may not have lived in this country long, but I keep my eyes and my ears open, and I like to know my neighbors in all walks of life. I have an affection for the old man and am convinced he has as much right as any of us sinners to live out his years in peace. So try not to worry, Harry Steer, and see if it doesn't all work out for the best."

How this might happen, Harry could not conceive; and he was much baffled by what might be the connection between Mr. Peters and John Tilt.

But in the end, Mr. Peters did indeed win the day. The

prime minister could not be prevailed upon to plead with a man he so cordially despised as he did Sir Nugent— but others, with the power to recommend elevation to the peerage, were persuaded to flatter him and offer innuendo and delicate half-promises of preferment if he would only cooperate in averting a national calamity. It was all done in a way that pledged nothing, but Sir Nugent, who had long believed a mere baronetcy to be a shabby ornament to the nobility of his house, leaped for the chance and forgot all about his determination to prosecute Harry to the fullest extent of the law. He agreed to the dropping of the charges, and sat down to wait for a title to be conferred upon him as reward.

He is waiting still.

Although this happy outcome may carry the appearance of encouraging vice in the young, it is a source of satisfaction to report that within a few days, therefore, Harry was on his way home, unscathed but for the fleas. His cousin Lee Steere Steere escorted him, for although Harry maintained that he was perfectly able to walk, despite the rigors and short rations of his days in jail, his kinsman was aware that all the influence of his prosperity and respectability would be required to secure Harry's father's acceptance of his miscreant son. Forgiveness was too much to ask of such a man, but Mr. Steere believed that once Harry was restored to his place in the family, habit would go far toward smoothing over outrage. And if Harry could be persuaded to work hard at Winchester, he might in time come to be regarded as the hope of his house once again.

In the gig on the way to Henfold, Mr. Steere ventured to make this representation to Harry, urging him to study hard and stay out of trouble. Harry, already well along the path toward idolizing Dr. Goddard, assured him that he had every intention of trying his utmost to succeed.

Upon their arrival, Mrs. Steer ran out before the others were fully on their feet and enfolded Harry in a strong embrace. She held on with determination even after Mr. Steer appeared on the doorstep, his face grim. She and their kinsman between them strove mightily to lend an everyday character to the scene, conversing in studiedly cheerful tones about the fineness of the day and the fairness of the harvest. Mr. Steere added what he had heard of praise from Dr. Goddard for Harry's courage, resourcefulness, and intelligence and his promise that Harry's place at Winchester was to be held for him.

At last, however, Mrs. Steer had to let go of her boy and their cousin had to depart, and then Harry's punishment must be faced. Never a man of clever words, his father knew only one way to express his disappointment, and Harry's beating was severe. The pain of his body, though, was considerably alleviated by the joy in his heart, for he was back in his rightful place and once again entitled to call it home. Isabella might—and did—complain that she was always good and never got the credit for it, and that Harry was always more highly valued than herself, but she earned herself only a stern "Hush!" from her mother.

The next day was once again market day in Darking, and Mrs. Steer judged it best to take Harry with her rather than leave him idling about the house or dragging his aching frame out to the fields in his father's wake, Mr. Marshall having been dismissed from his post upon Harry's arrest. Perhaps, she reasoned, the less Harry and his father saw of each other at first, the more smoothly their reconciliation would proceed. So Harry was faced with an unexpected holiday.

When she asked him to accompany her to market, however, he confessed his reluctance to meet the censorious eyes of the townspeople of Darking, having been so recently dragged through the streets in the guise of a felon. But his mother was having none of it.

"Now you are clean and dressed properly, ten to one nobody will even recognize you. And even if they do, they will see that you have been released and the charges dropped, and they will conclude it was all a misunderstanding. If you were to hide away at home, people would assume the worst and you might never live it down. No, you must hold up your head and show them you have nothing to be ashamed of."

In the event, Harry faced neither vilification nor acceptance, but simply obliviousness. No word of treason had leaked into the public mind. No one had seen anything sufficiently remarkable in the arrest of a dirty little boy to inquire into the nature of the crime, so there had been no gossip. Harry, the desperate criminal, moved among them and none the wiser. As for himself, he lacked the self-importance even to be disappointed by his failure to achieve notoriety.

It was a busy market; all Darking Hundred appeared to have come to town this day, and a festal spirit reigned in the streets. The bounty of this year's harvest was causing the echoes of the past year's misery to fade from people's minds. With each passing day, confidence grew stronger that there would be prosperity for all, and farmers and their wives flocked to the town to buy the goods they had long denied themselves—sugar and muslin, currants and lard and new tools to replace those broken. Through the open windows of the Three Tuns came the deafening shouts of sellers pitching their corn. Hawkers moved through the crowd, adding to the din: old Woodger, touting the freshness of his pasties in a cracked voice, his back more bent than ever; Mollie Fish with her impudent sallies and her blue apron; the broomdasher, the flower sellers, and the boys peddling the latest handbills.

Mrs. Steer entered the fray with the ease of long habit. She had half-grown turkeys to sell alongside her eggs, cheeses, and piles of excess beans from the garden; her cart was a popular stop on many a townswoman's circuit. Harry was kept busy supplying what they ordered and taking payment while his mother engaged civilly with each customer in turn, chatting about the minutiae of their children's lives.

At a pause in the activity Harry slipped away to the tobacconist's to purchase a peace offering for his father—using, though Mr. Steer would never know it, his ill-gotten gains from the first run of guineas—and he returned to find his aunt Steer and cousin Dick, now nearly recovered, hobnobbing with his mother. As she turned to attend to a customer, Dick whispered in Harry's ear, "The captain is well pleased with you; you stood strong."

Harry turned an incredulous stare on his cousin and caught a look of admiration in his eyes. He wondered how praise that would have made him swell with pride only a few weeks earlier could today leave him so unmoved. Where had the captain—or Dick, for that matter—been in his time of extremity? He realized that the moon was even now at the dark and wondered what the Tilts were up to. But he replied only, "Perhaps you will convey my farewells to the captain, as I leave for school next week."

Dick promised to do so and showed every indication of wishing to discuss Harry's adventures further, but fortunately he was forestalled by his mother's preparing to depart; so off he went, oblivious to Harry's true feelings. Mrs. Steer, with still a good deal to sell, asked Harry to perform some errands for her. He visited the chandler's, had some knives sharpened, purchased a placatory bag of gingerbread for Isabella, and collected powders ordered from the chemist's for his father's bilious complaint. Throughout, he remained untroubled by hostile notice—even when he skulked past a cluster of militiamen idling in front of the Wheatsheaf Inn. Their attention, for a mercy, was focused on a clutch of schoolgirls giggling past, sucking on lollipops.

It was when he purchased newspapers for his father that Harry received a shock. His eye fell upon a story about panic among the banks in the City after the Bank of England, during an audit, discovered that a portion of its gold reserve was unaccounted for. The bank's directors had issued public assurances that the amount was not fatal to their solvency, but even so, many banks that relied on them were experiencing an unusual rate of withdrawals. It was hoped that the panic would not spread into the country banks, which could not sustain a run on their funds.

Harry stopped outside the Three Tuns, unheeding as he was jostled by the farmers bustling in and out, and searched hastily through the pages of one paper after another. Only one had the story of the missing gold, but all the rest had some version of the same tale: On Tuesday evening, a Mr. G. B. of B______ Lodge, near Darking, Surrey—a director of the Royal Exchange Assurance Corporation, member of the Whig Club, member of Parliament for Bridport—had attempted to destroy himself. He took a boat at Blackwall in London and, just after passing under the London Bridge, jumped into the water; but he was pulled out by a passing boatman, despite struggling hard against his would-be rescuer. Once on shore, he was discovered to have a pistol, loaded but not fired, in his pocket; it was believed that he had first intended to end his life in that manner, but lacked the resolution to carry out his plan. After his second effort was foiled, by Wednesday morning Mr. B. had decamped from the metropolis and was believed to have sailed for the Continent that evening, with the aim of recruiting his health at one of the resorts for which the Austrian nation is justly famous.

Odd as it may seem for a person who had recently faced the prospect of hanging, Harry had not previously considered what might become of the man he had named a traitor. His imagination had not reached beyond "stopping" the crime. That a man should attempt to put a period to his existence as a result of Harry's words was a dreadful thing. For a moment he felt sick.

And yet it had not come to that. Mr. Barclay had survived and, like Harry, had even escaped punishment. Harry wondered why Mr. Barclay had not been taken up by the authorities. How had he remained at liberty once the information was laid? Had the Admiralty's need for secrecy been so pressing that he had simply been warned that his perfidy was unmasked, and left to make a gentleman's exit? This was rather disappointing; Harry could not help but feel that Mr. Barclay deserved at least as many flea bites as he had sustained, not to mention dwelling under the fear of the noose.

But perhaps, Harry reflected, being banished forever from his homeland was penalty enough. Harry remembered the pleasant meadows down by the River Mole that formed a part of Mr. Barclay's former demesne, the beautiful orchard across the river under the Whites, the river slipping peacefully by, and he thought perhaps it was. For the first time, Harry wondered about Mr. Barclay as a person. Did he love his home? Did he have a family? Had Harry perhaps deprived a son of his father?

Still, he knew he must not think in such terms: Mr. Barclay had started his own feet down the path to exile. He had set in motion the very events that led to his downfall. Harry folded up the newspapers and made his way back to his mother, and thence homeward.

Finis.

About Darking Hundred

Darking is—or was—a real place. It is in Surrey and is now known as Dorking. But in the year 1800, when the tales in this series are set, most of the residents pronounced the name "Darking."

A hundred *is an old administrative unit of British government that dates back to Anglo-Saxon times and continued into the nineteenth century. Land was divided into sections large enough to sustain one hundred households; the size of a hundred, therefore, depended on the productivity of the soil. The leading citizen of a hundred was known as its hundred-man; in 1800, the hundred-man for the Darking area was the Duke of Norfolk.*

There has never been a Darking Hundred: the market town of Dorking lies in Wotton Hundred, which includes the parishes of Dorking, Capel, Ockley, Wotton, and Abinger. The name Darking Hundred *is intended to signal that these stories are not entirely historical in an objective sense: they are realist but not entirely real. Some of the characters are historical figures (detailed on Darking's Web site, www.darkinghundred.com), but many never existed—though they might have done had the threads of their families' lives been differently woven. Elements of the stories are drawn from local popular lore and represent circumstances that ought to be true, even if they never actually happened.*

The Real and the True: A Historical Note

The Darking Hundred series owes everything to the indefatigable efforts of the Dorking Local History Group and their remarkable collection of studies of communities in the area. Their works are my delight and my inspiration. Thanks in large part to them, much is known about Dorking and its environs in the year 1800, though much else has been lost to time. But I am grateful for the gaps because they open the way for the writer of historical fiction.

My stories combine historical figures with invented characters, though this distinction is not always significant—for all the people who really lived I have needed to invent many of their words and actions. The places mentioned in the book all existed in 1800, and I have described them as accurately as possible.

I have tried to be true to the age and to all the facts I know about Darking and its neighborhood in 1800; but on occasion, when minor facts interfere with the story, they have been allowed to shift a bit. From my perspective, at this remove what feels true carries more weight than what was technically real at the time. One instance is placing John Tilt's household at Redlands Farm in the summer of 1800. It appears likely that by then he was no longer living at Redlands, having removed to his house in Capel and leased Redlands to the Cosens family. But for his one scene I preferred to place him in a more retired situation and amid a larger family group.

I feel a particular obligation to disclaim when it comes to the villain of the piece, George Barclay. *Treason* is a harsh word and a cruel accusation to lay at a man's door. It is important to state clearly that I have no evidence whatsoever that the real George Barclay was guilty of seeking to support the French cause by smuggling gold and secrets out of the country. Mr. Barclay was, by the only surviving public accounts, an arrogant and unsavory character who cheated his business partners and engaged in activities that brought shame upon his house. After these acts became public, he attempted suicide in the manner I have described, though he did so several years after 1800. My only excuse in exaggerating his infamy is that he was the person resident at Darking who most closely fitted the needs of my story. The nature of his business activities was such that he would have had the opportunity to commit these crimes, had he been so inclined. The historical record shows that London bankers financed both sides of the conflict during the Napoleonic wars—probably for no better reason than that it was profitable to do so—and military secrets did escape the country by means of smuggling networks. Any connection between those acts and Mr. Barclay is, however, purely fictionalizing speculation.

For more information about characters, places, and events, please visit www.darkinghundred.com, a repository of information about everything Darking.

Acknowledgments

My deepest gratitude goes to all my patient readers and listeners, some of whom have lived with *Coldharbour Gentlemen* almost as long as I have: Pam Palmer, Mary Sheldon, Christina Morland, Robin Schachat, Elaine Ober, Nina Kiskadden, Hilary Bok, Heli Perrett, Diana Love, Katherine Clements, and members of the Historical Novel Society's master class.

Coldharbour Gentlemen owes a special debt of gratitude to Pam Palmer, whose work on the Tilt family made this story possible and gave it direction. She has also welcomed and entertained me most kindly on my visits to Dorking. I hope she and other Tilt descendants enjoy this tale.

My work on Darking Hundred would not be possible without the librarians and archivists who guided me toward information and resources, first among them Jane le Cluse of the Dorking Museum Archive. Mary Day and other members of the Dorking and Mickleham local history groups also gave generously of their time and knowledge, taking me about and showing me secrets. And I owe a great deal to the generosity of institutions, from the Surrey History Centre to the National Portrait Gallery and the Yale Center for British Art, among a host of others, that have allowed me to use images from their collections to enrich the world of Darking Hundred on my Web site, www.darkinghundred.com.